DØ113503

Acknowledgements:

I firmly believe no author crafts a story without the support of family and friends. From inception to completion, family and friends are there, providing the love, guidance, motivation and feedback essential to taking the kernel of an idea to a polished publication. As such, it would be remiss of me not to thank the team that has kept me going. First and foremost I would like to thank my partner Kate. Thankyou for your unreserved patience and love, plus the many lonely Sundays and other days you spent by yourself, while I was glued to a computer screen. Thankyou Barb and Linda for your support and feedback—you give it unconditionally which makes it all the more precious to me. Joan, once again, thanks for allowing me to leave you in suspense, chapter by chapter. Your motivation took this story to another level. To Andi, my editor, I know I've said this already, but thankyou for your patience and feedback. I think we both know that, given the circumstances, this has been a long slog for me, made easier by your professionalism and guidance.

Finally, I would like to thank a woman who is no longer with us. I don't think I fully understood her standard salutation to me of "G'day missus", until it was too late. For me it was a heartfelt greeting. For her it was that and so much more. It was also recognition of all that really mattered was the happiness of her daughter—my partner, Kate; and everything else was merely white noise. Although gone from this world, she is in our thoughts everyday.

For Vano 1933-2005

Peace, perfect peace, with loved ones far away
~ E.H. Bickersteth 1825-1906

Love's Redemption

Helen Macpherson

Yellow Rose Books

Nederland, Texas

ISBN 978-1-935053-04-0
1-935053-04-3

First Printing 2008

9 8 7 6 5 4 3 2 1

Cover design by Donna Pawlowski

Published by:

Regal Crest Enterprises, LLC
4700 Highway 365, Suite A, PMB 210
Port Arthur, Texas 77642

Find us on the World Wide Web at
http://www.regalcrest.biz

Printed in the United States of America

Chapter
One

JO ASHBY NERVOUSLY plucked at her smooth skin wetsuit, as the *White Explorer* gently bobbed in the deep blue waters of the Great Australian Bight. She ran her hands over her wetsuit-encased thighs as the vessel's co-owner, Valerie Anderson, sat down beside her, regulator in hand.

"She's a lot calmer today than she was yesterday." Valerie used her fingernail to pick at a fleck of salt on the piece of scuba gear.

Jo watched Valerie's experienced hands play with the regulator, turning it this way and that, checking for any faults in the equipment. "Thank God for small mercies," Jo joked. "It's enough to be doing what I'm about to do, without adding choppy waters to it as well."

Valerie playfully nudged her shoulder. "You'll be all right. We'll be using equipment that'll allow you to talk with the surface, and with your cameraman in the other cage. I've done this hundreds of times. You'll be fine."

I'll be fine. I'll be fine. Now if I can keep on repeating that mantra then everything will be all right. Jo snorted. *Like hell it will. How did I get myself into this?* Valerie's reassuring hand patting her own halted her thoughts.

"You know if you don't want to do this, you don't have to. I can go down into the cage and your cameraman can get all the shots he needs."

Jo shook her head. "Thanks, but no. This is in keeping with the rest of my *Where Are They Now?* series. I've been actively involved in whatever my subject has chosen for a second career. I can't stop now, not on my second-last story."

Valerie chuckled. "Don't say I didn't offer," she paused at the sound of her husband's voice. Both women turned and watched him haul the scuba-diving tanks from within one of the deck's hidden compartments. "I'd better go and help John or he'll be complaining of a sore back tonight."

Jo watched the interaction between Valerie and her husband, which involved light-hearted banter, followed by a false argument revolving around Valerie and her ability to help lift the tanks. Valerie swatted John's back and they indulged in a quick make-up kiss. *Now that's what I need to find. Maybe we should get some shots of that.* She looked over her shoulder toward her cameraman, who was doing a final check on his equipment.

"Hey, Ben, do you think you could get some shots of the two of them together?"

Ben closed the waterproof compartment on his camera and shook his head. "Nope, got plenty of them already. How about we go over your introduction for this part of the story?" He stood and hefted the camera to his shoulder, planting his feet slightly apart to cater to the slight swell and gentle movement of the boat. He turned the camera in her direction, the green light on the top indicating he'd started filming.

"Now smile into the camera, cheeky chops." Ben's face came halfway around the side of the camera to see the look on her face.

Jo's green eyes twinkled. "I'll give you cheeky chops, you rude bugger." They shared a laugh before Jo settled back down. She centered herself and took a deep breath. Her body language exuded assurance as she expelled one last calming breath and looked at Ben.

"Hello and welcome to part two of the sixth episode in the series *Where Are They Now?* In part one we caught up with Valerie Anderson, once the Chairman of the Board for Sharman Industries, one of the largest gold and silver companies in the world. Last year, Valerie traded the sharks of the boardroom — with all their bluff and bravado — and a seven-figure salary to pursue the real thing. Valerie and her husband are the co-owners of Extreme Adrenaline Adventures, conducting shark tours, among other things." She continued to speak while Ben panned to where Valerie and John checked their equipment. "Ben, we'll edit voiceover once we're back in the studio. I just want to get a good narrative to go with the piece."

He nodded, not breaking his focus on the Andersons.

"As I promised in part one, today sees us in the waters of the Great Australian Bight, at the bottom of the continent." She paused. "Hey, Ben? Remind me to superimpose a small pop-up map on this footage. Most people have no idea where this place is."

"Hell, I didn't. Did you?" Ben's eye remained plastered to the camera's viewfinder.

"Well, I had an idea. Okay, back to voiceover." She rose and carefully walked across the deck, to where one of the shark cages stood. "As dangerous as the sharks of the boardroom can be, they're nothing compared to the real thing. And today we're meeting the most feared shark in the world when we shallow-dive in these cages." She lightly slapped the side of the cage with her open palm before confidently grasping one of the bars. "Today we're going to meet the great white, a shark found in a number of the world's oceans, but never as prevalently as the waters of the Great Australian Bight."

Valerie approached her. "That's right, Jo. And we grow them big down here."

Jo marveled at the way Valerie seemed to slip so easily into professional mode when the camera was on her. *She must have been a killer in the boardroom.* "Refresh my memory, Valerie. How big do they grow?"

"The largest substantiated catch was five metres, but I can tell you down here they've been known to grow to about eight metres."

Jo's eyes goggled. She heard Ben's soft laughter. "Don't forget, buddy, you're going to be down there as well, and at one hundred and ninety centimetres, I'm sure you make a much tastier morsel than me." Ben gulped, and the crew on the deck laughed at his nervousness. "Are we likely to see one that size today?"

Valerie shook her head. "Not likely. Years ago great whites weren't protected by sanctions, which resulted in a number of waters being fished out by shark hunters. I'm sure they're still out there, but these girls are probably too shy to come near a boat."

Jo raised her brows. "The females are usually bigger than the males?" Valerie nodded and Jo looked at Ben "Gee. Fancy you being eaten by a woman."

"Hey cheeky chops, that's your fantasy, not mine." Ben's comment elicited laughter from everyone.

"And your fantasy's watching me being eaten by a woman, right?" Jo retorted, her hands on her hips. "Anyway, enough of this. Let's get back to work. Valerie, the females are usually bigger than the males?" She repeated, cueing Valerie's answer.

"That's right. How about we get you down there to have a look?" Valerie walked across the deck, picked up a half-mask and returned to Jo. "You'll be wearing a mask, which will allow you full communication with me, Ben, and John, who'll be topside on the boat. It's an AquaNatter, which allows you to talk underwater. We'll attach it to your breathing tube and we'll record so you'll have commentary to match your footage. We'll also put an underwater camera over the side, so John will be able to see what's going on. If things go to hell in a hand basket then John and the crew will get you out of there."

"Great," Jo replied nervously as one of the deck hands helped her don her gear. She looked at Ben, as he was helped into the rest of his scuba equipment.

The minutes seemed to fly past and before Jo knew it, she and Valerie were lowered over the side of the boat. As the water enveloped her, she momentarily panicked and her mouth tightened on her mouthpiece. *Relax Jo, relax.* She practiced deep breathing while her heartbeat slowed to normal.

She watched as five metres away Ben's cage was lowered into the water. She crookedly smiled, her actions impeded by her mouthpiece. He had been with her from the beginning, and had jumped at the chance to film great whites. She waited while he picked his camera up from the bottom of the cage and raised it to his shoulder.

"Ben, can you see and hear me okay?"

Ben braced his feet against the bottom sides of the cage. "Loud and clear. Well, as clear as we can be. You see any sharks?"

"Not yet, Ben, but be patient," Valerie's tones flowed through Jo's earpiece. "I promise it won't be too long."

"Ben, let's get some narrative while we're waiting." Jo touched the side of the cage, trying to maintain her balance. "Down here is another world. The clarity is amazing. I can see past the cage of my cameraman, who is only a few metres away. The dappled effect you're seeing is from the sunlight above, as we're literally just below the surface of the water. Amazingly enough, even though the Australian Bight is pretty deep, the suits we're wearing make the water temperature almost bearable. Normally the temperatures around here are — holy crap!"

Jo's eyes widened within her mask as she watched the streamlined shadow approaching Ben's cage. At that distance, it was a darker blue than the water it swam through. The body shape and dorsal fin were unmistakable. "Ben, pan the camera around. There's one swimming toward you."

She watched him turn and then smiled as a string of curses flowed through her headset. The great white slowly floated past Ben and to the cage she and Valerie occupied. Its mouth was ajar, giving them an unimpeded view of the multiple rows of its teeth, perfectly designed for tearing flesh.

Jo started talking. "What you're seeing now has aptly earned its name as lord of the seas. Only as it swims past me can I begin to appreciate the deadly majesty of this creature. These cages are roughly two metres wide by two metres high and one-and-a-half metres deep, and yet I feel dwarfed by the size of the great white swimming around us. It's an unsettling feeling when her head is on one side of the cage and her tail is on the other side. She's truly a remarkable creature."

Valerie tapped Jo's shoulder. "I don't mean to interrupt but she's a he."

Jo looked at the shark swimming away from the cages, the light from the surface above playing across the darker colours of its back and dorsal fin. "How can you tell the difference?"

"Wait for him to come back this way and I'll show you." Almost on cue the shark slowly turned and headed back to the cages. "Watch as he passes." Valerie pointed at the underside of the fish. "See those two fins?"

Jo watched as the creature made another close pass. "You mean those big ones?"

"Not those. They're his pectoral fins. See the two smaller ones behind his pectoral fins? They're his pelvic fins. Each of them has an elongated piece that comes off the back of the fin, called a clasper. This is how we tell the difference. Females don't have them."

"Okay, thanks. Is this one of those big eight-metre sharks you were telling me about? He's huge."

"No, George is only about three and three-quarter metres long," Valerie said, laughing.

"Holy heck, if he's just that big, then I've no interest in meeting anything bigger. You called him George. Is he a regular?"

Valerie nodded.

"I'd better get back on the job. You okay over there, Ben?"

"As fine as one can be, feeling like they're a starter on a shark's lunch menu."

Jo chuckled. "We'll change the 'she' to a 'he' when we edit this at the studio. The shark you're seeing now is a regular named George. Valerie, how can you tell one shark from another?"

"It takes a while but, once you notice the slight differences, you can pick them out of a school of sharks. One of George's pectoral fins is shorter than the other. I don't know if it's a birth defect or if he lost it in a fight. He's a regular here and knows once the cages go under there'll always be some fish for him to eat." She turned to the back of the cage and pointed. "Just like Arthur. He's a regular, too."

Jo watched another shark swim in their direction. "George and Arthur. How did they get their names?"

"I named them after two of my directors who were particularly ruthless in their boardroom dealings. These two," she said, motioning at the sharks, "are relatively tame compared to them."

Jo slipped back into narrator mode. "Arthur has just swum by my cage. His black eye seemed to hold mine until the last moment. That time he was so close I felt like I could reach out and touch him." She held on to the bars and turned to see where the sharks had gone.

"You can touch him if you like. He'll make a few more passes yet, and you can touch him through the viewing port." Valerie motioned toward the port. "Both of them are used to it. Be ready, though. He may look smooth, but shark skin has the consistency of rough sandpaper."

Jo fought to keep the fear out of her voice. "Are you sure it's okay to touch them?"

"Absolutely."

Jo took a deep breath. "Okay, here goes. This pass by the cage should be close enough for me to touch him. Are you getting this, Ben?"

"Of course I am. Get on with it, you wimp."

Jo cautiously reached out and touched Arthur's side. "Wow, you're right. It really is like sandpaper."

"The scales are shaped like curved grooved teeth and this makes the skin a very tough armour. It's no wonder the only natural predators a great white has are the killer whale and, of course, humans."

"Thanks, Valerie." Jo returned to her role of narrator. "This is truly a remarkable experience and one I would recommend to all but the faint-hearted. George is heading my way now. Hopefully I'll get the chance to touch him, also." George slowly swam toward her cage, while at the same time Arthur headed toward Ben's cage. In the blink of an eye George and Arthur quickly darted away, disappearing into the depths below. "What's that about?" Jo queried.

Valerie looked through the bottom bars of the cage. "Strange. They usually hang around for much longer."

"Maybe they were scared away by that." Jo touched Valerie's arm to get her attention. Moving slowly toward them was a shark that literally dwarfed George and Arthur. "If you thought George and Arthur were large, the great white swimming toward us now makes them seem like gangling teenagers."

"John, can you see her through the underwater camera?" Valerie asked. "I don't think we've seen her before."

"No, she's a new one," came the tinny reply.

Jo sensed there was a lingering menace about the shark now swimming between the cages. George and Arthur were almost playful, but this one radiated palpable danger. "How big would you estimate her to be Valerie?" Jo watched the shark make another turn by the cage, this time closer than her last pass.

"It's hard to be accurate, but given her proportion to the cages I'd say she's at least five and three-quarters to six metres long."

Jo gulped. "Jesus, that's one large fish." The shark again returned, swimming even closer to the cage, brushing it as she went by. Jo steadied herself. "The shark's just made another pass and barely touched the cage but as you can see it was enough to make me nearly lose my balance. I can only imagine the force behind such an animal. These cages are safe, aren't they?"

"You'll be fine," Valerie replied. "They're made out of reinforced aluminum and can withstand quite a bit."

"Aluminum. Isn't that what I wrap food in?" Jo nervously joked.

"Sort of, but this is a lot tougher."

Valerie barely finished her last sentence when the shark returned, this time making a beeline for the cage. It bumped the side again with enough force to cause the two of them to bounce off each other.

"Jo, are you okay?" came Ben's panicked voice.

"I'm fine, just keep filming. This'll make great footage." She grabbed one of the bars to again steady herself. "She's just made another pass and it seems she's none too happy about us being here. Is this natural behaviour, Valerie?"

"Sort of. It's a shark's way of showing who's dominant. Just as a dog bares its teeth, so does a shark. That said, this shark's a little more demonstrative than some I've seen. John, maybe we should go topside for a little while. I've got a funny feeling about this one."

Jo looked to her right. "Here she comes again. I don't think she's going to veer." Jo screamed as the shark rammed headfirst into the cage, forcing its jaws through the eye-level viewing area. The enclosure tilted at the force of the impact and Jo fell back against Valerie, and they both lost their footing. The shark's body viciously writhed, as if she were attempting to force herself farther into the cage.

"Jo!" Ben's cry flooded her earpiece.

"I'm fine! I'm fine! Just keep filming. We are fine, aren't we, Valerie?" Jo's sentence ended in an unnaturally high pitch.

"I'm not so sure."

The shark disengaged itself from the cage and swim away out of view. They stood and examined the area where the beast had tried to make its forced entry.

"John, I think it might be a good idea to get us topside, now. I don't like the look of this shark. Jo, brace yourself. Here she comes again. John, get us out of here!"

Paralysed by the display of raw power, Jo stared as once again the shark rammed the bars. "The cage is bending," she yelled. "John, I agree with Valerie, now would be a *great* time to get us out of here."

"We're ready, we've just got to wait for her to let go, or we'll never be able to raise you. Get ready for a fast ascent."

"The faster the better." Jo stared into the bloody maw of the shark as she pulled her mammoth snout out of the cage. Almost simultaneously, the cage rose as it was hauled up and out of the water. Realising Ben was still underwater, Jo's relief rapidly turned to panic. She ripped the mouthpiece from her mouth. "What about Ben?"

Valerie also removed her mouthpiece and looked at the deck of the ship, as if assessing the crew's actions, and then focused on Jo. "He'll be fine. It was us she seemed to be fascinated with. Maybe it was a female thing," she joked.

"If it was, then that bitch had some serious issues." They shared a laugh while the cage finally came to rest on the deck of the boat. Before Jo could extricate herself, she watched the second cage being lowered to the deck. She breathed a sigh of relief as she shed her scuba gear. She awkwardly clambered out through the top and dropped to the deck of the boat.

"Whooee girl, that was bloody amazing!" An adrenaline rush over what had just happened replaced Ben's fear. Jo slightly bent over and reached behind to her neck, pulling the wetsuit hood over the top of her head. She jogged over to where Ben stood, almost losing her balance when Ben exuberantly ruffled his fingers in her burnished copper locks.

"Easy there buster. That hair *is* attached to my scalp, you know."

Jo rubbed a sore spot on her head.

"Sorry, but that was fantastic. I thought the thing was going to get right in the cage with the two of you."

"You're not the only one. I thought Valerie and I were goners for sure. Did you get film?" Ben nodded. "I can't wait to see the edited version. It can't be every day you get footage like that. This is certainly going to be a memorable *Where Are They Now.*" She thumped his back and they headed for the door to the galley.

"AS FOR ME, I'll take the sharks of the boardroom any day. They're babes in the woods compared to this lot. Tune in next time for the final installment of my series, *Where Are They Now?*" Jo hit the stop button on the editing suite remote, relaxed back into her chair, and rested her feet on the edge of the desk. "What do you think?"

Her editor, Ros Deakin, shook her head. "I don't know where to begin. That's fantastic footage and a definite ratings winner. Having said that, I'm not too comfortable that a good friend was almost fish food."

A dimpled cheeky grin lit up Jo's lightly tanned face. "Ros, you would've loved it." She laughed at the look on Ros's face. "Okay, maybe not, but it was a once in a lifetime experience, that's for sure."

Ros reached for her coffee and took a sip. "So what's your next project? Hang on, let me guess." She put the coffee cup down and picked up a pen from her desk, wielding it as if it were a microphone. "Welcome to my final installment of *Where Are They Now?* Today we follow a man who, until recently, had spent his entire life crafting exquisite crocodile skin shoes, which were eagerly snatched up by the world's elite. But he's left that all behind him now, swapping wrestling for a new shoe design to wrestling the actual thing. Yes, that's right. He now makes a living wrestling crocodiles." She finished, as if she were looking into a camera, and turned to Jo, a nonplussed look on her face.

Jo rolled her eyes. "Nothing so dramatic. Let me show you what I have in mind." She removed her legs from the desk and sat up in the chair before reaching forward and pressing the play button on the remote. The screen again came to life.

The rolling greens of a golf course filled the monitor followed by a close shot of a female golfer teeing off, her ball flying straight and true down the middle of a lush fairway. Jo's voice narrated the scene.

"Ten years ago this woman was on the verge of greatness. At twenty-five, Australian Lauren Wheatley had the golfing world at her feet. After taking up golf at sixteen she wasted no time in mastering the game, winning tournament after tournament." A collage of Lauren Wheatley victories followed. "Her last tournament was as good as won when she entered the final day, leading by eight under par. She only needed a top five finish to guarantee her a rookie spot on the much-coveted Ladies Professional Golf Tour. But in a spectacular example of how fickle life and sport can be, she imploded on the final nine." Matching the narrative were pictures of Lauren Wheatley missing putts and muffing bunker and fairway shots. The final shot was of a distraught Wheatley being led away from the eighteenth hole by her caddie, his arm around her shoulders. "That was the last game she ever played, mysteriously dropping out of the golfing world, never to be heard from again." The picture became a still shot of Lauren and her caddie, disappearing into a tunnel beneath stands surrounding the eighteenth hole, her putter in the foreground, lying on the side of the green, where she'd dropped it. The still caught Lauren in profile, taking one last look over her shoulder at what she left behind. "So, where is she now?"

Jo hit the pause button and turned to Ros. "What do you think?"

Ros released an exasperated breath as she rolled her eyes and shook her head. "Do you have a patent on the term "flogging a dead horse"? We've been over this already, when we tried to contact her at the beginning of this series. She never returned any of my calls or yours. Have you heard from her?"

Jo looked at Lauren's profile frozen on the screen, the sun-bleached brown hair partially obscuring her face. "No, but I do know there's more to this story than meets the eye. It's a story worth telling."

"Do you even know what she's doing at the moment, or where to find her?"

"Apparently, she's a Cradle Mountain guide, working and living in the park. Tell you what, why don't you let me fly down there and see if I can convince her to let us do her story?"

Ros leant back in her chair and folded her arms, a skeptical look on her face.

"How about this. If I can't get her to agree to the story, then I'll pay all the associated trip expenses. Come on Ros, please," Jo pleaded.

Ros held up her hands. "Okay, okay. You can give it a try. But don't blame me when you return with nothing to show for your venture except a bloody great credit card bill."

Jo smugly smiled. "Don't write me off just yet."

Chapter
Two

"HERE ARE YOUR keys, Miss Ashby. Once again, welcome to The Retreat. I hope you enjoy your stay."

Jo gratefully took the folder and keys from the desk clerk and, with the exception of a small map of directions to her cabin, stashed everything in her daypack. She walked through the carved wooden double doors of the lodge, across the verandah and to her car.

With only one misdirection, Jo came to a halt in front of the guest cabin that was to be her home for the duration of her stay. No sooner had she applied the brake than her phone rang. She struggled to turn off the engine while simultaneously groping around in her daypack for her mobile. She pulled the keys from the engine as she checked the caller ID on the screen.

"Hi, Ros. What's up?"

"I just wanted to make sure you got there safely and to find out what it's like."

Jo's ear filled with static from the call. "Hang on a minute. Bad reception. Let me get out of the car—right, that's a bit better. Yes, I made it safely." She scanned her surrounds. "The place is a series of guest cabins set up against the bush, with a main lodge."

"Sounds pretty swanky," Ros replied.

"It's not roughing it by any stretch. The main lodge is just that. It's lots of wood, leather, and comfy nooks, with a home-style touch to it. The cabins are self-sustaining with a little kitchenette, or at least that's what the brochure says. It'd be nice if I could actually get *inside*."

Laughter filtered down the line. "Okay, I can take a hint. Give me a call once you're settled and let me know what's going on."

"Will do, bye." Jo stashed her phone in her pack, grabbed her gear, and headed for her cabin which was as the brochure had promised. The main room incorporated a subtle mix of modern and rustic. The cool white walls were capably complemented by the Huon pine paneling, and a fireplace completed the room. She opened a door off the main room and gleefully rubbed her hands together. "Oooh, a spa. *You're* certainly going to get a workout while I'm here."

She walked across the room and opened a door that led to a small private balcony, replete with two carved wooden recliners. "What a beautiful view." Jo stepped through the door and gazed out across the Tasmanian wilderness. She watched a small bird settle on a branch to her left, before it began singing in high-pitched notes to other birds in the surrounding trees.

Jo braced her hands on the verandah's rail and smiled at the bird. "As much as I'd love to watch and listen to you for the rest of the afternoon, that's not going to get my unpacking done." She watched the bird flit to another branch, before she went back into the cabin to begin settling herself into what was to be her home for throughout her stay.

JO OPENED THE door to the guest bar and was immediately enveloped in a blast of warm air from the room's roaring log fire. She shrugged out of her jacket and placed it on a coffee table that stood near one of the groups of comfortable leather chairs dotting the room.

"Hi. Welcome to The Retreat's happy hour. I'll be with you in a minute."

Jo glanced at the bar counter just as the server disappeared around the corner. She was happy for the temporary solitude, and took the time to view the bar's intimate surrounds. The large stone fireplace dominated the room, and a semi-circle of stones surrounded it, strategically placed so people might sit by the fire. The hub-like striations on their well-worn surfaces looked to Jo like the fossilised vertebrae of a giant dinosaur. The honey-coloured, wood-paneled walls were in keeping with the theme of the lodge, as were the series of artworks and paintings adorning the walls. While Jo waited for the server's return, she scrutinised a group of old photographs, their occupants sporting clothing reminiscent of the early part of the twentieth century.

"That's Annie Hethrington, Marta Jung, and Kate and Gustav Weindorfer, a few years after the Weindorfers came to Cradle Mountain." The server came around from behind the bar. "Hi, I'm Ellie." She leant forward to get a better view of the picture, in turn subtly leaning into Jo's space. "That's Wombat Tarn in the background. It's also known as Wombat Pool." Ellie straightened. "What can I get you?" She flashed a smile and returned to the bar.

Jo followed Ellie and eased herself onto a bar stool. "May I have a gin and tonic?"

Ellie reached for a highball glass. "Coming right up."

"Thanks. Just put it under room two-twenty."

Ellie placed the drink and a plate of canapés in front of Jo on the shiny Tasmanian ash bar-top, and turned to enter the transaction into the computer. "Miss Ashby. Is that correct?"

Jo winced. "Sort of, except 'Miss' makes me feel like I'm in some bloody Edwardian novel. Would you mind calling me Jo?" She took a sip of her drink and reached for one of the salmon canapés, from where it rested on the plate.

Ellie smiled suggestively. "I wouldn't mind at all."

Jo's gaze met hers, taking in the open invitation they held. She cleared her throat and tried to defuse the moment. "So what's there to do around here of an evening?" The words were barely out of her mouth when she realized how they must have sounded.

Ellie leant back against the bar and raised one brow. "It depends on what you *want* to do."

Jo casually looked over her shoulder to confirm they were the only two in the bar before she looked back at Ellie. "Let's just keep it above the belt buckle, shall we? Thank you, but no thank you. Are there night activities for guests?"

Ellie acknowledged Jo's gentle refusal, and slipped back into her role as a server. "Normally there's a wine and cheese tasting or a Tasmanian animal night-viewing tour." Ellie turned and looked at the clock on the wall. "You're a bit late for the tour. It normally kicks off in the foyer at six-thirty and heads into the park from there. You might still be able to catch the wine and cheese tasting, though."

Jo took a slice of brie from the plate, and placed it on a wafer cracker. She sniffed the cheese and took a bite. Its creamy flavour exploded in her mouth. "If it's anything like this then that's something I'm definitely going to have to try, but maybe not tonight." She popped the remainder of the tasty morsel into her mouth, and washed it down with a sip from her drink. "Do you just meet somewhere, or do you have to sign up?"

"You sign up at the concierge's desk at reception. Both events are pretty popular. If you can, it's best to reserve a space on either of the activities the night before. Both are run by the Cradle Mountain National Park guides."

Jo took the opportunity to pursue Ellie's unwitting segue into the topic she wanted to discuss. "Do you know many of the guides here? How many are there?"

"There're a heap of part-time guides living in the towns around here. They come during the high season and leave again. Not counting them, there're about eight full-time guides who live in the staff rooms at The Retreat. The head guide actually lives in the park. They're a pretty decent bunch, with the exception of Geoffrey Blackson."

Jo's curiosity piqued. "What's wrong with him?"

"He's a misogynistic prick, that's all," Ellie replied dryly.

"Don't hold back. Say what you really mean."

Elli picked up a glass and began vigorously cleaning it with a towel. "Sorry about that. But he thinks he's God's gift to guiding. Without a doubt he's good at his craft, but his attitude to women and anyone who isn't white is pretty disgraceful."

"Why do they keep him on?"

"He's pretty careful. Plus, it helps if your father's a part owner of The Retreat. Just be careful about getting stuck in tight spaces with him. Aside from his personality he has roaming hands, especially with someone as beautiful as you." Ellie winked and placed the dry glass on a tray of similar glasses.

Jo held her hands up in mock surrender. "Enough already," she said, laughing along with Ellie. "He doesn't take the night tour, does he?"

"That'd interfere too much with his social life. The tour's normally led by the head guide, Lauren Wheatley. Now *there's* a beauty. Great physique and those eyes. Unsettling but beautiful at the same time."

Jo drained her glass. "Can I have the same again, please?" While Ellie prepared the drink, Jo again looked over her shoulder, checking to be sure they were still alone. "How do you get to be head guide?"

Ellie placed the drink down in front of Jo. "She's the longest continuous serving guide." She creased her forehead. "I think she's been here for just over nine years. That and her qualifications make her an easy pick. She's the only one who lives in the park, but here's the strange thing. She's got a modern cabin but instead she spends most of her time in Annie's hut. It's an old shack built around 1915, and it's got no mod cons whatsoever." Ellie shuddered. "I don't know if I could put up with that."

Jo retreated into her own thoughts. She looked up to see Ellie staring at her "What's she like?" Jo asked, attempting to redirect whatever Ellie was about to ask.

"She's nice, always polite to the guests. But I get the sense she's holding herself back. Because she keeps a lot to herself, quite a few of the guides and the staff think she's a snob. But I've had a couple of chats with her and that's not the case at all." Ellie wiped a cloth across the bar. "No doubt there's a mystery there. I just don't know what it is."

Jo popped another canapé into her mouth, mulling Ellie's words. *Maybe this isn't going to be as easy as I thought.* "Do you know what she did before she came here?"

"Wouldn't have a clue." Ellie leant forward on the bar. "Why all the questions?"

Jo stood and took a last sip from her drink, and checked the room, masking her questions by looking for her coat. "Just curious, I suppose. If I'm going to go on one of these tours, I like to know my guide's capable."

Ellie snorted. "She's more than capable. As a guide she's got a one hundred percent success record in all the rescues she's done on the mountain. She's never lost a single person. It's uncanny, really. But if you're interested in getting to know her on a personal level—" she shrugged her shoulders. "Good luck. She's never shown any great interest for male or *female* company."

"Thanks for the advice. I'd better go get myself signed up for tomorrow night." With a final wave in Ellie's direction, she picked up her coat and walked through the lodge to the reception area. The concierge's desk stood off to one side of the foyer, partially encased in a wooden nook carved to resemble the hollow trunk of a tree.

"Good evening, ma'am. Can I help you?"

"Hi. Can you tell me who's guiding the night-viewing tour tomorrow night?"

She waited as he consulted the schedule of events for the following day. "That'd be Lauren Wheatley. She's our head guide."

"Great. Can I sign up for the tour? I'm Jo Ashby, staying in room two-twenty."

"Certainly. We'll charge the expense to your room, Miss Ashby. The tour starts at six-thirty, but we ask you're here ten minutes before the tour kicks off."

"Thanks. Tomorrow at six-twenty it is." She struggled to stifle an unexpected yawn. "Sorry, it's been a long day."

The concierge smiled sympathetically. "The night air will do that to you. Have a good evening. We'll see you tomorrow."

JO CHECKED HER watch and realised she still had a little time before she had to check in for the night tour. She used it to contact Ros, which she did through her computer. Ros's face appeared on screen.

"Hello, stranger. How are things going down there?"

"Not too bad. I thought I'd call and let you know what I've been up to." Jo watched her sign something and hand it to someone off screen.

"Have you spoken with her yet?" Ros leant forward, a look of anticipation on her face. "Has she agreed to the project?"

Jo chuckled and shook her head. "No I haven't. I did some legwork last night and found out she normally guides an evening animal viewing tour, so I booked myself on one."

"Hell, woman, why not just find her and see if she's interested or not?"

Jo was accustomed to Ros's frustration, something her editor often displayed when they worked together. She shrugged off the criticism. "I don't think it's going to be as easy as you presume. From what I learnt last night, she keeps a lot to herself. Walking up to her front door and knocking on it isn't the way to get her to talk. I prefer to do this carefully or we might lose any possibility of filming her story."

Ros leant back in her chair and took a breath, the fingers of her hand impatiently strumming the armrest. "Okay, if you didn't see her today, what did you do?"

"I walked around Dove Lake and through the Ballroom Forest, just to get a feel for the place. This is the first time I've been here and I didn't realise just how beautiful it is. One moment I was walking along the edge of a glacial lake and the next minute I was in what looked like an ancient forest, with moss covering everything. It was a lot like that movie trilogy they did in New Zealand. Everywhere I looked was a carpet of green and gnarled trees. And that's just lower down. I can't wait to see what it looks like higher up. The walk was very calming. Maybe you should take some time off and come down here for a while. God only knows you could do with a break."

"There are days like this one when I could think of nothing better, but someone's got to hold the fort while you're off gallivanting around the countryside."

Jo checked her watch. "Speaking of gallivanting, I'd better be on my way or I'll miss my tour. I'll be in touch." After a quick goodbye from Ros, Jo shut down her laptop and made her way to reception.

AFTER SIGNING IN at the concierge's desk, Jo made herself comfortable in one of the large soft leather chairs dotting the foyer. She slowly scanned the small groups and couples who were also obviously waiting for the tour. She picked up a newspaper from the table beside her and reacquainted herself with the world's daily events. She was so engrossed in one of the articles that she didn't notice Lauren's entry.

"Hi everyone, and welcome to the night-viewing tour. My name's Lauren and I'll be your guide this evening."

Jo lowered her paper and then stared, open-mouthed, at Lauren. *She's not just beautiful, she's stunning!* She'd seen golfing photos of a younger Lauren and knew she was pretty. But the intervening years had filled out Lauren's young adult awkwardness with a quiet confidence and something she couldn't quite put a name to.

"We'll shortly be on our way, but we'll start off with a quick presentation on the park and what you're about to see. If you'll follow me, we'll go into the Fagus room and begin our evening." Lauren glanced at Jo. "Are you part of the tour?"

Jo realised she'd been gawking, somewhat like a cross between a village idiot and love-struck teen. She nodded and stood, inexplicably filled with warmth by Lauren's smile.

"Come on then," Lauren motioned and walked toward one of The Retreat's conference rooms. She waited as Jo stepped through, before closing the door and going to the front of the room.

"Welcome to you all. I see a few familiar faces, so what I'm about to cover might be old news to some, but it'll help the rest of you.

Cradle Mountain is part of the Cradle Mountain-Lake Saint Clair National Park which, in 1982, was placed on the world heritage list. About ten thousand years ago this area was covered with glacial ice, and that's been the main contributor in forming the landscape you'll see during your stay. The area was originally occupied by aborigines, and we've found evidence of their occupation throughout the park. Joseph Fossey is credited with naming Cradle Mountain in 1827. You're not going to see a lot of the landscape tonight, unless of course you can see in the dark." Laughter rippled through the group. "Hopefully what we *will* see are some of the park's night creatures. Just give me a moment to set up this screen."

Jo shifted in her seat, her fingers itching for her camera. She'd watched Lauren's face light up when she talked about the park, her enthusiasm making her more beautiful. *She might be aloof on some occasions, but she's clearly at ease with this group.*

Lauren wiped her hands and picked up a small remote. "Here we go." She pressed a button, and a small black-and-white creature filled the screen. "This is a Tassie devil. We might be lucky and see one of these tonight. Don't worry if we don't, though. There's a resident devil who's got a burrow under The Retreat's main building. On hot days, you can see him sunning himself beside the walkway to your huts. Don't be fooled by their cute looks, though. These things have a bite nine times more powerful than a dog's. It's no wonder the only thing they don't eat are echidna quills."

A picture of a small, furry four-legged, white-spotted brown animal appeared on the screen. "This is an eastern quoll and it's also found in the park, preferring to eat at night. It's a forest-dweller, making its nest under rocks or fallen logs. I'll take you to a couple of spots where we can find their nests." A member of the audience held up his hand.

"Isn't that the spotted-tail quoll?"

"They're very close, except the spotted-tail quoll has spots on its tail, whereas the eastern quoll doesn't." Lauren once more clicked the remote. "Many people say this next one reminds them of a mini kangaroo and they're not far wrong. They're known by their aboriginal name of pademelon, and they're found only in Tasmania. The males are much bigger than the females and can weigh up to twelve kilograms—that's twenty-six pounds for our overseas guests. But the female, which is clearly the cuter of the two, usually only weighs three point nine kilograms, or eight-and-a-half pounds." Several people laughed at her statement.

"I think I saw one of those outside my room tonight," Jo said, then uncontrollably blushed when Lauren's gaze fell on her.

"You probably did. They're pretty abundant around some of the huts set back against the forest." Lauren shifted her attention to the screen and then back to her audience. "This next one's a tree-dweller, like the ringtail possum. We should also be able to catch a glimpse of these tonight. What sets the ringtail apart from some of the other possums in the park is that they're active nest-builders." She paused and took a sip from her water bottle.

A picture of a squat grey furry four-legged animal appeared on screen. "Last, but not least is my favourite, the wombat. As you can see, they're built low to the ground. The ones here are not as big as the ones you'll find on the mainland, which I think adds to their appeal. At least it does to me."

Jo watched Lauren smile at the group. *I've only been with her less than ten minutes and I'm incredibly drawn to her. What the hell have I got myself into?*

"The wombat's a solitary creature that lives in burrows. It normally comes out at night to feed and then spends the daylight hours sleeping."

"Sounds like a great plan to me," someone said, again causing the room's occupants to laugh.

Lauren smiled. "These are the key animals I hope we'll see tonight. There are many more throughout the park, and if you're here for any length of time you might just see them. Anyway, let's head out, shall we?"

JO SIGHED AND shook her head as the small group once more made its way to their van. "It's uncanny how she finds these things. I could walk right by them and never see them."

"You're right," an elderly woman replied. "I didn't see that spotted quoll until we almost trod on it."

They reached the van and began to climb in. "Where to now, Lauren?" someone called through the darkness in the rear cabin.

"Let's go and find a wombat."

The vehicle slowly made its way along a dirt track, pulling on to a verge, next to open grassland. Lauren flicked on the interior lights and rested her arm on the top of the driver's seat as she partially turned her body toward the van's occupants. "This is where we're likely to find our wombats. As long as you're downwind of them you can get pretty close before they move. But I have to warn you, this is a game of patience, which, at times, can get a little cold. Anyone who doesn't want to get out can stay in the vehicle. There're blankets under your seats to keep you warm while the engine's off."

Jo was among the third of the van's occupants who ventured forth in search of a wombat.

"If you spread yourselves out along the edge of the road, I'll come by and help you try to find one," Lauren said as she closed the door of the van.

Jo walked away from the vehicle and stood in the bracing

mountain air. She folded her arms and looked up into the night sky, marveling at the myriad stars, accompanied by the glow of the full moon. She was so engrossed in trying to find the Southern Cross that she jumped at the sound of Lauren's voice.

"Trust me, you won't find them looking up there."

Jo smiled. "I know. It's just that the sky's so beautiful." They shared a quiet moment as they watched the heavens.

"Yes it is, but let's see if we can find you a wombat. Follow me." Lauren stepped off the road and into the rough calf-length grass, turning only once to be sure Jo followed her. They'd barely gone off the road when Lauren stopped, causing Jo to run into her back.

"Ooof, sorry, I was too busy looking where I was going."

Lauren softly laughed. "That's okay. It happens all the time." She lightly gripped Jo's arm. "There's a wombat just to our front. Crouch down and you'll be able to hear her munching the grass."

Jo barely heard Lauren's words. The touch of Lauren's hand through her jacket filled her with a long-forgotten warmth. Lauren retained the contact while the two of them crouched in the darkness silently watching the silhouette in front of them.

"Beautiful, isn't she?" Lauren whispered.

Jo looked at Lauren's face, lit by the soft blue glow of the full moon. "Yes," she replied, completely absorbed by the woman beside her.

Lauren turned and glanced at Jo, and for a moment a spark of recognition swept across Lauren's features in the dim light. She looked down to where her hand still held Jo's jacket, and she softly released her grip and stood. "We'd better get back."

Jo followed a now silent Lauren to the van and took her seat as Lauren addressed them from the van's open rear door.

"Team, that ends the animal viewing tour. We'll head back to The Retreat where a supper's ready for you in the bar. Given how cold it is, I think I'll take questions there rather than out here."

JO SIPPED HER port and nibbled a cube of sharp Tasmanian cheddar cheese while she watched Lauren circle the room, pausing at each of the small groups of people who had been part of the night's tour.

"Can I top that up for you?"

Jo turned and watched Ellie refill her glass. "Thank you."

Ellie tilted her head at Lauren. "She's a beauty, isn't she?"

Jo replied without thinking. "Yes, she is."

Ellie softly laughed. "And very aloof. I really don't think you'll get anywhere with her."

"Trust me when I tell you she might be a lovely woman, but I'm past my years of one night stands, even if she was available. That's definitely not my intent."

"Whatever your intent is, you'd better work it out because she's headed your way." Ellie stepped to the next group of guests, in turn filling their glasses.

"Have you any questions about tonight's tour?" Lauren popped a small piece of brie into her mouth.

Jo stalled her response by taking a sip of her drink, quickly taking the time to view her more closely. *Ellie was right. Lauren's eyes are amazing. They're almost the colour of honeycomb, lined with a ring of dark chocolate.* Jo blinked, realising Lauren was patiently waiting for a response. "No, but thanks for the evening. It was very informative. I'm amazed at how you managed to find all those animals. I could spend the next three-and-a-half weeks of my time here and never find what you pointed out tonight."

"Three-and-a-half weeks. That's a long time to stay here. What brings you to The Retreat?"

Deciding honesty was clearly the best policy, Jo answered, "Actually *you're* the reason I'm here." She watched Lauren's features shut down, almost as if someone had pulled an imaginary blind over her face.

Lauren nervously glanced around the room and at the clock above the fireplace. "What do you mean?"

"My name's Jo Ashby. I'm a reporter." She got no further.

"I don't give interviews anymore. I haven't done that for ten years," Lauren curtly whispered. "That part of me is in the past."

"Hang on. I'm not here to dredge up your past. I know you were an extremely promising golfer, but the focus of the series I'm doing is on what famous people are doing now."

"I'm not famous."

"You're right, you're not famous now, but by God, you were then." Jo quickly looked around their immediate surroundings, ensuring their conversation was still relatively private. "Look, people walk away from greatness for all sorts of reasons. That's not the complete focus of my story. I want to know what and why you're doing what you're doing now."

Lauren placed her glass on the table beside her. "Not now." Her eyes again drifted to the clock above the fire.

"Will you at least think about it? I can promise you it's not my intent to dredge up anything that'd make you uncomfortable. But, trust me; there *are* people out there who want to know where you went." She paused at the look of disbelief on Lauren's face. "It's true. We polled over two thousand people, asking them this: if they had the chance to know what certain people were up to now, who would they pick? You came up as number three on the list, which is why I'm here. Whether you like it or not, people are still interested in you."

Lauren's eyes scanned the room, realising a number of curious faces were now focused in their direction. "I'll think about it," she said noncommittally as she took a final look at the clock before quietly slipping from the room.

LAUREN DECELERATED as her four-wheel-drive vehicle hit the dirt road, signaling the entrance to the park. She drove through the crisp, black night, replaying the conversation she'd had with Jo. *Why now, after all these years? I've left that part of my life behind me.* She drove by the home the park authorities had allocated her, instead heading for Annie's hut, where she parked and got out.

Once inside, she used a torch to navigate around the darkness of the hut, lighting lamps as she went. The resulting soft glow seemed to bounce off the vertical wooden slats of the building's walls. She took off her daypack and placed it on the table, and wearily rubbed her neck. "I know you're here. Why won't you say something?"

"Who is she?" came a question from one of the room's still-darkened corners.

"She's a reporter after a story, that's all. I knew I'd have to face them again some time, but I don't think I was ready for it tonight. She's just interested in what I did before I came here."

"I think she's uncommonly interested in *you*," was the soft reply.

Lauren turned and looked in the direction of the voice. "I thought I felt you out there tonight." She waited for a reply that never came. "Look, she might be interested in me but she's definitely not the type of woman I want to be with. She strikes me as someone who takes risks in life and love, and that's something I've no intention of being a part of. Besides, it's you I want to be with. Surely you know that?" She moved toward the shadowy corner of the room and the figure waiting for her there.

Chapter Three

JO MUNCHED ON a piece of toast as she waited for the Web cam connection to come to life. She watched Ros adjust the Web cam's viewing field and settle back into her chair.

"Hey there. I was beginning to think you'd been eaten by a pack of Tassie devils or something."

"Not quite," Jo mumbled before she swallowed. "I've been busy trying to get the damned interview to work."

"How did the night-viewing thing go?"

"It went well, right up until the moment where I introduced myself as a journalist and it went downhill from there."

Ros took a sip from a cup that seemed to be a permanent extension of her hand. "What did she say?"

"She shut up like a clam, seemed obsessed with watching the clock, and made a quick exit shortly thereafter. Before she left I asked her if she'd think about the project and she said she would. But since then she seems to have disappeared into thin air. I thought she might've turned up for the viewing tour last night, so I camped out in the lobby, but someone else took it. I've even driven past her place inside the park and it seems to be empty." Jo picked up another slice of toast and took a bite.

Ros turned her face away from the screen and caressed her lips with her fingertips. Her contemplation complete, she returned her full gaze to Jo. "Are you still sure this is a good idea? I know this is a pet project and the stay down there is being paid out of your pocket. But how long do you intend to give it before you make a decision to squash this? I mean, there's still time to go after the multi-millionaire who gave his fortune away and now lives in a Buddhist monastery in the middle of the bush."

Jo vehemently shook her head. "I absolutely do *not* want to give up. Not just yet, anyway. There's more to this woman than meets the eye. She's hiding something and you can see it in the way she carries herself. I watched her last night during the tour, and she kept on doing this strange thing. It's like she weighs up everything she does before she does it, if you know what I mean. There's no spontaneity. At least give me a few more days. Maybe another week and we'll see if we're any closer to an interview."

Ros rubbed her chin, then rested her head on the splayed fingers of one hand. "What does she look like these days?"

Jo felt the heat of a flush on her cheeks. "She's quite stunning. She's about my height, maybe a little taller, sun-bleached light brown hair, eyes the colour of honeycomb, and a body that's obviously been kept in shape by all the Dove walking she does. I mean, when she was first on the golf scene she was pretty, but now she's beautiful." She baulked at the 'know it all' grin on Ros's face. "It's not what you think."

"Are you attracted to her?"

"You'd have to be dead not to be. Even a dyed in the wool heterosexual like you would find it hard not to be drawn in. She's got that quality about her."

"Be honest. Are you focused on the piece or the person?"

Jo leant back, ran both hands through her hair. "I won't deny I'm attracted to her, but that's not what I'm after. There's something deeper here, Ros, and I think it's a story worth telling."

"I don't need to tell you to be careful, but I can't help myself. So be bloody careful! You don't exactly have the best track record in matters of the heart."

"Thanks for your vote of confidence, *mate*," Jo replied in mock offence.

Ros winked. "I'll let you get back to it."

"Thanks. I'm heading to the store this morning to buy some food. This eating in the lodge and room service is starting to cut into my budget, not to mention blow out my waistline. I'll keep you posted."

JO STROLLED AROUND the small store filled with tourist paraphernalia, clothing, maps, books, and food. She picked up a baseball cap with an embroidered silhouette of Cradle Mountain on the front, and put it on. Pausing in front of a mirror, she nodded. Satisfied the colour of the cap didn't clash too much with her short, copper-burnished hair, she put it in the basket and moved on. Pulling open the door of the refrigerator, she grabbed a carton of orange juice and a carton of milk, put them in her basket, and headed for the checkout.

The cashier was fiddling with an empty paper spool, pulling it out of the machine then replacing it with a new one. "I'm sorry. I'll just be a moment."

"Take your time. I'm in no hurry." While Jo waited she couldn't help but overhear the conversation of the two couples behind her.

"We did the Dove Lake guided tour yesterday and it was absolutely beautiful. I really did enjoy myself, except for the fact it was supposed to be a two-hour tour but ended up being closer to three. The guide was very patient. But the slow people in our group held up the walk at times. We were so late in coming back I almost missed my spa appointment."

Jo rolled her eyes, then quickly schooled her features, managing to maintain an outwardly neutral look. *Stop the presses. Woman misses spa treatment. This could be the end of civilisation as we know it.*

The other woman behind Jo chipped in. "We had the same problem with the first walk we took. We had this guide, what was his name again? Blackson I think. At one stage I thought he was going to throttle one of the tour members. The whole thing took twice as long as it was supposed to. We weren't going to take another tour until we found out you can hire a guide for the day, and so that's what we did. There're no problems with having to worry about other group members not keeping up, because it's just the guide and you. It's not cheap, but you see more, and that makes it value for money."

Jo turned. "Excuse me, I didn't mean to eavesdrop, but did you say you could hire your own guide?"

The other woman nodded.

"How did you do it?" Jo pressed. The other woman looked her over, as if she were assessing whether Jo was capable of affording such a luxury. "You book through the concierge at reception, but you can only do it if you're a guest of the lodge."

Jo bridled at other woman's assumption, and barely managed to rein in what she really wanted to say. "It's a good thing I am, then. I have about three weeks remaining of my booking there." She silently high-fived herself at the look of surprise on the faces of the two couples, who now seemed to be calculating the cost of such a stay. "Thanks for the information."

"I'm ready now, ma'am."

Jo turned around and smiled at the clerk as she unloaded her groceries from her basket. After she paid, she made the short journey to the lodge's foyer and walked to the concierge's desk where she tapped the bell.

"Yes ma'am, how can I help you?"

Jo placed the two bags of groceries on the floor beside her and rubbed some warmth back into her hands. "I've heard I can hire a personal guide for the day."

"Yes, you can hire them for a half-day or a whole day, whichever you prefer. It's a little more costly than the normal tours we run, but you do see more."

"Money's not an issue. Can I nominate a guide for the day, or am I just given whoever's on?"

"We can do it either way. You can ask for him or her, so long as the guide isn't already booked on one of our tours."

"I did the night tour the other evening and was impressed by the depth of knowledge of your guide Lauren Wheatley. Is she booked for tomorrow?" Jo leant forward on the counter and tried to read the upside-down guide schedule in front of the concierge.

"No, she isn't and she's rostered for duty tomorrow. Would you like to book her?"

Jo smiled. "Yes please. For a day if I may. I'm in room two-twenty." She watched the concierge make a notation beside Lauren's name. "When would that start?"

"You need to be here by seven-thirty in the morning and the two of you head into the park from here. She'll have morning tea and lunch for you both, plus some water, but we ask that you also carry your own water. We also recommend you layer your clothes. The weather can change in a matter of minutes, especially once you get into the higher areas."

"Will do. I'll see you tomorrow." Jo picked up her bags and headed out the foyer. She strolled through the waist-high brush on one of the walking tracks leading to the cabins. As she walked, she couldn't help but wonder what tomorrow would bring. *If the mountain won't come to Jo then Jo must go to Lauren.*

JO FINISHED HER breakfast in the main lodge and headed into the foyer. She took a seat removed from the others, and waited for Lauren's arrival. She didn't have to wait long.

Lauren walked through the doors of the lodge to the reception. She shrugged a large pack from her shoulders and smiled at the young man behind the desk. "Hi Steve. I heard I'm doing a personal guided tour today."

"Yep, your guest's arrived. She's sitting just over there." He pointed in Jo's direction.

Lauren turned and when she saw Jo, the smile on her face disappeared, replaced with a flash of anger. Lauren silently closed her eyes, as if in frustration, then seemed to regain her control before walking toward Jo.

"Miss Ashby, it's great to see you again."

Jo choked back a snort at the words, which were in obvious contradiction to Lauren's feelings. "Please call me Jo. It's great to see you, too."

For a moment the shadow of a smile seemed to cross Lauren's face. "Before we step off, do you have enough water for an eight-to nine-hour trip? Do you have additional layers just in case the weather changes?"

Feeling as if she were being lectured in a manner an adult would speak to a child, Jo reacted. "Yes, I do. And I've even put my boots on the right feet this morning." She finished her last comment in a volume meant for Lauren's ears alone.

Lauren refused to take the bait. "Let's get going. We'll take my vehicle and head out to Dove Lake. That'll be our step-off point."

They walked out of the foyer to Lauren's four-wheel drive. Jo stowed her gear in the back seat and settled into the front passenger seat. Lauren turned the engine over, reversed out of the car park, and headed for the park's main entrance.

Lauren stole a sideways glance at Jo. "You don't give up, do you?"

Jo folded her arms over her chest and stared at Lauren. "I thought I'd have heard from you by now. If you never had the intention of getting back to me, then why didn't you just say so?"

"That's not the case. I've been a little busy, that's all." Lauren shifted gears, uttering a muffled curse at the crunching noise that emanated from the gearbox.

"Yes, it obviously takes a lot of effort to hide from me."

"I hate to break the news to you but I've other responsibilities here apart from making up my mind whether I want to expose to the general public a part of my life I've left behind. And I *wasn't* avoiding you as you seem to be implying."

"Lucky you haven't been, because otherwise it'd be a pain in the arse to be stuck with me all day, wouldn't it?"

"Wouldn't it just," Lauren replied through gritted teeth, glaring at Jo.

"Look out!"

Lauren whipped her head back to the windscreen, just in time to swerve around a wombat slowly making its way to greener grass on the other side of the road. "For God's sake!" She pulled the vehicle to the side, applied the brake, and rested her forehead on the steering wheel and attempted to bring herself back under control. Jo reached out and lightly touched her shoulder. "Are you okay?"

"Fine, just bloody fine," she quietly replied. "Look, you've paid for a day trip and it's my responsibility to get you through it without you being killed or, indeed, one of us killing the other. Can we set the interview thing to one side for the day?"

"The request's not going to go away. If it's not me interviewing you it'll be someone else. Sooner or later it's going to happen." Jo watched the wombat finally make it safely to the other side of the road.

"Just not today, okay?" Lauren pleaded.

Jo refused to acquiesce, preferring to redirect the conversation. "You're the guide. How about you show me what it is you do?"

Lauren pursed her lips and put the four-wheel drive into gear. "Let's do that, shall we?"

Jo pointed at a weather-beaten upright slab hut, its corrugated iron roof rusty from age, the small picket fence surrounding it bereft of any paint. "What's that?" She felt the speed of the vehicle suddenly increase as she posed her question.

"That's Annie's hut. It used to be owned by a woman who walked here in the early part of the twentieth century."

Jo nodded, thoughtful. "I remember now. Ellie pointed her out to me in a photo which is on the walls of the bar. She said you live there now."

Lauren's eyebrows rose. "You've been talking about me with the bartender?"

"No, it wasn't like that. She just mentioned you preferred this hut to the place you have in the park."

"You seem to have done your homework well. Who will you talk to next, the cashier at the shop?"

Jo sensed Lauren's discomfort at parts of her life being bandied about with someone she obviously regarded as a stranger. She attempted to defuse the situation. "I did that already. She says you get out here on the flats in the full moon and dance naked with the wombats."

Lauren stole a glance at the passenger seat and huffed. "We'll be at Dove Lake soon. Why don't you just enjoy the scenery. I'll be happy to answer any questions you have on *that* topic."

Rather than goad Lauren further, Jo did as requested and gazed around the park's surrounds. It wasn't long before they'd parked the car and headed for the sign-in hut, where a queue of walkers waited their turn to register their own walks.

Lauren pulled out a broad-brimmed cloth hat from the side of her pack and slipped it on. "We'll register our walk and be on our way." They silently waited in line, intermittently shuffling closer to the front. Lauren fiddled with the sternum strap on her daypack, refusing to meet Jo's eyes. "Have you walked before?"

"Been walking since I was a baby."

Lauren removed her sunglasses and wiped her forehead in exasperation. "That's not what I meant and you know it. Have you bushwalked before?"

"Why?" Jo innocently queried.

Lauren raised her face to the sky, attempting to control her temper. "Because your answer determines where we go today," she succinctly replied.

Jo belligerently put her hands on her hips and stared back at Lauren. "I have. Where would you like me to start?"

"The beginning would be good." Frustration glinted in Lauren's eyes. She turned at the tap on her shoulder from the walker behind her.

"Listen," the man said, "I'd like to start my walk today but before I can, I have to sign in. So how about you two newlyweds register and take your quarrel somewhere else?"

Lauren scowled at the curious eyes focused on them. She moved forward, checked her watch and picked up the pen, noting the time, number of people, and route they would take for the day. She replaced the pen and walked briskly across the dusty car park. "I'm assuming by your comments you've done this a few times," she called over her shoulder. "Let's see how good you are, shall we? We'll take the right path around Dove Lake, until we reach the Goat Track, and then we'll head up to Marion's Lookout. It's the shortest route although it can be little challenging. That is, if you're up to it."

"I'm right behind you. Where do we go from there?"

"We'll head up the Overland Track and across the Face Track to a little spot which hopefully shouldn't prove too difficult for you."

"Let's go." The words were barely out of Jo's mouth when Lauren took off at a fast clip. Jo matched her speed.

Skirting the edge of a pristine glacial lake, they soon reached a minor junction off the main path and Lauren pointed. "This is the quickest way up to Marion's Flat. Watch your step, it's steep in places."

"Let's do it." Jo followed, glad for the view Lauren's body heralded. She was also glad Lauren couldn't see the expression on her face. While Jo both climbed and hiked, she hadn't done it for a while and a constant burn began to settle into her thighs and butt muscles. *That bloody spa better work or there'll be tears and they won't be mine.*

Lauren paused and wiped the beads of perspiration from her forehead. She looked down at Jo. "Are you okay?"

Jo applied a three-point contact on a steep section, the stones still moist from the morning mist. She hefted herself up. "Couldn't be better."

"We're about halfway up. Watch this next part. It's the steepest bit." Lauren turned and continued her climb.

"Okay." Jo's thighs silently screamed at her to slow her pace. *This woman's a God damn mountain goat.* Despite her best attempts, Jo slowed down. After ten more minutes of solid scrambling she stopped and looked up, silently grateful to see Lauren waiting for her on what appeared to be a ledge. She had almost reached her when she lost her grip, and she struggled to find purchase on the moss-covered rock.

In an instant Lauren was beside her, steadying her from falling. "Are you okay?"

Jo wiped her mossy hand on the side of her trousers. "I'm fine. I just put my hand where it shouldn't be."

"Does that happen to you often?"

Jo raised her eyebrows. "You're making a joke, aren't you?"

The ghost of a smile crossed Lauren's face. "Yes, I was. I'm sorry. I should've taken things a little slower."

"And I should know better than to try and keep up with a mountain goat."

Lauren's eyes twinkled at the remark.

Five minutes later they reached the formed track signaling

Marion's Flat. Jo removed her daypack and tried to work the kinks out of her back.

Lauren took her own pack off and sat on one of the rounded boulders dotting the flat. "We'll take a ten-minute break here. Would you like a cup of tea?"

"No, I'm fine with water, but thank you." Jo positioned her backpack against one of the rocks, and leant back against it. As she sipped from her water bottle, she gazed at the park's namesake. Although she and Lauren were well above the valley floor, the jagged peaks of Cradle Mountain seemed to ascend toward the heavens. From where she sat it was as if some ancient being had taken a large bite out of the middle of the mountain, giving the peak the guise of a somewhat craggy smile.

Lauren motioned toward the mountain. "She's quite a sight, isn't she?"

"Yes, she is." Jo took another sip and looked around. Granite outcrops and hardy low alpine scrub dominated the sub-alpine plateau, interspersed with trees Jo didn't recognize.

Lauren tore the wrapper from an energy bar. "I can see by the way you handled yourself on the climb that you're experienced. But, honestly, now we're up here, can you tell me how experienced you are?"

"What? In walking?"

Lauren paused, the energy bar midway to her mouth. "*Yes*, walking. What else did you think I was talking about?"

Jo smirked, saving the answer to that question for another time. "Let's see. In Australia I've climbed Crater Bluff in the Warrumbungles and Uluru in the Northern Territory. I've walked the Milford Track in New Zealand, bugs and all. And I've also done one ascent of Mount Cook. I was within spitting distance of the peak of Mount McKinley but had to turn back."

"Why?" Lauren regarded her as she munched on her energy bar.

"I was part of a crew filming an ascent of Mount McKinley when my cameraman fell ill. He's not only my cameraman, he's my best friend and I wasn't willing to sacrifice his health for the thrill of being on the highest peak in North America." Jo shrugged. "It wasn't worth the risk."

"Many people would've completed the climb and then come back for him."

Jo stowed her water in her daypack. "I'm not one of them. His welfare was more important to me. Plus, his girlfriend at the time would've shot me if I came back without him." The two shared a laugh as Jo pointed to a small, golden-coloured tree. "What's that?"

"It's a Nothofagus, or fagus for short. It's one of my favourites." She walked over and picked up one of the small, waxy corrugated leaves from the ground and handed it to Jo. "At face value it's a pretty unassuming tree, only growing to about one hundred and eighty centimetres in height. But it's fairly ancient, proving a link between Antarctica, Australia, and South America, when the three continents were joined. It's unique because it's one of Australia's few native deciduous trees." Lauren returned to her backpack. "We'd better keep on going," she said as she shrugged into her pack. "I'll give you a running commentary along the way."

Relieved at the relative flatness of the next part of their journey, Jo also appreciated the way Lauren seemed to have loosened up. They walked side by side, after a while passing a small two-level wooden hut. "What's that?" Jo asked as they approached it.

"Kitchen hut. A lot of walkers doing the Overland Track to Lake Saint Clair stop here for a quick rest before starting their walk."

Jo pointed. "Why does it have one door on top of another?"

"It can really snow up here and when it does, this allows people to get through the top door, if the bottom door's blocked." Lauren slowed down. "We can stop here if you like, but I'd prefer to carry on. We've still got a little walking to do."

"No, let's keep going. Besides, by the looks of the people around the door, the place is full anyway."

"It fills up pretty quickly. We'll continue on around the Face Track. It's a track that sort of contours around the front of Cradle Mountain." Lauren glanced at the sky. "There's a place I'd like to show you. Not many walkers get to see it and, if the weather holds, it should be great."

Jo gestured at the path. "Let's go."

Another forty minutes of solid walking found both of them at a weather-worn, slightly concealed marker, high above Dove Lake.

"How are you traveling?" Lauren bent down and retied her shoelaces.

"Fine, but why have we stopped here?"

Lauren straightened. "This is the next part of the tour." She turned and pointed at a barely discernible steep track, leading up through the waist-high scrub and into a light fog. "Up there's Little Horn, and it's a great place to stop for a cup of tea. But it's a very steep climb. That's why it's not signposted. We don't advertise this route to inexperienced walkers. It's too dangerous."

Jo removed her cap and scratched her head. "I should be okay as long as we don't try and break a land speed record, like we did on Goat Track."

Lauren's face lit up with silent laughter. "I promise this will be very carefully done."

JO FLOPPED DOWN, exhausted by the exertion of the climb. As she caught her breath she surveyed her surroundings. Located at the base of a steep drop was Dove Lake, the walkers around the lake now resembling colourful ants. She shifted where she sat and stared into the gaping maw of Cradle Mountain. Farther in the distance stood yet another mountain. "What peak is that?"

Lauren's gaze tracked to where Jo was looking. "Mount Ossa. It's about twenty-five kilometres away, near the Overland Track to Lake Saint Clair." She pointed to something in the middle distance. "If you look hard you can just make out three walkers on the track."

Jo squinted and groaned. "As beautiful as it might be, they can have the track all to themselves. That spa of mine is so going to get a workout tonight."

Lauren rummaged through her backpack and pulled out a thermos of hot water. "Take a rest and I'll get some tea and muffins ready."

Jo rubbed her calves. "How high up are we?"

"We're actually not very high up. It's just the gradient of the climb making it feel that way. We're about thirteen hundred and forty metres up. If you climb the peak over there," Lauren motioned to a spire of granite not far from them, precariously tilted toward the mountain floor below, "You'd be at about thirteen hundred and sixty metres."

Jo grimaced. "It looks a little too risky for me."

"You don't strike me as the 'play it safe' type," Lauren said as she poured hot water over two teabags set in respective cups.

"I'm not, but I'm not stupid, either." She gratefully took the cup and muffin Lauren offered. "Have you climbed it?"

"Yes, but in summer and with ropes. It's a deceiving climb because you can get up there without help. But getting down without ropes is downright dangerous."

"I can understand why you don't sign-post this track. You'd spend most of your days rescuing people off that beauty." Jo munched on her muffin and washed it down with tea. "Why did you decide to become a guide?" Lauren's relaxed features suddenly shut down, as if a door had been closed. "Lauren, this is Jo the person asking, not Jo the reporter. I'm just interested, that's all." The silence between them seemed to go on for minutes. It startled Jo when Lauren finally answered.

"Apart from golf I'd always wanted to be a guide. Don't ask me why. Something appeals to me about telling people about this place, but it's also the open spaces. This isn't a nine-to-five job and it's as far away from the rat race as I can get." She finished her tea and muffin, stood up, and started to repack the gear from their morning tea. "Once you've finished we'll head down and to our next stop where we'll have lunch."

Jo drained the last of her tea and handed her cup to Lauren. *There goes that topic of discussion.* She stood and stashed the remains of her muffin in her jacket pocket for later eating. In silence, they headed back down the trail.

JO DROPPED HER pack and stared at the crystal clear water of the small lake below her, its foreshores dotted with what looked like miniature pine. Besides their heavy breathing from their exertions, the silence and image was one of absolute serenity. "This is beautiful," she whispered.

"Yes, it is. It's probably my favourite place on the mountain. Not many people come here, and it's a great place to just sit and contemplate. I don't know why, but I always feel peaceful here." Lauren pointed at one of the small trees around the waterline. "How old do you think that is?"

"I'm not a botanist but, given its size, it's about one hundred and eighty centimetres, isn't it?" Jo replied.

"Give or take a couple of centimetres."

Jo tilted her head to one side and the other, studying the tree. "I'd say it's about a year old."

Lauren lowered her pack to the ground. "Try closer to twenty. It's a King Billy pine and they have a very slow growth rate. They reach about thirty-six and a half metres when fully grown and have been known to live for about twelve hundred years."

"Hmm, looks can be deceiving, can't they?" Jo glanced at Lauren, daring her to respond. As the silence dragged on, Jo walked to the edge of the mirror-like reflection of the small glacial lake.

Lauren followed. "And just what's that supposed to mean?"

Jo dismissively waved her hand. "Forget it. You don't want to talk about it, remember?" She turned in time to see anger clearly written in Lauren's expression. Simultaneously, a cold shadow shrouded their surroundings. With the sun's sudden disappearance, Jo rubbed her arms to keep herself warm.

"No, come on, let's have it. You've been dancing around the edges of this discussion all day, now's your chance." Lauren replied, hands on her hips.

"Okay. Fine. Why did you do it? Why did you walk away when you did? You had everything in front of you. Fame, fortune, and God knows what else. Some people would give a limb to have just *half* that sort of talent. But instead, you walked away. Why?"

Lauren bent and picked up a smooth, flat rock. She viciously skimmed it across the surface of the lake before addressing Jo, her tone cold as the waters the stone sank into. "You don't know anything about my life, so don't pretend you do. I have my reasons for doing what I did, and I don't see the need to share my past with you or anyone else for that matter. Can't you understand?"

"I'll tell you what I understand. You had a talent and you let it go.

You had everything to play for and instead took the easy way out."
She hunched into the wind, which seemed to have arisen from
nowhere. Suddenly a strong gust hit her, forcing her to take a step
back. As she did she turned to the lake's now-choppy surface and her
eyes widened. *What's in the water? Is that a woman?*

For a moment, time stood still. Then, as if a fast-forward button
had been pressed, everything happened at once, and Jo fell toward the
frigid glacial waters.

"No, stop!" Lauren screamed. She pulled Jo toward her and away
from the lake's edge.

As quickly as the wind had come up it subsided. Reluctant to pull
away, Jo tightened her arms around Lauren, relishing her warmth and,
for a moment, it seemed Lauren tightened her grip as well

"Damn it," Lauren sighed, her irritation evident.

The moment broken, Jo pulled away. "I'm sorry for invading your
personal space but *you* grabbed *me*.

Lauren gesticulated back at the lake. "And if I hadn't, you'd be in
the bloody water by now."

Jo retrieved her pack. "Suddenly I don't feel like lunch. Why don't
you just get me down and you can go back to whatever it was you
were doing before I interrupted your life."

"That's fine by me." Lauren slapped the front of her trousers,
trying to remove some of the dust accumulated from the day's walk.

"Fine," Jo snapped, clicking the ends of her waist belt together.
She quietly cursed as her chilled fingers struggled with the pack's
smaller sternum straps.

She looked up, bewildered, when Lauren's hands encased her
own. Lauren carefully sealed the strap. "Look, I'm sorry I yelled. I
didn't mean to. There are just some things about me...well, that are
difficult to talk about."

Jo looked at Lauren's hands, amazed at how warm they were,
when hers were blocks of ice. She exhaled, breath shaky. "No, I'm the
one who should be sorry. You said you'd give me an answer about
whether I could interview you and I pushed you for it. I should never
have done that."

Lauren rubbed Jo's hands in her own. "I still owe you an answer.
Just give me a little more time. But for the moment we'd best be on our
way. We'll go down by Hansons Peak. You can start walking, but
when we get to Hansons Peak, I'll go first."

"That's fine by me."

Jo started toward the intersection of the main path they had taken
to arrive at the lake. Confused as to which way to go, she turned back
to where Lauren stood staring across the lake.

"Leave her alone." Lauren's voice carried through the serene air
to Jo, and across the now-still waters of Twisted Lakes.

JO STASHED HER backpack in the rear of the four-wheel drive and looked across at Lauren. "You were pretty quiet on the way down. Are you okay?"

"I'm fine. If you like, I can drop you off at your cabin rather than the lodge."

Jo eased her tired body into the passenger seat and groaned. "Thanks, that'd be great. My legs are reminding me it's been a while since I did this."

Lauren started the vehicle. "It looks like your spa's going to get a workout after all."

They made the trip to the cabin in silence, allowing Jo the opportunity to surreptitiously view Lauren. She seemed to be warring with something, her expression alternating between a scowl and frustration. They arrived at her cabin, and Lauren came around and opened the door for her. She retrieved Jo's pack from the back seat.

"You know, just because I don't share my golfing ability with the world doesn't mean I don't share it at all."

Jo took her pack from Lauren's hands, their fingers lightly brushing. "I'm sorry I said you were selfish. It was incredibly insensitive of me."

Lauren seemed to struggle with her next comment and she glanced around her surroundings as if in thought. Her gaze returned to Jo. "If you're really interested, I'll pick you up tomorrow and show you." She held up her hands in mock surrender. "I promise it doesn't involve climbing any mountains."

Jo smiled. "You're on. Where do you want me to meet you?"

"I can pick you up here at eight-thirty tomorrow morning if you like," Lauren said as she thrust her hands in her pockets, as if she were suddenly shy.

"It's a date." Jo stifled a giggle at the look on Lauren's face. "Not a date. An outing, if you like."

Lauren nervously smiled. "I'll see you then."

LAUREN WALKED THROUGH the door of the old cottage and slammed the door behind her. She threw her pack on the table and paced the cabin. "What the hell did you think you were doing? For Christ's sake, you could've killed her!"

A small ray of dusty sunlight played off the shadowy form that lingered near one of the cottage's windows. "She was in no harm," came a soft voice. "The worst that might have happened was she would have been a little wet. Given how heated she was becoming it might not have been a bad idea."

Lauren shook her finger at the figure. "Annie, you know damn well that's not what I'm talking about. What about the rock slips when we were coming down the chain link rail on Hansons Peak? She could've fallen to her death if one of those rocks had grazed her."

"She said some terrible things to you at the lake."

"They're words, that's all. They can only hurt me if I allow them to."

"I only did it for you. I'll always be there for you. You must know that."

"And I'll be there for you." Lauren's shoulders sagged, deflated by Annie's words.

"You look tired. Why don't you lie down?"

Surprised at the lethargy that seemed to seep unbidden into her bones, Lauren studied the bed. "I can't. I've got to set the fire and light the lamps."

"Leave it. We can do it after you've rested."

Almost on autopilot, Lauren collapsed on top of the bed, her eyes uncontrollably heavy. Her last waking thought was of the depression beside her, caused by another body, barely visible, and the feeling of arms that seemed to once again encircle her.

Chapter
Four

"HANG ON, I'LL be right there," Jo called in response to the knock on her door. She gingerly got up, nervously ran her hands over her hair and slowly walked across the room.

"Good morning." Lauren's smiling features were replaced by concern at sight of Jo. "You don't look too good. Are you okay?"

Jo ushered her into the cabin, noting Lauren's initial reticence as she stepped through the door. "I'm fine, just a little stiff from yesterday. It's been a while since I've really been in the outdoors and my body's reminding me I'm not as young as I used to be."

"You make it sound like you've got one foot in the grave." Lauren's eyes roamed over Jo's body, as if measuring how old she actually was. "I wouldn't put you much past, say, forty-nine."

The warmth flooding Jo's senses at Lauren's inspection was quickly replaced by shock until she read the laughter in Lauren's eyes. Jo reached out and lightly slapped her arm. "How about you take ten years off and you'll be closer to the mark."

Lauren's eyebrows rose. "Really? I wouldn't have put you any older than about thirty-five."

"It's all that good living. It keeps me young." Jo bent down to pick up her daypack, cringing when she straightened up. She rubbed a sore spot on her lower back. "Mind you, at the moment I feel about sixty-five."

"You know you don't have to do this today, if you're not up to it."

Jo glanced at Lauren, just in time to see a shadow of regret sweep across her features. "No, I'll be fine once I get some blood into these limbs." She walked across the room to retrieve her camera. After checking its charge, she stowed it in her pack.

Lauren nervously rubbed her hands against the front of her pants before putting them in her pockets. "What's that for?"

Jo's witty remark died on her lips as she turned and registered Lauren's body language. "I'm sorry. It's habit. I always travel with a camera."

Lauren removed her hands from her pockets and unconsciously wrung her hands. "Were you going to do some shooting today?"

"I was, if the opportunity presents itself. But if you're

uncomfortable with the idea then I can leave it here."

Lauren dismissively waved her hand. "No, it's okay."

Jo approached her and lightly touched her arm. "Listen, I still don't have any idea where I'm going with your story, but I thought it'd be nice to get some shots of wherever we end up. Trust me when I say any pictures involving you won't go any farther than my camera. I'm not paparazzi. As far as I'm concerned, some of those people are the lowest of the low. You can see what I shoot, if you like."

Lauren moved away, breaking the tenuous connection between them, much to Jo's chagrin. "Thanks, I appreciate that. Being photographed and filmed at inopportune moments was one of the things I was happy to leave behind." She checked her watch. "We'd better get going or we'll be late."

JO WATCHED LAUREN skillfully drive the winding country roads, alternating her focus between her and peering out the window at the passing scenery. "You know, I've been in some pretty places in the world but this is just..." she searched for the right word. "Peaceful. I can't explain it, but this is really relaxing. I don't think I've ever seen this many shades of green before."

Lauren negotiated a bend in the tree-lined road. "I know what you mean. It's one of the things that drew me to Tasmania in the first place. That and the wilderness here. It's still got a touch of 'the last frontier' about it, especially down on the southwest coast. Plus, for such a small state, the place is just full of history. History and great old buildings."

"Not too many people get the chance to see this sort of history, let alone live in it. Is that why you live in Annie's hut?" Jo paused at the look on Lauren's face. *There go those curtains again.*

"I don't live in Annie's hut."

Jo's brows furrowed. "I'm sorry. I was sure I heard that you spent a lot of your time there."

Lauren scowled. "I spend a lot of time there but I have a small house the park's allocated me. That's where I live."

A cold silence descended in the vehicle and Jo stared out the passenger window. *What did I say? All I was trying to do was make polite conversation, ask her a few questions. Oh crap.* She closed her eyes, rubbed her hand over her forehead, then turned to Lauren.

"I think we need to clear something up. I'm a naturally curious person and I think it's what makes me a good journalist. Even if it wasn't my job, I'd still be asking you the same kinds of questions. I'm not pumping you for information. If I wanted to, then I could've done that back at the lodge. The same rule applies with our discussions about my photos. I'd never publish anything about you without your approval."

Lauren relaxed a little. "I'm sorry. It's an instinctive reaction, especially given what you do for a living. I've been burned before talking to journalists who told me it was—" Lauren raised one hand off the steering wheel and curved two of her fingers as if to make a quotation mark, "off the record, only to see it in the papers the next day. I guess I was a little naïve when I was younger."

"I understand." *But do you trust anyone?* "I promise this is just me interested in you." Jo paused, then blushed at the way her last comment sounded. "I mean, that didn't quite come out the way it was supposed to." Her blush deepened at Lauren's smile. "Oh heck, I'll just stop for a moment so I can get my foot out of my mouth."

Lauren lightly laughed. "It's okay."

"So," Jo said, changing the subject. "What's the attraction with Annie's hut? Are you trying to relive the lives of our explorer forebearers?"

A slight gasp escaped Lauren's lips.

"Are you okay?"

Lauren rubbed her knee. "I'm fine, just an old war wound. I go to the hut to get away from it all."

Jo frowned. "From what I've seen of the hut it seems like it's been around for a while. How do you stop people from just wandering in when they feel like it?"

"The front door's the only access. These days it's bolted and I'm the only one who has a key. All the windows lock from the inside, so it's pretty secure from prying eyes or overnight campers." Lauren turned the vehicle off the main road and into a tree-lined driveway.

A stately old home came into view, its golden sandstone exterior balanced by the large green French double-shuttered windows on either side of the main portico entrance. "What a lovely house."

"If you think its lovely now, you should see it in spring. The gardens are landscaped in an English style and in September they're absolutely full of budding roses." Lauren slowed the vehicle. "Welcome to The Dales. It's the local golf club around these parts."

Jo stared at her, surprised. "I'd have never guessed you were taking me to a golf club. And just exactly where are 'these parts'?"

Lauren pulled into a parking space to the left of the clubhouse. "We're just outside of Sheffield. It's a small town that was settled by white man around the 1860s. We'll stop in there before we head back, if you like."

"Why *are* we here?" Jo looked down at her hiking outfit then at Lauren. "I'm not exactly dressed for golf."

"That's okay. We're not playing a round, especially not in boots like yours. The greenskeeper would have a fit if you walked on his pristine greens with those clodhoppers. Today we'll be on the driving range." Lauren opened the door and got out of the vehicle. Jo followed.

"You've come to drive some balls? I don't quite—" Before Jo could finish her sentence a young teenaged girl wheeled around the corner and hurtled herself at Lauren. "Can I carry your bag?"

Lauren stepped back, absorbing the impact of the girl. "Ooof, Karrie. Be careful or you'll knock me over."

A young teenage boy skidded to a halt on the pebbled drive beside Karrie. "Miss Wheatley, it was her turn last week. This week it's my turn."

Lauren ruffled the boy's hair. "Adam's right, Karrie, it *is* his turn. But let me get it out and onto the cart first. Karrie, can you go into the clubhouse and make sure the balls are ready?"

Jo stared, open-mouthed, at the interaction between Lauren and the two children. While Karrie headed to the clubhouse, Lauren lifted a blanket and hefted her golf clubs from the back of her vehicle and onto her cart. The clubs were barely secured in the cart when Adam began towing them around to what Jo presumed was the driving range.

Lauren's eyes twinkled at Jo's shock. "You know, you'll catch flies if you leave your mouth open like that."

"You teach golf to those two?" Jo pulled her backpack off the back seat.

Lauren put a golfing cap on and closed the door. "Yes, those two and these few as well." She headed around the side of the clubhouse.

Jo followed, still amazed. At least ten places on the driving range were occupied by children, varying in age from about twelve to sixteen. "You hold a golfing clinic."

"Yep. I do it once a week during most months of the year. It took me a while but I finally managed to convince the club manager to offer up some time and course space to kids who showed a talent for the game. This wasn't around when I was first starting out, and it's my way of giving a little back. We teach kids from all walks of life, not just those who can afford it. The club has pitched in by giving the less fortunate kids second-hand clubs, trimmed down by the club pro, so they fit the children."

"I'm amazed." *Now this would make a great story, if she'd only let me tell it.* "Have they any idea who you are?"

"I don't think the majority of the kids do. Most know I played a little when I was younger. Only Karrie and Adam know I was a decent amateur golfer and that's only because their mum used to follow the game." Lauren sat down and removed her boots, replacing them with a pair of golf shoes.

Jo looked at the kids and back to Lauren. "Anyone who could go as far as you did in such a short time is a little more than just decent."

Lauren shrugged and straightened. "I suppose, but now my focus is on the possible champions of tomorrow, not the ones who might have been." She clapped her hands together. "Okay you lot, you're not swinging away before you've warmed up, are you?"

Jo smiled at the moans of protest from Lauren's young charges. She found a spot away from the group and made herself comfortable, content to watch Lauren work her magic with her attentive crew.

For the next two hours she watched Lauren take them through their paces, adding praise for a ball well-hit and giving gentle advice when it was called for. The ease with which Lauren seemed to fit into the role warmed Jo's heart. *But it's more than that. She's at home with these kids. I've not seen her this relaxed, even in the short time I've known her.* She eased her camera from her bag and took a few impromptu shots of Lauren with the children. One required that she move from her position to get a better angle. She framed a shot of Lauren adjusting the stance of one of her pupils. Just as she was about to take the picture Lauren looked at Jo and smiled. "Perfect," Jo murmured, taking the shot before waving back at Lauren. She spent the rest of the lesson enjoying the sight of Lauren interacting with her young charges.

When Lauren finished, Jo walked over to her, hanging back as Lauren said her farewells to the children. One of the young boys stepped up to Lauren's cart.

"Do you want me to take this back to your car, Miss Wheatley?"

"No, it's okay, Brandon. I'm going to do a little hitting out myself." Lauren watched him head toward the car park, and then turned her attention to Jo. "Care to join me, Miss Ashby?"

"Oh, I don't think so. Besides, I'm not kitted out for golf, remember?"

Lauren pulled a driver from her bag. "Oh, come on. Surely you've hit a ball or two in your life, haven't you?"

Jo flashed her an "of course" look. "Yes, I have. I've played for about twenty years, on and off."

Lauren raised her eyebrows, clearly surprised. "You should have a pretty decent handicap, then."

"Yep. About thirteen." She grinned as Lauren almost dropped her driver. "That would be the sum total of the clubs in my bag. I'm a *very* social golfer. I like the game, but I've just never mastered its finer points. And, God only knows I'm hopeless at judging distances, and what club to use."

Lauren handed the driver to Jo. "All the same, why don't you show me what you can do with this?"

Accepting the challenge, Jo took the proffered club. She carefully placed a ball on the practice tee, drew back for the shot and hit the ball. It hooked badly and ended up on the fairway adjacent to the practice tees. "Bloody thing never goes straight. I swear these damn things have magnets in them. You," she pointed the driver in Lauren's direction, "stop laughing."

"I'm sorry, it's just you seemed so focused with your shot." Lauren took the driver. "Did you ever play softball?"

"Yes. Why?"

"Because you hit the ball like it's a softball. You need to hit it like a golf ball." Lauren bent down and placed another ball on the practice tee. "Like this."

Jo stepped back and watched Lauren drive a ball well past the two hundred and fifty yard marker on the range. "Wow. If you think you can teach me to do that, then we're going to be here for a bloody long time. That was amazing. How did you manage to get it to go that far?"

"By hitting it like a golf ball and *not* a softball. Let me show you." Lauren handed the club back. "Go on, address the ball."

Jo did her best to look like she was more than the weekend golfer she was. Her focus was shattered when Lauren's body encased hers from behind.

"I'm not going to correct too much in one sitting, but let's start with the basics." Lauren placed her hands on Jo's hips.

Jo gulped. *Thank God. I don't know whether this position's all that good for my libido!*

"First, let's adjust your hips so they're also parallel to the ball." Lauren's hands then gently gripped Jo's shoulders and aligned them. "Now your shoulders are facing in the right direction." Her hands slowly but surely traveled down Jo's arms.

Jo bit her lip, eternally grateful Lauren was seemingly unaware of the effect she was having. She stifled an overwhelming desire to push her backside against Lauren and instead tried to maintain focus on the club in her hand.

"Try and keep your arms straight, at least at the outset. Now pretend there's a rod that's been put down through the centre of your body and everything pivots around the rod." Lauren released her and stepped away. "Keep your head down and your focus on the ball. Like that. Now give it another try."

Despite the rapid beating of her heart, Jo managed to drive the ball a respectable distance.

Lauren clapped her shoulder. "See what you can do when you put your mind to it."

"Thanks." Jo handed the club back to Lauren. *If I could achieve things with just imagination then you'd be in a lot of trouble right now.* "I think I'll just sit down and let you finish your practice."

Lauren proceeded to hit a bucket of balls, never straying from the straight line of her first drive. Jo reveled in the view of her doing just that. Once Lauren finished, she checked in with clubhouse staff and they returned to her vehicle, where she stashed her clubs in the back before the two headed for the small town of Sheffield.

JO RELAXED INTO her seat as Lauren drove home. "Those paintings on the town's buildings were amazing. There were so many of them."

Lauren nodded. "That's why Sheffield's known as the town of murals. There're over thirty of them and they all tell a little of the history of the district."

"I particularly liked the one, on the wall of the corner store, of the rescue on Cradle Mountain. It was like a moving story on a static surface." Jo reached across and patted Lauren's leg. "Thanks for sharing them with me." She removed her hand as Lauren blushed at the contact.

"I'm glad you liked them. The rescue one's a favourite of mine as well."

In the silence, Jo struggled for a way to broach her next topic. She decided to just jump in. "Listen, I don't mean to ruin the day we've had, but I was wondering if you'd given any further thought to the piece I'd like to do on you. What you're doing now would make a really great story."

Lauren's hands gripped the steering wheel and she tilted her head from one side to the other as if she were releasing stress. "Can we discuss this at my place? I really need to focus on what I'm doing now."

Discussion, that's at least something. "Sure, that'd be good." Jo reclined the seat, closed her eyes, and marshalled her thoughts for what she felt was sure to be a battle to convince Lauren of the merits of telling her story.

JO STARTED AT Lauren's gentle shaking. "Wake up, sleepyhead. We're here."

Jo sat up, stretched, and looked around, trying to kick start her sleep-addled brain. "I thought we'd be going to Annie's hut."

"The fire's been out all day and it gets a little too cold to talk in there, especially when you're not used to it," Lauren deflected.

"I'd like to see it sometime."

"Maybe," Lauren absently replied, heading to the house with Jo in tow. She unlocked the door and stepped aside, motioning for Jo to enter. "Just put your gear down there. Can I get you a drink?"

Jo looked around the comfortable cabin, which was a slightly larger, better appointed version of her own accommodations. "I'll have a cup of tea if you're making it."

"Sure, have a seat. I'll be there in a moment." Before going any farther, Lauren turned on a two-way radio and then continued to the kitchen.

"I thought you were off duty today."

"I am, but I suppose it's a habit of mine. I always have it on when I'm in the cabin. Plus, as the head guide, it's always good to know if there's something going on. This frequency ties me back to the park's base, as well as to the portable radios carried by the guides in the park."

Jo listened as the static of the radio filled the room, its noise sounding out the daily guiding activity of the park. Making herself comfortable, she scanned through the shots on her digital camera, pleased at her day's labours, especially the photos of Lauren. "You know, you can look quite laid back when you want to be. These photos are very nice."

"Something tells me you might just be a little biased there," came the reply from the kitchen. "How do you take your tea?"

"With a little milk but no sugar, thanks." Jo continued flicking through the pictures, adjusting the lighting on one of them.

Lauren placed two cups of tea on the coffee table and took a seat next to Jo. She craned her neck toward the small screen on the back of the camera.

Jo finished adjusting the shot and handed the camera across to Lauren. "What do you think?"

Lauren smiled at the image on the camera's screen. "That's a great shot. Karrie's mum would love this."

Jo reached for her tea. "Have a look at the rest if you like. Just click the button to advance." She watched Lauren's face light up at each frame.

When she finished, Lauren handed the camera back. "Can I possibly purchase some of these? We're running low on funds and these would be great advertising for the golf fundraising brochure we're putting together."

"These aren't for sale but I'd happily provide you with whatever you need. What you're doing for those kids is fantastic. I don't know too many people who'd willingly give up their spare time, especially at no cost. Consider the photos a gift from me."

"Thank you," Lauren said, smiling. "They'll go a long way to making our brochure look more professional than it does at the moment."

Jo put down her cup. "You know, any story I did on you could only help the work you do with those kids. And don't give me that look! I'm not saying that just to blackmail you. It's the truth. Besides, as I said before, people wonder what happened to you. At least this way you'd get a say in how it's presented."

Lauren scanned the room, as she rubbed the back of her neck with one hand. "I've always been a private person. I'm just not very comfortable handing my life over for someone to film."

Jo rested her hand on Lauren's forearm. "Hang on a minute. You're not handing your life over to anyone. Anything filmed here would be professionally done and not intrusive in any way. You have my word."

Lauren returned her gaze to Jo, as if she were measuring the sincerity behind her words. "I'd only agree to the story if I had final say on what's actually shown on television."

"Yes, but if that's the case then I'm worried all we'd get were shots of your back. I can see it now," Jo shifted into interviewer mode. "Welcome to the final episode of *Where Are They Now?* So, where *is* Lauren Wheatley today? God knows, but I do have a great shot of her butt, as she ran head-long into the Tasmanian wilderness."

Lauren frowned then started laughing. Jo caught her gaze and the look that passed between them was inscrutable, yet still held a hint of possibility.

Jo gazed into Lauren's eyes, trying to measure her intent. "I know this may blow my chances of a story, but I've got to say it. You're definitely a mysterious woman. And lovely." She nervously chuckled. "But mysterious all the same. I've got a feeling that unlike so many other sports jocks I've interviewed there're multiple layers to you, as well as some places you never share."

Lauren rose from the couch, effectively breaking the moment. "I think I'd better be getting you back to the lodge."

"Lauren, this is Park base. Are you there?"

Lauren walked to the radio and picked up the handset. "Roger, base. This is Lauren. What's up?"

"We've just done a check of the log books and there's a lodge walker who hasn't signed back in. She left from the Waldheim car park and logged her destination as climbing Cradle Mountain. The weather's closing in and I'm afraid she's going to be stuck up there. Her name's Susan Gilmore."

"Hang on a minute." Lauren walked to the cabin's panoramic window and stared at the early dusk sky. She muttered a curse under her breath and returned to the radio. "You're right. It's starting to get ugly out here. Tonight might be the first snow of the season."

"Okay, if you wait there we'll send another guide to go with you and see if you can find her."

Lauren shook her head. "Don't worry. I'll go up alone."

"You know you can't do that. It's against the park rules."

Lauren huffed. "Since when have rules bothered me? And since when have I ever lost anyone during a rescue or failed to find someone on the mountain?"

Jo watched, amused, as Lauren repeatedly pressed the talk switch on the radio's microphone as the person on the other end tried to transmit.

"I'm sorry, Mark. You're breaking up. It must be the weather. I'll try and contact you later." She deliberately switched to another frequency and put the microphone down.

Lauren walked to a closet, Jo following, and opened it. An assortment of mountaineering gear was stuffed inside, clearly aimed for guiding and any type of rescue challenge the park might issue.

Lauren reached into the closet, flipped the lid on a large plastic container, and began to sort through its contents. She stashed an assortment of items in the side pouches and main area of her pack.

"You're not going alone, are you?"

"It wouldn't be the first time. I can handle it."

Jo glanced at the now silent radio and then back to the closet. "You've got enough rescue gear in there to equip a small Army. I'm dressed for hiking. Why not let me go with you?"

Lauren reached for a personal locator beacon, only answering Jo's question as an afterthought. "I work better alone. Besides, this is a rescue, not a tour."

Jo bridled. "Just what the hell does that mean? You think I'd make the suggestion if I wasn't capable of helping you? Do you really think you have a corner on the market on this sort of experience?"

The radio again crackled to life as Lauren started to answer.

"Damn it, Lauren, did you really think I'd fall for that trick? Stay where you are. We've called in Blackson and he's on his way to base right now."

Jo glanced at Lauren in time to see her scowl at the guide's name. "What's wrong?"

"We don't get along. We haven't since he propositioned me out on the mountain and I told him in no uncertain terms he wasn't equipped for my needs."

Jo motioned to the radio. "Then tell them you've got someone."

Lauren looked doubtfully at Jo. "There's a good chance we'll be out overnight. Are you up to it? I mean, have you ever trained for search and rescue?"

"Yes, actually." Jo headed to the gear and started pulling items from the container Lauren had used, to pack in her own kit. "It was a prerequisite for climbing Mount McKinley. The crew we were with wouldn't allow us to climb unless we first did a two-week course in search and rescue. I had to do the same thing for Mount Cook. While I'm not as well versed in it as you are, I do understand what needs to be done, and I'm more than capable of climbing. You saw that yesterday. Plus the aches and pains I had this morning are just about gone." *The last bit's only a little white lie.*

Partially satisfied, Lauren picked up the mike. "Mark, I've got someone here I can take with me. She's search and rescue trained and she cut her teeth on McKinley and Cook. I'm pretty sure she can keep up. We're out of here. I'll call you once we're on the move." She put the mike down. "I didn't tell them you were a guest at the lodge, or they'd never let you go." She opened another closet, pulled out cold weather gear and threw it over to Jo. "We're roughly the same size, give or take a few centimetres, so you might want to put this on. I've got a feeling it's going to be pretty cold up there."

Chapter
Five

LAUREN TURNED THE sheets of the register in the Waldheim car park, running her finger down each page. "There's a slight chance she didn't sign in at the lodge but did sign back in here. If that's the case, then she's not on the mountain." She slapped an open palm down on one of the pages. "There goes that idea."

"What do you mean?" Jo leant over Lauren's shoulder and looked down at the open page.

"She's still out there and she recorded her departure as seven this morning. A summit walk normally takes between six to eight hours, depending on how experienced the climber is, so she should've been back well before now." Lauren closed the book and headed to her vehicle.

Jo turned to follow, and then gazed up at the trees surrounding the car park. "It looks like the wind's picked up a bit."

Lauren followed Jo's gaze. "It's going to be pretty windy up there and bloody cold also. We'd better head out before that idiot Blackson turns up. Here." She handed a pack to Jo, thought again, and pulled it back. "Hang on. Let me check it one more time."

Jo waited as Lauren thoroughly checked the contents of her pack, reorganizing a few items in the process.

"It'd be better if you have these gloves in one of the outside pockets. It'll make it easier for you to get to them. I'll put those and your beanie in the right side pocket, and your water and snacks in the left, okay?"

Jo couldn't help but smile at Lauren's solicitousness. "I think I can remember that."

Lauren held up the pack, its straps facing Lauren. "Come over here and put this on and I'll check it for fit."

Lauren pulled one strap after another, adjusting in detail the fit of the pack to Jo's form. She finished her ministrations by straightening Jo's jacket down below the waist strap, where it had previously gathered.

"How does that feel?"

"Fine." Jo pulled a handkerchief from her pants pocket and

handed it to Lauren.

Clearly puzzled, Lauren looked at the handkerchief and then at Jo. "What's this for?"

"I just thought you might want to blow my nose," Jo replied.

Lauren raised an eyebrow, a ghost of a smile on her lips. "Does it need blowing?"

"No, but given you've checked just about everything else, except whether I have clean underwear on—which, by the way, I do—then I figure the last thing was blowing my nose before we headed off."

Without warning Lauren grasped the sternum strap on Jo's pack, and pulled her close. "It mightn't need blowing but there's a bit of dust on your nose."

Lauren shook out the handkerchief and brought it to her mouth. She dabbed the edge of the cloth with the tip of her tongue, while her other hand gently grasped Jo's chin.

Jo stifled a gasp as Lauren leant into her personal space, her soft touch burning Jo's chin. It was only a matter of seconds and Lauren nodded, as if in satisfaction at removing the phantom speck. Instead of moving away, Lauren gazed into Jo's eyes.

Oh, my God. It's like she's looking into my soul. Jo's eyes widened when Lauren's hand lightly stroked her skin, one finger barely trailing over the corner of her lower lip. Jo leant closer and closed her eyes, waiting for the kiss she wanted to follow. A sudden gust of wind blew through the clearing, causing Jo to almost lose her footing.

As Jo stepped back to balance herself, Lauren handed the handkerchief back to her. She stowed the item while Lauren turned and retrieved the second pack from the back of the vehicle.

Jo exhaled and fingered her waist strap, desperately searching for something to say. *And you're supposed to be the journalist.* "Which route do you intend to take?"

Lauren shrugged on her pack and shimmied her body, allowing the load to comfortably settle. "We'll take the Overland Track. It's the most likely path Susan would've taken if she left from here to climb Cradle Summit." Her tone was distant.

"Are there any other tracks she might've gone on?" Jo picked up her telescopic trekking pole and expanded it to a comfortable length.

"She signed out from here and this limits her options. The walking tracks in the park are either marked with a sign or they're a wood walkway. So I think it's safe to say she'd use one of these." Lauren locked the four-wheel drive and stowed the key in her pocket. "This leaves two other options. One's Horse Track but it's on the other side of Crater Lake, and would've added at least another hour to her trip. The other one reaches Marion's Lookout via the Wombat Pool Track. That's slightly easier than the Overland Track."

Jo frowned and thought over the three options. "Couldn't her delayed return have been caused by her taking the Horse one?

Alternatively, she may have chosen the easier option of Wombat Pool. What makes you so sure she took the one we're going to walk?"

Lauren angled her head to one side, as if she were considering the three options. She slightly nodded and again returned her gaze to Jo. "I'm pretty sure she took the Overland Track. The others are too out of the way for someone who's aiming to climb Cradle summit. We'd better head off."

JO'S FOOTING FALTERED as she left the formed walking path and moved on to the small rounded stones of a loose pebble beach. She followed Lauren around to the front of a wooden shed, its entry open to the lake, whose waters nearly lapped at the shed's entrance.

Lauren dropped her pack on the uneven floor of the boatshed and motioned to the water in front of her. "We're lucky at the moment the water in Crater Lake's so low. Normally we wouldn't be able to sit in here without getting our feet wet."

Jo lowered herself gratefully onto one of the weather-worn, lichen-covered wooden benches of the hut. "At least we're out of the wind for a while. How long are we going to be here?"

"Why?"

"I'd like to slip on some long johns if we've got enough time." Jo opened her pack and began to rummage through its contents.

"Ah, we've got enough time for that. If you like I can step outside while you change."

Jo looked up, Lauren's discomfort obvious on her face. "Why? Do you think I have something you don't?"

Lauren dipped her head. "No, I just thought you'd want your privacy."

"I'm fine. I've stripped down to my underwear in front of men when I've been on shoots and lived to tell the tale." Jo bent down to untie the laces on her boots.

"Yes, but did they?" Lauren muttered sotto voce.

Jo fingers paused at Lauren's barely audible comment. *Did she say what I just thought she said?* Bending over to mask her smile, Jo pulled off one of her boots and started on the other.

"I'll check in and let Mark know where we are." Lauren pulled a small radio from a side pocket on her pack. "Mark, it's Lauren."

"I was wondering when you were going to call in. Where are you?"

"We're in the boat shed at Crater Lake. I checked the book at Waldheim car park and she didn't sign back in there, either. I reckon she's taken the Overland Track to get to the summit. Hopefully we'll run into her as she heads down from the top."

"Here's hoping. If you haven't found her by then, can you give me a radio check when you reach Marion's Flat?"

"Will do, bye." Lauren clipped the radio onto the pack and turned to Jo. "Do you want a hot drink before we head out? It might be a while before we stop again."

Jo tucked her shirt back into her pants. "No, I'm fine, unless you want one." She reached down, picked up her jacket from the wooden ledge, and pulled it on.

"No, I'm good." Lauren looked out at the dusk sky. "We're quickly losing light. Get your head lamp while we have the chance."

After doing as Lauren suggested, they once again continued on the track. Lauren reached behind her back and pulled her trekking pole from where she had stashed it. She extended the pole and tested the tip against the ground. "It's a steady climb from here and a bit of a steep one as we head to Marion's Lookout."

Jo pulled her gloves from her side pocket and put them on. "You can really notice the drop in temperature, now the sun's all but disappeared. I hope Susan was well prepared for her walk."

"You never know. A couple of years ago I was guiding a small group around Face Track on a very foggy day. We stopped at Kitchen hut for a break when out of the fog walks this man and woman. They're both in jeans. He's wearing a polo shirt and she's in a t-shirt, which didn't even cover her waist. They've got one measly bottle of water between them and I asked them where they were heading. He said they were going to climb Cradle Mountain." Lauren shook her head. "You'd be amazed at what some people climb in. I just hope Susan was a bit more sensible."

"I know what you mean. I've seen similar things myself. It makes me wonder what some of these people were thinking." Jo looked at the sheer rock face on the other side of the lake, its tip reflecting the sun's final rays. "Is Crater Lake actually a volcanic crater?"

"No, but a lot of people think it is. It's a cirque created during Tasmania's last ice age. The steep walls are from glacial erosion, although I can see how people mistake it for the empty vent of an extinct volcano." Lauren lifted her face to the sky and held out her hand.

Jo turned to Lauren. "What's wrong?"

"We've got snow flurries. This doesn't bode well for what the weather's doing farther up. Here's hoping Susan's just resting in Kitchen hut."

JO ONCE AGAIN pulled the hood of her jacket over her head and trudged to where Lauren was finishing a radio check with Mark. "I'd forgotten how much I *love* snow. This stuff's getting in everywhere. Between the snow and the last little climb I thought I was going to be blown off the bloody mountain."

"The snow can be a pain some times, but you'll be happy to know we're past the worst bit. The climb up from Marion's Lookout can be a real challenge, even when the weather's fine," Lauren replied, her voice raised over the storm. "From here to Kitchen hut the going's pretty level."

"Given the wind, is it possible Susan was blown off while climbing up or down where we just came from?" She watched Lauren once again pause. *It's like she's asking someone.*

"No, she didn't fall here."

Jo's curiosity got the better of her. "Where did you go just now?"

"What do you mean?"

"It's the second time today you've done the little tilting and nodding thing with your head. How do you know she didn't fall here?" Jo braced herself as another gust of wind buffeted the two of them.

"I don't exactly know how to explain it to you. It's just a sense I get," Lauren replied.

Jo cocked her head and remembered the discussion she'd had with Ellie on the night of her arrival. "You're never wrong on rescues, are you?"

"Something like that. Come on or it's going to be *us* being blown off the mountain. Follow me. It's about a thirty-minute walk to the hut from here."

Their constant struggle against the ever-present wind and inclement conditions turned the half-hour walk into one closer to an hour. By the time Jo and Lauren arrived at the mountain hut, the snow had begun to pile around the lower door, and Lauren fought to open the door and peer in.

"Susan?" Lauren called up at the second floor, only to be greeted by windy silence. She dropped her pack and elbowed through the entrance. "I'll just make sure she's not asleep in the upper level."

"Okay." The top half of Lauren's body disappeared into the hole leading to the hut's second floor. A few moments passed until Lauren climbed down and shook her head. She pushed the door closed again, ensuring it was secure. "She's not here, which means she's still out there."

Jo roughly rubbed her gloved hands against the arms of her snow jacket. "I'm afraid if we don't find her soon, she'll end up dying of hypothermia."

"You're right. Let's hope—" Lauren paused, mid-sentence and suddenly turned back the way they'd just come. She nodded again.

There she goes again. It's almost like she's having a conversation with someone. I'm beginning to wonder whether this mountain living's unhinged her a bit.

"She's this way," Lauren pulled on her pack and moved headlong into the snow.

"We've just come from there. We've covered that ground," Jo

shouted over the wind as she hurried after her.

"I know, but there's a little side track that's not well sign-posted because it's a re-growth area." Lauren pointed at the ground. "Watch your footing here." She stepped off the formed path and onto a barely discernible secondary path.

Jo worked to match Lauren's pace through the scrub. Lauren paused before once again heading off in an alternate direction. *For God's sake, keep up with her. You'll never find your way back to the main path if you lose her now.*

Lauren stopped and grabbed Jo's arm. She pointed to a small brightly-coloured mound, ten metres in front of them. "There!" She jogged over to the huddled figure and knelt down. "Susan, can you hear me?"

The reflection of Jo's headlamp lit up Susan's obviously relieved features. "Yes. How did you find me? I thought I was gone for sure."

Lauren reassuringly rubbed Susan's arm. "Don't worry about that. Can you walk?"

"Not without help. I stepped into a hole while looking at an alpine strawberry plant. I don't think I've broken anything, but I'm pretty sure there's some sort of damage."

Lauren touched the bright orange emergency blanket Susan had wrapped around herself. "It's lucky you were equipped for your climb or you could've frozen by now." She reached into her pack and pulled out a basic ankle splint. "We'll immobilise your ankle here, boot and all, and try and get you out. Which foot is it?"

"Left."

"Jo, can you help me, please?" Lauren focused on Susan's foot.

Jo dropped her pack and knelt down. "What do you want me to do?"

"Can you support the ankle while I put this on? We'll stretcher-walk Susan back to Kitchen hut. There's no way we can make the trip down in this kind of weather. We'll overnight there and call in a rescue tomorrow."

JO SUPPORTED SUSAN'S form as Lauren struggled with the snowdrift against the door of Kitchen hut. After a battle that seemed to last forever in the cold conditions, Lauren pulled the door open and the three staggered inside.

Lauren removed her pack and placed it against a wall. "We'll settle you down here for the moment and then I'll get a better look at your ankle." She pulled a hurricane lamp from the hut's solitary shelf and lit it, the lamp's glow casting shadows off the vertical wood-slatted walls.

Jo helped Susan to where Lauren's pack lay, and eased her down onto the wooden floor. Susan settled against the pack. Recognition dawned on her face. "Aren't you Jo Ashby and Lauren Wheatley? Damn, a journalist and an ex-golfer. Cradle Mountain must be hard up for guides." She winced as she shifted, her movements causing the pain in her ankle to flare.

Jo smiled an 'I told you so' at Lauren. "What did you say to me the other day? Better close your mouth or you'll catch flies."

"Elevation's too high for flies," she deflected as she turned her attention to Susan. "Let's have a better look at your ankle." She removed the splint and proceeded to cut the laces of Susan's hiking boot. "Jo, can you get the compression bandage out of your pack? We're going to need to wrap this once we get the boot off."

Jo took the requested item out of its plastic bag. "Why don't we ice it before we bandage it? We can fill this with snow and place it on her ankle then strap and re-splint after the ice reduces the swelling a bit."

Lauren stood and took the bag from Jo. "Great idea." She headed back into the storm but returned within a few minutes.

She and Jo then began working to remove Susan's boot. After a couple of initial painful attempts, they succeeded.

Lauren sucked in a breath. "Swollen. By the looks of it, I'd say you've severely torn at least one of the ligaments in your ankle. The good news is, it's still painful. That's a good indicator it isn't a grade three tear."

Susan struggled to contain her pain, relief evident when Jo gently placed a cloth and then the snow-filled bag onto the swollen area. "Thanks, I think. I've got some pain pills in my pack, but we had to leave it behind."

Lauren stood. "No worries, I'll go and get it. Besides, you'll need it tomorrow when we get you down the mountain."

Jo rose and moved to where Lauren stood. "You're not going back out in that are you? How the blazes are you going to find her pack in this sort of weather?"

"The same way I found her and this hut. I'll be fine. Trust me." Lauren pulled on her jacket, zipped it up, and tightened her hood around her head. "I'll be back."

Jo closed the door behind her and turned to Susan.

"Is she going to be okay?" Susan asked.

"If her ability to find you is any indication, then she'll be fine. She knew exactly where you were, and for that you're lucky. I doubt anyone else would've been as accurate in this whiteout." Jo pulled a small gas bottle and camping stove from her pack. "Now, how about I fix us something to eat while we wait?"

THE RATTLE OF the door signaled Lauren's return. Jo rose. *The snow must have built up out there.* A concerted pushing from Jo's side resulted in her flying out the door, her fall cushioned by Lauren, who wrapped her arms around Jo as they both fell to the ground.

Lauren looked up at Jo's face, in close proximity to her own. "Is this your standard greeting when people return home?"

"It depends on who it is," Jo replied as she pushed herself up, hiding her reluctance. She held her hand out. "Care to come inside? It's warmer, you know."

Lauren took her hand, only dropping it at the curious look Susan gave them when they entered. Lauren pulled the radio off her pack and keyed the mike. "Mark, can you hear me?"

"Roger, where are you Lauren? Have you found her yet?"

"We're at Kitchen hut. Yes, we've found Susan. She's got what looks to be a grade two tear of at least one of the ligaments in her ankle. She can't put any weight on it, so we won't be able to get her down the mountain without helo support." Lauren pulled off one of her gloves and put it on her pack. She shifted the radio into her other hand and repeated the same action with the other glove.

"We can't fly in this weather. You'll have to wait until tomorrow morning."

"I figured as much. We've got food and I've got an extra sleeping bag so we'll be set for the night. I'll radio in tomorrow morning."

"We'll be waiting. Hopefully the storm will have passed by then. By the way, you never told me who the other person was who went with you. What's her name?"

Lauren winced in anticipation of where the discussion was heading. "Her name's Jo Ashby, she's a guest at The Retreat."

"She's a *what*? Lauren what the hell are you doing using guests for search and rescue?"

"She's not just a guest," Lauren countered.

"What do you mean?"

"She's an experienced walker plus she's also a journalist. And," Lauren paused and looked at the ceiling of the hut in exasperation before settling her gaze on Jo. "She's doing a story on me."

"This just gets better. I only hope she's as experienced as you say she is."

Lauren smiled at Jo and arched an eyebrow. "Trust me, she's experienced. Can you let the lodge know Susan's okay? I'll talk to you tomorrow morning."

"Okay, we'll hear from you then."

Lauren picked up Susan's pack and walked across to where Susan lay. She knelt down and put a hand on Susan's shoulder. "How are you feeling?"

"I'm feeling a bit foolish. I never should've gone off the track like I did." She gratefully took her pack from Lauren and searched its contents, pulling out a small box of painkillers. "Hopefully these might take a bit of the edge off the pain."

Jo also knelt beside Susan. "They haven't got any anti-inflammatories in them, have they? If they do, you won't be able to take them while your ankle's still swelling. The anti-inflammatories are likely to promote bleeding."

"No, they're just plain old painkillers. Once I've taken them, could you please help me into a sleeping bag? I'm just about dead on my feet or, more correctly, on my back."

"Sure," Lauren replied. "Just let me change my pack for yours and I'll pull your bag out."

Within a short while Susan lay snoring in the comfort of her sleeping bag, her pain occasionally evident through a grimace that intermittently crossed her features when she shifted.

Lauren rubbed the back of her neck in an attempt to release some of the strain of the evening's events. Jo noticed and quietly walked across and tapped Lauren's shoulder. "Can I get you a cup of tea or something?"

"That'd be lovely," Lauren said gratefully as she settled herself against one of the walls of the cabin.

Jo busied herself with the small camping stove, only occasionally stealing a glance in Lauren's direction. "Is tea okay?"

Lauren nodded.

Jo turned her attention back to the stove. "Did you mean what you said to Mark?"

"Hmm?"

"About the story. *Am* I doing a story on you or was your answer to Mark just a way to get him off your back?" Jo took a teabag and steeped it in a mug of hot water.

Lauren shrugged as if in resignation. "I figure it's the only way I'm ever going to hear the end of it. Besides, I think Susan recognising me made me wonder whether you were right about other people being interested in me."

Jo passed the cup to Lauren. "You thought I was using that as a sales pitch?"

Lauren blew on the warm liquid and took a sip. She returned her gaze to Jo. "I did wonder."

"I know there are plenty of journos who'd try such an approach, but I wouldn't deceive you like that," Jo quietly replied. She looked over her shoulder at Susan, ensuring she was still sleeping. The slight snoring emanating from the bag was answer enough. "Does your sexuality have anything to do with you not wanting me to do the story?"

"I suppose that's part of it. These days I'm not afraid of being labeled a lesbian but at the same time I don't see the need to share it with others." Lauren took a couple of sips and put the cup on a shelf above her, next to a small assortment of well-used iron pots and pans.

Jo closed the space between them and reached for Lauren's other hand, clasping it in her own. Lauren looked down at her hand and then back at her face. Jo squeezed her hand. "In the past I've done articles on gay athletes, but that's never been the story's centrepiece. I'm not interested in whether you're a lesbian or not." She caught herself. "I mean, I *am* interested, but not in terms of any story I'd do on you." She cleared her throat. "You understand what I mean, right?"

Lauren reached over and brushed a tendril of hair from Jo's eyes. "Yes, I do, on both counts."

Jo leant closer when suddenly her eye caught the movement of an iron pot precariously balanced on the ledge above her head. Almost in one action Lauren pushed Jo away and caught the pot before it crashed to the floor. She placed it back, this time flush against the wall the ledge was attached to. She wiped her hands, looked around the cabin and turned back to Jo. "The problem with having those things here is sometimes people don't put them back the way they should. Are you okay?"

Jo glanced at the pot that had almost fallen on her. "I'm fine," she said, shaken. "Tired but fine."

"Me, too. I think it's time we got some sleep." Lauren pulled a sleeping bag from inside her pack. "The winter-weight bag in the bottom of your pack should keep you warm. You'll find it a lot warmer if you strip down to your long johns." She paused at the look on Jo's face.

"Yes, mother, this isn't the first time I've had a sleepover in the bush, you know."

Lauren smiled and shook her head. "You're incorrigible, but I guess you already know that."

They laughed and then settled down for the night.

DESPITE LAUREN'S ADVICE about the sleeping bag, Jo found sleep tantalizingly elusive. Instead of the slumber she longed for, she tossed and turned for the better part of three hours and still couldn't get warm. Exasperated, she sat up in her bag, rubbed her face with her hands, and looked around the cabin and the shadows cast through the glow of a single lamp on the small centre table. She tilted her head to one side. *It sounds like the wind's died down. That's at least one good thing.*

She turned to where Susan lay, relieved to see she was still fast asleep. Jo shifted her position so she could see Lauren, who was also deep in slumber. *Obviously warm and snug if the look on her face is any indication.*

Hours before, Jo had stolen a glance as Lauren stripped down to her long johns and slipped into her sleeping bag. Now she was helpless to stop the myriad of fantasies filling her mind.

"Why couldn't it be just you and me stuck in this storm," she whispered at Lauren's quiescent form. "I bet I could find a way to get the two of us into one bag." Her less-than-pure thoughts were interrupted when the temperature of the hut dramatically dropped. The warmth generated by the three bodies within the cabin was replaced by a dank coldness. The hairs on the back of Jo's neck stood on end, a warning of something she couldn't quite see. She squinted, attempting to make out the corners of the cabin, and silently cursed when the lamp's glow didn't reach there. She looked up at the ledge, where the pot that had almost fallen on her earlier in the evening, now rested.

She studied it, puzzled. *I swear Lauren put that pot flush against the wall. What's it doing near the edge again?* Jo shivered and shifted her bag as far away from the ledge as possible. Satisfied, she pulled her pack closer, placing it between her and the pot, as if for protection. She snuggled back down into her bag and pulled the hood's string as tight as possible, just like she'd done as a child, when frightened by something she couldn't quite explain.

Chapter
Six

JO'S DREAMS OF open fires, fine wine, and intimate moments were interrupted by a soft kick to her foot. After pulling the sleeping bag's drawstring so tight in the early hours of the morning, she struggled to find its release clip.

Lauren placed a cup down within reach of Jo. "Is that a caterpillar or a person in there?"

Jo, finally free of her bag, yawned widely and scratched her head. She reached for the steaming cup beside her. "Thanks," she croaked before she took a sip. "That's better. How's Susan?"

"I didn't hear her last night. All things considered, I'm figuring she slept reasonably well. I don't know what she'll be like when I wake her, though. I figure her ankle's going to be pretty stiff and sore."

Jo stepped out of her bag, stretched, and reached for her outer clothes. "Why don't I get some more snow for her ankle before you wake her? At least we'll have it handy and, hopefully, it'll alleviate any pain she may have."

"Good idea. I'll get the door open while you get dressed," Lauren said as she walked across the cabin. She turned the old metal knob and put her shoulder to the door. "This thing's jammed solid." She opened the wooden window shutter and peered out. "Now I see why. I think the only way out of here's going to be through the upper exit, at least for the moment. I'll go and give that one a try."

Jo tracked Lauren's footfalls across the creaky floor above, followed by the opening of what was obviously the top door. She finished dressing and reached down to tie up her laces when there was a knock on the outside of the hut. She tucked the laces in the top of her socks and opened the window and peered outside. The surrounding countryside was covered with a white blanket. "Wow, it really must have come down last night."

"That's for sure. I'm going to have to move some of this snow from the front door so we can get Susan out. Normally when the snow's this high we use the top exit, but I don't think it's possible with her foot." Lauren pointed to the far wall. "Can you pass me the shovel and I'll clear the entrance?"

Jo grabbed the implement and a plastic bag and handed the two through the window. "Can you fill the bag before you start clearing? That way you can dig us out while I get Susan ready."

Lauren flashed her a smile. "I knew there was a reason I brought you along."

After a few minutes of effort on Lauren's part, Jo took the snow-filled bag from her and headed back to the small camping stove. She prepared a cup of tea for Susan, picked up the bag of snow, and knelt beside Susan's sleeping form.

"Hey, Susan. It's time to start getting you out of here."

Susan rolled over and a gasp escaped her lips. Her eyes watered from obvious pain.

"Let me help you get out of your bag and we'll get some ice on your ankle." Jo unzipped the sleeping bag as far as it would go and gently lifted Susan's injured leg out. She grabbed her pack and placed it under Susan's calf and injured ankle, further elevating the foot, and began to undo the bandage. "That's a pretty impressive bruise you've got there."

While the bandage had contained a fair degree of the swelling, Susan's ankle and instep were an ugly deep purple-blue, silent testimony to the extent of her injury.

Susan gritted her teeth and slightly turned her ankle to get a better look. "Looks like I did a good job of it." She grimaced once again, returning it to its previous position.

"We'll keep it elevated and hopefully the height and the ice will keep a bit of the pain away."

Although Jo placed a cloth over Susan's ankle, she still shivered when the bag came into contact with her limb. "I know this is good for me, but damn, that's cold." She reached for her tea. "Do you think I could take a couple more painkillers, just to take the edge off the ache?"

Jo placed a cold weather jacket around Susan's shoulders. "I'm not sure that's a good idea until you get some food in your belly and we work out when you're going to be picked up. I'd hate to think whatever you take up here hampers the medication you'll get when we get you off the mountain."

Both turned when the lower door was forcefully yanked open. Lauren stepped inside and propped the shovel against the wall.

"Fortunately, it's stopped snowing but we're going to have to call in a helicopter to get you out." Lauren joined Jo and Susan and carefully lifted the bag of snow. "By the looks of it, I don't think walking you down the mountain is an option." Lauren turned and pulled the radio off her pack. "Park base, this is Lauren."

"Lauren, this is Geoffrey. You must be feeling pretty proud of yourself. Yet another successful rescue."

Lauren threw a look at Susan and Jo, then stepped out of the hut.

Jo reassuringly patted Susan's shoulder and casually walked to the door, hoping to surreptitiously overhear Lauren's conversation.

"Stow the attitude, Geoff. Susan's awake and stable but not able to walk. I'm sure you're aware of most of that from the report you received when you took over this morning," she replied in a lowered voice. "We need an air evacuation. When can we get a chopper in here?"

"Okay, love, just let me check."

Jo heard Lauren mutter 'I'm not your love' under her breath, then pick up a handful of snow and pack it into a small ball, throwing it flat and hard at a nearby shrub. She was part-way through repeating the action when the radio again came to life.

"The chopper's good to go, but you'll need to move her clear of the hut so it's not damaged by the downdraft. Also, regulations won't allow the helo to land where you are, so you'll have to strap her into an under-slung basket stretcher. There'll be an ambulance waiting at Dove Lake car park, and it'll take her to the hospital in Launceston."

"Give me twenty minutes and I'll scope out an area and get back to you." Lauren turned off the radio.

Jo walked to Lauren. "A little hot under the collar, aren't we?"

"Just saving battery power. You know how it is." They laughed. "I've got an idea where I want to move Susan for the evacuation, but I just want to check it first. We should be easy to spot in the clearing I'm thinking of. Especially if the snow's as thick there as it is here."

Jo put her hands in her jacket pockets. "Unless you need a hand I'll go and finish getting her ready."

Lauren shook her head.

"Then I'll give her a quick bite to eat, and get her dressed for the trip."

Jo walked back into the cabin and checked the bag of snow on Susan's ankle. "By the sound of things it shouldn't be too long before you're out of here. The chopper can't land, so you'll have to be put in a basket stretcher."

"What's that? Are they safe? What about the conditions?"

"It's an orange stretcher with high sides, just like a basket. There's a bit of padding you lie on and three straps to keep you tied down and stable. Trust me, they're as safe as houses. A friend of mine was evacuated off Mount Cook in New Zealand using one and she said it was a great ride. A little cold but fun all the same. As for the conditions, they're a bit overcast but fine." Jo once again fired up the stove. "We've got about a twenty minute wait. Are you hungry?"

Susan rubbed her belly. "Strangely enough, I could eat a horse."

Jo made a show of thoroughly checking her pack. "Sorry, we're all out of horse." She held up a dehydrated food packet. "How about some oatmeal instead?"

"Sounds fine to me."

Jo put the oatmeal and water in a metal mug on the stove. "Once you're finished we'll get you up and ready."

It wasn't long before Lauren returned, having identified an area for the helicopter to hover over. She radioed the coordinates to Geoffrey before joining Jo and Susan for a hurried breakfast. Stashing their gear, Jo and Lauren prepared Susan for the next part of her journey.

They supported Susan between them as they waited for the helicopter's arrival. The first view of the chopper was of it rising from the location of Dove Lake, the orange basket stretcher gently swaying below, between the helo's skids.

"Can you support Susan while I go out and steady the basket?"

"Sure."

"I'll give you the thumbs up when it's okay to bring her in."

Lauren walked through the mid-thigh-high snow to the spot marked for the stretcher's put-down. After one false grab at the stretcher, which nearly knocked Lauren's head off, much to Jo's consternation, she finally had the basket under control. She motioned Jo toward her.

Jo clasped her arm around Susan's waist. "Put all your weight on me. This is going to hurt, but once we've strapped you in you should be down in the car park in no time." They followed the path Lauren had made through the snow.

Susan sucked in a breath. "They'd better have some damn good drugs in the bloody ambulance."

"I'm sure they will," Jo reassured her.

Jo and Lauren worked quickly to make certain Susan was secure and comfortable as possible in the basket. Once satisfied she was ready to be lifted, Lauren stepped back and gave the thumbs-up to the co-pilot observing her from the door of the helicopter.

Jo patted Susan's shoulder. "You'll be fine. Good luck at the hospital." She stepped back when the helicopter lifted the basket free of the snow. Slowly the chopper circled and headed back the way it came.

Jo pulled her beanie from her pocket, and put it on her head. "That's enough fun for one day."

"That's for sure," Lauren replied. "Let's get ours and Susan's gear together and head out."

"CAN WE STOP here for a moment?" Jo plaintively said as they approached the boat hut where they'd rested the previous evening. "I just need to get some of this white muck out of my gaiters."

Lauren checked the overcast sky. "Sure. I don't think we're going to get another dump for a while. Besides, after trudging through the snow and slush I'm sure we could both do with a break. Would you like a something warm to drink before we head off again?"

"I think I'll take you up on that this time." Jo lightly slapped the snow sticking to her gaiters and stomped her feet to rid herself of the remaining residue. Satisfied with her efforts, she removed her damp gloves and liners, vigorously rubbed her hands and put them under her armpits. "My hands feel like blocks of ice."

Lauren fiddled with the camper's stove she'd retrieved from her pack. "I completely sympathise with you. I can wear double liners and the best waterproof gloves, but my hands can still feel frozen solid sometimes."

Jo smiled. "You know what they say. 'Cold hands, warm heart.' "

Lauren shook her head and smiled back. "Given where you've climbed, surely you'd be used to worse conditions than this," she said, dissembling Jo's previous comment.

"I am, but it doesn't mean it gets any easier, or my hands stay any warmer. I thought I was going to lose a finger to frostbite when I climbed Mount McKinley. Fortunately, my cameraman had a wealth of spare gloves and liners. With the number he had you'd have thought he was going to set up shop on the mountain."

Lauren pulled two cups from her pack and placed a teabag in each of them. "He sounds like quite the enterprising fellow. Although I'm not sure he'd have seen much business at six thousand metres."

Jo bit her lip, struggling to find a way to broach the next topic. She watched Lauren squeeze a small amount of condensed milk from a tube into each of the mugs while waiting for the water to boil. *Here goes nothing.* "Last night you said you'd agree to tell your story to me. Does your offer still hold?" She paused at the slightly sullen look on Lauren's face. "I mean, given the circumstances you were under up there, I can understand if you want to say no."

Lauren lowered her head before returning her gaze to Jo. "I said I would and my word's my bond. As long as what you said the other day still applies."

Jo furrowed her brows, trying to recall their conversation. "What did I say again?"

Lauren poured a measure of water into the two mugs and handed one to Jo. "The bit about having final say on what was shown. You can understand there are certain parts of my life I'd prefer to remain private."

"Sure, not a problem." Jo covered her excitement by taking a sip of her tea. "Ah, that feels like it's defrosting me from within."

"How do you deal with it?" Lauren leant back on her pack and cradled her cup in her hands.

Jo tilted her head. "Deal with what?"

"Being a lesbian and working in such a visible industry like television."

"I know I've had to be careful about my private life, but I think I've gotten away with it because I'm not in the mainstream media. You know, on the box every night being seen by millions of people. I pity the people who are, because they normally end up leading incredibly closeted lives." Jo looked out at the stillness of the lake, keeping her voice devoid of emotion. "I even remember a female reporter for prime time news who ended up getting married just to cover up her lesbian life," she looked down at the cup in her hands. "I don't think I'd ever do that." Jo cleared her throat, reached into her pack, and pulled out an energy bar. She ripped the top of the bar and broke it in half, offering a piece to Lauren.

"Thanks. I didn't get much breakfast this morning." Lauren took a bite of the bar.

"No problem. Remember the cameraman I told you about, the one who fell ill summiting Mount McKinley?"

Lauren nodded. "Yes."

"I'd like to get in touch with him and see if he's available to film your story." Jo watched as Lauren seemed to retreat into herself. She leant across and rested her hand on Lauren's knee. "He's my best friend, and I'd trust him with my life. His principles are similar to mine, and I think it's why we get on so well. Plus, my lifestyle isn't an issue to him. Trust me with this, please."

Lauren silently chewed the energy bar, as if she were mulling over the idea. She reached down and picked up her cup and drained its contents. "I trust you but, like I said, I've been burnt before."

I get the feeling that's a story all of its own. "If it'd make you feel any more comfortable I can have a contract drawn up, stipulating everything we've discussed. We can wait until you've agreed on the terms before we start even the first frame of filming." Jo removed her hand from Lauren's knee and pulled on her liners and gloves, waiting for an answer.

"It won't be necessary. I think I can trust you," Lauren replied, her voice barely above a whisper.

"I get the feeling that's a big concession from you. I won't let you down, I promise."

Lauren piled snow around the stove element to cool it down. Satisfied, she stowed it in her pack. "Thanks. I don't know about you but I could do with a hot shower and sitting here isn't getting me closer to one."

Jo handed her empty cup to Lauren, then stood and pulled on her backpack. "Amen to that. I can hear my spa calling my name."

JO SANK INTO the comfort of one of Lauren's four-wheel drive's front seats and moaned. "God, that feels good." She bent down and rubbed one of her calves. "I really am out of shape."

Lauren laughed and turned on the engine. "You sure don't look it."

Jo's glance shot to Lauren's face, just in time to see the blush on her cheeks.

"I mean, we'll make a mountain woman out of you yet." Lauren looked at the sky then turned on the headlights. She checked her watch. "I can't believe how overcast it still is. It's only just after ten in the morning and yet it looks like dusk."

"You're right, it does. This is just the sort of day for long hot baths and staying in bed, both of which I intend to do when I get back to the cabin."

Lauren cleared her throat. She checked the rear vision mirror and put the four-wheel drive into reverse. "I can drop you off at your cabin if you like. It'd save you the walk from the main lodge."

"That'd be great, thanks." Jo looked out her window at the surrounding grasslands, lightly dusted with last evening's snow. "It looks like a maniac's been let loose with a bloody great container of talcum powder."

"You wait until it really snows here. In a good year the snow level comes down much lower than last night's dump."

Lauren paused at the intersecting track to the main road, waiting for a convoy of small buses to pass. Jo glanced toward Annie's hut and frowned. She craned her neck and squinted at the wooden structure. "Is there a light on in Annie's hut?"

Lauren surreptitiously glanced at the hut then back to the road. Jo saw Lauren's grip tightened on the steering wheel.

"Someone must've lit one for me."

Jo frowned and looked at Lauren and then at the weather-beaten structure. "But I thought you said the place was secure and only you had the key. How could someone light a lamp for you if they can't get in?"

"Maybe I left the door open or something. Look, I don't know about you but I'm pretty beat. Can we have this conversation when I'm a bit more awake?"

"Sure. It just seemed strange, that's all." *And, besides, from what I've learnt of you so far you don't strike me as someone who'd leave a door unlocked.*

LAUREN UNLOCKED THE front door of Annie's hut and went in. On a small table by one of the hut's windows sat a lamp, its soft glow lighting the corner of the room.

"Would you care to explain your actions last night?" Lauren demanded, her hands on her hips.

"And what actions would those be? The ones where I helped you locate the woman?" came the ghostly reply.

Lauren impatiently tapped her foot and took a deep breath.

"Don't be obtuse. You know exactly what I'm talking about. I know it was you in the car park and it was you with the pot in the hut. If the pot had hit Jo's head I'd have had two casualties instead of one."

"You're calling her by her first name now?"

Lauren watched Annie's shadowy form pace from one side of the room to the other. "What's that supposed to mean? Of course I'm calling her by her name."

"Do you like her?"

Lauren massaged her shoulder, attempting to loosen the knot caused by carrying hers and Susan's pack down the mountain. "Of course I like her. She's a nice person."

Annie turned and pointed at Lauren. "Now who's being obtuse? You know what I mean. Do you *like* her?"

Lauren sat down at the small table in the centre of the room and ran her hands through her hair. "Maybe I do and maybe I don't. I just don't know at the moment."

"Where does that leave me?"

Lauren looked to where Annie's form stood. "It leaves you where you've always been. Just because I like Jo doesn't mean I don't like you." She suddenly stood, causing the chair to skitter across the floor. "But, damn it, what we have now is about as good as it'll ever get, isn't it?"

Annie's form moved toward Lauren. "Maybe that's the case, but at least I'll always be here for you. Will she? Can you be sure she's not just interested in you merely for what she can get out of the story she's doing on you?"

Lauren shook her head and turned away. "Jo's not like that."

"How do you know? How can you be so sure?"

"I just do." Lauren rubbed one hand across her face, silently beginning to question whether she had let Jo in too easily.

"Are you as sure of her as you were with Patricia?"

Lauren wheeled. "Don't you *dare* bring up her name. I never want to hear it again, do you understand?"

"I'm sorry. I didn't mean to upset you. I just know from what you've told me how much that woman hurt you and I don't want to see someone do the same to you again. Can you forgive me?"

"Of course I can," Lauren walked to the lamp. She blew out the flame, trimmed the wick, and headed for the door. "I'm going to the main cabin to have a shower."

"Are you coming back?" Annie's voice was tinged with doubt.

"Of course I am. I always do, don't I?" Lauren softly replied, closing the door behind her.

"MY GOD, THE explorer returns! I was beginning to wonder whether you'd been swallowed up by the Tasmanian wilderness."

Jo laughed at Ros's comments while adjusting the screen of her computer. "You should be so lucky. No, I'm fine. I'm a little tired but fine all the same."

Ros grabbed a small handful of hard-covered chocolate candy from the bowl on her desk. "Have you convinced the recluse of the golfing world to let you do her story?"

"Let's just say you'd better be mailing the company's credit details down here, so I can let reception know to bill my trip up to you and not me."

"Yes!" Ros pumped her fist in the air. "That's great news. When do you start?"

Jo tightened the sash around her plush, white bathrobe. "I've got to get in touch with Ben first, to see if he's available to do the filming. He's my first choice, and plus Lauren's still a little skittish about the whole thing. I'd hate to get halfway through filming with someone I didn't know and have her frightened off because of some small reason or another."

"Is she likely to do that?"

Jo pulled her legs on to the couch and tucked them beneath her. "I don't know. She's a very private person but I can't help thinking the privacy's got more to do with caution than shyness."

Ros sorted through her candy bowl, found a blue one, and popped it in her mouth. "So, how are *other* things going with her? I mean, is there any hope of a future between the two of you?"

"I don't think I'm chasing a complete dead end if that's what you mean. She's gay but, just like the rest of her life, she's very private about it. I know you won't but please don't discuss what I told you with anyone."

Ros reassuringly waved her hand. "I won't. I know you're a professional and will deliver a great story, but where does that leave you personally?"

"I'm not sure. And, given where she is and the way she handles herself, I don't know if she'd be interested in a relationship. She seems to have capably filled her life with other things to do. I mean, she works as a guide most days and, on her days off, gives her free time to teach kids at a golfing clinic. I don't think it leaves much space for romance."

"Does she seem interested in you?"

Jo shrugged. "She holds herself back, like she's protecting herself. I've sensed there's an interest there but there's also a reticence. It's as if she's always looking over her shoulder. It's strange, that's for sure."

Ros leant back in her chair. "I'd like to give you some advice but my track record with love is about as woeful as yours." They shared a laugh. "Take care. I'd hate to see you hurt."

"Thanks. At least as the absolute minimum, I can promise you what she's doing now is going to make a great story. I'll be in touch."

Jo switched off her Web cam, picked up her mobile, and punched in Ben's number.

"Hi Ben, it's Jo."

"Hey squirt, what're you up to?"

Jo smiled. "Don't give me that. You're not much taller than I am. Are you on a project at the moment?"

"No, what did you have in mind?"

"I'm down in Tassie and I've secured Lauren Wheatley for *Where Are They Now?*, and I need a cameraman. Are you free?"

"It depends. Is she good-looking?"

Jo groaned and rose from the couch. "You're a disgrace, and you're full of it, but you know that, don't you?"

"Stop it, I'm blushing," he said, chuckling. "Seriously, though. Yes, I'm free. When do you want to start filming?"

Jo peered out the sliding glass door to her balcony at the grey sky. "I figure the sooner the better. When can you get down here?"

"I'll catch the first flight out tomorrow if you like. Where do you want me to fly into?"

"Devonport's closer but connections out of Melbourne can be a nightmare. How about we shoot for tomorrow afternoon? Hang on a minute." Jo moved to her laptop and began to search for fares on the Internet. "Where are you flying out of?"

"I'm just outside of Sydney, so Mascot's the closest airport."

"There's a Sky Rider flight leaving Sydney around midday. It gets into Launceston at four tomorrow afternoon. I'll meet you at the airport." She read the details to Ben, concurrently jotting them down on a small notepad.

"Sounds like a plan. You make the bookings and I'll pick up the ticket at the airport. See you tomorrow."

JO THREW HER bag in the passenger seat of her car and checked her watch, mentally calculating how long it would take her to get to Launceston airport. "Just enough time to pay a visit to Lauren to let her know what's going on." She closed the cabin door and started down the stairs. "Who are you fooling Ashby? You'd use any excuse to get a chance to talk with her." She got into the car, put it in gear, and headed to Lauren's cabin.

As she drove through the gates of the park the snow that had fallen two nights ago was barely noticeable. The slight warmth of the ground had melted the light cover, and the only immediate evidence of its presence was the muddy slush on the shaded sides of the dirt road. She pulled up to where Lauren's four-wheel drive was normally parked, got out, and knocked on the cabin door. She fought hard to control her disappointment when her knocking went unanswered. "Maybe she's down at Annie's hut."

Jo pulled out of the driveway and headed to the wooden hut, only to be disappointed again. She didn't need to get out to see the lock on the front door was still secure. She turned the car around and headed back the way she came toward the lodge. *I might as well check the booking I made yesterday for Ben's room. At least it'll give me an opportunity to ask what I really want to ask.*

She went through the main doors of the lodge and walked to reception. On cue one of the staff walked through the internal office door located behind the counter.

"Can I help you, ma'am?"

"Can you confirm if the room I booked for Mr. Redbourne is ready?"

Jo waited as the staff member's fingers danced across the keyboard in front of her. "Yes ma'am, it is. Is there anything else I can help you with?"

"I was wondering if I could get in touch with Lauren Wheatley. I'm Jo Ashby."

The receptionist's eyes widened. "You're the guest who helped Lauren with the rescue the other night. Congratulations. I'm sure you'll be happy to know Miss Gilmore's doing well. Her ankle was severely strained but, thankfully, no broken bones."

"That's great news." Jo impatiently looked around, as if doing so would afford her a glimpse of Lauren. She returned her gaze to the receptionist. "Anyway, is there any chance of me getting in touch with Miss Wheatley? Is she doing a tour today?"

"No she's not. She left early this morning for a couple of days' break to play some golf down in Hobart." The receptionist paused and scanned the room. "You know she was a great golfer once," she whispered. "She still plays, especially after she's finished a rescue. I suppose it helps her to let off some steam."

Jo fought to contain her surprise. "Yes, I've no doubt it does." She thanked the receptionist and walked out the door, shaking her head at the latest piece of the puzzle that was Lauren Wheatley.

Chapter
Seven

JO HEADED DOWN the stairs leading into The Retreat's guest bar, Ben just behind her. She walked to the bar's serving area and rang the small bell on the counter.

"You have to ring for service here?" Ben scanned the bar's comfortable surrounds.

"Not normally. But I've discovered during the weeknights the server manages both this area and the tavern on the other side." Jo reached across, snagged a cashew from the courtesy bowl on the counter, and popped it into her mouth.

Ellie walked through the doorway between the two areas. "Hi, Jo. What can I get you?"

Ben smirked. "Trust you to be on first name terms with the bar staff—ow!" He yelped when Jo swatted his shoulder.

"It's not like that at all," she countered. "Ellie was here the night I arrived and so I introduced myself."

"So she did." Ellie refilled the bowl of cashews. "Mind you, she didn't tell me what she did or that she'd make herself so well known in the short time she's been here. Her rescue's the talk of the lodge."

"It wasn't my rescue, it was Lauren's. I just happened to be in the right place at the right time to lend a hand." Jo gestured toward Ben. "This is my cameraman, Ben Redbourne."

"G'day Ellie, it's great to meet you. Where is everyone?"

"It's off-season, so there aren't a lot of guests around on a weekday. We had a group in earlier but they've headed off for the night-viewing tour. The place will fill up again in a couple of hours when they return. In the meantime, it's just the three of us. What's your poison?"

"I'll have one of Tasmania's finest beers." Ben turned to Jo. "And what about you, short stuff?"

Jo lightly kicked his shin. "I'm not short, you bloody great tree trunk. I'll have a beer also. Thanks, Ellie."

"Not a problem. Take a seat and I'll bring them over."

To afford them a little privacy, Jo herded Ben to one of the corner nooks farthest from the bar.

Ben sat down and plopped his feet on the large cloth ottoman in front of him. "You didn't tell me you were part of a rescue. What happened?"

Jo nonchalantly shrugged. "It was just a case of good luck rather than planning on my behalf. I was at Lauren's place when she got the call that someone was missing and I offered my services."

"I bet you did," Ben replied, dodging Jo's mock blow. "So what's she like?"

"Hopefully she'll be here soon so you can see for yourself. Can you do me a favour? Keep control of your sometimes less-than-pure mouth. She's a little skittish about the whole interview idea and the last thing I want is for you to scare her off. Especially not when we're this close."

"You don't need to convince me. You're the one who seems a bit edgy about the whole idea. I swear, during the drive from the airport, if you'd questioned me one more time on whether my camera gear survived the journey I was going to strangle you." Ben reached across and lightly shook Jo's shoulder. "I know you're anxious to get the story. Trust me, we'll get it. But you can't let your impatience get the better of you, as it sometimes has a tendency to do. As for me scaring Lauren off—" he leant back and placed his hands behind his head. "I'll be the epitome of diplomacy."

Jo snorted. "You couldn't even spell the word, let alone practice it."

"What?" Ben innocently asked. "Epitome?"

Ellie placed two mugs of beer and a bowl of mixed nuts on the small table between them. "Here you go. Let me know if you need anything else."

Ben picked up his drink, took a sip and smacked his lips. "Ah, that's better. Thanks."

Jo took a sip of her drink as she waited for Ellie to return to the bar. "Just be careful how you treat Lauren. God knows it took me long enough to understand your warped sense of humour. She mightn't be ready for it just yet."

Ben held up his hands. "Okay, I get it. There's no need to tell me again. But is she good-looking?"

Jo rolled her eyes. "See, that's just what I mean, you big oaf." She scowled at the teasing look in Ben's eyes. As she made an attempt to reach across and slap him again, she caught sight of Lauren as she walked down the stairs leading into the bar. Jo smiled and motioned her head to where Lauren stood. "You tell me. Is she beautiful?"

Ben looked over his shoulder and quickly stood as Lauren approached. "Good evening, Miss Wheatley. I'm Ben Redbourne, Jo's cameraman." He courteously extended his hand. "It's a pleasure to meet you."

Lauren graciously took his proffered hand. "Please call me

Lauren." She looked at Jo and shyly smiled. "Hi."

"No worries. Call me Ben. Can I get you anything to drink?"

"Just a juice, thanks."

"One juice, coming right up." Ben went to the bar, affording the two women a moment of privacy.

Jo motioned at the chair beside her. "How are you?" She watched Lauren take a seat and nervously look around her surroundings. Lauren started to answer when Ben returned and sat down opposite them.

"Your drink's on its way. Jo tells me you're the head guide here. How do you become head guide of this part of Cradle Mountain National Park?"

Lauren eased back into her chair. "It's partly the time I've been working here and also my university degree. When I first arrived I began my undergrad studies in Natural Resource Management, and followed it with a Master's in Natural Resources. Not all the guides have degrees but we share a common interest in the environment and keeping the park as pristine as we can."

"It sounds like a long way from swinging a golf club," Ben replied.

Lauren rose. "Yes, it is. I'll just go and check on my drink."

Jo watched her walk toward the bar. "She's nervous about something."

Ben leant into Jo's space. "She might be nervous, but she's a stunner."

Jo took a sip of her drink. "I don't mean to burst your bubble but I don't think she'd be interested in you."

"What?" Ben glanced to where Lauren waited for her drink and back at Jo. "You mean she bats on your team?" He sighed. "Why are all the good-looking ones unavailable?"

"What do you care? You're married. Shhh, she's coming. Do you think you could make yourself scarce for a couple of minutes while I try and work out what's wrong?"

"Sure. I'll go and check on tomorrow's forecast. Back in a bit."

Lauren placed her drink on the table and sat down. "Where's he going?"

"He's checking on tomorrow's weather."

Lauren frowned. "I could've told him what it's going to be like."

Jo placed her hand over Lauren's. "I figured you'd know but I wanted a quiet moment to find out what's wrong. You look like you're ready to bolt."

She watched the interplay of emotions across Lauren's face, pleased when Lauren made no attempt to remove her hand from where it rested under Jo's, on the chair's armrest.

Lauren reached over and lightly stroked Jo's hand. "I'm fine. Just a little nervous."

Jo's breathing quickened as she looked down at their hands. The room faded into the background and she had the overwhelming desire to link Lauren's fingers with her own. She slowly looked up and into Lauren's eyes, surprised at what she saw there. "Lauren," she started.

Ben loudly cleared his throat as he sat down and Jo removed her hand from Lauren's.

Ben sipped his beer and returned the mug to the coaster on the table. "They say it's going to be a clear day tomorrow. It'll be a little cold but sunny."

"Yes, I know," Lauren replied.

"It should make a great day for filming, if you're okay with it."

Lauren nodded, a noncommittal expression on her face.

Jo pushed on, sensing it was going to be the only way she'd make Lauren understand everything was going to be okay. "What I'd like to do is an introductory interview in the lodge here, possibly in the Cowle Lounge next door. Then I'd like to get some footage of you taking a tour."

Lauren picked up her juice. "To commercially film in the park, you need a permit, and you must carry it with you at all times. Have you got one?"

"I got one today, before I headed out to pick up Ben." Jo didn't miss the look of disappointment that flitted across Lauren's face. She pressed on. "Do you have any tours tomorrow?"

"Yes, I'm taking a group through Waldheim Chalet tomorrow morning."

Jo rubbed her hands together. "That'll work. If you're free in the afternoon I'd like to do a short walk, maybe to Wombat Pool."

Ben eagerly leant forward. "That'd make fantastic footage. I've got a framed photo of it in my room and the colours are fantastic. I'd also like to get some shots of where you live, as well as inside Annie's hut. On the trip from the airport, Jo mentioned you spend a lot of time there. Having the hut as a backdrop would help bring the piece together."

Lauren folded her arms across her chest and crossed her legs. "I don't mind the opening interview or the tour. And I'm okay with you filming my home in the park but I won't agree to you filming inside Annie's hut."

Ben frowned, sat back in his chair, and looked questioningly at Jo.

Jo quickly glanced at Ben and back at Lauren, her frustration building at Lauren's stubbornness. "I don't understand. It's only a hut. You've my word we'll be careful about how we film in there."

Lauren pursed her lips and shook her head. "I want no filming in Annie's hut. That's a deal breaker."

Jo fought to tamp down her impatience. "What is it with you and the hut? Every time I try to raise anything to do with it you try your darnedest to change the subject. For God's sake, it's only a building."

Ben looked back and forth at them. "Calm down, Jo. There's got to be a way around this. Lauren, would you agree to me filming the outside of the hut? So I can put that part of the story in perspective?"

Lauren rubbed a hand across her forehead. She closed her eyes, sighed, and returned her gaze to Ben. "Okay," she softly replied.

Jo counted to ten and slowly let out an exasperated breath. "Fine. To give the story some perspective I'd also like to get some footage of you on the golf course, playing a round of golf."

Lauren stared, steely-eyed, at Jo. "I don't do that anymore."

"*Really*? So what is the game called that you play on your days off, to let off steam?" Jo challenged.

Lauren's hands gripped the sides of her chair. "And this is why I don't want someone filming my life. What I do is private, but obviously it isn't to *you*."

Ben rapped on the table to get their attention. "Look, I think things are getting a little out of hand here. I'm not about exposing your private life and I don't think Jo is, either." He rose from his chair. "How about we take a time out for a moment and just all calm down. I'm going to go and check out the Cowle Lounge for tomorrow's filming. In the meantime, why don't the two of you work out whatever bug it is you've both got up your respective arses?" He picked up his beer and took the stairs, two at a time.

Jo leant forward in her chair, rested her elbows on her thighs and clasped her shaky hands together, as if in prayer. She rested her chin on her fingertips, struggling to find a way ahead. She looked sideways at Lauren. "I'm sorry I lost my temper. I shouldn't have blurted out what I did."

Lauren reached forward and placed her hand on Jo's shoulder. "I'm sorry, too. I shouldn't have reacted the way I did."

Jo straightened and turned to Lauren, struggling to find words for what she wanted to say. "When I started this story, it was the final part of my series and that's all. I'd wrap up the filming and just move on. But now I'm finding it increasingly difficult to do. I can't help but feel more for you than just an interview subject. I'm sorry if you're uncomfortable with this. It's been a very long time since I've felt this way about anyone."

Lauren's eyes widened in surprise, before she looked down at their intertwined hands.

How can I convince her she isn't just a fling for me? The grip of their hands was testimony of Lauren's internal struggle. Lauren closed her eyes for a moment before returning her gaze to Jo.

"You're a beautiful and obviously talented woman, but—" Lauren removed her hand from Jo's and sighed. "I can't allow such a relationship to happen. I hope you can understand."

Jo hopes were dashed by Lauren's forced reluctance. She sadly smiled and offered her hand. "Can we at least be friends?"

"I'd like that."

What started as a shake became something more as they both held the clasp, regretful that the release of the other's hand would signal the end of something that never really had the chance to begin.

"Have you two kissed and made up yet?" Ben mischievously asked when he sat down.

Lauren dropped Jo's hand and leant back in her chair.

Jo scowled. "Can you keep your mind above your belt buckle? We were just shaking hands."

"Okay, no need to get bent out of shape about it. Have we ironed out the kinks in this story?" Ben picked through the bowl of nuts in front of him.

Jo slapped his hand. "Just take a handful and *then* sort through them, you grub." She looked at Lauren, questioning, and received a slight nod in return. "Yes, we have. We'll start filming tomorrow. I'd like to do the initial interview first. Can we fit it in before your morning tour?"

"Sure. It doesn't start until ten-thirty, so I could be here by nine if you like. I'd better get going." Lauren rose, as did Jo and Ben.

"That sounds fine. We'll meet you in the Cowle Lounge." Jo smiled, trying to hide her disappointment at Lauren's earlier rebuff.

Ben shook Lauren's hand. "It's nice to meet you. We'll see you tomorrow." Both Jo and Ben remained standing as Lauren left the bar. "And, Jo, here I was thinking your anxiety had to do with wrapping up the final story of your series. I haven't seen you this flustered since you started that thing you had with Lise Cowley. When were you going to tell me you're in love with Lauren?"

Jo glared at him. "I am *not* in love with her," she furiously whispered.

"If you're not, then it's something a hell of a lot like it. What if I said 'falling in love with her'? Would that be a more accurate assessment?"

Jo refused to be drawn by Ben's probing and instead reached down and picked up her coat and put it on. "I'm going to bed. I'll see you tomorrow."

"Pleasant dreams." He ducked the cashew Jo threw in his direction.

LAUREN REACHED FOR the lamp and matches resting on the ledge just inside Annie's hut. She placed the lamp on the table, removed the glass chimney, and struck a match, only to have it blown out by a cold gust of wind. After five failed attempts she straightened and put her hands on her hips. "Will you at least let me try and light this damn thing? You mightn't need light, but I do." She once more bent over the lamp and struck a match, this time successfully getting the wick to flare.

"Where have you been this evening?"

Lauren turned to the form framed in the bedroom doorway. "I told you where I was going. Why do you need to ask me again?"

Annie moved closer to Lauren, her lithe body, short curly hair, and weather-tanned face barely visible in the lamp's glow. "You've been there all this time?"

Lauren returned the matches to the ledge by the door. "There was a lot to talk about. Jo wanted to go over what we'd be filming over the next few days."

"How convenient it must be, having you all to herself for such a long time."

Lauren wheeled. "We weren't by ourselves. Her cameraman was there." She paused at the look of disbelief on Annie's face. Lauren closed her eyes and pinched the bridge of her nose. "You make this so hard. Sometimes I feel like I'm losing my mind. Every time I look sideways at someone you're reading something into it." She turned at the sound of her keys being swept off the table.

Annie jabbed her finger, as if in accusation. "But there is something to it this time, isn't there?"

Lauren gritted her teeth and shook her head, attempting to answer without raising her voice. "Damn it, there could be if I wanted it to be. That much I *do* know."

The lamp on the table flickered and the temperature inside the hut suddenly dropped. "Then why don't you?"

Lauren thrust her hands into her pockets at the sudden loss of warmth. "God, you can be so difficult."

Annie moved to Lauren. "Are you saying you're not happy? How do you think I feel? How can I be entirely happy when you spend so much time with her?"

Lauren threw her hands up in desperation. "How can I be entirely happy with someone I can't even hold?"

"If that's how you feel, why don't you just leave?"

Lauren moved to the table. "You've called me on this before and I told you then I won't continue taking your accusations. Don't force me into making a decision that could be a final one."

Annie backed into one of the shadowy corners of the room. "You make your own decisions."

"Fine. I will!" For the briefest of moments the light from the lamp was gone, throwing the cabin into temporary darkness. It came to life again then, almost as quickly, it was extinguished. Lauren searched the cabin, trying to see or sense Annie's presence. "Annie, are you there?" She walked to the corner where Annie had last been. "I'm sorry. I shouldn't have said those things." The silence in the hut was deafening. "You know I need you. You'll never leave me and I need that." Lauren hung her head, realising she'd gone too far. She bent down and picked up her keys and put them in the pocket of her jacket. She straightened, reached across the table and trimmed the lamp's wick, then headed for the door and the warmth of her modern home.

JO WAITED AS Ben pulled the camera from the back seat of her small rental car. "The interview in the Cowle Lounge worked well."

"It sure did. Lauren seems a lot more relaxed than she was last night." Ben closed the car's door. "Did you get the written permissions from the people on the Waldheim tour?"

Jo grabbed her clipboard off the roof of the car. "Yes, I managed to get them before we headed out of the foyer. They all seemed pretty excited about the idea."

"I think I'll get some exterior shots before Lauren arrives with the group."

Jo watched Ben set up his equipment to one side of the path leading to the Waldheim Chalet. She looked at the weather-worn building, nestled among a copse of overhanging trees. Made entirely of wood, two small verandas complemented its shingled roof and sides. She turned at the sound of an engine and looked back over her shoulder at Ben. "You'd better get your filming done. I think Lauren and the tour group are about to arrive."

Jo walked to where the small van parked and waited while Lauren helped her group from the vehicle. She watched Lauren glance around her surroundings, as if she were expecting more guests for the tour. "How are you going?"

Lauren released a shaky breath. "I'm fine. Just not used to all the attention again. I had more questions on the trip here about why I was being filmed than what I did about the actual park."

Jo patted her shoulder. "You'll be fine. I'm sure they'll be all ears once you start talking about the chalet. You've a great voice, you know."

Lauren blushed and ducked her head. "I think you're a bit biased, but thanks for the compliment." She looked at the group making their way across the small wooden bridge and path leading up to the chalet. "What's next?"

Jo motioned her forward. "We'll mic you up and do a quick sound check before we start. We'll have to do it again when we get inside, but it shouldn't be too intrusive."

"Let's do it."

Ben walked across to them and held up a small portable microphone and body pack. "This'll feel a little funny at first but I figure it isn't the first time you've worn one of these things."

"It's been a while. I'm happy to see they're a little smaller than I remember."

Ben handed the body pack to Jo and he proceeded to clip the mic onto Lauren's jacket. "Jo, can you turn the mic on and put the pack in the small of Lauren's back? I'll go and check the sound level."

"Sure."

He walked back to his camera.

Jo watched him before focusing on Lauren again, hoping she at least appeared confident. It wasn't as if this was the first time she'd done this. *But this is with someone you're terribly attracted to.* She casually lifted up the back of Lauren's jacket and clipped the pack snugly to her heavy cotton trousers. As she adjusted the small receiver she heard Lauren softly chuckle. She pulled down the jacket. "What's that about?"

"I'm sorry. You just seem to be doing that so carefully. I guess it puts a different spin on getting your hands on someone's pants."

A flush worked its way up Jo's neck at Lauren's innuendo. She recovered from her shock and smiled wickedly. *Turnabout's fair play.* "I think the saying's got more to do with getting my hands *into* someone's pants, although that can always be arranged."

"Yep, ladies, the mic's working fine," Ben called out, a cheeky look on his face.

Jo laughed at the blush on Lauren's features. Lauren cleared her throat and pulled her jacket into place. "I think I have some tourists waiting."

Jo followed Lauren as she walked to the group, taking a place to one side, out of camera range so she could watch Lauren talk.

"Welcome to Waldheim Chalet, ladies and gentlemen. Let me start by saying what you see in front of you isn't the original building. It fell into disrepair in the 1960s. However, using the original floor plan and working only with natural materials, the building was pulled down and rebuilt in 1976, back to its original state." She paused and pointed at a man with his hand raised. "Yes?"

"Was it Waldheim who built it?"

"No, Waldheim — or 'forest home' — is the name of the chalet. The man who built the original was Gustav Weindorfer, an Austrian who migrated to Australia in 1900. He's often regarded as one of Tasmania's earliest conservationists. He was the first person to envision the idea of a national park that everyone could enjoy." Lauren pulled a laminated photo from her jacket and handed it to the closest person in the tour group.

"What I'm passing around is a photocopy of an early picture of Gustav and Kate Weindorfer. He and his wife first visited here in 1910 and were absolutely taken with the area's beauty. Weindorfer managed to purchase two hundred acres of the surrounding land and built the chalet where its replica stands today. He first opened it in the summer of 1913 and played host to twenty-five guests. The original house was only three rooms. Over time, and with demand, this grew to eight rooms and associated outbuildings."

"Is this the original version or the one with all the additional rooms?" a voice called out from the back.

"This is a reproduction of the original three-room building, consisting of a combined living-dining room and two bedrooms. One bedroom was the Weindorfers' and the other was for any couples who were honeymooning. The rest of the people would bed down in the large common living-dining room. Unfortunately, Kate died in 1916. Gustav never remarried and lived here for the rest of his life. He died in 1932 and he's buried in the small forest behind the chalet." Lauren nodded to a woman with her hand raised.

"You said he purchased two hundred acres. How did the park get so big?"

"After his wife's death, Gustav continued to petition the local government for the preservation of the park. He finally got his wish, and in 1922, one hundred and fifty-eight thousand acres, stretching from Cradle Mountain to Lake Saint Clair, were set aside as a scenic reserve. Today the same land forms part of the Tasmanian Wilderness World Heritage area. Let's head inside and I'll show you where Gustav entertained his guests with wombat stew and songs."

Lauren ushered the group through the building's entrance.

Jo lightly touched Lauren's arm. "Can you wait just a moment? Ben's got to set up and check for lighting and sound."

Lauren smiled. "Not a problem." She moved around the group and entertained them while Ben prepared for the interior shoot. He gave her a thumbs-up and she nodded and discreetly moved to Lauren's side. "We're ready."

Jo again stood to one side and watched Lauren speak for another fifteen minutes on Weindorfer and the contributions he made to Cradle Mountain and Tasmanian conservation. She was grateful for the opportunity to observe Lauren. Jo smiled at the way she interacted with the group and blushed on more than one occasion when Lauren's gaze settled on her.

"Okay, feel free to have a look around the chalet and the outbuildings. If you can meet me by the back door in about ten minutes I'll then take you on a short walk to Weindorfer's grave." Lauren waited for the group to disperse and then walked to Jo and Ben. "How did everything go?"

"Great," Ben closed down his camera. "I'll head out the back and check the lighting at the grave site. Then we can move straight into filming without interrupting your talk."

"Great," Lauren replied. "Just go out the back door and take a right. The track to his grave is sign-posted. I'll see you there shortly, but I'll mingle here first and see if there're any other questions."

Lauren moved to the first small group and it wasn't long before she was answering another series of questions. Jo smiled and wandered around the interior of the chalet, pausing at the various boards filled with information and photographs from days gone by.

She walked inside the small "honeymoon" room and giggled at the bed that dominated it, leaving barely enough space to reach the shuttered window at the foot. She gazed at the view in front of her. The surrounding trees created a sense of wonderland, its silence blanketed by a carpet of lush green grass and moss. The only sound came from the burble of a small creek, which ran in front of the cottage, a small distance from where Jo stood. She was jolted back into the present by a soft touch to her shoulder.

"This would've been such a peaceful place back then. No cars, few tourists, and no worries," Lauren softly said.

"It would've been a lot more peaceful if you were the lucky guests who got this room." Lauren's hand remained where it had initially come to rest and a little charge raced down Jo's back. *Friends touch like this, right?* She glanced over her shoulder, noting Lauren stood perilously close. Jo turned to face her. "But there isn't a lot of space." She checked her watch in an effort to mask her overwhelming desire to pull Lauren to her and onto the bed. "It's almost time for you to start your tour again. We'd better get going. Excuse me." Jo eased past Lauren, swallowing a gulp when she brushed Lauren. She looked back at Lauren's enigmatic smile and the silent laughter in her soft golden eyes. "You deliberately did that, didn't you?"

"Now, why would I do such a thing?" Finally out in the broader part of the room, Lauren sidestepped Jo and sauntered toward the back door of the chalet.

"I swear she's going to kill me," Jo softly muttered as she followed.

"THAT SHOULD JUST about wrap it up." Ben called from behind the camera. "The shots of the two of you in front of Wombat Pool should turn out great. I'm amazed how still the water is. It's almost like a mirror."

"It's pretty well protected from any of the prevailing winds." Lauren removed the microphone from her jacket and the mini receiver from the small of her back and handed them to Jo.

"It's a beautiful spot, there's no doubt about that." Jo moved closer to Lauren, ensuring both microphones were off and they were out of Ben's hearing. She marked a leisurely trail over Lauren's body with her eyes. "Natural beauty as well as a walking, talking beauty. You can't beat those two together."

"You know—" Lauren stopped at the sound of other voices coming up the track. She stepped away from Jo and looked in the direction of the voices.

"Hey, here's one of those lemon myrtle trees. See if you can grab some of the leaves for a cup of tea," a woman said.

Lauren's features darkened when one of the three women left the wooden path and walked through the undergrowth with little thought about what she was treading on.

"Excuse me," Lauren said in an overly professional tone, "but the park requirements are that you remain on the path at all times. You're not allowed to pick anything from the native bushes, either. If you're after some leaves for lemon myrtle tea, then it'd probably be a lot better if you bought them at the store just outside the main entry into the park."

The woman who'd left the track stopped and turned back to Lauren. "And who the hell are you?" she demanded, hands on hips.

"Lauren Wheatley, the head guide for Cradle Mountain and I'd really appreciate it if you'd return to the walkway."

Jo moved to stand beside Lauren and placed a soothing hand in the small of her back, out of sight of the three other women.

The woman casually returned to the path, disdain on her features. "So, it's *ranger girl*, saving nature's day is it?" She looked behind Lauren to where Jo stood and lasciviously smiled. "Hey there, are you a ranger too?"

"No, I'm just a friend." Jo stepped back.

The woman moved past Lauren and to Jo. "My friends and I'd be happy for your company," the woman replied, not bothering to mask the suggestion in her words. "We're walking the Overland Track tomorrow and we'd be more than willing to have you to join us."

Jo quickly cast a glance at Lauren, surprised at the mixture of anger and jealousy mirrored in Lauren's face. "No, thanks. I've got other things planned for tomorrow."

Lauren shouldered herself in between Jo and the other woman. "Excuse me, but do you have passes to walk the track?"

"What are you, my keeper? Of course we've got passes." She looked around Lauren at Jo. "We're gonna conquer the track in five days, walking there and back. Come along if you want." When Jo didn't reply she shrugged "Oh well, your loss." She turned to where her two companions stood. "Let's go back to the bar. It should be happy hour by now." The three abruptly turned and headed back the way they'd come.

Lauren took a notepad from her jacket, flipped it open, and started making notes.

"What are you doing?"

"I'm writing down some information on those three. I'll check with the park headquarters to see if they actually do have passes."

"I'm sure they do, and I'm sure they're qualified walkers, even if they were boorish just then."

Lauren finished her notes, stowed the pad in her jacket and turned to Jo. "That may be the case, but they're not walking for the love of nature, they're walking to conquer."

Jo frowned at the melancholy mood that seemed to have

descended over Lauren. "I think they were only trying to big note themselves. Besides, throughout history haven't people always tried to conquer things?"

"Does it need to include conquering nature? What did it do to them?" Lauren shrugged on her pack and headed down the track.

Jo turned to where Ben was finishing up stowing the camera. "Are you okay?"

Ben waved dismissively. "Sure, you head off and I'll catch up. I'll just be a minute."

Jo nodded and trotted after Lauren. "Hey, slow down. You're going as fast as day one again."

Lauren stood and waited. "Have you ever reached the peak of Mount Cook?"

"Yes, why?"

"When you reached the top, how did you feel?"

Jo thought back to a moment five years ago when, after what had been a difficult climb, she finally stood on the summit's peak. "Exhilarated, like I was on top of the world and yet very humbled by how little I was in the greater scheme of things."

"Did you stand there and feel or say you'd conquered Mount Cook?"

"Of course not. I had to get back down and it's not a good idea to upset the mountain gods like that."

Despite Jo's efforts to lighten the mood, a frown still remained on Lauren's face. "Mount Cook isn't something you conquer. It's nature in its wildest moment."

With sudden clarity Jo understood Lauren. "I see what you mean."

Lauren moved away. "I've seen people like those three whose sole aim is to conquer anything at all costs, with no thought about the people or the beauty around them or what they're doing. People like them exist in all parts of life and they disgust me."

Jo watched the interplay of emotions on Lauren's face, her conviction made clear by her words. She caught up with her and softly stroked her arm. "Is that what happened? Did someone try to conquer you?"

Lauren looked down at Jo's hand and up to her face. The anger and frustration Lauren so recently displayed seemed to vanish at Jo's touch. She calmly reached out and lightly stroked Jo's chin. "That's a story for another day."

"What's a story for another day?" Ben huffed, finally catching up.

Jo and Lauren smiled as Jo slapped Ben's back. "Nothing you need to worry about. I think that's enough for now. Let's head back to the lodge."

JO WALKED TO her cabin, escorted by Lauren. "Thanks for dropping us off."

Lauren smiled. "No worries. He looked pretty tired after lugging all his equipment around for the better part of the day."

"He'll be fine once he's had a shower and a beer." Jo unlocked the door and opened it. She hesitated and turned back to Lauren. "Do you want to come in and finish the story you started on the mountain? I've been told I'm a great listener." She reached in and flicked on the light in the cabin's foyer. Indecision flickered across Lauren's face. *It's like she's torn between wanting to come in and wanting to run.*

"No, it's okay. We'll keep it for another time. Besides, if we're climbing Cradle Mountain tomorrow you need to get your rest and so do I. Talking all hours of the night isn't the best way to start a major climb."

"You know we've plenty of footage now to base the story on. There's no need to go tomorrow if you don't want to."

"I never miss an opportunity to get outside, especially with someone I enjoy spending time with." Lauren's gaze lingered on Jo's face as she stepped away from the door. "Anyway, I'll see you tomorrow," she said and walked to her four-wheel drive.

Jo watched her get into the driver's seat. "Of course you will. Unless I immolate from sexual frustration beforehand," Jo muttered, closing the door behind her.

Chapter
Eight

LAUREN CAME THROUGH the front doors of The Retreat and waved at the man standing behind the concierge's desk. "Hi, Ron. I've got a walk planned today for myself and two others, and I'm wondering if you'd check with the kitchen to see if the lunches are ready."

"Sure. Where are you off to?"

"We're doing the Cradle Mountain summit, so I figure it's going to be a long day. Thankfully, my guests are a bit more agile than the last group I took a month ago."

He grimaced. "I remember. The group that bit off more than they could chew. If I recall correctly, you never made the summit. So, who are the lucky ones today?"

"They're Retreat guests: Jo Ashby —"

"Hang on," Ron interrupted. "Wasn't she the one who was with you on the rescue you did a few days ago?" Lauren nodded, a smile lighting her features. "I could think of a worse person to be stuck overnight with, in a mountain hut. But I expect you're used to such living conditions. How's the heat in Annie's hut, now that the days are cooling down?"

Lauren baulked at Ron's question and gathered herself. *You should realise by now the majority of the staff know you spend most of your time there.* "It's been a little chilly, but I haven't been there for the last couple of nights."

Ron grinned. "Getting a bit old to be roughing it, eh? Anyway, Jo's one good-looking woman."

"Yes, she is and she's also great to talk to. She's quite an accomplished climber in her own right."

Ron crossed his arms, a knowing smile on his lips. "*Really?* Care to share anything with me?"

She struggled to hide her blush. "How about you focus on checking the lunch orders for me? I'm sure Ms. Ashby and Mr. Redbourne will need feeding sometime during their walk."

"Ben Redbourne? I could swear he was at the reception desk just a minute ago. He looked like he was checking out."

Lauren wheeled and scanned the room, her eyes finally coming to rest on Ben, bent over a pile of luggage. She headed over to him. "Hi. What's going on?" Lauren tried to contain the nervous tremor in her voice.

Still bent over his bag, Ben looked over his shoulder at Lauren. "We're leaving."

Despite her outward appearance, Lauren's stomach seemed to plummet twenty floors, and she fought to control the bile rising in her throat. Her surroundings closed in around her and, for the briefest of moments, she swore she heard Annie's laughter echoing off the walls of the room. *I thought I could trust you, Jo.* She thickly swallowed. "Why? Have you got enough film for the story?"

"We got a fair bit yesterday." Ben closed the flap on the bag and straightened. His eyes widened in surprise and he reached out to steady Lauren. "Are you okay? You're as white as a sheet. Do you want to sit down?"

Lauren closed her eyes and ran her fingers through her hair. "No, I'm okay. Just too many things on my mind, that's all."

"We're heading back to the mainland because Jo's mum's been in a car accident. It happened a couple of days ago but it took her family a while to track her down. We're flying out from Launceston today."

Ben's words jolted Lauren back to the present. "Is her mum okay?"

"She's a little battered and bruised and she's broken her leg but other than that, she's apparently stable."

Lauren impatiently scanned the foyer. "Where's Jo?"

"She's still in her room. I'm down here checking out for the two of us, so we can get away a little faster."

"I'll go and see if she's okay." Lauren started to walk away and then turned toward the concierge desk where Ron stood. "I won't need those lunches now. One of the two people who were supposed to be climbing has a family emergency. Can you contact Park headquarters for me and let them know I won't be walking the summit today and I'm taking a rest day? I'll check in tomorrow."

He offered a wave. "No worries."

Lauren barely heard his response as she strode out the door of the lodge and to her four-wheel drive. She closed the door and rested her head against the steering wheel, attempting to calm the anxiety coursing through her. Although she'd been floored by Ben's words, what rocked her was her response to Jo's sudden departure. She raised her head and sighed. *You thought you'd been deceived again, didn't you?* As she sat and collected her thoughts, what surprised her more was the overwhelming feeling of loneliness that momentarily enveloped her at the thought of Jo leaving Cradle Mountain. Relieved she'd regained at least a modicum of composure, she reversed out of the car park and headed for Jo's cabin.

JO ONCE AGAIN blew her nose and rose to answer the knock on her cabin door. She took a deep breath and pulled the door open, only to have her emotions crumble at the sight of Lauren's worried face.

Jo was never sure who moved first, but almost simultaneously they walked into each other's arms. Lauren tightly held Jo as she uncontrollably sobbed, and minutes seemed to pass before Jo managed to gather herself.

"I'm sorry about this," Jo said, voice muffled against Lauren's down jacket.

Lauren lightly stroked Jo's back. "It's okay. Don't be sorry. Ben told me about your mum and I fully understand why you're feeling the way you do."

Jo eased herself out of the embrace enough to look at Lauren. "But I know we were supposed to be doing the summit walk today."

Lauren cupped Jo's face with her hands. "It's not important now. What's important is getting you fit for travel. We can climb any time." Lauren leant forward and placed a tender kiss on Jo's forehead as she pulled her into another hug.

Jo released a shaky breath. "Thanks for being here just now. I think I'd allowed everything to build up and I just needed to let go."

"Then I'm happy I could help." Lauren turned and closed the door, then took Jo's hand. "Why don't we go inside and sit down for a bit?"

With their hands entwined, Jo walked with Lauren to the sofa and sat down. She was quietly relieved when Lauren made no attempt to release her grip.

Lauren tucked one leg under the other and faced Jo. "Do you know what happened?"

"The news I've got is pretty sketchy, but mum was involved in a car accident. Something about another car running a red light then running into her. She's stable but her leg's broken." Jo blew her nose and crumpled up the tissue, which she placed with the already large pile on the coffee table. "I lost my father a couple of years ago to a drunk driver. With the amount of alcohol in the other driver's blood he should've been dead, but instead he killed my father in a head-on collision. The bastard was on the wrong side of the road." She shook her head. "When I got the news about mum I couldn't help but think the worst."

Lauren softly stroked Jo's arm, her hand finally coming to rest on Jo's shoulder. "I understand. Not long after I walked away from the golfing circuit I lost both my parents in an aircraft accident. I still regret the time I spent away from the two of them, wrapped up like I was in tournament life. It's just me now and I suppose it's part of the reason I am who I am today."

Despite her own pain Jo struggled to conceal her surprise at Lauren's willingness to share something so obviously private with her. She gently rubbed her thumb across the back of Lauren's hand. "I'm sorry to hear that, but I know your parents would be proud of you. They raised an incredibly talented and remarkable woman, and I'm sure they're looking down on you today, smiling each time they do." Jo paused at the distant expression that suddenly masked Lauren's face. "Are you okay?"

"I'm fine. Dredging up old memories does this to me, I suppose. When does your plane leave?" she queried, deflecting the conversation away from any further discussion about the ghostly presence of her parents.

"It's an afternoon flight, but between the drive to Launceston airport and the security screening to get on the plane, I thought Ben and I should get away early."

"I could drive you if you like. You shouldn't be driving feeling like you do."

Jo smiled. "It's okay. I've got the hire car I have to return. And besides, Ben can drive."

Lauren reached out and tenderly stroked the side of Jo's face. "I know Ben can drive you, but I'd like to, if it's okay with you. Ben can still drive the hire car. Surely he'll understand."

Jo froze, mesmerized as Lauren lowered her face toward her own, only closing her eyes when Lauren's lips softly touched hers. She leant into the kiss and lightly stroked Lauren's neck, sensing that even though Lauren had initiated the kiss, she was still holding back.

Lauren slightly pulled away "Are you coming back?" Her voice was barely loud enough for Jo to hear.

Jo gently took Lauren's hand and raised it to her lips. She placed a kiss on Lauren's open palm then cupped the hand to her own face. "I'll be back for the story, but more importantly, I'll be back for you. There's still a lot we need to work out, and I'd like the chance to do that."

Lauren lowered her head as if in doubt and Jo placed the tip of two fingers under Lauren's chin and raised her face. "I *am* coming back."

"I'd like that," Lauren quietly replied. She reluctantly rose, breaking the contact between them. "Right now, though, we better get you down to the foyer or Ben will be wondering where we've gotten to."

JO THANKED THE taxi driver and made her way up the stairs of her mother's Victorian-style home. She lowered her bags to the ground then reached up and banged the brass door-knocker. While she waited she looked out at the night sky of Sydney. The black expanse of the harbour was surrounded on either side by a foreshore of brightly coloured lights, like stars in the night sky. As she looked up at the shining half-moon, her thoughts wandered to the first outing she'd shared with Lauren. The veranda light interrupted her reminiscing, and she turned as the front door was opened by Andrew Longman, a friend of her mother's. Jo's eyes widened at Andrew's presence. *What are you doing here at this time in the night?* She composed herself. "Hi, Andrew, how are you?"

He bent and picked up Jo's bags then stepped aside, letting her through. "Fine, thanks. How about yourself?"

"Busy as always," Jo walked down the hallway, glancing into the kitchen as she passed. She stopped and scanned the pile of pots and pans, evidence of the remnants of the evening's dinner.

"Sorry about the mess. I was just finishing up with getting Margaret, er, your mum comfortable. This was my next chore."

Jo stepped into the kitchen and placed her daypack on the bench top. "Trust me, her efforts often leave the kitchen a lot worse." They laughed, easing the slight tension in the room. "How's Mum?"

"She's fine. The pain's still there but they discharged her with some pretty potent painkillers. Would you like a juice? You must be parched from all that flying."

"Yes, please." She gratefully took the bottle from Andrew and loosened the lid. "If she's still in so much pain, why is she at home?"

Andrew shrugged. "You tell me. She's *your* mother. Once her condition stabilised she wanted nothing more than to be out of hospital. But the doctors insisted she couldn't go home unless there was someone there to look after her. With your sister still tying up loose ends in Perth, and us still trying to track you down, your mum called me and requested that I spring her from the sterile asylum. Her words, not mine."

Jo smiled. "Sounds like Mum, all right."

"Anyway, I was free so I volunteered to stay here until you or Emma arrived. It's been a full-on job, but thankfully she hasn't tired of me yet."

Jo took a long drink from her bottle, her actions affording her time to register Andrew's words. *This is a one-bedroom Victorian. Where did you sleep?* She mentally slapped herself. At least Andrew had been here for her mum. *And besides, whose business is it if Mum's sleeping with someone?*

She looked across at Andrew and realised he was waiting for her. "We'd better head up and see how she is," Jo said.

"I gave her some pills a little while ago." He mounted the stairs, and Jo followed. "I expect she might be a little groggy when you see her."

He lightly knocked on the bedroom door. "Margaret, love, look who I found skulking on the front verandah." He stood aside, so Jo could enter.

She plastered a brave smile on her face and walked into the room.

"Hi, Mum. I thought I'd warned you about biting off more than you could chew." Her attempt at bravado wilted at the sight of her bruised and broken mother, sitting with her leg in a full cast, propped up on pillows. Tears welled in Jo's eyes.

Margaret opened her arms. "Oh, pumpkin, come here. It's not as bad as it looks."

Jo crossed the room and lightly rested in her mother's embrace, fearful of causing more harm.

"And besides, these pain pills are wonderful."

Andrew cleared his throat. "Ladies, I think I'll leave you to it."

"There's no need for you to go," Margaret said.

Jo eased herself out of her mother's arms and blew her nose.

"No, it's okay. I'm sure Jo would appreciate some time with you. And besides, I'll never get a word in once you two women start talking girl talk. I'll just wash the dishes and be off."

Jo shoved her handkerchief back in her pocket. "It's okay. I can do those. It's the least I can do after what you've done for Mum."

"It was hardly an effort. I'll just say a quick goodbye and get my things." He walked over to the bed and leant over as if to kiss Margaret but in the last instant, he caught himself. He patted her hand instead.

"I'll give you a call tomorrow to see when it'd be okay for me to come over."

Margaret smiled up at him. "I'd like that. Thanks for being my knight in shining armour."

Andrew straightened and put his hands in his pockets. "I think those drugs are starting to addle your brain. I'll see you later."

Jo followed him back down the stairs. She waited as he opened the study door and retrieved a sleeping bag and a deflated air mattress.

"Comfortable room, this office," Andrew said, a knowing smile on his face.

Jo quirked her mouth. "I suppose it is. Is there anything I need to know about Mum's treatment?"

"The hospital released her with a couple of pages of instructions, but the key things are that she keep her leg elevated and she doesn't spend all her time in bed. Her movement should be gradual. I got her into the bathroom the past two days, and it's about all she can tolerate at the moment. Check on her toes now and then, just to make sure both feet are the same temperature. And her pain pills are on her dresser." He tucked his bag and airbed under one arm and opened the door with the other. "She's had what she needs for tonight and she should drop off to sleep soon."

Jo patted his back. "Thanks, Andrew, you're a godsend."

"No problem. She's a very special woman."

He walked to his car and she gave him a final wave as he headed out the driveway. She closed the door and went back up the stairs. She quietly opened her mother's door and smiled at the hazy expression on her mother's face. "Can I get you anything?"

Margaret slowly blinked. "No, I'm fine, pumpkin. Why don't you get changed and hop into bed with me?"

Jo hesitated. "Are you sure? I don't want to bump anything. I can sleep on the sofa bed downstairs."

"God, even Andrew wouldn't sleep on such a wafer-thin piece of foam. Plus, this is a king-sized bed. If I can have Liam, plus you two girls in this bed when you were young then I'm sure I can manage it now. Besides, my leg's in a cast so I'm more likely to cause damage to you than you to me."

Jo kissed her mum's forehead, aware it was taking all of her mother's energy to stay awake. "Okay. I'll have a quick shower and then I'll be in. Our girl talk, as Andrew put it, will have to wait until tomorrow."

"Okay dear. He's a lovely man, Andrew," Margaret barely managed as her eyes lost the fight with the painkillers.

Jo moved to her side of the bed and turned on the bedside lamp. She switched off her mother's lamp and quietly made her way to a well-deserved shower.

JO LOOKED ACROSS at the clock on the far bedroom wall and chuckled. "I think Andrew had the right idea, leaving last night when he did."

Margaret took a sip of water and placed the glass back on her bedside stand. "What do you mean?"

"Remember he mentioned getting out of here last night before we started our—" Jo raised her hands and formed a quotation mark with two fingers from each hand—"girl talk? I'm sure he'd be stunned to know we've been at it now for two hours."

"There was a lot to talk about," Margaret huffed. "It's been so long since we've done this, there was bound to be plenty to catch up on. And we haven't even started on what you're currently doing." She shifted her position in the bed.

Jo reached and steadied the pillow under her mother's injured leg. "Are you okay? Do you need some more pain pills?"

"No, I'm fine. It's just that sitting here for so long makes my backside feel as if it's going numb. Andrew was great for getting me comfortable after my morning bath. He's a master at plumping up those pillows just right."

Jo awkwardly cleared her throat. *Dare I ask how the bathing part of the day's activities were achieved?* "Let me have a go at fixing them. I can't say I'll be as good at it as Andrew." She took the plunge. "It was nice of him to help you with your bath every morning," she said, not meeting her mother's eyes.

Margaret tilted her head and softly smiled. "Why don't you ask me what you really want to ask?"

Jo feigned innocence. "What do you mean?"

"I'm sure you're keen to know whether we're sleeping together."

"I am not," Jo blustered. "It's none of my business."

Margaret laughed. "It's never stopped you in the past. Why start now?"

Jo's face reddened and she sat on the bed, cross-legged, facing her mum. "You always knew how to figure me out. I'm just curious to know how things are between the two of you."

Margaret looked away from Jo and down at the duvet. She preoccupied herself with smoothing out a wrinkle in the duvet's cover, deliberately avoiding Jo's gaze.

Jo reached out and stilled her mother's hand with her own. "If things are progressing with Andrew beyond friendship, then I'm happy for you." She put a finger under her mother's chin and raised it so she was again looking at her. "And I'm sure Dad would also be happy. From what you've told me about him, Andrew's a great guy."

Margaret sighed. "I just don't know. He's not like Liam but we seem to get on so well. I sense he's keen to take things further but he's waiting for me to make the first move. And I don't know if I'm ready. Liam hasn't been gone long."

"Mum, I know you and Dad were high school sweethearts but he's been gone over two years now. If there's one thing I know, it's that Dad wouldn't want you to spend the rest of your life alone. He'd want you to move on."

Margaret brushed away a tear and smiled. "When did you get so well-versed in matters of the heart?"

Jo threw her hands up, exasperated. "I'm far from being well-versed, that's for sure. Dad's death shattered me and for weeks it was hard for me to find a way ahead without him in my life. But it was also a wake-up call in terms of relationships. Before his death I hadn't been in a steady relationship for so long—and I wasn't looking for one either, not after Lise. His death reminded me life is too short and you never really know whether you're going to be here from one day to the next. It made me realise I had to move on. If someone came along then I had to be willing to give it a go."

Margaret frowned. "Lise. She was the reporter, wasn't she?"

Jo nodded.

"You never really told me what happened with her."

"She married her male news anchor, except she neglected to tell *me*. The first I knew about the wedding was when it was the lead story on prime time evening news. Until then I had no idea. Everything seemed to be going so well." Jo shrugged, rueful. "But obviously I was wrong and I'd been royally fooled. I couldn't leave the house fast enough."

"I remember when you arrived at my door you'd left quite a lot of your gear behind."

"I only took my clothes and left everything else. It was part of my old life and I wanted no reminders of it. It was a struggle to get myself set up again." She shook her head, her eyes focused on that part of her past. "You know she never once called me to see how I was. It was as if I never existed." Jo held her mum's gaze with her own. "I see her on the television every now and then, still the lead reporter for the evening news, and still married."

Margaret patted Jo's arm. "It's in the past and good riddance. Are you seeing anyone now?"

Jo smiled, recalling the moment she had shared with Lauren the day before. "I've met someone I really like but it's a bit difficult at the moment."

"How so?"

"Lauren's the subject of the last episode of the series I'm currently doing."

Margaret frowned. "How does that make it difficult?"

Jo lay back on the bed, placed her arms behind her head, and stared at the ceiling. "She's a complex person and not easy to read. She's a guide at Cradle Mountain National Park but she's also an ex-golfer. She's a great conversationalist but can clam up at the drop of a hat. She's also incredibly good-looking. I'm pretty sure she's interested in me and I'd really like to start something with her, but it's like she's holding back, as if she's afraid if she lets go emotionally then she'll be hurt. At the beginning, I thought there was someone else but I don't think that's it." Jo smiled, a flush racing through her veins. "She kissed me for the first time yesterday morning."

"It's a start."

"Yes and no. It was a very tender kiss, as if she was trying to calm me. But at the same time I sensed passion behind it. She's really the first person I've felt like this about since Lise." Jo covered her face with her hands. "God, I sound like a love-struck teenager."

"You'll be fine. Just go with it and see where it leads." Margaret leant back and stifled a gasp.

Jo immediately sat up. "Are you sure you're okay?"

Margaret nodded, her eyes closed as if hiding her pain. "I think it's about time for another couple of pills."

Jo eased off the bed and retrieved her mother's pills from the dresser. She popped the lid and shook two tablets into her hand. She picked up the glass of water and handed it to her. "Here you go,"

Margaret gratefully took the pills and washed them down. "Thanks, pumpkin. Hopefully they'll start to work in about twenty minutes or so."

While her mother settled back onto the bed Jo adjusted the duvet. "How about once those kick in we get you showered and changed? If

I'm not wrong Andrew will pay you a visit today and I'd hate for him to see you looking all disheveled." She raised her eyebrows, teasing.

"That'd be lovely," Margaret said, ignoring the jibe. "What are your plans for the day?"

"I need to pick up my car from my place and then I've got to meet with my editor to let her know how things are going. I also need to contact Ben and find out when would be a good time to sit down and view the film he's shot so far. But it can wait until Andrew gets here, so for the moment you're stuck with me."

Margaret chuckled. "I'm sure I can cope."

"Do you know when Emma's arriving?"

"She's due in tomorrow afternoon from Perth. Her work's cleared her for as much carer's leave that she needs to look after me."

Jo laughed. "With the three Ashby women in one household, we'll be lucky if we can coax poor Andrew through the front door. I'd better get your bath underway or we'll still be here when he arrives."

JO SMILED WHEN Ben opened the door to the house that also served as his editing studio.

"G'day, stranger," he said, gesturing for Jo to enter. "How're things going?" He called over his shoulder as they walked down the hallway and into the kitchen.

"I've been looking after Mum and catching up on old times. Emma got in a couple of days after I did, so it's been one non-stop gab fest. It's been years since the three of us have been together."

Ben held up his hands in mock horror. "Three women in one house. Spare me the details. I've just brewed a fresh pot of coffee. Do you want a cup?"

Jo settled onto one of the breakfast bay's high stools. "That'd be great. White and one, thanks. Have you looked at the film yet?"

Ben nodded, handing a cup to Jo. "I had my first look at it yesterday afternoon."

"So is everything all right with it?" Jo took a sip of her drink.

Ben tilted his head and shrugged. "I suppose it depends on what your definition of 'all right' is."

"What do you mean?"

"It's easier if I show you." Ben picked up his mug and headed for the door.

Jo grabbed hers and followed him through the house to his editing suite, which was a mini-version of what could be found in any television station she'd ever worked in.

"Take a seat and I'll set it up."

Jo settled into her chair as Ben flipped a number of switches and turned a couple of dials. The screen came to life with a picture of Jo interviewing Lauren in the Cowle Lounge. "That looks great. You really did a good job with the lighting there."

Ben leant back in his chair and tapped his foot. "Keep watching."

The footage moved from the interview to the scene outside the Waldheim Chalet. Jo frowned, leant forward, and squinted her eyes at the screen. "What's that between Lauren and me? It looks like the film's scratched or something. Is there something wrong with it?"

"Just keep watching," Ben replied.

Jo sat, her frustration growing at the presence of the indistinct white shape. "There it is again. The last scene of her in the hut was fine. But once we're outside..." she pointed to the side of the main picture. "And there when I'm interviewing her at Wombat Pool — it comes back again. Is it something to do with the lighting?"

Ben hit the pause button. "It's got nothing to do with the lighting."

"Is it a flaw in the film?"

Ben shook his head. "It isn't a flaw. I've seen this sort of thing before."

"What do you mean?"

"You remember a couple of years ago when you wanted me for your mining project and I wasn't available because I was doing that haunted house shoot?"

"The one at the Pelham property — Gleneagle, wasn't it? Isn't it reputed to be Australia's most haunted house?"

"That's the one. It's supposedly haunted by at least four people. Two are the Pelham parents who first owned the farm. Their carriage has apparently been seen with them in it, crossing the small creek bordering the entrance to the property. As the story goes, they were killed during a thunderstorm that swelled the creek. Their carriage rolled into the water and they drowned." Ben took a sip of his coffee. "The other ghosts are two women who lived there until they died, Catriona Pelham, the only daughter, and Katherine Flynn. The women have apparently been known to greet people at the front door."

"What's that got to do with our current piece?"

"The medium I did the shoot with insisted the marks on the film were the ghosts of Gleneagle. The Gleneagle shapes were almost exactly like the ones on the footage I shot at Cradle Mountain."

Jo folded her arms. "You're saying we've captured a ghost on film," she scoffed.

"Don't be so quick to dismiss this. I was every bit as skeptical as you when I started the Gleneagle shoot, but by the end of it I was convinced. It was mid-summer when we filmed and, given the entire house was made of sandstone, the rooms were always moderately warm. Despite that, I'll never forget standing in the parlour one particularly hot morning when all of a sudden the temperature dropped way below normal. Another time I was in the kitchen with the medium, laughing at his suggestion of a ghostly presence, when a large pewter jug fell off a shelf. There was no way that thing could have moved without help. I'm telling you Jo, I think there's a ghost and it seems to be attracted to you and Lauren."

Jo ran her fingers through her hair, recalling her time with Lauren. She paled as a chill shot down her spine. The incident at Twisted Lakes, the pot in the hut, the sudden cold, and the way Lauren always seemed to be listening for something all began to make sense. *Lauren's reluctance to talk about Annie's hut has something to do with all of this, and I'm going to get to the bottom of it, one way or another.* Her eyes widened as another memory of Lauren's strange actions hit her. "Do you remember much about the Gleneagle shoot?"

"Remember it?" Ben turned in his chair and rolled himself across the polished wooden floor toward a bookcase holding his library of tapes. "I still have the footage." He sorted through the stack, pulled out the one he'd been searching for and held it up. "Let me run it for you."

He ejected the Cradle Mountain tape and inserted the other one.

Jo watched the opening credits roll down the monitor. "This is an unedited copy of the Gleneagle shoot?"

"Yep. Let me fast forward to the good bits."

Jo watched in disbelief when a marking, disturbingly similar to the one on the Cradle Mountain film, dominated the screen.

Ben pointed at the monitor. "See what I mean? Just watch a little more of this and then I'll put the other one back in and we can compare."

Jo silently watched the footage. The scene changed to include the man Jo assumed was the medium. She reached out and laid a restraining hand on Ben's arm. "Hang on. Let me just watch this for a bit."

Jo was astounded, watching the medium speak to other members of the cast and then halt, as if someone were speaking to him, although no one was. "What's he doing?"

"He did a lot of looking around him. It got spooky after a while. He said when he did he was speaking with his spirit guide. It was all a bit strange, if you ask me."

Jo stifled a gasp. *Just like Lauren does.*

Ben pressed the stop button and the screen went blank as Ben changed back to the Cradle Mountain tape. He hit the rewind button, taking the film to the footage he shot at Wombat Pool. "See? They're almost the same marks."

Numb, Jo watched the footage. "Can you make me a copy?"

"I've already got a copy burnt to disc. Why?"

"I'd like to talk to Lauren about what's on the film. I wonder whether she's aware something's been following us around, although given some of her actions I wouldn't be surprised if she didn't at least have an idea."

"When are you heading back?"

"I'll be flying out in a couple of days or so. Now that Emma's here and getting herself settled I feel like the odd one out. Plus, with her medical training she's more than capable of looking after Mum."

Ben pulled a disc in its case from the collection in his drawer and handed it to Jo. "Are you going to mention this to Ros before you fly out?"

Jo frowned. "I'd forgotten about that, but I think I'm going to have to. In the least this shape on the film means we're going to have to do some more shooting, and that's time and money." Jo stowed the disc in her pack.

Ben shut off the screen in front of him. "Is there any chance Ros will put an end to any more work on this?"

Jo shrugged. "I honestly don't know. I have no idea how she'll react to the idea of a ghost." Jo checked her watch. "I'll see if she's available today to talk this over. When I know where we stand I'll let you know. Either way I'm still intending to fly out tomorrow."

"No worries. Just let me know what Ros decides. If we're still filming and, if it's okay with you, I'll join you there at the end of the week. I've got a couple of loose ends I need to tie up here first."

"Thanks." Jo rose. "The end of the week's fine. It'll give me time to talk to Lauren and work out just what's been going on."

Ben grinned. "What I'd give to be a fly on the wall when *that* conversation takes place."

Chapter
Nine

JO LIGHTLY KICKED a stone out of her path as she strolled along the dirt track to Lauren's park-allocated accommodations. As she walked down the road, she marveled at the beauty around her. Aside from the occasional passing car, Jo's journey was broken only by the wind rustling through the trees on either side of the road, and the occasional sound of a bird calling out to other birds in the surrounding trees.

She pulled a bottle of water from her pack and took a long drink as she rounded the final bend in the road to Lauren's cabin. She walked down the path and up the stairs onto the cabin's small verandah. Taking a breath, Jo pushed the doorbell and then waited, hearing only its echo. She walked back down the steps and around to where Lauren's four-wheel drive would normally be parked, and found the space empty. Jo sighed. *The man at the front desk said she was off today. Hopefully she isn't too far away. I suppose I'd better make myself comfortable.* She sat down on the shaded front porch to wait for Lauren's return.

As she sat, her mind wandered to her discussion with Ben about the footage. *She must at least sense something. Especially given how she does the same thing the medium was doing—like she's talking to someone.* Puzzled, Jo stared off into the forest, thinking. The sound of an engine interrupted her thoughts, and she looked up to see Lauren turn into the driveway.

Lauren brought the vehicle to a halt, waving at Jo at the same time. Smiling, she jumped out and went over to Jo, pulling her into a hug. "You didn't tell me you were heading back, but I'm glad you're here. I was beginning to wonder what was going on, especially since I haven't heard from you for the past few days."

"I wanted to surprise you."

"You certainly did." Lauren loosened her grip slightly and looked at Jo. "Is your mum okay?"

"She's fine. My sister Emma arrived the other day. She's a critical care nurse and her employer's given her the time off to look after Mum."

"Are you all right? You seem a bit preoccupied."

"It must have been the walk out here. It was a little hotter and longer than I expected," Jo vaguely replied.

Lauren bent down, picked up Jo's small daypack, and headed up the stairs. "Why don't we go inside and I'll fix us a cool drink?" As she stepped into the cabin she switched on the park's radio.

Jo followed, looking toward where the radio slowly came to life. She accompanied Lauren into the kitchen, and took a seat at the breakfast bay.

Lauren reached into the cupboard, pulled out two tall glasses, and placed them on the counter. She walked to the fridge, opened it, and took her time scanning its contents. "I'm glad everything's okay," she said over her shoulder. "You should've called me. I would have come and picked you up from the airport."

"It's okay. I had to hire a car so I could pick Ben up when he comes back. He had some loose ends to tie up in Sydney. I said I'd head on down to Cradle Mountain and he'll fly down in a couple of days."

Lauren held up a cardboard carton. "Sorry, tomorrow's shopping day so I don't have a great choice of drinks. Will orange juice do?"

Jo nodded and watched Lauren pour two generous amounts of juice into the glasses. Jo took the glass Lauren offered and took a long sip, searching for a way to bring up what she really wanted to talk about. "How's the weather been since I've been gone?" She inwardly cringed at her inane comment.

"Not too bad. We had a bit of weird weather a couple of days ago. It was strange for this time of the year, anyway. We went from a really cold day to an incredibly hot one." Lauren shrugged. "Maybe it was autumn's last gasp before winter begins to really set in."

Seeing an opening, Jo changed the subject. "Talking of strange, when I was home I scoped out my narrative for the footage we've shot so far. When I looked at what we'd shot, there were some weird moments in there and it got me thinking not only about the film, but our time together here."

Lauren put the juice back in the fridge. "What do you mean?"

Jo waited for Lauren to turn around. "You know, like the day at Twisted Lakes when I almost fell in. One moment it was calm and the next moment the wind was blowing a gale."

"But we didn't film there," Lauren replied.

"I know, but there were things like that on the film and it got me thinking."

Lauren dismissively waved her hand. "It's the nature of the weather around here. It can change at the drop of a hat."

Jo uncomfortably shifted in her chair. "Okay, what about when we were about to head out from Waldheim car park on the Gilmore rescue? The trees around us should have shielded us from any wind and yet when you were helping me with my pack I was nearly blown off my feet."

"I think you're exaggerating. And besides, there're wind tunnels caused by gusts, trying to find a way around the trees. We were hit by one, that's all." Lauren swallowed the remainder of her juice and turned to the sink.

Jo rubbed the back of her neck, attempting to tamp down her frustration at Lauren's trivialising of her questions. "What about the pot in the hut?"

Lauren looked over her shoulder. "Hmm?"

"You remember the pot that nearly fell off the shelf? The one you barely managed to catch before it hit me."

Lauren turned, her features guarded as if she were deliberately measuring her response.

"Obviously the person who used it last didn't put it back flush against the wall. When did you say Ben would be back?"

Jo refused to be swayed by Lauren's attempts to redirect the conversation. "What about the thing you do when we're walking?"

Lauren shook her head. "I have no idea what you're talking about."

Jo released an exasperated breath. "*Yes*, you do. The thing where one minute you're talking and the next minute you stop, like someone's talking to you. You did it the first night on the animal-viewing tour and God only knows how many times thereafter."

Lauren leant back against the kitchen counter. "I was collecting my thoughts, nothing more than that."

"Pretty well done if I say so myself, especially how collecting your thoughts always seems to coincide with something happening. It's almost as if you're talking to an invisible person."

Lauren's face reddened. "You sound like you got a bit too much of the sun on your walk out here. You're allowing your imagination to get the better of you."

Jo took a sip as the tension slowly mounted between them. "You reckon that's what it is?"

Lauren bit her lip and tilted her head. "Yes, I do."

Jo placed the glass on the counter and stood up. "If that's all there is to it, then why don't we pay a visit to Annie's hut?"

Lauren walked across to Jo and braced her hands on the counter. "If you're trying to say something then why don't you just go ahead and get it off your chest?"

"Okay. Is there a ghost haunting the mountain and park?"

Lauren pushed off the counter. She walked past Jo and into the lounge. "Now I know you've had too much sun. Listen to yourself. You sound crazy. Misplaced pots and changes in weather don't amount to a ghost. You're allowing an overactive imagination to get out of hand."

Jo's anger flared at Lauren's condescending and dismissive tone. She walked to where Lauren stood with her back to her. "Two weeks ago I would've believed you, but we've got footage. Footage that Ben says is disturbingly similar to film he took on a previous shoot while investigating a haunted house."

Lauren wheeled. "You said I'd have final say on the footage to be used. If the film's damaged, then I don't want it shown."

"If that's the bloody case, then given the number of times this damn shadow thing turns up, we're going to have next to nothing to work with." Jo eyes barely caught the pain on Lauren's face as Lauren again turned and headed toward one of the cabin's windows.

Jo closed her eyes and released a shaky breath. She walked over to Lauren and placed her hand between Lauren's shoulder blades. "Tell me what's going on."

Lauren's finger traced a smudge on the window's glass as she lowered her head. "It's Annie."

Jo frowned. "Who's Annie?"

Lauren turned. "Her name's Annie Hethrington. She came to Cradle Mountain with a friend of hers, Marta Jung."

Jo furrowed her brow. "I've heard those names somewhere before."

"You'd have heard them from me the day of the tour at Waldheim Chalet. The one Ben filmed. They were friends of Gustav and Kate Weindorfer. They first came to Cradle Mountain in nineteen-thirteen."

Jo gasped. "Their photo's on the wall of The Retreat's bar, isn't it?"

Lauren nodded.

Jo stared at her. "Then Annie *is* a ghost?"

"Yes, she is." Lauren dropped her gaze. "From what I can gather she and Marta were, as they called it back then, close companions. They were feminists for their own era. Annie was one of Australia's first female lawyers and Marta was a skilled golfer. The research I did on Marta said she could drive a ball as far as a man." Lauren walked to the sofa and sat down.

Jo sat down and turned her body to face Lauren. "What happened?"

"From what I've read and the little Annie's told me, the two of them went walking on the mountain and some sort of argument erupted between them. Annie said they headed off in opposite directions. When Annie came to her senses she tried to find Marta but she couldn't. She headed back down the mountain to get Gustav and Kate to help in the search. Despite three days of looking, Marta was never seen again. Annie was devastated and vowed never to leave the mountain until she found Marta's body. The history books say she was often found on the mountain, searching for her. Gustav and a friend of his built a hut for her, Annie's hut, and she lived there until her death in the 1930s."

Jo rubbed her forehead as she tried to take in Lauren's words. It was one thing for Ben to suggest marks on a film amounted to a ghostly presence, but it was completely different to hear Lauren speak as if Annie were flesh and bone. "If Annie's been dead for so long, how did you meet her?"

Lauren looked down at her hands and returned her gaze to Jo's face. "I met her shortly after I came to the mountain, after campers had illegally used Annie's hut. They'd spent the day on the mountain and were walking home when it began to rain. Rather than return to the lodge, they broke the hut's front door, so they could get in out of the downpour. Apparently they weren't in there very long before they turned up, white and shaken, at the Park's headquarters, insisting something had happened to them in Annie's hut. I was on night shift and went down to check the damage. It was the first time I met her."

"What do you mean, 'met' her?"

"After I got the door back on its hinges I went into the hut to see if they'd done any other damage. The campers had started a fire in the fireplace, most likely to dry out their clothes. I was worried that leaving it burning and unwatched might cause further damage to the cabin so I put it out. When the last flames were extinguished, I realised I'd left my torch in the four-wheel drive and I was in darkness.

Lauren strained her eyes, trying to catch any residual light in the hut. She reached out in front of her as she slowly shuffled around, attempting to get her bearings in the unfamiliar room.

She had barely taken four steps when her shin collided with an overturned chair and she fell heavily against the wooden floor.

As she struggled to get up, the air in the room seemed to shift and she froze in place.

"Are you all right?"

"Who's there?" Lauren groped at the empty air around her, making an effort to locate the direction the words had come from.

"Don't be afraid. I won't hurt you. I'll help you find your way to the door, just follow the sound of my voice."

Lauren eased herself off the floor and blindly turned, waiting for any discernible sound. A feather light touch brushed her forearm and then it was gone.

"Come this way. Carefully, now."

Lauren held her hand out in front of her in early warning of any other objects she might run into. The cabin's front door opened and she walked out on to the hut's verandah and into the grey light of the evening. She looked around, endeavouring to see where her rescuer had gone. "Where are you?"

"I'm right here. I'll always be here for you. All you need do is ask for me when you're in the park and I'll be there."

"Who are you?"

"Just a friend," was the soft reply, as it was carried away on the evening wind.

"I didn't find out her name until later, when I visited the cabin in broad daylight and she spoke to me. At first I thought I was going crazy. But then I heard her again on the mountain one day, during a rescue. She knew exactly where the person was and led me straight there," Lauren said. "After that, I did further research on her and found out what had happened."

"That explains your one hundred per cent success rate in rescues."

Lauren self-consciously nodded. "I don't know why, but she's always there for me."

Jo frowned. "Did they ever find Marta's body?"

Lauren rubbed her shoulder in an obvious effort to ease the stress held there.

"No, they didn't. And once the hut was built, Annie barely left the park's surrounds."

"Have you ever thought she helps you because it's her way of reconciling with the fact she could never find Marta?"

Lauren shrugged. "I suppose that's part of it."

Jo frowned. "What's the other part?"

Lauren shifted in her seat. "I think she cares for me. The first night she said she'd always be there for me and she has been. The only time I'm aware she's not with me," she gestured around the cabin, "is in here and outside the official park boundary. Over the years we've developed a close bond."

"The one allowing you to find people?"

"Yes, but it's more," Lauren awkwardly replied, avoiding Jo's gaze.

Jo frowned. *What the blazes is going on?* She put her head in her hands, thinking, and then it hit her. She slowly raised her head. "Are you saying you love her?"

Deliberately refusing to meet Jo's eyes, Lauren stood and paced the room, her hands thrust deeply into her pockets. "I suppose I do."

Jo's eyes widened. "I'm sorry, but this is just a bit hard to take in right now. You're saying you love her? But how can you love a ghost?"

Lauren turned to Jo and folded her arms. "Whenever I've needed her she's been there, ever since the first night. No matter how bad things seem, I can always rely on her."

Speechless, Jo stared in disbelief.

"What, you don't believe me? I don't see how it matters either way," Lauren defensively countered.

Jo crossed to where Lauren stood. "That's not love, it's

dependence. How can you love something you can't even touch?"

"What would you know? She'll never hurt me and, besides, at least she'll never leave me!"

Jo stepped back, momentarily struck by the vehemence behind Lauren's words. "Is that what you want?"

Lauren lowered her head, as if in defeat.

Jo lightly touched Lauren's cheek. "What happened to you? Who hurt you so badly that this is what you've come to?"

"It's a long story," Lauren replied, deflated.

Jo guided her back to the sofa and sat her down. "I've got plenty of time," she said as she took a seat beside her.

The silence between them became so prolonged that Jo began to wonder whether Lauren would ever reply. She jumped when Lauren finally spoke.

"It happened on the last day I played in a tournament." Lauren turned to face Jo. "How much research did you do about the final competition I played in?"

"What do you mean?"

"Why I was there," Lauren replied.

Jo made herself comfortable on the sofa. "You mean the reason an amateur was playing in a professionals-only association tournament?"

Lauren nodded.

"I know it's unusual and it's not normally done."

"That's right. It was an open secret I was on the verge of turning pro and, to put it bluntly, the association needed publicity for the women's tour. The tournament's main sponsor invited me to play. Back then it was one of the few ways an amateur could play in a professionals-only tournament. Of course, they'd cleared it with the association, who in turn made the offer even more enticing."

Jo frowned. "How so?"

"If I finished in the top five I'd be offered automatic entry to the tour, instead of having to qualify for exempt status."

"I didn't know that, but it makes sense." Jo pursed her lips in thought. "If I remember correctly, back then the women's tour was having publicity problems. Two of its high-profile players were outed as lesbians. And publicity problems amounted to sponsor problems."

"What they wanted was a presentable, clean-cut, and supposedly straight woman to champion the tour." Lauren ruefully chuckled. "If only they knew."

"You knew you were gay back then?"

"Yes, but I was in the closet. There were a few of us on the amateur circuit. But we were well aware that to ensure a professional tour spot we had to be discreet. Very discreet." Lauren broke Jo's warm gaze. She silently stroked her lower lip with one finger, her face distant. "It was on the amateur circuit that I fell in love for the first time."

Jo reached across and placed a reassuring hand on Lauren's thigh. "Who was she?"

"Her name was Patricia — Pat Morgan. She was a professional golfer."

"If she was a professional golfer, how did you meet her on the amateur circuit?"

"There're a number of games open to professional and amateur golfers and it was one of those where we met. She was a pretty decent golfer, but she'd hit a rough patch and had been forced to increase the number of tournaments she played to keep her card."

"I'm not sure I follow you."

"Pat was driven by her need to get into the association's Hall of Fame. Since the Hall's inception in 1950, only twenty-two players and one honorary have been inducted. Only two of those players weren't Americans, and neither of those two was British. Part of the qualifying criteria is you must have been an active tour member for at least ten years. If she lost her card she'd also lose her active status and have to start from scratch."

"Given the competitiveness of the women's tour, I'm assuming that's easier said than done," Jo commented.

Lauren nodded. "She played in the lesser tournaments to maintain her points, which in turn maintained her card. I met her at one of those tournaments. She was older than I by a few years. But back then she was charming and funny and she seemed more than eager to help me improve my game."

Jo snorted. "I suppose the fact you had a body women would kill for and looks to match didn't enter into the equation?"

Lauren held up her hand. "She didn't seduce me. I knew what I was getting myself into, or at least I thought I did. Besides, we always seemed to do well when we played together. Plus, it was the first time anyone had really paid any sort of attention to me and I fell in love." She ran her fingers through her hair. "In retrospect I wonder if she really did love me."

"Why do you say that?"

Lauren smiled sadly and reached down to cover Jo's hand with her own. "That gets me to my last tournament. It was the final major of the touring year and Pat needed a win to have enough points to secure her card. Finishing second wouldn't be enough. We were paired in the championship round."

Jo felt her anger boil to the surface. "Let me guess, you were first and she was second. She knew for you a top-five finish would guarantee you a tour card and she convinced you to relinquish first place for her."

Lauren lowered her head and nodded.

Jo gritted her teeth and took a deep breath, trying to rein in her temper. "How *bloody* convenient."

"She said if I loved her I'd allow her to win." Lauren paused as Jo cursed. "I was young and in love for the first time and what she was saying made sense. I mean, besides Pat, I was four clear shots from anyone else. There was little chance of anyone catching me or her."

Jo shook her head. "I don't get it. What happened to you? You were eight under par on the final day when there was a rain delay between the front and back nine. What went wrong?"

"I took a shower, that's what went wrong."

Lauren hurried toward the shelter of the Clubhouse, her caddie Nat Gilmartin following closely behind. She gratefully accepted two towels from one of the tournament helpers, and threw one at Nat and then wiped her face and arms with the other.

"With all the lightning around, I didn't think we were going to get the ninth hole in."

Nat wiped the back of his neck, allowing the towel to rest on his shoulders. "You're right, there. It was as if when you sank your putt it was the signal for the heavens to open up. Hey, eight under, kiddo. You've just about got it in the bag."

Lauren bit back a grin. "Don't jinx me."

"Not the way you're playing. I've never seen you go after a course like you have today. Besides, other than Pat, the closest players are four shots away. I think I can safely say our next tournament's going to be on the professional tour. No more roach motels for us."

"You'll come with me?" Lauren shyly asked.

Nat playfully flicked at Lauren with his damp towel. "Through thick and thin, kiddo."

Lauren looked around the group of women golfers and their caddies. "Did you see where Pat and her caddie went?"

"I thought I heard Pat mention to Sue something about going to grab a quick bite to eat."

Lauren shivered and rubbed her arms. "The officials said the delay would be between fifteen to thirty minutes. I think I'll go and take a shower to try and warm up. How about I meet you in fifteen minutes in the bistro?"

Nat picked up Lauren's clubs and slung the bag's strap over his shoulder. "I might do the same. I'll see you there."

Lauren walked into the women's changing room and picked up two complimentary towels. She went past the rows of lockers until she reached hers, discreetly marked by the small card slipped into the slot on the locker's door. She glanced around, quickly stripped out of her wet gear, and wrapped herself in a towel. Lauren keyed in the locker's combination and grabbed her toiletry bag, stashed her wet clothes, and headed to the showers, whistling as she went.

Standing in the shower stall and toweling off after her wash, she heard the distinct timbre of Pat's voice, sharing a joke with her caddie.

She smiled at the prospect of Pat and she being on the professional tour together. At least they'd be able to see a hell of a lot more of each other. She squeezed moisturiser into her hand and began to apply it to her arms, in turn surreptitiously listening to the conversation between them.

"What's the plan, Pat? You're one behind Lauren. When will the change occur?"

Pat shrugged. "We'll wait until the seventeenth hole. That way we'll know where we stand once we're the only group left on the course. I suppose she'll drop a shot or something. We haven't really gone into specifics about how it will happen."

Sue laughed. "I'd say you've got it just about wrapped up."

Pat thoughtlessly dropped the towel she'd been using to dry her hair and kicked it under a locker bench. "You better believe it. This'll be my stepping stone back to the professional tour on a full time basis. It'll bring me just that bit closer to the Hall of Fame."

Sue nudged Pat. "I'd say your stepping stone's been the brilliant young golfer you've been sleeping with. It looks like the two of you will have a lot more time together once she hits the pro circuit."

"Yes, there is that problem. How to get rid of her? She's been a wonderful stepping stone and a gratifying fuck, but now it's time to move on. Besides, there's only been one openly gay woman in the Hall of Fame. I can't afford anyone finding out about me." Pat stroked her pale angular chin squinting introspectively. "I'll wait until after the win to tell her it's over. We're currently booked to fly back to the U.S. with her and her damned caddie. Change our bookings, will you?

Lauren slid down the shower stall and slumped to the floor in disbelief. She thrust a fist against her mouth to contain the sob that threatened to break forth, as she listened to the footfalls of the two women as they left the changing room.

She couldn't be sure how long she sat there, but the intercom, announcing the resumption of play in ten minutes, broke her trance. She struggled off the floor and headed for her locker. She dressed on autopilot, and went out to the club's foyer.

"Lauren, there you are. What happened to the bite to eat?" Nat's question faded as he looked at Lauren's pale face. "Are you okay? You look like you've seen a ghost."

"I'm fine, just a little tired. Let's go," Lauren headed out the door and toward the tenth tee.

Lauren looked down at her hands. "If you've seen the footage then you know the rest."

Jo fought back the overwhelming desire to throw something. "That bitch! How could she do such a thing to you?"

"I don't know. I was devastated. Those nine holes were the longest of my life. All the way through them she treated me like nothing had happened. If I hadn't overheard what I did then I'd have been none the wiser." Lauren bitterly laughed. "She even had the gall to ask me before we teed off on the tenth how I was going to drop a shot for her. I ended up dropping five in all, while the rest of the field went by me. By the eighteenth I was a complete wreck, but I'm sure you've seen the film."

Jo rubbed Lauren's arm. "I'm sorry she hurt you. I did see the game, but I can't say I paid her too much attention. My focus was on you. You can bet I'm going to have another look at it though, if for no other reason than to know who it is I'm going to bitch-slap if I ever run into her."

Lauren softly smiled. "Nat knew about the two of us, but I didn't tell him what I'd heard in the changing room. After he'd helped me down the tunnel away from the eighteenth hole he went back to get my putter. He overheard Sue ask Pat where I'd gone to. Apparently Pat said I'd faded into the background, which she was grateful for because she didn't like break-up scenes anyway."

Jo paced, barely managing to keep herself from screaming in anger and frustration. "Do you know what happened to her?"

"I've no idea. After that game I didn't go near a golf course for two years. I don't even know if she's still on the circuit or whether she secured her precious spot in the Hall of Fame. I just don't care." She rubbed her face with her hands. When I was on the golfing tour I was pretty young and naïve. I was the great Australian golfing hope and I had many people around me, asking me to promote this or attend some function or event. You probably find this hard to believe, but I thought they were really interested in me."

"I don't find it hard to believe at all," Jo replied. "Fame attracts its share of hangers-on and, given who you were, I'd say you had your fair share of them."

Lauren sighed. "It was the first time I'd had people really interested in me. And Pat's words were a wake-up call. They showed me how false everything was, even love. If that wasn't enough, the days after the tournament proved it. With the exception of Nat, no one, not even the media, who were usually hungry for a story, called to ask what was wrong."

Jo sat beside Lauren and reached for her hand. "I'm sorry you had to go through that crap at such a young age. Were your parents there for you?"

Lauren's eyes misted and she pulled a handkerchief out of her pocket and blew her nose. "They were, but it wasn't long after I walked away from the circuit that they died. It was the last straw for me. I lost the ability to trust and love because of what happened. After a while it became second nature for me not to trust or fall in love, because it was too hard to deal with the deceit and loss that came with it."

Jo softly stroked their entwined hands. "Christ, with everything that's happened to you, it's a wonder you didn't end up having a nervous breakdown. But how did you end up at Cradle Mountain?"

"Cradle Mountain had been a holiday retreat for my family when I was a teenager. I always found it a very peaceful, almost spiritual place." She glanced around the room, as if recalling sweeter times. "Whenever I was on the tour and things got too much I'd think of Cradle Mountain and it would ground me."

"Coming here was an escape for you?"

"Yes and no. Here I always felt safe. I was just fortunate I could combine my time here with my next career."

Jo mulled over Lauren's words. "Didn't anyone ask why you were here? I mean, you were a pretty recognisable person back then. Surely it caused some questions?"

Lauren shrugged. "I was well known on the mainland but not really here. Every so often, in the months after I arrived, someone would recognise me when I was working. But as time passed fewer people knew who I was, and the arrangement suited me fine. I didn't want to be known as the great Lauren Wheatley anymore."

Lauren scanned the room, her face reflecting the pain of her young adult years. Knowing it wasn't the time for words, Jo held her tongue, and the two sat in silence, each lost in her own thoughts.

Lauren finally broke the silence. "Sorry to unload on you."

Jo reassuringly patted Lauren's thigh. "Don't be silly. There's nothing to be sorry about. I'm glad I could be here for you."

Lauren released a heavy sigh. "You said you had footage of Annie. Do you have it with you?"

"Yes." Jo crossed the room to her daypack. She pulled out the disc, opened the case, and held it out to Lauren. "Do you want to see it?"

Lauren stood up and took it. "Yes. Give me a minute and I'll put it in my player."

They took a seat on the sofa and silently watched the footage, replete with the indistinct shape that occurred at regular intervals on the film.

As the recording finished, Jo picked up the remote and switched it off. "Is that how you see Annie?"

Lauren tilted her head and frowned. "Not really. Sometimes I don't see anyone, but I know she's there, like a presence. Sometimes it's like she's in my head and other times I can see her."

"What does she look like?"

"She's a little bit taller than me with boyish features. Her hair's short and curly brown and she's always in loose trousers and a blouse. I suppose it's a hell of a lot easier to bushwalk that way than in a dress."

Jo took Lauren's hand. She nervously licked her lips, searching for a way to broach the next topic. "Those incidents and the one at the lake. Was she there?"

Lauren's gaze at Jo was unwavering. "Yes."

"Is she dangerous?" Jo paused at the shocked look on Lauren's face. "I mean, a woman's got to know what she's up against, right?" she lightly joked.

"She's not dangerous, just jealous." Lauren lowered her gaze before once again meeting Jo's. "You're the first person I've shown any real interest in since I got here."

"You mean up until me, you've held everyone else at arm's length?"

"I didn't want the hurt I'd experienced with Pat and the loss of my parents." Lauren shrugged. "Keeping everyone at arm's length was my way of dealing with the situation." She shifted in her seat. "Remember I told you how I met Annie?"

"Yes, the camper incident," Jo replied.

"What I didn't tell you was it was one of the lowest points in my life. I felt like I was living on autopilot, from one day to the next, fearful of letting anyone in. The night when Annie said what she did, it seemed to calm me. She offered something better than what Pat, the golfing tour, or anyone else could give. She offered security and, as difficult as it may seem to you, love."

Jo stroked their entwined hands. "I'm sorry for what I said earlier about dependence. It didn't come out the way I wanted it to." Jo gazed around the room, searching for answers. "But it's still not the way to live your life. I *know* there's something between us, but if you love Annie, where does that leave you and me?"

"A big part of me wants to believe you'd never hurt me." Lauren's eyes began to fill with tears. "I've been like this for so long, it's hard to take the leap of faith you're asking me to. But I really want to."

Lauren's struggle was written on her face. Jo softly brushed Lauren's tears away. "I want that, also. I'm a patient woman and I'll be here as long as it takes me to convince you, or you send me packing."

"Trust me when I tell you I'm definitely not sending you packing. Not just yet, anyway."

They silently stared at each other, weighing up the morning's discussion. Jo's stomach broke the moment, grumbling loudly. They chuckled.

Lauren stood and offered her hand to Jo. "How about we head up to the tavern for something to eat?"

Jo let her pull her to her feet. "That sounds like a great idea."

Chapter
Ten

JO SAT CROSS-LEGGED, waiting for her Web cam connection with Ros to activate. She had just put a spoonful of cereal into her mouth when the screen came alive.

Ros checked her watch and looked at Jo. "Hmm, ten o'clock is a little late for breakfast, isn't it?"

Jo chewed, simultaneously wiping the milk dribbling down her chin. She swallowed and set the bowl on the table in front of her. "It normally is, but Ben called at about eleven-thirty last night to tell me he'd finally arrived. He also wanted to know if he could catch up on some sleep before we started filming and I said okay, hence my late start."

"I thought you were supposed to pick him up?"

"I was but I wasn't expecting him until tomorrow. He caught the park shuttle, which had to wait for a number of other flights to arrive before it left for The Retreat."

Ros alternated her attention between signing the documents in front of her and addressing Jo. "How's everything going? What have you been up to while you've been waiting for Ben?"

"I've done a fair share of walking around the park." Jo rubbed her calves, remembering the amount of ground she and Lauren had covered. "Lauren took a small group to the top of Cradle summit yesterday and I tagged along. I took a camcorder unit in my pack and got some footage. I have to tell you though, by the time I reached the top of the mountain, that camera, small as it was, felt like it weighed as much as a full-blown unit."

Ros arranged the stack of papers in front of her and handed them to someone off-screen. "Have you checked the footage?"

"I did a quick check when I got home and there's no distortion on the film. I'll need to record voiceover for it, but I can do it with Ben when we get into the main studio in Sydney. I'll also have him do a thorough check of the film now he's back." Jo leant forward, picked up a glass of juice and took a sip.

"So there was no sign of, you know, Annie?"

Jo chuckled. "At least you can say her name now. I thought you were going to have a cow when I told you in Sydney."

"What did you expect? You've always known horror films scared the crap out of me. The idea of something following me around," Ros shuddered, "just turns my blood cold."

"I told you, Lauren says Annie's not like that. Protective, yes. Jealous, definitely. But malignant, absolutely not."

"I'll take your word on that one. I have to say I've heard of lover's triangles, but yours just beats the band. So, was she there?"

Jo rolled her eyes. "No. Even when we were in the park Lauren commented on the fact that Annie wasn't around. Normally she at least makes herself known to Lauren." Jo scratched her head. "Lauren says she senses she's still close by. But the two of them haven't spoken in well over a week."

Ros pursed her lips as if in thought. "Is Annie at the old cabin?"

"If she is then she's not showing herself. Lauren said she'd gone back there a few times but she's not felt anything."

"Maybe she's moved on. You know, like you see in the movies, gone over to the other side."

"I'd have to whack you if you were here now," Jo said, laughing. "Seriously though, it's like she's giving Lauren the silent treatment." Jo shrugged. "Looking at the relative benefits of her absence, at least it's given me and Lauren plenty of time to do some great walks together."

Ros gave her an "oh really?" look. "It sounds like it. How are things on the personal side?"

Jo sighed. "They're better since we had that talk I told you about." *Well, not all of the details, just the key ones.* "I think she's really trying to make an effort to see that I'm not out to hurt her. It's baby steps at best, but I'm willing to be patient."

"I expect it's the best you can hope for at this point. At least she hasn't sent you packing." Ros frowned. "I don't mean to state the obvious, but what happens when you finish filming?"

Jo fiddled with the signet ring on her finger and then returned her gaze to the screen. "I don't know. To tell you the truth, I hadn't given it much thought."

Ros smiled. "You might want to, my friend. Have you ever thought your relatively short stay there might be a contributing factor to why Lauren's reluctant to commit to anything more than a strong friendship?"

Jo closed her eyes, then looked back at Ros. "See, that's why I'm so bad at this relationship stuff. I really hadn't thought it through." She chewed on her thumbnail. "But I suppose I'm going to have to consider what the future is between us. That is, if we ever manage to start something to build a future on."

"I'm sure you'll both come around to each other in the end." Ros checked her watch. "Talking about time, when were you meeting Ben?"

Jo looked over her shoulder to the digital alarm clock beside her bed. "I'm supposed to meet him and Lauren in the Cowle Lounge in about forty-five minutes."

"You'd better get a move on if you're going to meet them in something other than your bathrobe."

"Ever the slave driver, aren't you? I'll keep you posted on how everything's going." Jo reached toward the laptop's built-in mouse to break the connection.

"Hey, just one more quick thing before you go," Ros said.

Jo paused. "What?"

"I might be your boss, but I'm still your friend, and if you ever want to talk to me about what's going on between you and Lauren then just call, day or night."

"Thanks," Jo quietly said. "I really appreciate it."

Ros made a shooing motion at Jo. "Now, get on and finish this final piece before you send me and the company broke."

JO RECLINED INTO one of the soft leather sofas dotting the lounge. She watched a staff member gather an armful of kindling from a box, partially hidden behind the door leading to the verandah. Just as she rose, the door swung open and a man stepped through it, causing the kindling to fly out of her arms and land on the floor.

"For heaven's sake, why don't you watch where you're going?" He ran his hand over his near shoulder-length, slicked-back blond hair.

Jo stared at him, disgusted. *It was you who caused the wood to go flying, not her, you boor. And where have I heard that voice before?* She silently watched the exchange, the woman profusely apologising and simultaneously picking up the wood, while at the same time the man made no attempt to help her.

"You need to be more careful or you might hurt someone." As he finished he scanned the room, his gaze coming to rest on Jo. He smiled and headed over to where she sat.

Oh crap, just what I need. Someone who obviously thinks he's God's gift to women. As he swaggered closer Jo stifled the desire to say what she was thinking. *Ugh, look at those turkey jowls. You may have been handsome once, but now you look as if you've gone to seed.*

He halted in front of her and she looked up at him, barely containing her irritation.

"Hello, I don't think we've met," he held out his hand. "I'm Geoffrey Blackson."

Despite not wishing to do so, Jo reluctantly extended her hand. *Ellie and Lauren were spot on about you. Just the way you're looking at me makes me want to go and take a shower.* "Hello," she coolly replied, hoping he'd pick up on her disinterest. Unfortunately he didn't.

"I'm one of the main guides working here."

So, what do you expect me to do now, genuflect? "How nice," she said noncommittally, pulling her hand from his and unconsciously rubbing it against her pants leg.

Geoffrey's gaze lingered on the vee of her shirt. "Would you like to join me for coffee?"

His wandering eyes were not lost on Jo. "No, thank you. I'm waiting for someone."

"Oh well, maybe another time," he replied as he smoothed his hair back.

She smiled, thin-lipped. *Is never a good time for you?*

"I told you my name but you didn't tell me yours." Geoffrey needled. Realising she was unlikely to get rid of him until she answered his question, Jo said, "Jo Ashby." She picked up the paper from the table beside her.

He started, surprised, and his dun brown eyes seemed to darken just a fraction more. "Oh, of course. You were the unfortunate soul stuck with Lauren Wheatley during her recent rescue."

Jo opened her mouth to dispel his slant on the matter, but Geoffrey dismissively waved his hand. "You want to watch yourself on the mountain with her. She might have a perfect success rate in rescues. But one day her luck's going to run out and then God knows what will happen."

He consulted his watch, clearly oblivious to Jo's mounting anger. "I'd better get going." He reached down and patted her shoulder, his touch lingering beyond what was appropriate. "Any time you want a tour," he lowered his voice, "up close and personal, just let me know."

His greasy smile was the last Jo saw of him as he left her, and she shivered in revulsion. "Not until hell freezes over," she muttered.

A soft hand came to rest on Jo's shoulder. "Good morning. You sure picked a good spot." Lauren moved around and sat down in the chair opposite Jo's. She frowned at the look on Jo's face. "Are you okay?"

"I'm fine. I just had the misfortune of meeting Geoffrey Blackson. What a creep."

Laurens eyes flashed in anger as she searched the room. "Are you okay?"

Jo patted Lauren's knee. "His type doesn't scare me." Seeing Lauren's focus was still elsewhere, she elected to steer the conversation to the matter at hand. "Are you sure it's okay to get some filming in this morning?"

"It's no problem. My first party of walkers isn't until two, so we've plenty of time. Did Ben mention what he had in mind?"

"No, he was pretty brain dead when he got in last night but he said he'd meet us here to go over the morning's filming." Jo instinctively looked up when one of the doors to the lounge opened and Ben walked or, more correctly, limped through it.

"G'day, you two. Sorry I'm late." He carefully manoeuvred his way around the leather sofa and placed his camera on the coffee table.

Jo pointed at the brace on his knee. "What the blazes have you been up to?"

"What can I say? I fell over in a bar in Sydney, chasing a good-looking woman." He smiled roguishly and sat down. "You know how it is, you just can't keep a good man down."

"Yes, well chasing good-looking women can be a dangerous occupation," Lauren replied, casting a meaningful glance at Jo, who fought to control her blush.

Jo looked a Lauren, cleared her throat, and then returned her focus to Ben. "Not as dangerous as trying to explain your shenanigans to your wife."

Ben pleadingly held up his hands. "Hey! She was the good-looking woman."

Jo laughed. She motioned toward his brace. "How serious is it?"

"It's just a bit of a strain. The doc says I'll have to wear this for a couple of weeks, but it should be okay. Don't worry, though. I can still do filming, just not any climbing that's too strenuous." Ben bent down and tightened the lower strap holding the brace in place. "Speaking of filming, I've some good news. I managed to edit the footage we took at Waldheim. You'd have to look pretty hard to see that there's anything out of place with the film."

Jo caught the look of relief on Lauren's face. She focused on Ben again. "What about Wombat Pool?"

"That bit I wasn't too successful with. The shape is way too prevalent around the two of you. We're going to have to re-shoot there."

Jo dubiously looked at Ben's brace. "Can you get up there with your knee the way it is?"

"No." He turned to Lauren. "This is your home turf. Do you have any suggestions where we might do a re-shoot?"

She thought for a moment. "There's a place called Pencil Pine falls. It's just near the Park Visitors' Centre, and there's an access ramp all the way down to a viewing platform. Do you think you could manage?"

"It shouldn't be a problem. What's the lighting like?"

Lauren looked toward one of the large glass double glazed windows gracing the walls of the room and back to Ben. "At this time of the day it shouldn't be too bad, but if you leave it any later you're going to need some sort of artificial lighting. It makes a pretty good backdrop, with the falls in the background and the surrounding lichen-covered trees."

"You're beginning to sound more like a journalist than a park ranger," Jo joked. "So..." she tentatively began. "What about the possibility of there being *damage* to this film?"

Lauren leant forward and patted Jo's knee. "The falls are outside the confines of the park."

Ben broke in. "Okay. But just in case, I've teed up with a mate who works at the local television station in Devonport to give me access to his editing suite, so I can check the film. It shouldn't be a problem." Ben mimicked Lauren's actions and reached for Jo's knee.

She smacked his hand away and stuck her tongue out at him. "That mightn't be a problem but you'll have your other knee in a brace if you're not careful," she warned.

Ben sighed in defeat. "Okay, I get it." He glanced at Lauren. "Jo mentioned you teach kids in a golfing clinic. Is there any chance of getting footage of you and the kids together?"

"Your timing's uncanny. I'm doing a day clinic tomorrow if you want to tag along. All I ask is that you set up to one side, away from the kids. It was difficult enough to hold their attention when Jo was there snapping photos of them." Lauren rolled her eyes. "God only knows what they'll be like with someone filming them."

"We'll set up in a discreet location, so hopefully it won't be too much of an interference," Jo assured her.

Lauren flashed her a quick smile. "While I think about it, you might want to pack a change of clothes. The weatherman's forecasting a chance of rain tomorrow. It's a fairly long journey there and back and not one you want to be doing in wet clothing."

"Darn, and here I was hoping to see some wet t-shirt action." Ben dodged the sofa pillow flung in his direction.

Jo stood. "Before you get yourself into any more trouble, I suggest we head out and do this shoot, while the light's still good. Are you right to carry the camera?"

Ben steadied himself and picked up the piece of equipment. "No problem. Lauren, lead the way."

JO WATCHED FROM the rear seat as Lauren pulled into her parking space at The Dales golf course. Jo sat in the back, giving Ben greater space to stretch his injured knee.

The vehicle had barely come to a halt when it was surrounded by a group of children, all calling Lauren's name.

"It seems you have quite a fan club." Ben unclipped his seat belt and opened his door.

Lauren did the same. "They're a great bunch of kids and sometimes just a little too full of beans for me."

Jo smiled to herself as she got out and joined Lauren at the rear of the vehicle. "I'm sure you can more than handle them and, besides," she nudged Lauren's side, "you know you love it."

"Hi, Miss Wheatley," Karrie said, shifting from one foot to the other in anticipation. "Can I carry your bag today?"

"Not today, Karrie. But thanks. There're a few other things I need to get out of the back here, and it might take a few minutes." A chorus of groans erupted from the young group and Lauren held her hands up to quiet them. "How about you get your gear and I'll meet you at the driving range. Scott, do you think you could lead the group in a warm-up drill?"

"No problem, Miss Wheatley." He slung his golf bag onto his shoulder. It was almost as large as he was. "Come on, everyone. Last one around has to collect the ball buckets."

Jo barely managed to stifle a laugh as the kids half-carried, half-dragged their bags around the side of the clubhouse.

Ben limped over and unconsciously rubbed his knee. "What's the plan?"

Lauren looked to the sky and scratched her chin. "Today's normally a lesson on the practice fairway just past the third hole. But if the weather does take a turn for the worse I don't want to have to be herding a whole lot of soaking children back to their parents. We might do some hazard work instead."

Jo retrieved Ben's tripod from the vehicle. "Where do you normally do hazard practice?"

"It's on the other side and to the rear of the driving range, about a five-minute walk." Lauren lifted her golf bag clear of the four-wheel drive.

"I think I'll hire a cart rather than lug all my gear over there," Ben mused.

"Not a problem." Lauren pointed to a set of doors. "Go through there and turn to the left. At the counter ask for Eric and just tell him you're with me and ask for a cart. He shouldn't have any problem finding you one, especially since it's mid-week." She picked up her bag "We'll meet you at the back of the driving range."

Jo rummaged through her daypack, pulled out her camera, and closed the back door. "What constitutes a hazard?" She asked as she followed Lauren around the side of the clubhouse.

"Hazards usually refer to bunkers either on the side of a fairway or near the putting green. They can also be a copse of trees or tall grass. There're also water hazards such as lakes, small streams, or ponds."

Jo moaned in exasperation. "Water hazards are the bane of my existence. I can literally be kilometres away from water and yet it's uncanny how my ball always seems to find the damned stuff. I swear there are water magnets in all my golf balls."

Lauren laughed and playfully bumped Jo's shoulder with her own. "Don't I know it. My ball found its way to water on more occasions than I care to remember when I was playing. Today, though, I'm going to start the day with some simple bunker drills. It's a bit of fun and hopefully it'll take the kid's attention off Ben and his filming."

Jo patted Lauren's arm. "Don't worry. We'll try and set up far enough away so as to not disturb you."

"But still close enough so you can watch me, like you did when we were last here?"

Jo turned her gaze to the grass underfoot. "I didn't realize I'd been so obvious," she said sheepishly.

"It's okay," Lauren softly replied as one of the parents of the children approached the two of them. "I enjoyed it." She winked and shifted her bag's weight on her shoulder. She met the woman halfway. "Hi, Pam, let me introduce you to a friend of mine. Jo Ashby, this is Pam Hanson, Karrie and Adam's mum."

Still recovering from Lauren's earlier comment, Jo extended her hand. "Hi. It's nice to meet you."

"You're the photographer who did the great shot of Karrie. Thank you very much. It's a beautiful picture."

"No problem. My pleasure." They walked to where the group of children was engaged in warm-up exercises. "Lauren mentioned you needed some shots for a promotional brochure and I was more than happy to help. From what I saw on the first day, some of these kids are really talented."

Pam smiled. "They are. Though I can't help but think some of them could get so much further with appropriate sponsorship or funding."

"It's true." Lauren placed her bag down near the rag tag bags of her young charges. "When I first started playing, funding was a huge problem for me. If only we could get some support for these kids then maybe," she motioned to the assortment of old bags and clubs, "we could equip them with better gear."

Karrie walked over to them. "Miss Wheatley, you could get some money if you entered the Gracemere Wells Pro-Am charity golf tournament."

"What's that?" Jo glanced first at Lauren then back at Karrie.

"It's an annual tournament sponsored by the Gracemere Wells Foundation," Lauren explained. It's played at different courses in Australia and it coincides with when the big-name players are down here for the Oceania Ladies Masters. I competed in it once when I was still on tour. There's no prize money for the players. Instead, the winner elects a charity of her choice to donate her winnings to." Lauren reached down and ruffled Karrie's hair. "I'm a bit too rusty to be playing serious golf, young lady. Besides, I'm not on the tour at the moment so I'd need a sponsor's exemption to play."

"Exemption to play in what?" Ben asked as he walked toward them. He reached out his hand to Pam. "Hi. Ben Redbourne."

"I'm Pam Hanson. We were just talking about the possibility of Lauren playing in a charity tournament if we could get her a sponsor's exemption."

Jo barely caught the look of surprise on Lauren's face at Pam's words.

Ben rubbed his hands together. "It sounds like a great idea. It'd certainly make for some great footage."

Jo opened her mouth to add her support but snapped it shut at the warning look in Lauren's eyes.

Pam continued, obviously oblivious to Lauren's reaction. "This year it's being played at the Royal Tasmanian Golf Course, just outside Hobart. In fact, I was speaking with Jim Sattler last night, and he mentioned that his sister's one of the executives managing the Pro-Am this year."

"Who's Jim Sattler?" Ben looked from Lauren to Pam.

"He's The Dales Club President," Lauren replied. "Pam, even if he does have a word to his sister, there's no guarantee she can convince a sponsor to give me an exemption."

"But what if she can?" Pam insisted. "Would you at least consider it?"

Lauren picked up her bag. "I'll think about it. But right now I've got a lesson to teach. Ben, if you take the buggy and follow the path around to the right, you'll find a series of bunkers. That's where we're headed." She looked around her at the group of young teenagers who'd witnessed the exchange between the adults of the group. "Okay, it's hazard practice today, starting off with bunkers. Last one over there gets to rake the bunkers at the end of the session. See you in a couple of hours, Pam."

Pam waved and headed back toward the clubhouse, flipping open her mobile phone as she went.

Jo silently walked beside Lauren as they made their way across the manicured grass.

"Thanks for not saying anything back there," Lauren stated flatly.

"I sort of sensed you're not too keen on the idea, but can it really hurt? I mean if there's money to be earned, it might help the kids."

Lauren shifted her bag from one shoulder to the other. "I know. Just let me think about it, okay?"

Jo glanced at the group of children, ensuring that the last one rounded a copse of trees. She reached out and softly grasped Lauren's arm. "I understand it's completely your decision but I'm here if you want to talk about it."

"I really appreciate that," Lauren gently replied. "But for the moment I think I'm going to need all my focus to keep these kids from going crazy over a cameraman."

They parted company, with Jo heading toward Ben, and Lauren to where her young charges waited for her. It wasn't long before the equipment was set up and Ben started filming. For the next hour Jo watched Lauren put the children through hazard training, every now and then flashing a smile in her direction.

Lauren clearly had the patience of a saint. Despite Jo's best efforts to place Ben in a position where he could unobtrusively shoot footage, the kids' focus was clearly more on him than on the lesson. As they had throughout the afternoon, Lauren's eyes once again found hers, and they shared a mutual shrug.

Lauren addressed the group. "Okay, team. There have been some good bunker shots today. The key to remember with a splash bunker shot is you want to hit the sand behind the ball by imagining an island around it. Your aim is to slice under the ball and let the sand do the work." Lauren executed a perfect splash shot, and the ball rolled to a stop mere inches from the hole on the practice green. "Now, pick up your balls and one of you rake the bunker, please."

Jo walked over to where Lauren was wiping her sand wedge off before she stowed it in the bag compartment. "I'm sorry. They still seem to be preoccupied with Ben."

Lauren sighed. "It's kids and cameras, I suppose. It's a bad combination."

"Is that the end of the lesson?"

"Just one more, but this one should be a fun way to end the session. I don't expect many of them to master this but at least a few of the older ones might, and they should enjoy themselves in the process." Lauren pulled out a pitching wedge and removed its cover. "Okay you rabble, over to the water and we'll do a quick instruction on those kinds of hazards."

They trooped over to a small pond whose water was the colour of tea. Jo found herself a spot in the shade and made herself comfortable.

Lauren sat down with the group and began to remove her golf shoes and socks. "Here's the first lesson to learn about playing a water hazard. Never leave your shoes and socks on." The kids giggled as Lauren rolled up her slacks. Once finished, she dropped an old ball into the water, about a metre from the hazard's edge. "The second lesson is this. If water completely covers your ball, then pick it up and take a penalty stroke. You'll waste more time trying to hit it out than the one stroke you earn by picking it up. And besides, you'll end up soaked trying that."

Lauren moved over to the fringe of the pond and placed a ball on the muddy bank, where three-quarters of the ball's surface remained above the water line. "It's a ball like this you might want to take a shot at. Just remember, at least half the ball must be above the water line."

Jo laughed along with the students when Lauren entered the water to address the ball, her laughter earning her a raised eyebrow from Lauren, who made a show of focusing on the ball.

"In terms of hitting this, you use the same principles you do with a splash bunker shot. Be forward in your stance and make a steep swing. You'll contact the water about an inch behind the ball. Step back and I'll show you what it looks like."

Lauren checked the pin location and then her stance. While she went through her pre-shot routine, Jo glanced over at Ben, and was relieved to see he was still filming. She looked back just in time to see Lauren get soaked from the backsplash her swing created. She laughed out loud at Lauren's drenched shirt. She quickly brought her hand to her mouth, trying to stifle any further mirth.

Lauren turned and smiled wickedly. She held out her club. "Does anyone want to give my last shot a go?" There were no takers so she held her club out to Jo. "What about you, Miss Ashby?"

"No thanks, but I'd pay good money to see you do it again."

Lauren walked up the bank toward the giggling children and shook her body, dispersing a light spray of the water on the group. "I don't know about money, but who'd like to see Miss Ashby try that shot?"

Jo's laughter died in her throat at the chorus of children's voices, all egging her on. Lauren's eyes seemed to twinkle as she held the club out to Jo. "Come on, Miss Ashby," she teased. "Anyone can do it."

Ben gave Jo an eager thumbs-up.

She shook her head and took the club to the cheers of Lauren's young charges. "Okay," Jo relented. "I'll do it, Miss Wheatley. But only if you'll give me a hand." She removed her shoes and socks and joined Lauren on the bank. "You're going to pay for this," she whispered to Lauren as she stepped into the frigid water. Her toes sank into the dank mud of the small pond. "How disgusting." Her comment elicited another round of children's laughter.

"Don't worry. You'll get used to it." Lauren waggled her eyebrows and, like she'd done at their first outing at the club, she positioned herself against Jo's back and reached around to steady Jo's hands on the club.

"I could get used to this," Jo said in a tone only Lauren could hear.

Lauren cleared her throat. "Same here," she said near Jo's ear. "Okay, then. Now grip down on the club and make it a nice fluid swing. Don't forget to follow through."

Jo barely registered Lauren's instructions, the feel of her body on her back and her comment disrupting any concentration she might have harboured. She swung down toward the water, missing the ball completely. In doing so she overbalanced, and she and Lauren both fell backward into the muddy water.

Jo came up first, spluttering, and trying to wipe her hair from her face. Sitting in the cold water she glanced over her shoulder, saw Lauren, and started laughing, along with the children on the bank. A clump of water reeds covered most of Lauren's face. "You look like some kind of creature from the deep," Jo managed, gasping with laughter. A distant rumble of thunder silenced them all.

Lauren tossed the reeds in Jo's direction. "Thanks for the

compliment. You *did* pack a change of clothes didn't you?"

Jo gained her feet and offered Lauren her hand to help her up. "Thank God I did. It's the end of the lesson for the day, I take it?"

Lauren slogged out of the water. One of the kids handed her a golf towel. "Yes, it's the end of the day for the lot of you." She waved the smelly towel in the direction of her students. "Good work. But next week we'll be back again and you're all going to have a practice at playing water hazards, so bring plenty of dry clothes and towels with you. I'll see you then."

Jo handed Lauren her club, gratefully accepting a towel in return.

Ben hobbled over. "You two were great! Jo, you should have seen the look on your face when you surfaced. It was priceless."

"Thanks, *mate*. Where would I be without friends like you?" Jo bent down and retrieved her shoes and socks. "And as for you," she waved her socks in Lauren's direction. "You're a bad influence. Where are the showers?"

Lauren laughed. "They're in the women's bathroom but there's only one. Let's head back to the carpark and grab our bags and I'll show you. Ben, if you like I'll leave the back of the four-wheel drive open. Once you've stowed your gear, head to the bar and we'll meet you there."

"A drink after a hard day's work. Sounds like my sort of job," he called over his shoulder, limping to his golf cart.

Jo accompanied Lauren to the vehicle, where they grabbed their packs and headed inside.

Lauren opened the door to the ladies' bathroom and stepped aside to allow Jo to pass. The entrance foyer was small, a door positioned on either side. Lauren gestured with her head to the left. "The toilets are through there." She motioned to the other. "And the shower and changing room is through here."

Jo entered the compact changing room. Two wooden benches were positioned between two rows of lockers that faced each other. Jo looked around the corner of one of the rows of lockers. "I take it that's our shower?" She turned, catching Lauren blushing. "I mean *the* shower," she stammered, realising what she'd inadvertently implied.

Lauren set her pack on a bench. "Uh, yes. How about you have the first wash?" She charted the conversation into safer waters. "You seem to have got the most mud on you."

"Okay." Jo reached down to the bottom of her polo top and paused. "Do you have anything we could put our clothes in? I mean, the dampness doesn't bother me but the aroma leaves a lot to be desired."

"Sure. I've got a couple of plastic bags in my golf bag. I'll be right back."

Jo waited for her to leave then quickly stripped down, grateful to be free of the clinging clothes and the odor. She'd barely finished wrapping a towel around her when she heard the outer door and then saw the door to the changing room open. Lauren's expression sent a warm glow of pleasure down her spine. "Uh — here." Lauren held out a bag to Jo, gazing anywhere but at her.

Jo pretended not to notice Lauren's discomfiture. "Thanks. I'll just put all this in here and hit the shower." She gingerly placed her wet clothes in the bag, then grabbed her soap and shampoo.

"Great idea," Lauren muttered. "I'll get changed and follow you. I mean, I'll have a shower after you've finished."

Jo stifled a laugh as she shuffled past a bright red Lauren, their bodies brushing as she did so. She opened the door to the small shower stall, stepped inside, and placed her towel on the hook on the back of the door. Jo reached around the curtain, turned on the water and waited for it to reach the desired temperature. Grabbing her soap, she stepped under the stream of warmth, grateful as the water sluiced the mud from her body.

She shampooed her hair, replaying Lauren's actions during the training drill and her reaction to seeing her in a towel. *I know she wants to take this slowly, but this is killing me! The looks and soft touches she's given me during our walks are enough to test a saint. Not to mention her holding me during the hazard drill. Thank God there were others around. Otherwise...* Jo released a frustrated sigh and turned her face into the cascading water, in the process turning the temperature down a bit.

Finished, she turned the water off and stepped out of the stall to towel off. *It's probably a safer option to dry myself here than next to Lauren.* She secured the towel around her, grabbed her soap and shampoo and headed back to the change room.

"Thank God," she said conversationally. "The idea of sitting in wet clothes all the way back —" Jo momentarily lost the ability to speak when she came around the row of lockers, and found Lauren in only a towel. Despite her best intentions, she found herself unashamedly staring at the barely concealed beauty in front of her. She'd always been aware of Lauren's physique, but seeing her like this brought it even more to the fore. *She really does keep herself in shape. Look at those shoulders and arms.* Jo silently groaned. *I think I need another shower. A cold one.*

Lauren smiled, as if aware of the effect she was having on Jo. "To Cradle Mountain," she finished Jo's sentence. "I know what you mean." She picked up her toiletries bag and moved past Jo in the confined change space, her eyes never leaving Jo's. "I won't be long."

Jo watched her round the corner to the showers. Relieved to finally be alone she arched her neck, trying to rid it of tension. "God, give me strength," she muttered. She let the towel drop to her waist, holding it there as she searched her pack for her underwear. She had only enough time to pull it up to cover herself when she heard Lauren's footsteps.

"Hey, can I borrow your soap? I forgot to pack mine." As Lauren wheeled around the lockers she came to a sudden halt. Her eyes traced a path up Jo's partially naked form.

Jo made no attempt to cover herself. She watched, quietly pleased when Lauren's eyes seemed to be unable to pull themselves away from Jo's naked back. She waited until Lauren's gaze once again met hers and she softly smiled. "No problem." She reached down to pick up the soap, aware that her actions would reveal even more of her body. She moved over to Lauren and held out the soap.

As Lauren reached for the soap, her hand closed over Jo's. She looked down to where Jo's fingers lightly covered her hand and slowly back to Jo's face. Lauren nervously licked her lips.

"Do you like what you see?" Jo softly asked, her eyes never leaving Lauren's.

Lauren stepped perilously closer. "Yes, I do," Lauren replied, lowering her face to Jo's waiting lips. "Very much."

At the sound of the outer door to the women's bathroom opening, Lauren quickly stepped back and looked toward the door leading to the change room. She breathed a sigh of relief when the door to the toilets closed. She looked back at Jo and took the soap from her hand. "I think I'd better go and wash."

"I'll meet you outside," Jo replied, knowing the moment between them had passed, but unwilling to completely let it go. "Maybe we can talk about this later?"

"I'd like that," Lauren gazed back at Jo as she made her way to the showers.

JO WATCHED AS Lauren manoeuvred the vehicle into the parking lot in front of The Retreat and pulled the key from the ignition. She spared a glance at Jo seated in the rear and turned to Ben. "I'm just going to confirm my schedule."

"What's in the works for you tomorrow?" Ben unfastened his seatbelt.

"I'm scheduled for a very early start on a summit climb. A couple's paid handsomely to be on top of the summit when the sun hits Smithies Peak, Weindorfers Tower, and Little Horn. On a clear day it makes a spectacular photograph, but it also means a very early start for me." She got out and gallantly opened the rear door for Jo.

Jo nodded her thanks. *I wonder if she realizes what she just did.* "Are they experienced climbers?"

"Yes. They were here last year and we tried then. Unfortunately, at the moment when the shot was right it clouded over and stayed overcast for the next five days of their holiday. Apparently they plotted this trip to optimize the possibility of getting the shot they're after."

"They're obviously pretty serious about what they do." Ben eased himself out of the vehicle. "While you're doing that, we'll head down to the tavern. You're joining us for dinner, I hope?"

Lauren looked at Jo and back to Ben. "Sure. It'll make a nice change from baked beans and toast. I'll be there in a moment."

Jo watched Lauren walk toward the front of the lodge, recalling how she looked in a towel.

Ben bumped her. "Hey. What's with the silly grin?"

Jo shrugged. "Nothing. Let's go and get a table." They walked around the verandah to the tavern.

"Is everything okay between you and Lauren? You hardly said a handful of words to each other on the way home. I thought you might've been pissed at her getting you all wet."

In more ways than one, Jo thought as she opened the door to the tavern. "Not at all. I think she enjoyed making me her crash test dummy. The kids seemed to like it."

Ben slid along the wooden bench. "That's good. Because it'll make great footage."

Jo opened her mouth to say something as Lauren joined them at the table. "What'll make great footage?"

"Oh, just the two of you falling back into the water." Ben leant back against the corner wall of the tavern, a smug look on his face.

Lauren stared at him. "You actually filmed that?"

"You betcha. You should have seen the look on Jo's face." He folded his arms over his chest. "Priceless."

Lauren laughed. "Is it possible to get a still? I'd love it as a photograph."

Jo playfully slapped Lauren's arm and scowled at Ben. "I am a serious journalist. What are the two of you trying to do? Ruin my reputation?" She looked at a chuckling Ben and gazed at Lauren, and was surprised to see Lauren's raised eyebrow, as if in invitation.

Jo sighed in mock exasperation. "I need a drink. What are you two reprobates having? Hang on — Ben, let me guess. One of those fine Tasmanian beers," Ben nodded. "And Lauren, what would you like?"

"Lemonade will be fine for the moment." Lauren's eyes twinkled mischievously.

Jo flashed her a grin and walked to the bar.

Ellie nodded at her. "Hello stranger. I haven't seen much of you lately. What can I get you?"

"I'll have a gin and tonic, Ben will have his normal beer and Lauren would like a glass of lemonade."

"No problem." Ellie reached for a large glass and placed some ice in it. She motioned at Lauren. "It's good to see her coming out of her shell. You two seem to get along well together."

Jo blushed. "I think she just needed someone who was persistent enough to get past the barriers she set up, and see her for who she is."

Ellie placed the gin and tonic and lemonade on a tray in front of Jo. "All the same, it's good to see." She grabbed a pint glass, placed it under the beer tap and pulled the handle. The result was more foam than beer and Ellie muttered something that sounded like a curse. "It looks like this one's just about empty. Give me a moment and I'll pull his beer from the keg in the other bar."

"No problem." Jo took a sip from her gin and tonic and waited for Ellie to return. She reviewed the day's events, feeling a flush of pleasure at the growing intimacy between her and Lauren.

"Hello there. This is a great little spot, isn't it?"

Jo blinked and swivelled toward the woman who'd sat down beside her. Her dark brown hair was pulled into a ponytail, in turn highlighting the woman's rounded features. "Yes," Jo answered. "It's a nice place to unwind after a day in the park."

"Are you a guest here?" The woman edged a little closer into Jo's personal space.

Jo looked to where the woman's knee now brushed her thigh. "Ah, yes I am." *Ellie, where are you?*

"So am I. Why don't you let me buy you another one of whatever you're drinking?"

Jesus, what is it about this place? Do I have a sign on me that says "lesbian" or something? "Thanks, but no thanks. I'm here with friends."

"Why don't I join you?"

Jo searched her mind for another diplomatic excuse to extract herself from the brown-headed woman, when she felt a hand in the small of her back.

Lauren bent down, her eyes never leaving those of the other woman. "Jo, why don't you let me pay for these and I'll see you back at the table."

Jo slid off the stool, barely managing to hide her pleased surprise at Lauren's obvious possessiveness. She lightly trailed her hand down Lauren's arm. "Sure. See you there."

The other woman shrugged, as if in apology. "Sorry. Why didn't you say you were taken?"

"Here's your lager, Jo." Ellie placed the beer on the tray, her eyebrow raised.

Jo picked up the tray of drinks. "Thanks, Ellie. I'll see you back at the table, Lauren."

Jo weaved around the tables back to where Ben sat. It was clear by the look on his face that he'd witnessed the whole incident.

"So *that's* how it is between the two of you? Obviously you've been doing more than just walking." He leant back against the wall and grinned.

"Ben, you're such a bloke sometimes. And before you ask, I'm not going to give you a run-down on what's going on." She placed the beer just out of his reach. "And if you mention a word of this when

Lauren returns then, as I live and breathe, I swear to God you'll wear your beer *and* the glass."

"Now I know it's serious, with such threats from you." He quickly picked up his beer and pulled it away from Jo's hand, spilling some of it. "Don't worry. I won't say a thing. It's just a quiet meal between three close friends. Some closer than others." He winked at a scowling Jo and raised the glass to his lips.

JO GAZED OUT the passenger-side window as Lauren drove her to her cabin. Lauren's soft touch on her thigh interrupted her preoccupation. "Are you okay?"

Jo glanced over at her. "I'm fine. I was just thinking about dinner."

Lauren turned left onto a side road. "Ben seemed to be in fine form. I could hardly see his limp when he headed to his room in the lodge."

"It's the beer. I'm glad we finished up when we did. He can get a little rowdy when he gets one too many under his belt."

Lauren came to a halt in front of Jo's cabin, turned the engine off, and repositioned herself in her seat to face Jo. "Are you okay with what I did at the bar? You seemed a little quiet after I got back to the table."

Jo reached across the cabin's interior and took Lauren's hand. "I'm absolutely okay with what you did. Just a little taken aback, that's all."

Lauren dipped her head slightly. "I was a bit surprised at what I did, too. It was as if one minute I was talking with Ben and I turned and saw her trying to get into your lap. I suppose I just reacted without thinking."

"Hey," Jo waited for Lauren to raise her head. "I'm happy you did. She seemed clueless about my attempts to tell her I wasn't interested." She squeezed Lauren's fingers. "I know you've got an early start tomorrow, but do you want to come in for coffee?"

"That'd be great. If you like, we can talk some more about the golf tournament." Lauren got out of the four-wheel drive and they went inside.

Jo prepared their coffee and snagged the jar of cookies off the bench top. She walked into the lounge room as Lauren closed the door to the wood burning stove. Jo placed the two cups and cookies on the table, sat down on the sofa, and waited for Lauren to join her.

Lauren stood and wiped her hands on her pants. She moved to the sofa and sat down. "You know I'd do anything for those kids, but I don't know if my entering a tournament is going to result in the fairytale ending they're hoping for."

"I think you underestimate yourself. I know you still play and I'm betting you're as good as you've ever been." Jo reached for her coffee. "A bit rusty, but good all the same."

"I do still play, but not in tournaments and not against anyone else. I've no real gauge of how I'd stand up against a professional field."

Jo looked over the rim of her coffee cup at Lauren and pursed her lips. "Do you keep score when you play?"

Lauren avoided Jo's gaze. "Yes. Why?"

"What do you score? On average, I mean."

"Somewhere between," the remainder of Lauren's sentence was incoherent.

Jo put her cup down and reached for Lauren's hand. "Do you want to try again, in a language I can understand?"

"I normally score between two and sometimes four under par."

Jo's eyes widened. "Holy crap! And you think such a score *isn't* a gauge of your ability? You could literally walk onto the tour tomorrow."

Lauren pulled her hand from Jo's grasp. "I don't want to. That's not who I am now."

"I'm sorry, that didn't come out the way I meant it to. I was just surprised you can still maintain such an average and yet only occasionally play golf. Wherever you ended in the tournament, the kids would still love you for who you are." *And so would I,* a quiet voice deep inside her added. She again took Lauren's hand. "Would you at least give it a go?"

Lauren looked at the fire and back at Jo. "I will but only for the kids and only on one condition."

"What's that?"

"You caddy for me."

Jo blinked. "Are you insane? I'm a social golfer at best and I've never caddied before."

"Yes, but as you've just mentioned, if I'm consistently under par without a caddy then I don't think your presence is going to do any harm." Lauren smiled, a wicked edge to it. "You *can* carry a golf bag, can't you?"

Jo scowled at Lauren's obvious entrapment. "Of course I can, but it's not the point. You need someone who can offer you the support you need."

Lauren reached along the back of the sofa and softly stroked Jo's neck. "You've offered me more support than anyone has in a long time. I couldn't think of anyone else I'd rather have caddy for me than you."

Jo's heartbeat sped up and she leant into Lauren's intimate touch. She entwined her fingers with Lauren's, pulled their hands to her lips, and kissed Lauren's fingertips. "So," she whispered, "am I taken?"

Lauren pulled Jo toward her. "What do you think?"

Jo's body hummed when Lauren's lips met hers. Caught in the moment, she eased herself between Lauren's legs, at the same time pushing Lauren down onto the sofa. She gently teased Lauren's lips with her tongue and moaned when Lauren opened her mouth.

Lauren pulled her close as Jo lightly stroked her tongue with her own. Struggling not to push with her hips and increase the sensuous contact between the two of them, Jo deepened the kiss as Lauren's hands snagged her shirt free of her shorts.

Jo sat up, pulling her shirt completely off. She reached behind to remove her bra, but Lauren stopped her.

"Let me do that," Lauren whispered, finishing what Jo had started. She peeled the bra from Jo's arms and reached up, softly cupping Jo's breasts.

Jo threw her head back and leant into the contact, rejoicing as Lauren slowly stroked her nipples. "God, that feels good," she sighed, pulling Lauren's polo top from the front of her pants. She slid her hand under the shirt, caressed Lauren's muscled abdomen and moaned again. "Oh lord, a washboard stomach. I should've known." She once again settled herself between Lauren's legs, raised Lauren's shirt, and began lightly nipping at her soft skin.

Lauren's hips surged at Jo's touch and then she growled, low in her throat. "Honey, we've got to stop."

"Hmm," Jo continued to nuzzle Lauren's stomach, as her hands blazed a teasing trail toward Lauren's breasts.

"I'm sorry, but we have to stop now or I won't be able to stop at all."

Jo frowned and studied Lauren's face. "What do you mean?"

Lauren edged herself out from under Jo. "I mean, if we don't stop now there's going to be two really pissed-off people tomorrow who were expecting to climb the summit."

"What about this pissed-off woman *here*," Jo plaintively cried.

Lauren gazed longingly at her, the backs of her fingers tracing a lingering path between Jo's breasts and down to the top of her shorts. "Trust me when I tell you there are other things I'd rather be doing right now. Can we pick this up another time? Please?"

"Those two had better bloody-well turn up for their walk tomorrow or there'll be tears and they won't be mine. And as for picking this up again, next time make sure your calendar's clear," Jo huffed, grabbing the front of Lauren's shirt and pulling her in for one final kiss.

Chapter
Eleven

JO STRUGGLED TO find a comfortable spot on her shoulder for the golf bag's padded strap. "What have you got in here, bricks?"

Lauren glanced sideways at Jo as they headed to the tenth hole tee. "No, just the standard number of clubs and golf stuff. A couple of boulders, maybe," she added with a mischievous tone. "You sure you're up to this?"

"Of course I am. Even if it means I'll start the tournament being five-eight and end it at five-two."

Lauren turned and looked back the way they'd come and then toward their next tee. "It's a quiet day today. Why don't we call into the clubhouse for a quick drink?"

"I thought you'd never ask." Jo shifted the bag again to her other shoulder.

Lauren opened the door of the clubhouse with a flourish. "Do you want me to take those?"

Jo struggled to get both herself and the bag through into the foyer. "No," she said pridefully, grabbing the handle on the bag to steady it. "I can manage." She bounced her way through the doorway.

Lauren smothered a smile. "That was quite an entrance," she said, gesturing at the far wall. "Just put the clubs in the rack over there."

Divested of her burden, Jo followed Lauren into the bistro area of the clubhouse. The room itself was elegant and yet, at the same time, casual. Golf memorabilia adorned the deep green walls, which were complemented by the red plaid carpet of the floor. The Huon pine fireplace and bar lightened the room, helping give it a casual air.

"What can I get you?"

Jo pulled the cap from her head. From the look of amusement on Lauren's face, it was clear she had a bad case of hat head. "Lemonade will be fine. And don't you dare laugh or I'll be forced to hit you. Just remember, *I'm* the one carrying the bag of blunt objects."

Lauren held her hands up in mock defeat. "Okay, I know when I'm beat. Why don't you grab a table and I'll get the drinks."

Jo moved through the bistro to a table discreetly tucked away near the fire. She sat down and ran her fingers through her hair, trying to bring some semblance of order to it. As she did so she thought back on the morning so far. *It's been a great opportunity for just the two of us to get to know each other a little better. I swear she knows more about me now than just about anyone but Mum.* She smiled. *It's nice to be able to share those things and also have her share some of herself.*

Lauren placed a drink in front of Jo and sat down. "Why the silly grin?"

"Oh, nothing. Just happy thoughts."

"Where's Ben today?" Lauren took a sip of her drink.

"He's in Devonport, working with his friend on the film we took the other day. You still haven't told me how your walk went yesterday. How did it finish up?" Jo took her glass and pressed it to her forehead, sighing with pleasure at its cool surface.

"It went well. The day was lovely and the couple got some great shots. We came back via Lake Hanson, so I was pretty worn out by the time I got home. Sorry I didn't call you."

"No problem. I understand." Jo wiped the light sheen of condensation on her forehead, as she tried to measure Lauren's words. There was definitely something more than friendship between the two of them. *But does it mean Lauren thinks I expected to hear from her last night? Is this the way it's supposed to be? Damn. I'm so rusty at this relationship thing.* She looked up and realized Lauren was scrutinizing her. "I mean, I also had things to do. I spent the better part of yesterday working on the narrative for the program. Did you have any *company* during the walk?"

"Not directly, but I can sense she's still around. She's just not talking to me."

"I meant to ask you before, but are you fey or something?" Jo took a sip of her drink.

Lauren tilted her head, her brow furrowed. "I'm sorry, what do you mean?"

"You know. Sense things others normally don't."

"I don't know. I've never really given it much thought. But I do know I can sometimes pick up on things before others do." Lauren shrugged and a far away smile graced her features. "I used to drive Mum crazy as a kid, especially when I'd finish her sentences."

"I've never really been exposed to it, although my mum did say that her mum, Grandma Davis, was pretty fey." Jo scratched her chin in thought. "In fact, I remember Mum telling me about a time when she was a teenager. She walked in on Grandma Davis, who seemed to be talking to no one. Mum asked her what she was doing and Grandma told her that she was talking to Great Granddad Davis, except Mum knew he'd been dead for over five years. It unsettled her at first. But she said after a while she got used to it."

Lauren nodded. "I didn't have much to do with that sort of thing until I met Annie."

Jo set her glass on the table. "My professional exposure with psychic ability didn't really happen until I did a piece on it. I think it gave me a greater understanding of the possibility for some people to possess such latent capabilities."

"What do you mean?"

Jo thought on her response. "Now this is only Jo's theory on psychic ability." She paused. "I figure it's not so different than people who have the ability to play a piano. Most of us can manage chopsticks with two fingers and that's about it. But for some people it's a natural talent. Sure, they have to work on their discipline to maximise their talent, but the natural skill's always there. I believe talent like that is just a part of the brain that's more developed than in the rest of us mere mortals. I figure psychic ability's much the same. Just another door of the brain that's open for some but not all. I've no doubt it's a key reason as to why Annie first connected with you."

Lauren lightly rubbed the side of her neck as if in thought. "She certainly doesn't seem to be doing much connecting at the moment."

"Does that bother you?"

"I'd be lying if I said it didn't. I mean she's been a part of me for so long and now she's not. I miss her company."

Jo fought her instinctive jealousy in response to Lauren's candour. She scanned the bistro and then reached across and patted Lauren's hand. "I'm sure she'll be back."

"We'll see." Lauren picked up her glass, drained its contents and stood. "For the moment, though, we'd better get back out there, especially if I'm supposed to be playing in a tournament the weekend after next."

Jo's eyes widened. "You got the sponsor's exemption?"

Lauren smiled. "Pam Hanson left a message on my answering machine last night. Apparently the DeVrie foundation, one of the tournament's major sponsors, is more than happy to give me an exemption, especially when they were told the reason that I wanted to play."

Jo threw her arm across Lauren's back and lightly hugged her. "When were you going to tell me? That's fantastic news."

"I thought I'd surprise you today. I mean, it was a lucky break and I'm grateful for it." Lauren wagged her finger at Jo. "However, just because I've got a start doesn't mean I'll win."

As they walked to where Lauren's golf bag rested, Jo found she was secretly pleased at Lauren wanting to surprise her. She hefted the golf bag back to her shoulder. "A girl can only hope, can't she? Is there a hotel close by to the Royal Tasmanian Golf Course?"

Lauren again held the door for Jo. "That's the other good thing about a sponsor's exemption." They headed toward the next tee. "My caddie and I get free accommodations."

"Hmm," Jo shifted the bag on her shoulder.

Lauren reached out and gently stopped Jo's progress. "What's wrong?"

"I was just wondering how you wanted to play things between you and me during the tournament."

Lauren pulled Jo toward a grove of large eucalyptus trees. "I'm not twenty-five anymore and I certainly don't have to worry about losing sponsorship over my sexuality." She reached out and softly trailed her fingers down the side of Jo's face. "I'd like to be discreet but definitely not dismissive. That's why I got us adjoining rooms."

Jo leant against the tree. "I'm sorry about this. It's been a while since I've seriously been with someone and it takes a bit of adjusting. My last relationship required a heck of a lot of discretion because of my ex's job as a news reporter. I just wondered if it was going to be the same at the tournament."

Lauren removed Jo's cap from her head and placed a feather-light kiss on her forehead. "People will see what they want to see and come to their own conclusions. I don't intend to waste my time worrying about what they think."

"Thanks for the reassurance," Jo replied as Lauren placed her cap back on her head.

"You've told me a lot about yourself but you haven't said much about your ex," Lauren said as they continued their walk to the tenth tee.

Jo snorted. "The less said the better."

"I'd like to hear about her some time."

"Some time, just not today." Jo steered the conversation to a safer topic. "Now this is the bit where I'm supposed to give you a club and test the wind by throwing grass into the air before offering you some sage words, isn't it?"

Lauren pretended to think. "Yes, it is."

"Then let's give it a go." Jo pulled the course card from her pocket. "This is a par five. It's four hundred and ninety-five yards and has a dog leg to the left halfway down the fairway. The picture here says there're fairway bunkers just around the dogleg, both left and right." Jo put the bag down and made a show of plucking a small tuft of grass. She stood and threw it in the air above her head, while Lauren stifled a laugh at her antics. "There's a little breeze from right to left, so it should help. Or something." She pulled Lauren's driver from her bag, removed the head cover, and handed it to her. "Now for the sage advice." She moved closer to Lauren, close enough so their bodies touched. Jo leant toward Lauren's ear. "Stay on the green stuff and hit the crap out of the ball."

Lauren burst out laughing. "Maybe we should work on that part of the caddying relationship."

"I'm sorry, but it's about as sage as I get, at least when it comes to golf." Jo picked up the bag and moved behind the tee to observe

Lauren's shot.

Lauren began her pre-shot routine. She seemed to focus her attention on a point in the distance, before moving away from where her ball sat on the tee. She tilted her head from side to side, as if releasing nervous tension, and then she took a practice swing. Lauren nodded and made a deep-throated sound, as if satisfied with her effort. She again walked to where her ball waited to be hit. After one final look in the direction of her shot, she addressed the ball and drew the driver fully back, before smoothly unwinding and impacting with the ball.

Jo watched, amazed, as the ball drew slightly to the left around the fairway's dogleg. "How the hell do you manage to hit it so far when you hardly look like you're hitting the ball at all?"

Lauren bent down and picked up her tee and handed her driver back to Jo. "There's a trick to it. You see, it's not about hitting the cover off the ball. It's about one smooth motion over and over again. It's the secret to consistent shots in golf. It's pretty boring when you think about it, doing the same thing each time." Lauren smiled at the disbelieving look on Jo's face. "Have you ever seen seventy- and eighty-year-olds play golf?"

Jo stowed the club back in the bag. "I have to say they're not really the sort of people I enjoy watching playing golf. What's your point?"

They began their walk in the general direction of Lauren's ball. "Good players can consistently drive a ball a long distance without the strength of a twenty-year-old. It's one smooth motion, not just power."

"It might be for the likes of you, but for the rest of us hackers it's all about hitting the crap out of the ball," Jo replied.

"It's just something I'm going to have to work on with you, isn't it?" Lauren commented with long-suffering patience. They rounded the fairway, the tenth hole flag barely discernible in the distance. "I should be able to get it on the green from here. Oh, shit."

Jo looked toward where Lauren's attention was focused. Sitting in the middle of the left fairway bunker was Lauren's ball. She lightly patted Lauren's back. "Look at it this way. Anyone can hit all this green stuff, but it takes real skill to find a little bit of sand." They laughed as they headed to where Lauren's ball lay.

LAUREN'S FOUR-WHEEL drive reverberated over the cattle grid, signaling the initial entry into the park. Jo was jolted awake by the loud vibration. She stretched her arms and yawned.

"Welcome back to the land of the living, sleepyhead." Lauren weaved her way around a series of traffic chicanes, strategically placed to slow vehicles entering the park.

"I didn't even realise I'd dropped off." Jo rubbed her eyes. "I must have been a bit tired after lugging that brick of yours around all afternoon."

"You poor baby." Lauren patted Jo's leg.

Jo gazed at the surrounding countryside and was surprised by what she found. "There's a For Sale sign on the block of land over there. How can that be if it's in a national park?"

Lauren downshifted and manoeuvred through another group of traffic barriers. "It's because the land borders the actual park. Just as The Retreat can build just outside the park boundaries, it's also okay for people to sell land just outside the perimeter."

"It would be a pretty tempting offer for a developer."

Lauren shook her head. "Not as tempting as you'd think. There're strict building ordinances around these parts and at the moment, the area has met its quota for commercial buildings. Whoever builds here would only be allowed to put up a private residence."

"What a great way to stop the area from turning into an ugly commercial sprawl." Jo yawned again.

"Are you too tired to come and have a look at the wombat cam my team and I set up?"

"Not at all. Why a wombat cam?"

"Aside from the obvious, this is a wombat I rescued as a juvenile when it was still in its mother's pouch. Unfortunately, her mother had been hit by a car. I mustn't have been too far behind whoever hit her because the mother's body was still warm when I found it. When I was checking the body I found she was carrying a joey."

"She was carrying a baby kangaroo?"

Lauren chuckled. "No. Contrary to popular belief, 'joey' can refer to any small animal and not exclusively a kangaroo, although most people only use the term when they think of kangaroos or wallabies."

"I never knew that."

"There you go. You learn a new thing every day." Lauren waved at the ranger who occupied the booth at the official entry to Cradle Mountain National Park. "Anyway, after I rescued her, I raised her until she was old enough to set out on her own. We then fitted her with a GPS collar and released her inside the park. Once she started burrowing we thought we'd install a series of cameras in her warren, to keep track of how she was coping. I can even show you the warren if you like. It seems the two of us get along well because she's taken up residence not far from the back door of my cabin."

Jo suggestively arched a brow. "I have to say, looking at your wombat cam sounds like a variation of 'come up to my room and look at my etchings.'"

"Trust *you* to think that way," Lauren joked.

"You're just lucky you didn't make the offer to Ben. I won't damage your sensibilities with what *his* response might have been."

Lauren winced. "I can just imagine." She steered into her parking bay and got out. "Come inside and we'll check to see if she's still in her burrow."

Lauren switched on the park's radio when they got inside and the room slowly filled with the muted conversations of park headquarters and guides. She adjusted the volume and walked to a part of the room dominated by a myriad of electronic equipment, topped by a small television monitor. "Come and have a seat and I'll see if her ladyship's in residence."

Jo took the proffered seat. "Is that what you call her?"

Lauren chuckled. "No. I originally called her Fluff, because when I found her that was about all there was to her. She got the nickname 'her ladyship' because of her antics when I'd feed her."

"What did she do?"

"I swear she had her meal schedule down to the exact minute. If I wasn't there to feed her then she certainly let me know about it." The act of reaching down to flick a series of switches on the console caused Lauren's body to brush against Jo's shoulder and Jo unconsciously leant into the contact as she watched the monitor come to life. Her breathing hitched when Lauren leant beside her.

"What should I be looking for," she stammered, deliciously unsettled by Lauren's proximity.

"They're only black-and-white screens, but you should be looking for a small, grey furry object. It'll be Fluff."

Chills shot down Jo's back as Lauren's breath tickled her ear, her concentration on the screen severely impeded by Lauren's actions. Her breathing hitched as Lauren continued flicking through a series of screens, seemingly oblivious to the effect she was having.

"In all, there are five cameras that'll allow us to map out the entire burrow." Lauren paused on one view, and adjusted the focus. "There she is," she whispered into Jo's ear.

"I see," Jo replied, her attention directed on the woman beside her rather than the small creature on the screen. She turned her head, her lips brushing Lauren's cheek. "I take it back," she said, quietly pleased at Lauren's slight shudder.

Lauren shifted her gaze from the monitor to Jo's face. "Take back what?"

Jo gulped at the charged air that encircled them. "Your pick-up line," Jo smiled, leaning toward Lauren's lips. "You can show me your wombats any time." She brushed her lips against Lauren's.

Lauren responded and gently pulled Jo from the chair, deepening their contact.

Jo ran one hand through the hair at the nape of Lauren's neck, her other softly stroking Lauren's back. Jo teased Lauren's lips with her tongue, seeking entry.

Lauren moaned at the contact and arched toward Jo, cupping her backside with her hands, pulling Jo in closer. She reached for the back of Jo's polo shirt and began to slowly pull it free of Jo's pants.

Jo nuzzled Lauren's neck, alternating between kisses and light nips on Lauren's delicate skin. She groaned when Lauren's strong hands mapped a path over her back. "Maybe we should find somewhere a bit more suitable than this. Because I swear I don't know whether I'm going to be able to continue to stand if you keep touching me like this."

"That sounds like a great idea," Lauren whispered into Jo's ear before sucking the lobe.

"Lauren, this is park base. Are you there?"

"Don't answer it," Jo desperately murmured, all the while knowing Lauren would.

Lauren cursed in frustration and loosened their embrace. She lightly kissed Jo's ear. "Their timing sucks but I have to take this."

"They're just lucky they got to you *now*," Jo grumbled. "Because, I swear, in ten more minutes I wouldn't have allowed you to answer the bloody thing."

Lauren looked over her shoulder at Jo. "I don't think I would've wanted to," she replied, her flushed face evidence of her own desire. She took a ragged breath, slowly released it and moved to the radio.

"Park base, this is Lauren. What's up?"

"Hi Lauren, it's Dave. We've just completed our closing check of the park's sign-in register, and we've got someone who hasn't signed back in."

Lauren frowned. "A solo walker or a group?"

"It's a solo walker, a guy named Robert Gibson. He recorded his walk as being the Dove Lake and Lake Hanson walk, via Twisted Lakes. He signed out this morning at eight, so he should have been well and truly back by now."

Lauren checked her watch and frowned. "You're right. It's about a five- to six-hour walk and he's two hours overdue. Have we got anyone near there?"

"Geoffrey Blackson was taking an afternoon Dove Lake tour, but I can't raise him on the radio. I'm assuming he's finished for the day and has headed home."

"It looks like I'm off for a walk." Lauren released the radio's talk switch and glanced at Jo. "Did you happen to pack your hiking boots?"

Jo nodded. "I didn't know what we were doing when we got back to the park, so I packed them just in case."

Lauren suggestively raised one brow, the radio message momentarily forgotten. "I'd love to know what else you packed, just in case."

Jo trailed her fingers down Lauren's arm. "And if you're a good girl then you might just find out."

"Lauren, are you there?"

Lauren again picked up the radio's mouthpiece. She turned back to Jo. "I know you must be tired from today's golf, but do you feel up to a walk?"

Jo smiled. She reached up and tenderly cupped Lauren's cheek. "What girl could refuse such an offer?" She leant in and lightly kissed Lauren's cheek before she went to retrieve her boots from her daypack.

"Lauren, I've checked our on-call roster. We can have the on-call guide meet you at your cabin in about thirty minutes."

"Don't worry about it. I've got someone here who can help." Lauren looked out the large glass window, offering her an unimpeded view of Cradle Mountain. "Besides, from the look of those clouds, the weather's closing in pretty quickly. I don't think I can afford to wait, especially given the climb to Hansons Peak. I'll give you a radio check every thirty minutes. I'll turn the radio off between so I can conserve power."

"You're not using one of the guests of The Retreat again, are you?"

"Yes, I am, and she's more than happy to come with me. If you get any flak over this then tell them it was my decision. I'll check in with you before we step off."

Lauren rummaged in the cupboard containing her climbing and hiking gear. She picked up a canary yellow pack and walked over to Jo, who finished double tying her bootlace. She stood and took the pack. "Same thing again?"

"Yes, but this time we'll leave from Dove Lake. It's a shorter walk than from Waldheim car park."

Jo put on the backpack and tested it for weight distribution, nodding at the snug yet comfortable fit. "Are we likely to have any guests when we're walking?"

Lauren paused. "Annie's always accompanied me on rescues. But this time, well, I just don't know. She hasn't spoken to me in quite a while."

"Let's just hope she's there for you this time." Jo gazed out the large glass window, toward the lightly mist-shrouded Hansons Peak. *And here's hoping we don't have the same problem with rock fall that we had with our last descent.*

Chapter
Twelve

JO SCANNED THE Dove Lake car park, dotted with just under a dozen cars. "It looks like Robert Gibson isn't the only one we'll be searching for."

Lauren closed the door to the back of her vehicle and examined her surrounds. "Not necessarily so. A lot of walkers who go from Lake Saint Clair have a friend pre-position their vehicle at this car park. She moved to a beat-up, mud-spattered truck and peered at the dashboard. "See the card on the dash?" Jo nodded. "It details the walkers' name and when he or she is due to arrive at Dove Lake. Part of the responsibilities of the on-duty guide include, before the park's opening and closing time, to check the vehicles and their cards to see if anyone's overdue."

"That makes sense," Jo pulled on her rain jacket. "Given some of the tracks around here, it'd be easy to step in a hole and break an ankle or a leg."

Lauren donned her gloves and pulled on her beanie. "Speaking of breaking things, how's your mother doing?" She began a final check of her pack.

"She's fine but getting a little tired over the fuss my sister's making. She was happy to be able to get rid of her for a little while yesterday, so she and Andrew might have some time to themselves." Jo contemplatively pursed her lips. "He seems to be spending a lot of time there lately."

"Who's Andrew?"

Jo snapped the sternum strap buckle shut on her pack. "He's a friend of Mum's. I think he's the first guy she's been interested in since dad died. I sense she wants to take things farther, but when we spoke while I was there, she was afraid of what my dad would think." Jo pulled on her gloves as she considered the developments between her mum and Andrew.

As if reading her mind, Lauren moved to Jo's side and touched her arm. "And what do *you* think?"

Jo shrugged. "I don't know. The night when I arrived home after Mum's accident and found Andrew at the house I was a bit curious but resentful about what was going on. But when I see the two of them together, it's a neat fit. They complement each other very well. But still, she's holding herself back." Jo wanly smiled. "Sort of reminds me of someone else I know."

The sound of thunder reverberated around them. "That's not good." Lauren checked the temperature gauge and barometer on her watch and frowned. "We're sure to get a storm before we get off the mountain."

Jo extended her telescopic walking stick. "We'd better get going, then." She steadied herself as a chilling wind blew off Dove Lake. "Is Annie here?"

Lauren seemed to centre herself, then gaze at the old wooden boatshed at the foot of the lake. "I can sense she's here, but she doesn't seem to want to talk." Lauren sighed. "I suppose this time it's going to be just you and me."

Jo stared at the boat shed. *I can't sense a bloody thing except this cold wind.* She shivered at the idea of a ghost tracking their every move. She turned back to Lauren. "What's the plan?"

"We'll head along the left fork of the Dove Lake track for a little bit and then we'll begin the climb to Hansons Peak. From there we'll follow the track to Twisted Lakes and then on to Lake Hanson."

Jo pulled a Cradle Mountain map from her pocket and followed Lauren's path. "Wouldn't it be more logical to head to Lake Hanson first, given this would be his last stop before heading back down again?"

"Normally it would be, but with the wind down here and the approaching storm, if we have to climb up Hansons Peak, which we have to do sooner or later, then I'd prefer we do it now. If the storm hits us bad, then climbing down the peak could be fairly dangerous."

"I recall it was tricky when the weather was good. It was pretty scary with those rocks falling like they did the first day you took me walking."

Lauren suddenly occupied herself with checking the tension of her pack's hip belt. "Let's get going. Why don't you head down the left path and I'll do a quick radio check and catch up with you."

Confused by Lauren's sudden verbal and emotional shifting of gears, Jo looked at Lauren, who refused to meet her gaze. "Sure, I'll walk slowly until you catch up."

Taking her time, Jo walked to the first bend on the track, roughly two-hundred metres from where she'd set off. Before rounding the bend she turned, surprised to see Lauren still standing, staring at the weather beaten hut. The direction of the wind allowed Jo to catch Lauren's words.

"I know you're here."

Jo gasped and then turned, moving around the bend and away from Lauren's immediate view. She shook her head. *Oh crap, God only knows what Annie's got in store.*

JO STRUGGLED TO find a spot out of the wind and sleet that seemed to go right through her. For the fifth time during the climb she tightened the strap around her wrist, attempting to stymie any more sleet from finding its way into the minute space between her jacket and glove.

"Here, let me," Lauren shouted over the wind.

"Thanks," Jo yelled. "I think you were spot-on with your suggestion to climb the peak first." She squinted at the slowly darkening sky. "Given this weather, I'd hate to be doing the ascent or descent at night."

Lauren patted down the re-closable fastener. "We only need the temperature to drop a little more and this whole face of the mountain will ice up, making it impossible to use this path to go down until it gets some morning sun on it. Fortunately, the route around Lake Hanson, although wet, is a bit more protected and not too bad."

"Robert Gibson seems to have made it this far. Any idea on where we might find him?"

Lauren seemed to focus herself, as she'd done during the previous rescue. "No, and Annie's still not saying anything, either." She retrieved her radio out of her pack. "I'll call base and give them a report. Maybe they've heard something."

As Jo listened to Lauren's voice over the wind, she stared down the track leading to Twisted Lakes and frowned. *I could've sworn I saw something on the track just then.* She closed her eyes, shook her head and looked again. Whatever she thought was there was now gone. Lauren's hand on her forearm jolted her out of her preoccupied state.

"Are you okay?"

"I'm fine. I just thought I saw something." Jo stood and put her pack back on.

"It was probably brush blowing across the track. Your eyes can play tricks on you up here." Lauren closed the flap over the pouch that held the radio. "Dave says he's had no further news. I suppose we'd better keep moving. "

Jo picked up her walking stick. "You head out and I'll be right behind you."

Lauren carefully picked her way across the small track, back to where it joined the main track which led to Twisted Lakes. Jo's focus once again returned to a point back down the path, where she'd thought she'd seen something only moments before. *It might well have been a bit of bush, but since when does a bush resemble the shape of a person?*

Their battle against the deteriorating conditions seemed to go on forever. Jo couldn't be sure just how long she'd struggled behind Lauren's form, attempting to gain some respite from the sleet and wind. Despite her best efforts, she was at odds to keep up with Lauren.

Jo tugged her neck gaiter up farther, trying to cover at least part of her face from the unrelenting onslaught of the sleet. She endeavoured to walk to where Lauren stood. "Thank God for this bloody pole. I'd have been on my backside at least three times by now if I didn't have it."

Lauren turned her back to the sleet and moved as close as possible to Jo, affording her some degree of shelter. "I think I'd have done the same. Unfortunately, this part of the mountain's pretty well exposed. Twisted Lakes is a beautiful place on a good day but on days like this it's just downright ugly. I'm going to do a quick check of the foreshore, just in case Robert's holed up somewhere." She pointed at a small copse of King Billy pine. "Why don't you go and wait over there? It'll probably give you as much shelter from the wind as you're going to get at the moment."

"Okay, but don't be too long." Jo leant into the wind and staggered, her drunken gait steering her to the small group of trees forty metres off the main track. Lauren's bright yellow jacket helped Jo track her progress around the lake. Despite Lauren's skill, it was obvious she was fighting her own battle against the elements, every so often disappearing into a fold of the ground before reappearing again. As she watched her disappear over another rise an instinctive sense told Jo she was no longer alone. Despite her neck muff, she felt the hairs on the back of her neck rise and she hurriedly surveyed her surroundings. Her eyes finally came to rest on a point near the lake's shore, roughly ten metres in front of her. She gasped as a wraithlike figure seemed to materialise from the water.

It made no move toward her, seemingly content to watch her from afar. Jo glanced at where Lauren had previously been. *Where are you?* She stared again at the semi-transparent form, its hands on its waist, a disdainful expression on its face.

The condescending smile was enough to dispel the fear that gripped Jo, replacing it with anger. "What the bloody hell do you think you're doing? If you care for Lauren as much as she says you do, then why don't you go and damned-well help her?" The silent form remained in its place.

"Now I know I'm losing my mind, trying to get a response out of a ghost." Jo watched the wraith suddenly peer over its shoulder and disappear. She followed its gaze, releasing a shaky breath when Lauren topped the rise of a small mound and headed to her side.

"He doesn't seem to be around here." Lauren's eyes widened when she saw Jo. "Are you all right?"

Jo rubbed her arms, attempting to warm herself. "I'm fine, but I think I just got my first view of Annie."

Lauren wheeled and scanned the landscape. She turned back to Jo. "Are you okay?"

"Yes. She seemed to be more content to just watch me. You remember when I said I thought I saw something at Hansons Peak?"

Lauren nodded a response.

"Well, I'm beginning to believe it was her then, too. She's following us."

Lauren rubbed her gloved hand across the back of her covered neck. "I thought so. I felt something at the car park before we left. It looks like she's giving me the silent treatment."

Jo reached out and pulled Lauren's hand into her own. "At least she's here for you, even if she's not helping with the search."

Lauren took a deep breath and slowly released it, as if trying to calm herself. "Speaking of which, I need to report back in." She reached into the side of her pack and turned the radio on. "Dave, we've reached Twisted Lakes but there's no sign of him."

"Lauren, thank heavens you called. Blackson found Gibson. Geoffrey said he heard my initial call to you and headed out again. He said he found him off the main Lake Hanson track, which wasn't surprising, given he said a number of the markers on the track are missing."

Lauren's jaw clenched. "If he heard what was happening, why did he maintain radio silence?"

"I don't know."

Lauren swore. "Is Gibson okay?"

"Yes, just feeling a little foolish. I had him taken to the lodge doctor to check him over."

"Is Blackson still there?"

"No, but he's on duty first up tomorrow if you want to talk to him."

Lauren kicked a stone, sending it flying into the bush. "You're damned right I do."

"I think I'll make myself scarce for that discussion," Dave said dryly. What are your plans?"

"We'll head back down via Lake Hanson."

"If what Geoffrey's saying is true, walking an unmarked track in this weather is too risky."

Lauren looked at the temperature gauge on her watch and scowled. "We can't go down via Hansons Peak, either. The temperature's dropped below freezing here. The descent would be far too icy. I guess we'll hole up in Rodway hut."

"Okay. Keep us posted."

"Will do. Out." Lauren placed the radio back in her pack. She checked their surroundings.

Jo did the same. "Why didn't we see Geoffrey's lodge vehicle at the Dove Lake car park?"

Lauren, tight-lipped, shook her head. "I can only assume he used his own vehicle. If he'd used one of the guide's vehicles then it would've been easy to spot among the others."

"The weather seems to have gotten a hell of a lot worse since we arrived here. I swear the visibility's down to about five metres." Jo clapped her hands together, attempting to elicit some warmth. "What do we do now?"

"We get on the main track and head toward Rodway hut. It's not as well appointed as Kitchen hut, but it'll at least get us out of the wind."

Just as she finished talking, another strong gust buffeted them. "It sounds like a fine idea to me," Jo agreed.

Despite their best efforts, the deteriorating conditions made it impossible to locate the main track to shelter. After thirty minutes of searching they were no closer to Rodway hut. With the snow beginning to blow around them, Lauren pulled Jo back to a small copse of King Billy pine.

"I can't find the damned track. And in this weather, we're just as likely to walk off the edge of the mountain as find it."

Jo shivered. "It's like we're walking in circles. What do you want to do?"

"I've got an idea." Lauren stepped a short distance away from Jo and gazed out into the storm. "Annie, I know you're out there and I know you've been following us. I can't find the track to Rodway hut and I know you can find it for me."

With every passing minute the weather worsened. Jo watched the frustration and panic grow on Lauren's face, her concern for the two of them evident. *Annie, why are you doing this to her?* She walked to where Lauren stood. "It's all right. We'll just bed down here."

Lauren firmly shook her head. "It won't be all right. It's too cold. If we sleep here you'll die of hyperthermia and it'll be my fault."

"That's crap and you know it," Jo tried anger to calm Lauren's panicked state. "I made a conscious decision to go with you and that's all there is to it. If anyone or anything's at fault it's this damned weather and that bloody stupid guide Blackson." Try as she might, her words didn't seem to have the effect she was hoping for.

Her anger rising, Jo stepped away from Lauren and put her hands on her hips. "Listen you bitch! I know you're out there. I saw you by Twisted Lakes not long ago. Lauren says you told her you love her. You sure as hell picked a bloody fine way of showing it! Or is this all part of your plan to see Lauren dead so the two of you can be together for the rest of your lives? If that's so then I've got a news flash for you, sister. If she dies there's a decent possibility I'll also die. And if that happens I swear I'll be right behind you, following your every move. If you think I'm annoying now, you should see me when I'm part of *your* world!"

Jo caught herself as an unusually strong gust of wind hit her. She laboured to walk to Lauren, using every ounce of energy to get there. She reached Lauren's side in time to see her nod.

"It seems your speech had the desired effect. Come on." Lauren turned one hundred and eighty degrees and headed into the storm, with Jo tucked in behind her. After a five-minute struggle they finally reached the path.

Twenty minutes later they were inside Rodway hut. Lauren locked the door behind them then shrugged out of her pack and collapsed onto it as Jo did the same.

After a short rest, Jo pulled a small lantern from her pack, turned it on, and checked the room. Its Spartan, wooden walls held no shelves or windows. There was no table, either. She looked at Lauren's hunched form and reached across and touched her thigh. "Are you okay?"

"I'm fine. Just a little tired. I'd better let base know we got here."

While Lauren finished her call Jo pulled a camping stove from her pack. She poured water from her canteen into a metal mug and began heating water for soup mix. As she stirred the water, she felt the hairs on the back of her neck once again stand up. She peered at the figure now occupying one corner of the hut. "Lauren," she said quietly, "We have company."

Lauren turned in the direction Jo was motioning with her head. There stood an unmistakable form. "It's Annie." Lauren rose and placed herself between Jo and the ethereal shape.

Jo stared at the ghostly presence through the scant lighting of the hut. *She could almost be a living and breathing woman.* Her thin, androgynous figure was clothed in baggy dark trousers and a formless light-coloured shirt, her curly brown hair barely reaching the bottom of her ears. *I can understand how you'd fall for her, Lauren. She must have been a beauty in her day.* Jo's focus returned to the present and their most recent predicament. Recalling how close she and Lauren had come to disaster, her anger again began to bubble to the surface and she stood.

"Finally, I'm graced with your presence," Jo said. "It's a fine time to be showing yourself now, once all the drama's over."

"There was no need to show myself before," Annie calmly replied.

"How bloody convenient." Jo accusingly pointed at Annie. "You knew all along Robert Gibson had been rescued, you *had* to have known."

Annie seemingly leant against the wall of the hut, crossing one ankle over the other. "Yes I did."

"And yet you still put Lauren's life at stake. The same woman you're supposed to love." Jo snorted. "If you ask me, it's a hell of a strange way to show your feelings for her."

Annie glanced at Lauren and back at Jo. "She knows I love her and it's all that matters."

"You wouldn't know the meaning of the word. It's not love you have for Lauren, it's dependence. The woman you really loved died years ago and now you thoughtlessly tie Lauren to a love she can never fully have. As far as I'm concerned, it's nothing more than selfishness."

Jo stepped back as Annie moved toward her.

"Annie, she didn't mean it," Lauren said, attempting to defuse the situation.

Annie softly smiled at Lauren and again settled her steely gaze on Jo. "This is what Lauren wants, isn't it?"

Jo looked at Lauren, whose gaze moved from her to Annie. "Lauren?"

"I do want Annie, but I want you as well," Lauren softly replied.

Jo gritted her teeth. "Is it Annie or the security she represents that you truly crave?"

"Imagine you being the one to talk about security," Annie interjected. "At least I can offer that much to her."

"What's your point?" Jo demanded.

"You're a newspaper reporter or journalist, aren't you?"

Jo baulked at the question and then remembered she was talking with a ghost who'd died in the 1930s, some twenty years before mainstream television arrived in Australia. Opting not to belabour the point, she answered in the affirmative.

Annie pointed an accusing finger at Jo. "If that's the case, wouldn't it also be true to say when your work is finished here you'll be heading home once again? Where does that leave Lauren?"

Jo's face drained of colour, realising how easily she'd been drawn into a corner. She glanced at Lauren, silently trying to convey how she felt for her. "I want Lauren to be part of my life, but there're a number of issues we've yet to work through." *Damn it.* Lauren's face seemed to clam up at her answer. "Distance isn't an issue. I'll always be there for her."

Annie harrumphed. "Then it's no different than how Lauren and I are, is it?"

"Enough," Lauren shouted. "I'm not a piece of meat the two of you can haggle over and, after the day I've had, I just want to sleep. If the two of you want to continue this argument you can take it outside."

Jo moved over to Lauren, only to have her turn away. She pursed her lips and turned back to where Annie stood, but she had vanished.

"Lauren, you know it's not like that, don't you?" Jo quietly asked.

"Honestly, at this point I don't know what to think."

"There are a number of things we need to talk about and I understand now's not a good time. But I don't want to lose you. That's the one thing I'm sure of. I'm willing to work through everything, if you'll just let me."

The sizzle of an overflowing mug of soup interrupted them. Jo softly cursed as she bent down and turned the stove off. "Cooking would also be one of those things I need to work through," she muttered, trying to lighten the mood. "Can we at least talk about it?"

Lauren shook her sleeping bag out, settled it on the floor, and slipped out of her boots. "Not right now. Maybe when we're back down the mountain and we each have some time. Right now I really need some sleep."

Lauren climbed into her sleeping bag and rolled over, putting her back to Jo. Sad and shaken, Jo started cleaning up the mess the soup made. *Trust me when I say it's one conversation we're going to have, ghost or no ghost.*

THE FOLLOWING MORNING, despite Jo's best attempts to draw Lauren into conversation about the previous evening, Lauren remained tight-lipped. Their descent was rapid and mostly silent.

Jo tried once again to strike up a conversation in the vehicle. "We made good time coming down."

"Yes, we did." Lauren downshifted to negotiate the turn onto the main park road. "Despite the fog."

Jo murmured an agreement, watching out the window at the light shroud of mist that dominated the bush, turning the surrounds into something akin to a picture taken through a soft lens.

"If you don't mind," Lauren continued, "I'd like to head for Park base to speak with Geoffrey before tourists start filling up the centre." Lauren accelerated now that they were on the recently-graded main dirt track. "At this time of the year, the person who mans the park radio is also responsible for manning the tourist centre, and I want to avoid a scene."

I doubt if you'd listen to me if I said no. "No, that's fine."

With the speed they were doing, it wasn't long before they reached their destination. The vehicle had barely stopped when Lauren was out and heading for the entrance. Jo quickly unbuckled her belt and jogged after her.

Lauren marched across the Park centre, her target a door on the back wall. She whipped it open, causing it to slam against the wall.

Geoffrey jumped out of his seat, spilling the contents of his mug down the front of his shirt.

"What the hell did you think you were doing last night?" Lauren demanded, stopping a mere arms-length away from him.

Geoffrey held his shirt from his body in an obvious attempt to stop the liquid from burning his skin. "My bloody job," he sneered. "There's no need for you to be pissed just because I pulled off the rescue and you didn't."

"I couldn't give a great God-damn about who rescued Gibson. What I'm furious about is you were obviously the guide closest enough to effect a rescue. Yet not once, during related radio traffic on the park channel, did you make yourself known. Your actions last night nearly caused two deaths on the mountain. Mine—" she jerked her thumb over her shoulder "—and Jo's."

Geoffrey glanced behind Lauren at Jo and smirked. "On a first-name basis with the guests now, are you?" He raked Jo's form with his gaze. "I see how it is."

Lauren clenched and unclenched her fists. "Only a perverted mind like yours could put such a spin on something like that. Aside from the fact she's an experienced mountaineer, she's a journalist doing a story on me, nothing more."

Jo's stomach sank at Lauren's words. As she opened her mouth in defense, Geoffrey huffed.

"How convenient."

Lauren stepped dangerously close to him. "This time you've gone too far. By not advising Dave or me you'd started the rescue, you risked more lives than what's necessary. You haven't heard the end of this," Lauren practically snarled.

"And what do you propose to do about it?" he challenged.

"I'll see you thrown out of this park as a guide, if it's the last thing I do."

Geoffrey disdainfully laughed, smirking. "Strong words, but you know you haven't got the authority to throw me out."

Jo put a restraining hand on Lauren's arm, halting what she figured was Lauren's next action—to throttle Geoffrey.

"Is he right in what he says?"

Lauren lowered her voice to a dangerous, cold tone. "As long as his father's part owner of The Retreat and, despite the complaints made against him, my word alone won't be enough to see him fired."

"Miss Wheatley might not be able to fire you Geoffrey, but I certainly can."

They all turned to the imposing figure dominating the entranceway into the office.

"Mr. Blackson," Lauren said at the same time Geoffrey said, "Dad." Mr. Blackson senior glared at his son before his gaze settled on Jo. He walked toward her. "Miss Ashby, isn't it?"

Jo smiled and held out her hand. *You're not a bit like your son.* "Mr. Blackson, it's a pleasure to meet you."

He took Jo's hand. "The pleasure's mine. I'd been told you were doing a story on Lauren and had been meaning to catch up with you. I'm sorry the circumstances weren't a little more jovial."

His no-nonsense glare again settled on his son. "From Dave's brief to me last night, you not only jeopardised Lauren's safety through your thoughtless actions, but you also threatened a journalist who happens to also be a guest here."

"Dad, I can explain," Geoffrey took a step toward his father who, in turn, imperiously held up his hand.

"And, if that wasn't enough, Robert Gibson is a golfing partner and good friend of mine. As the CEO of the DeVrie foundation, he's just given Miss Wheatley an exemption to play in a charity golfing match I have a lot of interest in. Lauren's right. This time you've gone way too far."

"But if she wasn't so pig-headed about wanting to save everyone on the mountain," Geoffrey whined, only to be cut off.

"You can go now, Geoffrey. And feel free to leave any of the Park's property behind." Mr. Blackson turned away.

Geoffrey shot a look of pure hatred at Lauren and she took a step back. He strode to the door, gripped the handle and turned it. "It was a crappy job to start with. I should've left this dead end behind a long time ago." He stepped through, slamming the door behind him.

Mr. Blackson glanced over his shoulder and back at Lauren, an apologetic look on his face. "I'm sorry, Lauren, but Geoffrey's untimely departure leaves the Park centre unmanned."

Lauren smiled. "It's okay, sir, I can hold down the centre until I can get in contact with one of our temporary guides."

He turned to Jo. "Unfortunately, I walked down here Miss Ashby, otherwise I'd offer you a lift back to your cabin."

Jo looked across at Lauren, recalling her earlier words to Geoffrey. She turned to Mr. Blackson. "It's okay. The walk will do me good. I'll leave the rescue pack in the vehicle so I should make good time," she replied without inflection. Jo smiled at him, sparing a final glance in Lauren's direction as she walked toward the door. "Besides, it'll give me time to do my job as a journalist." One final look in Lauren's direction assured Jo that Lauren had understood the double meaning behind her words. She stepped through the door and softly closed it behind her.

Chapter
Thirteen

JO WENT THROUGH the sliding door onto her cabin's private deck. She placed a mug of hot chocolate on a small wooden table and eased herself into one of the verandah's wooden chairs. The interaction between her and Lauren over the past week since the rescue had left Jo bewildered. She punched a well-used speed dial number on her cell and pressed the phone to her ear, smiling when a familiar voice answered.

"Margaret Ashby speaking."

"Hi, Mum, how are you feeling?" Jo stretched her legs out in front of her.

"Hang on a minute, love. Let me get settled."

Jo's ear filled with her mother's small grunts and obvious movement to find a comfortable position for her broken leg.

"There, that's better."

"Where are you?"

"I've graciously been given leave from my bed by your overly-solicitous sister," Margaret replied.

"At least you're out of bed and that's got to be a relief. How's your leg?"

"I had my check-up with the doctor, and it went well. He said the bone's knitting just fine, and he replaced my current cast with a lighter full-length cast in a lovely shade of pale blue. Of course, Andrew made fun of me on the drive home, suggesting the change of casts was no more than a fashion statement."

Jo's brow furrowed. "I thought Emma would've taken you."

"Trust me, she wanted to, but I was afraid she'd give the poor doctor the first, second, and third degree about my injury."

Jo laughed at Emma's well-known antics. She pulled her jacket around her as a cool breeze whispered its way through the trees. "How are things with Andrew?" She blew on her hot chocolate and took a sip.

Margaret's sigh filtered down the line. "Things have changed a bit between us since the accident."

Jo frowned. "In what way?"

"Not in a bad way. But I think Andrew would like to move things along. It's as if the crash was a wake-up call for him."

Jo shifted in her seat, feeling somewhat unsettled discussing her mother's love life, but sensing she needed to speak to someone about it. "How were things between you before the crash?"

"They were great. We spent a lot of time together, going out to lunch and dinner. He'd often come over to my place for a meal."

"What's changed?"

"He spends a lot more time with me. That is, when Emma allows him." Margaret softly chuckled and then stopped. "But the other night he kissed me," she whispered in a conspiratorial tone.

Jo bit back the laugh threatening to spill forth. "You mean you haven't—he hadn't kissed you before?"

"Well, not like that."

"Mum, how long have the two of you been seeing each other?"

"Listen, missy, it's not like things are for you these days. Things move a little slower for us and, besides, I'm not sure if the time is right."

"From what you've already said, it's been a good three months, hasn't it?" Silence was the only response from the other end of the line.

A few moments later, Margaret spoke again. "But what about your father?"

Jo closed her eyes and lightly drew her fingers through her hair. "Mum, I think Dad would absolutely understand. He'd be hurt to realise you're holding yourself back, especially after so long. And, what's more, you're still young. I'm *sure* he'd understand."

Margaret sniffled and cleared her throat. "We'll see how things go. How are things between you and Lauren?"

Jo flopped back into the chair, wondering how much she should tell her mother. "It's a little complicated."

"What do you mean?"

Jo sighed. "There's sort of someone else but there isn't."

"Now you're confusing me. What's going on?"

Jo looked across the bush, to the direction of the snow-capped Cradle Mountain. *Here goes nothing.* "Mum, what I'm about to tell you is going to make you wonder whether I'm crazy."

Margaret laughed. "My dear, I've thought you were crazy for a number of years now. What makes you think telling me now will be any different?"

Jo scrunched her face, attempting to work out the best way to explain herself.

"Jo, you're scaring me. What is it?"

"The someone else is a ghost who lives in the park and follows Lauren around," Jo said in a rush, bracing herself for her mother's answer.

"Lauren is in love with a ghost," was Margaret's deadpan response.

"Yes, she is, but up until a week ago I thought she was falling for me."

"Hang on a minute. Before we move on to you and Lauren, how do you know the ghost is real?"

"I've seen her. Her name's Annie Hethrington and she lived here in the early twentieth century. There's a small hut in the park that used to be her home."

"Well," Margaret said, her tone tentative. "I have to say I haven't had a conversation like this since Mum died. It took me a bit to get used to her talking to dead people but, all the same, I was a bit disappointed I didn't inherit her talent."

Jo pensively ran one finger around her mug of hot chocolate. "Don't be too disappointed. If I have any of Grandma's talent it seems a pretty hit and miss affair at the moment. Lauren's the one Annie seems to connect with. And besides, I know you said Grandma Davis was fey but I've never had to deal with a ghost and now I am, at least as far as Annie's concerned."

"You speak about her as if you've been formally introduced," Margaret's curiosity was evident in her tone.

Jo nervously cleared her throat. "We weren't formally introduced, but I did have an argument with her."

Laughter echoed through the phone's earpiece. "Now why does that not surprise me?"

"Mum, do you think I'm crazy telling you this?"

"My dear, if it was anyone else telling me, I'd be highly skeptical. But given your grandmother's ability, I'm assuming it must have skipped my generation, but not yours. What did you argue about?"

Jo relayed to her mother an abridged version of the events surrounding the previous week's rescue and the scene in the Park centre office the following morning.

"How had things been going between you and Lauren until then?"

Jo's face reddened. "Let's just say we'd progressed beyond kissing and, if it weren't for radio interruptions and tour groups, we may have gotten a little further. But, during the rescue, Annie called me on what I was going to do once I finished the piece on Lauren, and everything seemed to go downhill from there."

"You say that was a week ago. Have you seen Lauren since?"

Jo expelled a frustrated breath. "I have, but it's very confusing. It's like she's keeping me at arm's length, but it's a struggle for her. I've tried to get closer again, but she shies away."

"What were your plans when you'd finished with the story?"

"This is going to sound like I'm positively clueless, but I really hadn't given it much thought." Jo massaged the back of her neck. "Obviously, I should have. And when Annie confronted me on my imminent departure to the mainland, I'm sure I must have looked like a deer caught in headlights when Lauren looked at me. I couldn't have handled the situation any worse if I'd scripted it myself."

"Do you love her?"

Once again Jo stared silently out at the park's rugged scenery. "Yes. And I think it's why this past week's hurt so much."

"Have you told her?"

"No, I haven't, and now I don't know if it'd be worth the pain of her rejection."

"If she wanted to reject you she'd have done it a week ago. It's up to you, but I think you should tell her. If for no other reason than to allow you to move on if her response isn't what you hoped. Have you given the distance issue much thought?"

Jo rubbed her brow. "I'm working on an idea but it's a little early to go into detail."

"I think you need to find Lauren and set things straight."

"I'm afraid it'll have to wait a little while." Jo checked her watch. "Ben's due to pick me up in about half an hour. We're heading out early to the charity golf tournament I told you about last time I called. Ben wants to check the course for camera shots while it's still light and I want to get some footage before the tournament kicks off. Lauren's on duty and she'll meet us there."

"I'd better let you go, then. But, sweetie, don't let what's between you and Lauren pass. You may end up regretting it for the rest of your life."

Jo sighed. "Thanks, Mum, but *you* should listen to some of your own advice and move things along with Andrew. I know Dad would want you to be happy."

"We'll see. Now go on and get yourself organized. Call me next week if you can. I love you."

"Will do. I love you too. Bye." Jo stood and stretched, working the kinks out of her back. She reached down, picked up her cup and went inside.

LAUREN DROPPED HER daypack on the verandah of Annie's hut and reached into her pocket. She pulled her keys out and inserted one into the padlock on the cabin's front door. She furtively glanced over her shoulder and walked inside, checking the interior in the early afternoon lighting.

Lauren's eyes scanned the cabin's main room. "Annie?"

Silence was her only answer.

She walked across the main room to the bedroom, set back to the rear of the cabin. Stopping in front of a well-worn nightstand, she opened the top drawer, then bent down and sorted through the drawer's contents.

"What are you looking for?"

Lauren straightened and turned toward the room's entrance. "I thought you were here."

Annie smiled. "Yes, you were always good at knowing when I was around. What are you searching for in there?"

"I'm looking for the golf ball you gave me." Lauren riffled through the drawer again.

"Marta's lucky golf ball?"

"That's the one—here it is." Lauren held up a small, dull white spheroid Haskell ball, its dimples in convex low relief to the surface, unlike the concave dimples of its modern counterpart. "Thank you for this. It'll always be a special part of my golf gear."

Annie moved into the room. "Marta would be happy I gave it to you, especially given your skill as a golfer."

"From what you've told me, Marta was no slouch, either. I'm sure I would've liked her," Lauren absently replied.

"What's wrong?"

Lauren shrugged and partially turned herself away from Annie. "I'm a little preoccupied with the charity golf tournament in Hobart. The first round starts tomorrow."

"Where's Jo?"

"I'd never bring her here. This is *your* home." Lauren stowed the golf ball in her pants pocket.

"I know you wouldn't, but it's not what I asked."

Lauren returned to the hut's main room. "She left early with her cameraman. I suppose there's setting up that needs to be done before the tournament starts."

Annie followed her. "How are things between the two of you?"

Lauren looked at Annie and struggled to contain the pain written on her own face. "They're safe."

For a moment time seemed to stand still. Annie stared across the room at her and then looked around the hut, as if searching for something. The silence between them was only broken by the laughter from a company of kookaburras in a tree close by.

Annie sighed heavily. "Safe isn't enough, and I was wrong to suggest it was."

Lauren warily watched her. "What do you mean?"

"You know I'll always be here for you. But—" Annie hesitated and bowed her head. "You need to find someone where *you* are. I can't offer you everything I'd like to and it's not fair to either of us."

Lauren forcefully shook her head. "That's not the case. You said it yourself. Once Jo's finished, she'll leave, so what can she offer me? Once she's gone I'll be here and she'll be on the mainland, and the distance is just too great."

Annie moved over to Lauren. "Marta and I argued a lot, but none more so than when she would leave for months at a time to pursue her golf career. But she always came back, no matter how far away she went. I'm sure Jo would be more than willing to do the same."

Lauren fought to contain a tear that threatened to fall. She struggled to escape Annie's loving gaze.

"I know you care for her a lot," Annie said softly. "It's been written on your face from the very beginning. Honestly, it's what hurt me the most at the start. But you need to give this a try, if not for your sake, then mine. I couldn't stand the thought of me standing between you and happiness. And, if the look on your face is any judge, you're certainly not happy at the moment."

Lauren sadly shook her head. "It may already be too late."

Annie reached across the distance between the two of them and reached out, as if to brush away the solitary tear. She looked at her hand, as if in regret, and lowered it. "It's only too late if you want it to be. Speak to her. Find out what she intends to do once her story's completed."

"I don't know. I'll have to see where things lead."

"They'll be leading nowhere if you don't start your journey. The roads may have improved from my last trip to Hobart, but I'll wager it's still a bit of a drive."

Lauren wanly smiled. "It is, and you're right. I'd better get going."

Annie looked at the pocket that contained Marta's golf ball. "Just remember, whatever happens, I'll be there for you."

"I know." With a final, fond smile Lauren turned and walked through the cabin's entrance.

LAUREN NERVOUSLY PATTED down the collar of her long-sleeved lilac golf shirt and smoothed the front of her tan slacks. Satisfied, she once again glanced at the adjoining entry to Jo's room. From the sounds of activity resonating through the door for the past hour, she knew Jo was awake.

She resolutely exhaled, walked across the room, and lightly tapped on the door, stepping back when it was opened.

"Hey," Jo said, the ghost of a smile on her face. "When did you get in?"

"Pretty late last night. There was an accident on the Midlands Highway. By the time I got in, I didn't see a light under your door and I didn't want to disturb you, so I went to bed. You want to come in?" Lauren motioned for Jo to enter.

"It would've been okay if you knocked. I'm a light sleeper," Jo said as she accepted Lauren's offer.

Lauren hated the forced nature of the conversation between them. She rubbed one hand along her forearm and jumped at Jo's light touch.

"Are you okay?"

Lauren grimaced. "Its just I haven't been in this situation for so long. It's hard to get used to it again."

Jo knitted her brows. "What, the golf tournament?"

"That, too," Lauren replied. She steeled herself. "I was thinking about us. I've been pretty evasive this past week and it's not been entirely fair to you."

Jo smiled, but it seemed forced, like the conversation. "I'd be lying if I said it was okay. To be honest, it's been a long week for me also. But trust me when I tell you I understand."

Lauren sighed. "I think there're still a couple of things I need to work through."

Jo turned at the sound of a cart passing outside the room. She glanced back at Lauren and motioned with her head toward the door. "It sounds like some lucky soul's having room service delivered. Have you had breakfast yet?"

"No, I was waiting to see if you wanted to have breakfast together downstairs." Lauren failed to conceal the insecurity in her tone.

"I'd love to. And besides," Jo mock-punched Lauren's shoulder, "if I'm to caddy for you today I'm going to need all the energy I can muster. And that means food." She headed back to the door.

Lauren reached out and lightly grabbed Jo's arm. "Before we head down, can I ask a favour?"

Jo turned, a curious expression on her face. "Sure. What?"

"Would it be too much to ask for a hug?"

Jo wrapped her arms around Lauren's waist and rested her head on her chest.

Lauren pulled Jo closer, basking in the warmth and security she felt radiating from her. Holding Jo, she thought about the discussion she'd had with Annie the previous day. *She was right. This was one thing I could never do with her, but how do I get back to where we started?* Jo's rumbling stomach broke the silence.

Lauren laughed as she disengaged herself from Jo's embrace. "I think we need to get you down to breakfast before you faint from lack of food."

"Sorry. Ben and I spent a lot of time yesterday scoping for the shoot. By the time we'd finished and showered for dinner the restaurant had closed and we had to make do with bar snacks instead."

Lauren picked up her hotel room key card and stowed it in her back pocket. She ushered Jo out the door and to the elevators. "Then we'd better get you a good breakfast." She pressed the elevator's down button. "I'd hate to have you stumble and break something out there." She stood aside when the elevator doors opened, and motioned for Jo to enter.

Lauren caught the look that flashed across Jo's features as she walked past. "What's on your mind?" She pressed the ground floor button and the doors closed.

Jo shrugged. "When you said 'break,' it reminded me of my mum. I spoke to her yesterday before I headed out here with Ben."

"Is her leg okay?"

"It's fine. It's her heart that's giving her trouble," Jo absently replied.

Lauren grabbed Jo's arm. "What are you doing here if she's having heart trouble? Your mum's more important than this tournament. Let me drive you to the airport."

"Hang on. I mean, her heart in the emotional sense, not the physical sense."

Lauren let go of Jo, relieved. "What's the problem?"

"You remember I told you about Andrew?"

"Yeah."

"It seems he wants to take things a little farther but Mum's holding back, as if she's afraid of the consequences."

Lauren nervously swallowed at the uncanny similarity between Jo's mother's situation and their own. "Is Andrew only looking for gratification?"

"I don't think so. Mum and I are a lot alike when it comes to making love with another person. We're only ever intimate with someone we love," she quietly replied, her eyes searching Lauren's face.

Lauren's eyes widened at Jo's comment, and her heartbeat seemed to speed up. She thought about what they'd started that evening in Jo's cabin a couple of weeks ago. *I'm sure if it hadn't been for me having to take those two guests to the top of Cradle Mountain the following morning, then we would've made love. Does she mean—* Lauren intently returned Jo's gaze, searching her face for any hint of innuendo. She found none and heart pounding, she moved toward Jo. Simultaneously, the elevator doors opened to a crowded foyer.

Jo smiled ruefully and shrugged when people began to fill the elevator for its return journey. "We'd better get out of this thing or we'll end up in our rooms again and we may *never* get to breakfast." She stepped around Lauren and out of the elevator.

Lauren stared at Jo's retreating back as she headed to the restaurant. *Am I reading too much into this?* Hopeful, she hurried after Jo.

WHILE THEY WAITED to be seated, Jo glanced around the restaurant, which was full of competitors and staff for the golf tournament. As she did she thought about Lauren's reaction to her words. While she hadn't really made a declaration, she'd made her feelings crystal clear. And, by the look on Lauren's face, Lauren had a reasonably firm idea of what those feelings were. *Mum, you'd be proud of me. I finally put it all out there. Well, sort of. I suppose now I just wait and see where things go from here.*

A red-faced and slightly flustered restaurant manager approached, interrupting Jo's reverie. "I'm sorry, ma'am, but we only have a table for four. If you like, you could wait for a table for two to open up."

"No, that's fine. From the crowd in here you look like you've got your work cut out for you." Jo followed him around a series of tables, to one situated by a window that afforded views down a fairway.

He pulled out a chair and motioned for Jo to sit. "Yes, it's been pretty hectic so far. We're only serving the buffet this morning, but I can assure you it'll more than satisfy your needs. Can I start you with coffee?"

"Thanks, that'd be great. Lauren?"

"None for me, thanks. You don't happen to have any herbal teas, do you?"

"Yes ma'am, we do. I'll have your server bring over a pot of water and our herbal tea box." he motioned to Jo. "And I'll get you a pot of coffee."

Jo nodded her thanks as she watched him walk back through the crowded restaurant. She returned her focus to Lauren. "I thought you drank coffee or black tea."

"I do. But they make me a bit twitchy when I drink it before a tournament. I have enough of my own nerves without adding artificial stimulants." She settled herself in her chair. "How did things go yesterday with Ben?"

"We got a lot done. In the afternoon there was a meeting of the camera crews and accredited media covering the tournament. I was surprised at how many major stations are covering the event." Jo smoothed her napkin over her lap. "In fact, there are still a few media people who are due to arrive this morning. Apparently, they're being briefed after the meeting of players and caddies. That's after breakfast."

Lauren shifted, a pained expression on her face.

"What's wrong?"

Lauren slightly stood and reached her hand under the table, a determined look upon her face. Her look was replaced with relief as she sat down and placed a small, worn ball on the table.

Jo frowned and reached across, picking it up. She rubbed her finger over the ball's raised surface. "I'm pretty familiar with golf but I don't think I've ever seen anything like this before. What is it?"

"It's a Haskell ball, the precursor to the golf ball of today." Lauren reached an open palm across the table and Jo dropped the ball into it. "The model was successfully used by a guy to win a golf major and it became the rage to use them. This one—" she tossed the ball into the air, closing her fingers around it as it came to rest in her palm

" — was a ball Marta gave to Annie. Not long after I met Annie I told her about my past as a golfer and she gave it to me. It was Marta's lucky ball and I normally keep it in Annie's hut."

Jo looked at the ball enclosed in Lauren's palm, and up at Lauren's face. She opened her mouth to respond just as the restaurant manager returned with a pot of coffee. She waited for him to finish pouring while a myriad of thoughts filled her mind, not the least of which was an overwhelming, jealous urge she was helpless to check. She nodded her thanks to the manager and he moved away.

Jo poured a splash of milk into her cup. She emptied a packet of sugar into her mug and stirred. "So did you see her?" Jo's focus remained on the small whirlpool she was creating in her cup.

"Yes."

Jo's shoulders slumped as she removed the spoon from the coffee cup, her measured actions masking how she really felt. Her resignation was interrupted by Lauren's soft touch on her arm.

"It was an interesting conversation." Lauren kept her hand on Jo's arm.

Jo gritted her teeth and raised her gaze to Lauren's face, a terse reply already forming on her lips. Lauren quickly removed her hand.

"Before you say anything, you should know she agrees with you."

"Agrees with me about what?" she hedged.

Lauren glanced around at the people seated at tables close to their own, seemingly relieved they were all engaged in their own conversations. She leant forward toward Jo. "She told me safety in love was not the way to live my life and she understands that now."

Jo's jaw dropped at the potential implication of Lauren's words. As she struggled to form a response, a man approached their table. "Lauren Wheatley?"

Lauren's focus shifted from Jo's face to the man now standing by the side of the table. She gasped and stood. "Nat!" She wrapped him in a hug then released him, stepping back to give him some room. "How are you? You haven't aged a bit." She looked at Jo. "Where are my manners? Jo Ashby, this is Nat Gilmartin. He used to caddy for me when I was on the circuit."

Jo stood and took Nat's outstretched hand. "I remember. It's nice to meet you. Are you caddying for anyone today?"

"Yes, actually. She's young and new to the circuit. She's every bit as impetuous," he nodded his head at Lauren and lowered his voice, "as this one was. But her game's nowhere near how Lauren's was."

Lauren blushed at Nat's praise. "Would you like to join us for breakfast?" Almost on cue, a woman passed by their table, her plate laden with bacon, eggs, and baked beans. Jo fought to conceal the longing look she gave the food.

Lauren reached across and lightly slapped Jo's stomach. "Maybe you should get some food into you before you faint."

Jo grinned. "That sounds like a good idea. Can I get you some juice?"

"Just a small glass of orange juice, please. We'll wait for you here," Lauren motioned for Nat to take a seat. She smiled as Jo successfully negotiated the room to the buffet area before she returned her gaze to Nat.

"How does Jo fit into all of this?" Nat settled himself into his chair.

"She's a journalist doing a story on me for a series she's been filming. She's also my caddy for the tournament."

"You mean you're actually playing in this?"

"As strange as it may seem, yes." Lauren nodded toward Jo. "And a lot of getting me here has to do with her. I give a golf clinic to kids in central Tasmania, near where I work, and the clinic's a little short of money. After a bit of convincing and wrangling for a sponsor's exemption, I'm here. Part of the deal is she caddies for me."

Nat looked across the room to where Jo filled a couple of glasses from a pitcher of juice. He returned his gaze to Lauren and raised his brow. "Is there anything else between you?"

Lauren leant back in her chair and sighed. "I don't know. I may have blown my chances already by giving too many mixed messages."

Nat chuckled. "If the way she looks at you is anything to go by, then I'd say you're still in the running."

Lauren shrugged. "Maybe. I hope so."

"It's more than maybe. I'd bank my reputation on it." Nat looked over his shoulder then back to Lauren. "Thanks for the breakfast invite, but I'd better check in with my young prodigy." They both stood and Nat extended his hand. "Good luck, Lauren. I don't know if you've been keeping up with your game. But if you're anywhere near as skilled as you used to be, then my rookie and the rest of the field have their work cut out for them."

Lauren smiled, embarrassed. "Thanks, Nat. I'll see you at the after-breakfast meeting."

JO SCANNED THE briefing room and waved to Ben as he crossed the room to where they stood, off to the centre of the rapidly-filling area.

Ben opened his arms and swaggered the remaining few steps toward them. "How are my two lovely ladies this morning?" He let out a wolf whistle. "Jo, what a lovely body-hugging pullover you're wearing. It should make for a great shoot."

Jo rolled her eyes. "We're fine, thank you. I thought you were going to join us at breakfast."

"You remember yesterday, when we had those issues about trying to frame a shot at the third tee?"

"Don't remind me. I've never seen you so anally retentive about a shot."

Ben huffed. "Criticise me now, woman, but you'll be thanking me later when you see the footage. I went out there again this morning and found just the spot. I had breakfast before I headed out."

The tapping of a microphone at the front of the room quieted those in attendance.

"Ladies and gentlemen, welcome to the Gracemere Wells Pro-Am Charity Golf Tournament. I'm Matthew Snell, the organiser for this event. I'd like to thank you all for making the time to be here today." He glanced across an audience filled with people from the current women's golf tour. "I'm sure you've read the tournament information we sent to you in your acceptance pack. However, let me just clarify a couple of things. This is a charity tournament and all players are required to complete the form listing their nominated charity and hand this in before teeing off today. This is also an officially sanctioned tournament, so points will count toward the women's tour, even if you don't get paid for your sterling efforts here."

He paused as a ripple of laughter moved through the room. "It's a two-day, stroke-play tournament of sixty players, competing in pairs. Given that there are only two rounds, the first cut will be at the end of the day, and will reduce the field to thirty players. If necessary, we'll have a sudden-death playoff of those players who are tied and borderline on the cut. You have another two hours before the first couple tees off. The pairs were picked randomly, and you'll find your tee time and opponent on the board by the left exit door at the front of the room here."

Jo's glance followed Matthew Snell's arm as he gestured and she nudged Lauren. "If you like, I'll check it out when the meeting's over, while you grab your clubs from your room," she whispered.

"Sounds like a plan. I'd like to loosen up just a little before I tee off. Can I get anything from your room?"

"I left my cap and sunglasses on my bed. Could you pick them up for me?"

Lauren nodded and they returned their attention to Snell, who cleared his throat at the low-level hubbub filling the room. "I can hear you're all eager to get away, but before we break, does anyone have any further questions for me?"

Jo was distantly aware of the rustle of people arriving in the rear of the room, but her immediate focus remained on getting to the player board to find out Lauren's opponent and tee time. Squinting in the direction of the board her blood suddenly ran cold at the voice that echoed from the rear entrance.

"I understand there's another media briefing for latecomers. Can you tell me where that'll be held?"

Jo whipped her head around and searched the area from where

the voice came. Her face drained of colour.
    "Oh my God. It's Lise."

Chapter
Fourteen

JO'S BREATH FROZE in her lungs as she stared at Lise, who hadn't yet seen Jo in the crowd. As Lise waited for an answer from the organiser, Jo's mind filled with a kaleidoscope of images of the last time she'd seen Lise. Recalling those final days, she fought to control the bile that rose in her throat.

"The morning briefing for media latecomers will be held in the Derwent room, next door to this one. Turn left on your way out the door," Matthew Snell replied.

Ben lightly grasped Jo's shoulders. "Hey, steady there mate, you'll end up tripping over someone."

Lauren's eyes followed Jo's gaze. "Who's Lise?"

Jo, fighting off her sudden light-headedness, eased herself into Ben's calming grip. "My ex."

Lise turned, as if she'd heard the conversation across the crowded room and, at the sight of Jo, a myriad of emotions crossed Lise's face. At first curious, then surprised, she seemed to stare at Jo, an expression of profound sorrow replacing her surprise.

Lauren looked first at Lise, then at Jo. "She's the news reporter you mentioned?"

"Yes." Jo rubbed her temples as Lauren's eyes narrowed to mere slits, her steely gaze focused on Lise, who was speaking to someone beside her.

Ben nodded his head in Lise's direction. "I suppose the bitch is back."

Jo fought to disguise her own emotions. "That's enough, Ben."

Lise glanced once more in her direction then turned, and headed left out the door to the latecomers' media briefing.

"I should've realised there was always a chance she'd be here, especially given the coverage the tournament's receiving."

Lauren's eyes tracked Lise's departure. "What happened between the two of you?"

Jo hesitated, her emotions in turmoil over Lise's sudden appearance.

Ben snorted. "She got a safer offer, that's what happened."

Lauren turned her attention to him. "Safer?"

Jo bit back a retort and instead changed the subject. "I'll go and check the board to see when we're teeing off."

Ben put a restraining hand on her shoulder. "Hold on, cheeky chops," he said gently, using his pet name for her. "I'll do that."

"Thanks." Lauren acknowledged him as she lightly touched Jo's arm. "Why don't we head upstairs and pick up the rest of the gear?"

Jo nodded absently as Lauren checked her watch and addressed Ben again. "We'll meet you in the main foyer in, say, twenty minutes?"

"Sounds like a plan. It'll give me enough time to pick up my camera gear after checking the board."

Ben made his way through the milling crowd and Lauren turned to Jo. "Let's go upstairs," she said, her tone comforting.

LAUREN GLARED AT the elevator doors as they closed, silently frustrated that she and Jo weren't the only occupants. From the shell-shocked expression on Jo's face, it was evident she was shaken at seeing her ex. Lauren fought an overwhelming desire to hold and protect her from the pain she was clearly feeling, opting to wait until they had some privacy.

The elevator doors opened and Lauren followed Jo silently down the hall. She slipped her hotel key card from her back pocket and opened the door then gently grasped Jo's elbow and led her inside, motioning at one of the room's plush chairs. Jo sat down, still quiet.

"Would you like a glass of water?"

Jo nodded, stiffly. "Thanks. There's a bottle by my bed."

Lauren retrieved the bottle, along with Jo's cap and sunglasses. She unscrewed the bottle's top and handed it to Jo before she took a seat on the foot of her bed, opposite her. "Do you want to talk about it?"

Jo took a sip of her water, her shoulders slumped. "There's not much to say." She wiped away the beads of water on her upper lip. "I thought the two of us would be together forever."

Lauren ran her finger across the logo on the front of Jo's cap before looking up at Jo. "Was there someone else?"

Jo bitterly chuckled. "In a manner of speaking. I thought everything was fine but obviously I was wrong. She was a news reporter for one of the big television stations on the mainland. We'd been together for about three years and I couldn't have been happier. I mean, we were very discreet because of her position in the media. But hell, we'd even talked about a commitment ceremony and having kids. And then things changed." Jo stared at the bottle. "I had a shoot at Franz Josef glacier in New Zealand and was gone for a week. When I left, everything was as it had always been. I was returning on a

Sunday, and Lise had even planned a dinner for the two of us." Jo took another sip of water, her eyes distant. "I came home around five-thirty and she wasn't there, so I figured she was getting groceries. After I unpacked I grabbed a beer and turned on the evening news. I almost choked at the lead story. It was an announcement that one of the channel's news reporters had married the station's primetime news anchor. There was Lise, in all her virginal white glory, smiling at the cameras as she hung on his arm. They interviewed her and she said they'd been secretly planning it for months."

Lauren reached out and reassuringly stroked Jo's arm, sadness and anger welling in her throat. "I can't begin to imagine how you felt."

"I felt betrayed and sick. I barely made it to the bathroom before I brought up my lunch and a good part of my breakfast. That night I gathered my gear into my bags and walked out, leaving everything else behind."

"I'm so sorry you were hurt like that." *You bitch, Lise. What I wouldn't give to have two minutes alone in a dark room with you right now.* Lauren again fought to mask her emotions. "I can't begin to imagine how awful that must have been for you, having to leave like you did."

"I wanted nothing that would remind me of her. The whole house was full of things we'd bought together." Jo cleared her throat and took another sip of water.

"Did you see her after that day?"

Jo shook her head. "No. And she didn't even call to try and explain what happened, nor was I was in any state of mind to call her to find out what went wrong. But over the years I've seen her every now and then on the evening news. She's still a news reporter and still married to that man. Funny thing is, she always wanted to be a news anchor. I suppose she never managed to convince management she was anchor material. Since the break-up, I've never seen her close up. Until this morning. I really didn't think I'd be affected the way I was," she finished, sadness in her voice.

Anxiety rippled through Lauren's heart. "You must have loved her deeply."

"Yes. Completely." Jo screwed the cap back on the now-empty water bottle. "It was one of the happiest times of my life. I mean, yes, the relationship was risky because of her high media profile but we always worked around it. Obviously, it wasn't enough for her, and she opted for the safe alternative."

Lauren softly bit her bottom lip, uncertain how to deal with Jo's past but knowing she must. "I don't know how anyone could bale for something safer, like Lise did." She blinked at the almost accusing, yet inscrutable look on Jo's face and something dawned on her. She leant toward Jo. "Is that what you think I was doing with Annie? Playing it safe?"

Jo took Lauren's hand. "Not entirely. Obviously, the safe issue was a subconscious knee-jerk response to *my* previous relationship, not yours. I never really realized it until now."

Lauren softly ran her fingers over Jo's hand. "You must have looked for it in your partners since the break-up with Lise."

Jo looked at their hands. "There hasn't been anyone since then. I've had a few liaisons, but no one I've wanted to give my heart to." She raised her eyes to Lauren's face. "Until now."

Lauren's anxiety dissipated like leaves in a wind. She closed the distance between them, lightly touching her lips to Jo's. Warmth filled her, racing out to her extremities as her heart beat in a staccato rhythm. She deepened the kiss, trying to convey feelings she hadn't yet been able put into words, tenderly stroking the back of Jo's neck before she reluctantly pulled away.

"We'd better get downstairs," she whispered hoarsely, "but trust me when I say we'll definitely pick this up later."

Jo took her cap from Lauren and placed it on her head. "I'd like that."

Lauren stood and pulled Jo to her feet as well. "Are you okay?"

Jo looked down at her watch and glanced around the room, her thoughts obviously elsewhere. "We should get going." Jo turned to the door.

Lauren reached out, gently halting Jo's progress. "Hey. Are you okay?"

Jo managed a wan smile and squeezed Lauren's fingers. "I'm fine. Just a little shaken, but fine. We'd better head down or Ben will be wondering where we've gotten to." She released Lauren's hand and opened the door.

Lauren grabbed her clubs, and followed Jo out of the room and to the elevators. She studied Jo's back, feeling a wave of uncertainty. *At the moment, Ben's worries are the least of my concerns.*

JO SMILED WHEN she caught sight of Ben nervously checking his watch while he stood on the opposite side of the foyer from the elevators. She and Lauren wove their way through the group, finally reaching his side.

"There you are," he said, obviously relieved. "I was wondering if you were ever going to make it down."

Lauren lowered her bag and looked at her watch. "We're only a couple of minutes late. What time do I tee off?"

"You're about three-quarters of the way through the field and you tee off at eleven-thirty." He pulled out a small notepad and flipped through the pages. "You're playing with Jackie Kim."

Lauren shrugged and smiled. "I can't say I've ever heard of her, but it's not surprising."

"One of the other caddies said she's a young player, new to the tour. She's from Korea."

"Oh, well that makes sense. There's a stable of young Korean players who are on the circuit. Korea's obviously investing good money toward the future of golf."

Jo scanned the foyer, filled with players and their caddies. "I expect we'll get to see how good she is in a couple of hours." She turned to Lauren. "What do you want to do now?"

"I'd like to do some driving and putting practice before we start."

Jo picked up Lauren's golf bag. "Lead the way." She turned to Ben. "What are your plans?"

Ben picked up his camera, which he'd set on the floor by his side. "If it's not too obtrusive, I'd like to get some shots of Lauren when she's practicing, followed by a quick interview afterward."

"Sure," Lauren consented. "It shouldn't be a problem. But, you'll be restricted to the media area, behind the ropes of the driving range. It's as much a safety measure as it is a courtesy to other players who are warming up."

"No problem. Once I've finished with you guys I'll head out on to the course," Ben replied.

Lauren turned to Jo. "You okay carrying the bag?"

Jo shifted her body, allowing the strap to rest on a meatier part of her shoulder. "Yes. Just like last time I carried this brick. And, besides, there's no time like the present."

The ghost of a smile hovered on Lauren's lips. She straightened the cap on Jo's head, her fingers trailing down Jo's cheek when she finished her task. "There certainly isn't. Let's get going."

JO STOOD WATCHING as the group before them teed off. She then followed Lauren into the area reserved for introductions to the crowd. Jo lowered her shoulders and moved her head in a slow circle, attempting to loosen the knot forming in her shoulder muscles.

Lauren brushed Jo's lower back with her fingers. "How are you doing?"

Jo stopped and smiled. "I'm fine. Just getting rid of some nervous tension. I can't believe how calm you are."

Lauren smiled back and shrugged, nonchalant. "I'm certainly not as nervous as I used to be but I think it's got more to do with the fact there's no great pressure on me to perform today. Don't get me wrong. I'll be over the moon if I can get some money for the kids. But it's not the same as when you're competing to either gain or retain your exempt status on the tour."

"What does that mean?"

Lauren pulled her arm across the front of her body and parallel to the ground, in turn stretching her muscles. "It's a bit too convoluted to explain without going into detail. Generally, if you have exempt status, you have immediate entry into certain major tournaments." She repeated the same action with the other arm. "Non-exempt is like second on the rung. I can go over it with you later if you like."

"Okay, but I think I get the idea." Jo paused when the announcer's voice introduced the first golfer from the group in front of them then she continued, "How do you feel about teeing-off three-quarters of the way through the field?"

"Some people are suspicious about where they start in a tournament, but it's never really bothered me. It doesn't really matter where or when you start. It's how you finish that counts."

Lauren winked at her and they both fell silent as the first woman to be introduced went into her routine before addressing the ball on the tee. Jo scanned the throng of media positioned on the opposite side of the tee to where she and Lauren currently stood. Her gaze fell on Lise, who was standing in the section reserved for media, a confused expression on her face.

Lauren gently nudged her. "I'll bet she's wondering why you're carrying a bag," she whispered.

"I've no doubt," Jo softly replied. Though it was odd to see Lise in these circumstances, Jo decided she'd much rather be on the fairway with Lauren than in the crowd with Lise.

"She looks like she could blow away in the wind," Lauren commented.

Jo's eyes trailed Lise's body. Her chiseled cheekbones were offset by closely cropped blond hair, cut in an androgynous, pixie-like bob. "I never knew what it was about her. She could eat a horse and still look like an advance party for a famine. She hasn't changed much," Jo said. "Physically, at least."

The soft whack of a ball and the cheers from the crowd signaled a solid shot. The announcer introduced the second player.

"She obviously knows you're here. How are you going to handle it?"

Jo looked down to Lauren's golf bag and unzipped and unclipped the top cover, stowing it in one of the bag's many pockets. "I'll handle it when the time comes. Are you ready?" she queried, deflecting any further conversation about Lise.

"As ready as I'll ever be." Lauren reached into her pocket, pulled out the ancient Haskell ball, and tossed it to Jo.

Jo caught it and rubbed the dimpled surface. "You carry it with you?"

"Yep, of course I do. It's Marta's lucky ball, so hopefully it'll mean good luck for me." Lauren reached into a side pocket on the bag and pulled out a modern variant of the Haskell.

Jo chuckled. "And here I was, thinking you didn't rely on suspicions and charms to get you through the tournament."

"It can't do any harm, can it?" Lauren arched an eyebrow and smiled.

Jo bumped her with her hip. "Of course it won't, you big brave golfer, you."

They quieted when Lauren's partner for the round was introduced to the crowd. Jo moved to Lauren's side, her lips close to Lauren's ear. "She seems like a good kid. I tried to talk to her earlier but she doesn't seem to speak much English."

Jackie Kim hit the ball squarely, laying it up a distance along the middle of the fairway.

"She doesn't have to," Lauren said wryly. "She can let the clubs do the talking for her." She ran a hand through her hair and glanced at Jo. "Here goes nothing."

Jo reassuringly patted her shoulder. "You'll be fine."

"Ladies and Gentlemen, playing with Miss Kim today, with a sponsor's exemption, is Miss Lauren Wheatley."

Jo shouldered the bag and followed Lauren through on to the first tee. The clapping greeting their entrance was more than mere polite recognition of the player next to tee off. This was confirmed when Jo caught the snippets of conversation around the edge of the tee.

"Lauren Wheatley. I'm sure I've heard her name before."

"She was famous on the tour about ten years ago and then dropped out of sight. No one quite knows why."

After acknowledging the crowd Lauren looked at Jo expectantly, seemingly oblivious to the whispers around her. Jo pulled Lauren's driver from the bag, removed the head cover, and offered it to her. Lauren smiled and nodded her thanks. Gathering herself, she headed on to the tee proper.

The crowd fell silent as the field marshals surrounding the tee held up their "quiet" signs.

While Lauren went through her pre-shot routine, Jo glanced at the scorecard and the small diagram of the first hole. It was a par four, calling for a long tee shot to the left side of the fairway, followed by a short iron shot onto the green. A large bunker dominated the right side of the fairway. *Stay left, Lauren. Those look to be in play given the distance you hit the ball.*

She looked up in time to see Lauren address the ball and set herself up for the drive. Lauren took one final look down the fairway and waggled the head of the club, as if to relax. She drew the driver back in a smooth, athletic motion until the head of the club and shaft were parallel and horizontal to the ground. To Jo it seemed as if for just a fraction of a second Lauren paused, mid-motion, before she brought the club down and connected with the ball, the impact resulting in a whack that signaled a clean hit off the tee. Lauren finally looked up and acknowledged the appreciative applause from the crowd.

Jo took the driver and stowed it in the bag. "Great shot," she said, smiling proudly. "Right where you want to be for your next shot to the green."

Lauren loosened the back of her golfing glove and walked down the steep embankment to the fairway. "Thanks, but there're a few more to go yet."

LAUREN WIPED THE head of her seven iron off with her hand then used a tee to remove dirt from the grooves on its face.

Jo held out her hand. "Shouldn't I be doing that?"

Lauren looked up, the remnants of concentration on her face. "Sure, if you really want to." She handed the club over. "It does help keep me focused, though, when there's a delay in play."

Jo unclipped a towel from the side of the golf bag, and used the small brush stitched onto one of the towel's corners to clean the club face. "What do you think the hold-up is?"

Lauren looked down the fairway, where players were still in the process of putting out on the green and shrugged. "It could be anything. The players in front could've been slow, or one of the two up there may have muffed a shot. I mean, this looks like a simple hole on paper, but it's fairly tricky."

Jo handed the club back. "In what way?"

"The fairway's pretty narrow and the three bunkers over there—" Lauren pointed to the right side of the fairway—"are very much in play if you don't stay just left of centre."

"Which we did, but surely even a fairway bunker wouldn't hold them up too much, would it?" Jo clipped the towel back onto the bag.

"Not if they've played this course before. The trickiest part on this hole is the green."

As if confirming Lauren's observation, a ball hit by one of the other players rolled off the green and out of sight. "It looks like it slopes a bit," Jo said dubiously.

Lauren grinned. "That's an understatement. If there was a green that could break you on this course, it's this one. Apart from being very narrow, the left and right approaches slope sharply. Miss the hole and your ball may well roll right off."

"So the intent is to hit a shot to the rear of the green and putt from there?"

"If only. You can't do that, either. You can't see it from here, but there's the mother of all deep bunkers back there, just waiting for an unsuspecting golfer. The aim is to lay up and try and chip the ball on to the front of the green."

Jo reached into one of the bag's side pockets and pulled out a snack bar. "Hence the use of your seven iron." She tore the top off the wrapper, took a bite, and offered the bar to Lauren.

"No, thanks. And yes, that's what I'm hoping to do."

As play on the green dragged on, Lauren used the opportunity to practice the swing she'd eventually make.

Bored with the wait, Jo checked the fairway parallel to their own. Her gaze fell on an electronic score board, positioned near the green of the adjoining fairway. She removed her sunglasses and squinted, trying to make out the names on the board. She stared, amazed and excited when she saw Lauren's name, with a score of three under next to her name. "She's tied for the lead with four other players," she softly uttered.

Jo looked back to where Lauren was rehearsing, oblivious to the news on the leader board. She checked the board again, but the list had spooled to another group of player's names.

"It looks like play's cleared up ahead." Lauren approached her ball.

Jo moved the bag out of the way. "Now I get to see you put your theory into practice."

Lauren grinned and hefted her club in preparation for her address. Jo stood out of Lauren's line of sight as she went through the routine she'd gone through over the past hour. Just as she began her follow-through, a cell phone rang, it's warbling breaking the early afternoon silence. Too late to check her swing, Lauren shanked the ball to the right.

"If wishing could make it so," she said, sighing, as she handed her club back to Jo and raised a warning finger in the direction of the sound.

In spite of a couple of tough spots, Lauren maintained a good score. As they walked down the eighteenth fairway, Lauren acknowledged the appreciative crowd while making her way to the final green. Jo consulted her scorecard. "You're four under. Not a bad round for someone who doesn't play the tour any more," she teased.

Lauren waved at an enthusiastic group of women. "Thanks. Everything just seemed to click today."

"If you birdie this one you'll be five under."

Lauren grinned. "It's good to see your ability to add and subtract hasn't been affected by the weight of my bag." She moved just in time to dodge a swat from Jo. "Seriously though, I've got a long putt that could be tricky, especially if I miss the hole. I'd be happy if I two-putt this one."

Jo looked down the fairway at the advertising that filled the electronic score board. Though she'd seen the leader board on the front nine, she hadn't seen another list of the leading players since then, despite her best efforts. *Surely four under would have to put her in a reasonable position to at least not miss the cut?*

Lauren glanced at Jo. "What are you looking for?"

"I'm trying to make out the leader board at the eighteenth hole.

Do you ever look at them when you're playing?" She removed her sunglasses and tried to get a better view of the screen.

"Uh, no. I make a habit of *not* looking at them when I'm playing. And once I'm finished, I don't need to look. The reporters who used to interview me after the end of the day's play were always keen to let me know where I finished in the field, good or bad." Lauren removed her golf glove and handed it to Jo.

Jo took it and followed Lauren around to the edge of the left side of the green, where Lauren's ball lay. She pulled out the putter, handed it to Lauren, and crouched behind her to get a read on the green between Lauren's ball and the hole. "It's long but it looks pretty straight-forward."

Lauren nodded, thoughtfully. "I think I'll putt a little to the left and see whether I can make the birdie."

As they stood, Jo squeezed Lauren's shoulder. "Good luck. Not that you need it though."

Lauren's opponent's ball was farther away, so she made the first putt. Lauren waited for Jackie Kim to complete her shot before she crouched down to get one final read on the green.

Jo's eyes scanned the leader board and her face broke into a bigger smile. *She's still co-leader. I can't wait to tell her.* She glanced to where Lauren was setting up for her shot before returning her focus back to the leader board. As she stared at the screen, it spooled to the next list of players. *Two more players at four under. So a total of seven all up.* She read the name of the final player in the group of seven leaders and failed to hide a gasp just as Lauren connected with the ball.

Lauren looked up clearly broadcasting her annoyance. "Are you all right?"

Jo tore her eyes away from the screen to where Lauren's ball had stopped, less than a foot away from the hole. "Oh crap. I'm sorry. I lost my concentration and now it looks like I've blown your attempt at a birdie."

Lauren glanced at where the ball lay tantalisingly close to the hole then back at Jo. "Got carried away looking at the leader screen, did we," she said, a teasing grin on her face.

"I'm sorry. I did," Jo replied, still shaken by what she'd seen there.

"Hey, it's okay. It's only a game. Besides, it's why I don't look at the damned thing. The one time I did I spent the rest of the day wondering where I was in the field and who I was up against the in the following round." As Jackie Kim holed her putt, Lauren moved to her own ball.

"It's a good thing you didn't look at it today, then," Jo muttered as she followed Lauren across the green. *If you were preoccupied by where you were in the field, then I guarantee you'd be even more preoccupied if you knew Patricia Morgan was a co-leader.* Jo removed her cap and vigorously scratched her head. *Do I tell her or not? Maybe once we get back to the room.*

Lauren bent and retrieved the ball from the cup. She straightened and acknowledged the applause from the crowd, tossing the ball to the group of women who had followed her throughout the day.

Jo took the putter and motioned with her head at the women. "Looks like you've got yourself a fan club."

Lauren chuckled and shrugged. "God knows why." She walked over to Jackie Kim and shook her hand, congratulating her on her day's play.

Jo shook Jackie's caddie's hand as Jackie spoke, in halting English, with Lauren.

"She's a damned good player," Jackie's caddie said, shaking Jo's hand and motioning to Lauren.

Jo graciously acknowledged his praise. "Pretty good, considering she doesn't play on the tour anymore."

The caddie shook his head in disbelief. "You've got to be joking. She's a co-leader for the round today and she doesn't play regularly? Pity the lot of us if she did." He picked up his golf bag and headed over to Kim.

Lauren gave Jo a small hug. "Thanks for your help today. It was fun to have you out there."

Jo picked up the golf bag and smiled. "I was happy to be here," she said, meaning it. As they moved off the green, Jo took a deep breath. "But there's something you might want to know."

"Hold that thought. I've got to give my card to the marshal." Lauren made one final notation on her card. "I've got par for the last hole, leaving me at four under. Is that what you've got?"

Jo pulled out her copy and looked it over. "Yep."

Lauren signed off. "Great. Hang on and I'll hand this over." She headed off toward the marshal and, a few minutes later, was back at Jo's side.

"What was it you wanted to say earlier?" she asked as they moved through the tunnel under the stands surrounding the eighteenth green.

"I was looking at the leader board when you were putting and —" Jo's words were cut short at Lauren's soft curse.

"Damn, if there's one thing I hate most about playing golf it's the after-round interviews. Hopefully they won't take too long."

Jo followed Lauren as she moved along the bank of reporters, spending a few minutes with each one, politely answering the questions they had for her. They'd almost managed to negotiate the long line when a voice from the past brought a bitter taste to her mouth.

"Excuse me, Miss Wheatley, could I have a few words, please?"

Jo watched Lauren wheel, the anger on her face proof she'd

remembered the sound of Lise's voice from earlier that day. Jo moved out of the way so she was close enough to witness the interview, yet be out of camera range.

Lauren barely managed to school her features, recognising the green light on top of the camera next to Lise as the standard signal she was being recorded. "Yes?" She made no effort to hide the contempt in her voice.

"I'm Lise Cowley with the *Evening Hour* news. Congratulations on your play today. You must be pleased at finishing as a co-leader."

Lauren spared a glance at Jo and then her steely gaze returned to Lise. "Yes, I am. Thank you."

Lise frowned, seemingly flustered by Lauren's demeanor. Lise covered her nervousness by looking down at her notes. "You haven't played for a number of years. Can I ask what brings you here today, for this tournament?"

As Lauren opened her mouth to answer, the voices of two young children cut through the tense air surrounding the interview.

"Miss Wheatley," squealed Adam and Karrie Hanson as they climbed under the rope barriers and ran to her side, their mother struggling to follow them.

Lauren held up her hand to the harried marshal who was closing in on the trespassing group. "It's okay, I know them." He nodded and moved away.

"Hi, Lauren," Pam Hanson managed between puffs of breath. "I'm sorry I couldn't keep a tight rein on these two. Once they saw you they were off."

Lauren smiled. "No worries," she reached down and ruffled Adam's hair. "It's good to see you all." Lauren turned back to Lise.

"These two are why I'm here today, and many more just like them. We have a wealth of sporting talent in this country. But unless you play a major code, and golf isn't in that league, then it's a struggle to make ends meet." Lauren reached down and touched Adam's shoulder. "This young man is fourteen, but he already has a handicap of eight. His sister—" Lauren lightly touched Karrie's shoulder—"is thirteen and plays off a handicap of five. Despite their ability and others like them, most of them are playing with second-hand clubs, often too big for them. Anything I gain out of my play this weekend will be going straight to kids like these."

Pam touched the shoulders of her children and then looked across at Lauren. "I'd better get these two out of your way, but..." she lowered her voice, "thanks for the free advertising."

Lauren smiled. "No problem." As the family walked away Lauren turned back to Lise.

"Thank you for your time, Miss Wheatley." Lise turned to her cameraman. "That's a wrap. Take five and I'll catch you at the beverage tent." The cameraman walked away and Lise returned her gaze to Lauren. "Where did you find your caddie?"

"She's doing an article on me and agreed to caddy for me," Lauren replied, her tone like ice as anger flashed in her eyes.

"Can I interview her?" Lise nodded to where Jo stood. "It'd present a different angle to the story."

Jo's mouth was barely open when Lauren answered for her. "No, you can't. There's work she needs to finish as my caddie. Excuse me." Lauren turned and walked away. "Come on, Jo," she called over her shoulder.

Jo's face reddened at Lauren's reaction to Lise's request. She spared a glance in Lise's direction and then hurried after a fast-retreating Lauren. Finally managing to catch her on the quiet path leading from the course to the hotel, Jo grasped Lauren's forearm, trying to make her stop. "What was that about? Don't you think I could've answered for myself?"

The muscles in Lauren's jaw clenched then unclenched. "I didn't want her to hurt you any more than she already has."

Jo reached up and gently placed her fingers against Lauren's lips. "I know, but don't you think I can take care of myself?"

Lauren's face went blank as she stepped away from Jo's soft touch. She reached around and picked up her golf bag where Jo had propped it against a tree trunk. "I'm going to the driving range."

Jo studied her, frustration wrapping itself around her guts. "Do you want me to come along?"

"No, I'll be fine by myself." Lauren hefted the bag to her shoulder.

Jo searched Lauren's face, trying to discern a reason for Lauren's sudden dismissal. "I've a meeting with Ben in a little while," she said.

"I'm going for a massage after practice. I'll catch up with you at the buffet tonight."

Jo clenched her jaw, fighting to keep her frustration and irritation at Lauren's actions in check. "Fine. I'll see you there." She stepped around Lauren and continued toward the hotel, clasping and unclasping her fingers as she went in an effort to control her feelings. *Damn. I forgot to tell her about Patricia Morgan.* Jo turned but the path was empty, Lauren and her golf bag already gone.

JO SNORTED AT the "know it all" look on Ben's face. "Okay, so you were right."

Ben smugly smiled. "I told you the shot was worth the effort I put into it." He pressed the replay button and Lauren's form once again filled the screen.

Jo watched it in slow motion, as Lauren connected with the ball, a vista of the broad blue Derwent River serving as a fitting backdrop. Despite this afternoon's scene, Jo's heart skipped a beat at Lauren's athletic grace and beauty. *Now, Lauren, if I can only counter your bloody jealous streak.*

"Penny for your thoughts," Ben hit the stop button on the mobile editing suite he'd borrowed from one of the local networks.

"I was just thinking about Lauren."

"How are things going?" Ben retrieved the tape from the machine and stowed it in its cover.

Jo scratched the side of her head. "It's got its ups and downs."

"Do you want to talk about it?"

Jo exhaled. "I'm in love with her, but this morning's events threw me for a loop. Lise was the last person I expected to see here. Then this afternoon, when we were leaving the course, Lise interviewed Lauren and it went downhill from there."

Ben slapped his leg. "Damn, don't tell me I missed a fight between the two of them? My money would be on Lauren. Especially with a bag of blunt objects to back her up."

Jo laughed at Ben's efforts to lighten the moment. "No, it wasn't like that. She was just incredibly jealous. Then when I tried to talk to her about it, it was as if I was at fault. I tell you there're times when I don't know what she feels for me. I can't help but wonder if it's worth the pain and effort."

Ben covered Jo's hand with his own. "Don't run from this one. She's a keeper, Lauren is, even if it does take her a while to tell you she loves you. She does, you know. She's just taking her time about saying anything."

Jo looked around the confines of the small van then back at Ben, trying to change the subject. "So what are you doing tonight?"

Ben rolled his eyes. "Okay, I can take a hint. Keep out of it. I'm going to grab a quick bite to eat and then finish today's editing. What about you?"

"I've got the function tonight, but I still need to call Ros." Jo shook her head. "There are five voice messages from her on my cell." She stood. "I'd better go and try to ring her before she sends the police out after me."

"I'll leave you to it. Catch you later," Ben popped another tape into the editing machine.

Jo stepped out of the van and looked at the late afternoon sky. The orange glow of the slowly setting sun spread across the fairways, highlighting the kangaroos grazing on the lush carpet of green. Jo sighed heavily, thinking about Lise, Lauren, and the distance between them all. *What ever happened to the simple girl meets girl and they ride off into the sunset together, without all the crap in between?* Her gaze lingered on the kangaroos for a few moments longer then she turned, and walked to the hotel.

Chapter
Fifteen

LAUREN DEPOSITED HER clubs and bag just inside the entrance to her room. "Those damned things never seem to get any lighter," she grumbled as she tossed her cap across the bed. It landed on the chair where Jo had sat earlier that morning.

She kicked off her shoes and stripped off her sweat-soaked shirt, trying to figure out what she was feeling. *What's wrong with you, Wheatley? She wasn't expecting her ex to be here, and she doesn't seem to be interested in her anymore, so why the green-eyed monster act? After all, you're the one she was kissing this morning, not Lise.*

Lauren padded to the door separating their rooms. She pressed her ear to it and lightly knocked. No answer. *She must still be at the meeting with Ben.*

Her shoulders slumped and she wandered to the bar fridge. After looking at her choices, she pulled out a bottle of water. As she did so, she bent her head and sniffed. "Better have a shower before I head out to my massage. God only knows I wouldn't want to touch a body that smelled like *this*." She took a swig of the water, stripped off the rest of her clothes, and headed for the shower, anxious about Jo and feeling badly about how she'd acted earlier. *Well, hopefully I'll be able to make it right.*

LAUREN EXITED THE elevator into the foyer, wearing a loose-fitting t-shirt and shorts, in preparation for her massage. She headed down the hallway toward the hotel's day spa, passing the room where the golfers and caddies had met earlier.

She slowed and glanced in. Matthew Snell was busy putting something on the same board that had listed pairings for the day's play.

Curiosity got the better of her and she walked over to him. He was too preoccupied with the board in front of him and didn't look up.

"Are those the pairings for tomorrow?"

He jumped, dropping the sheet in his hand. He picked it up and turned to Lauren. "I'm sorry. I didn't hear you come in." He scrutinized her face. "It's Miss Wheatley, isn't it?"

Lauren held out her hand. "Yes, it is."

Matthew took her hand. "It's a pleasure to finally meet you. I was surprised when I read your name on the list, after so many years of being off the tour."

Lauren shrugged, smiling. "I was lucky to get a sponsor's exemption. I didn't think I'd be here myself."

He chuckled. "I expect I have to add my congratulations as well. You're one of seven players tied for the lead."

Lauren craned her neck to see the list he'd just posted. "*Are* they the pairings?"

"No, just the final field." He finished pinning a second sheet of paper onto the board. "The pairings will be drawn at the function tonight and posted here afterward. The start times will also—" he was interrupted by the walkie talkie on his hip.

Lauren stepped away to afford him some privacy, though she caught snippets of his conversation as she absently scanned the room.

He finished and returned the radio to his belt. "I'm sorry, but it seems there's a minor drama with the seating arrangements for tonight. If you'll excuse me." He was already heading for the door as Lauren started to reply. She closed her mouth, and instead walked to the board listing the final field. Scanning the group, her eyes came to rest on one name among the list of seven leaders and it was as if someone had punched her in the gut. A sick feeling filled her stomach, and she closed her eyes and took a deep breath, trying to calm herself. Despite her best efforts, nothing would change the name that was indelibly burned into the inside of her eyelids. *Pat. Damn it, what the hell are you doing here?* She opened her eyes and released a long, shuddering breath and scanned the room, almost expecting her past to materialise, right then, in front of her. "Can this day get any worse?" she muttered to the empty room. She headed to the door and her massage. Though it couldn't remove Pat from the tournament, it might help alleviate the tension that now occupied every part of her being.

JO SCANNED THE faces in the crowded function room, in search of Lauren. Disappointment gripped her when she didn't find her. Lauren's actions and the discussion they'd shared on the path had left her strangely hollow. She felt a hand on her elbow and turned.

"Hi, Jo. I see Lauren lived up to her old abilities today, didn't she?"

"Oh, hi, Nat. Definitely, though I think she was as surprised as anybody. And with seven leaders, it makes for an interesting day of golf tomorrow." Jo continued inspecting the room.

"I don't think Lauren's arrived yet," Nat said. "I ran into her near the day spa a short time ago. She said she might be late." He took a sip from his glass and studied Jo, as if measuring his next comments.

"Do you recognise any of the names of the seven leaders, other than Lauren's?"

Jo returned Nat's gaze. *I know you know about Lauren and Pat, but what did Lauren say this morning about us?* "If you're asking if I know Patricia Morgan as a golfer, I don't. But Lauren's told me enough about her for me to know what this might mean." She glanced at the carpet then back at him. "To tell you the truth, I don't know if Lauren knows Pat's playing yet."

Nat patted Jo's arm. "What happened was a long time ago. As much pain as it caused Lauren, I'm sure she's managed to get over it by now."

Jo tried to swallow the lump in her throat. *If you only knew the truth.* "Maybe. I wonder what's — " she halted mid-sentence at the loud laughter emanating from a group seated a couple of tables away. Jo turned and watched Pat Morgan hold court over a group of younger golfers, her heavy British accent sounding like fingernails on a chalkboard to Jo's ears. For a moment Pat's cobalt eyes met hers and Pat raised her eyebrows, as if in invitation, her fingers toying with her short, ebony hair. Jo's years of journalism kicked in and she reined in an overwhelming desire to sneer at her and, instead, she turned back to Nat. "I think I'll go and get a drink at the bar and check in a little later to see if Lauren's arrived."

Nat gestured at Pat's group. "Don't worry about her. She doesn't pose a threat to Lauren on or *off* the field. You head to the bar. If I see Lauren, I'll let her know where you are."

Jo thanked him and left the rowdy function room. Walking across the foyer to the hotel's tavern, her thoughts strayed to the emphasis Nat had placed on the word 'off'. *That bitch has unknowingly affected Lauren for the past ten years. I can't see that influence stopping any time soon.* She walked across the room to the Tasmanian Myrtle-paneled bar and hitched one of her feet on the brass rail running down its length.

"What can I get you?" The server placed a bowl of rice crackers in front of her.

Jo scrutinised the ice-filled bowl of sparkling wines on the corner of the bar. "A glass of sparkling, please."

He pulled a glass flute from the rack over his head. "Do you have a preference?"

"Tasmanian sparkling brut, if there's any."

He tilted the glass in her direction and winked. "I know just the one."

While the barman busied himself with his task, Jo idly looked around the room, dotted with booths affording an even greater degree of privacy in the already subtly lit surroundings. Her attention settled on a woman sitting by herself, her hands cradling her head.

Jo paid for her drink and approached the lone woman. "I thought you'd be at the function by now."

Lise raised her head, her slack features indicating that she'd obviously been in the bar a while. Lise leant out of the booth, made an exaggerated, but wobbly inspection of the room, and then leant back against the booth's padding. "You can talk for yourself, now? I thought your golfer friend did all the talking for you. Where is she, then?"

Jo refused to rise to Lise's obvious baiting. "Can I sit down?"

Lise raised her drink to her lips. "It's a free world."

Jo settled herself opposite Lise and watched her drain one of three full drinks in front of her. A pervading smell of strong grain alcohol wafted from Lise's direction.

"Where is she?" Lise slurred, placing the empty low-ball on the table in front of her.

"Busy. She's a little preoccupied at the moment. She hasn't played in years and I think it's been a big day for her." Jo knew there were elements of honesty in what she'd said, even if it wasn't the absolute truth about what had happened between them after the finish of the day's play.

Lise snorted. "She treated you like baggage this afternoon. I've seen people treat their dogs in a better manner than she did you."

Jo took a sip from her wine in an attempt to stave off her rising anger. She placed her flute on the table and gazed unwaveringly at Lise. "It's not like that. Not at all."

Lise laughed disdainfully, a harsh sound that stopped as quickly as it started. "It was *exactly* like that." She jabbed her finger at Jo. "Like you were something she could easily discard, without too much thought."

Her control finally broken, Jo leant across the table into Lise's personal space. "And you'd know all about discarding people, *wouldn't* you, given the bloody practice you've had," she clearly enunciated each word. "Coming from the likes of you, it's a damned hypocritical statement."

Lise reached for one of the two full glasses on the table in front of her and took a long gulp of the amber-coloured liquid. "For Christ's sake. It was for the best, and you know it."

Jo's face flushed with anger. "Whose best? Because it certainly wasn't mine!" She shook her head in disgust. "Christ Lise, we had three years together. Then out of the blue you were gone, with no warning. The morning I left for New Zealand we were talking about commitment ceremonies. Imagine my surprise when I came home to find you'd moved on without me, and with your bloody male anchor for God's sake! Damn it, I thought we were happy together. Obviously, I was wrong."

Silence fell over the booth as Jo fought to regain control of her emotions. She glared across at Lise, whose face was blank as she took yet another sip of her drink.

"You've held that in for way too long, haven't you?" Lise's finger trailed through the small pool of water on the table created by the condensation from her drinks.

Jo reached across and halted Lise's hand. "Yes I have, but I'd have given anything to be able to speak with you about your decision all those years ago. If there was one thing we were always good at, it was talking to each other."

Lise stared at her, then lowered her gaze to the table. "It was the biggest mistake I ever made," she said softly.

Offended, Jo yanked her hand back. "I don't need to hear any more of this."

Lise grabbed Jo's arm. "No. I should've never married him. *That's* the mistake I made. You were *never* a mistake."

Jo took a deep breath and settled back down in the booth. "Then why did you do it?"

"It was my fault. I was after something I should've known I'd never get." Lise took a large gulp from her second drink, and shook her head as the contents of the hard alcohol settled inside her. "The network's performance against the other networks was sagging and they were hoping for something that would kick-start their ratings again. They offered me a co-anchor position if I agreed to marry the anchor."

Jo stared at her in disbelief. "Why would you ever agree to such a thing?"

Lise's unfocussed gaze looked around the booth, as if searching for an answer. "I wanted the media recognition and the network guaranteed that if we married they'd make me a co-anchor." She scornfully laughed. "And they did, for three weeks. But then the ratings came in and it showed I was the more popular member of the new team. My co-anchoring husband gave the studio an ultimatum. It was either me or him." She slumped against the back of the booth. "And so I returned to reporting, under some bloody false pretense of wanting to return to my roots. What a load of crap that was."

A deep sadness settled across Jo's heart. "What about the marriage?"

"I was locked in. If we separated then it would've been revealed for the stunt it was, and my credibility in the industry would be ruined. And now," Lise sighed, "it's a marriage of convenience. Christ, what a fool I was." She drained the remainder of her drink, pushed the glass next to the other empty one and pulled another full glass to her. "I haven't been happy since we were together. It's something I've had to live with since I left you."

LAUREN WALKED INTO the bar from the side entrance that adjoined the function room. By sheer luck she'd run into Nat, who'd mentioned where Jo had headed. *It's about time I apologise for my big mouth and crappy behavior.*

She saw two people in a booth, leaning toward each other, as if in intimate conversation. Lauren's blood turned to ice as she recognised Jo and Lise. She turned to the bar and settled herself on a stool as the barman approached her. "I'll have a gin and tonic," she said, trying to keep from snapping at him. Or crying. Emotions roiled through her chest.

"Do you have any preference for your gin?" He placed a coaster in front of her.

"Something nice and strong." Waiting for her drink, she glared at the booth occupied by the two women. *What the hell are you playing at Jo?*

The barman placed the drink in front of her. "That'll be seven dollars, please."

Lauren picked up the glass and took a long sip, savouring how the gin coursed down her throat. A movement in her peripheral vision signaled that she was no longer alone.

A hand reached across Lauren, barely brushing her arm in the process. "I'll pay for her drink." Pat placed a ten-dollar note on the counter in front of the barman. "Keep the change."

He picked up the note, acknowledged the tip, and moved away to afford them some privacy.

Pat settled on the stool beside Lauren, her knees touching Lauren's thigh. "So, you still like a gin and tonic before dinner. It's good to see some things never change."

Lauren glowered at Pat, barely managing to keep her anger in check. The misfortune of seeing Pat's name earlier and the massage had at least given her more than ample time to prepare herself for the inevitable confrontation. *You no longer have a hold on me. Why has it taken me so long to realise that?* "You couldn't be *more* wrong. A lot has changed."

Pat chuckled, shimmying off the edge of her barstool, and moving closer. "You're right. You've grown into a striking woman." She casually trailed her fingers down Lauren's arm and Lauren gritted her teeth, wishing she'd just stayed home.

A FAMILIAR VOICE and grating laughter broke Jo's focus on Lise. She looked across the room at the bar where Lauren sat, her face in shadow. Jo clenched her jaw when Pat sidled off the barstool. *Shit, why don't you just jump into her lap and be done with it!* As Pat slowly moved her fingers down Lauren's arm, Jo half-rose from the booth. *That's it. You've crossed the line now, woman!* A glass scraped across the table and Jo glanced back at Lise, who had just drained almost all of its contents.

Lise plunked the glass on to the table and raked her fingers through her hair. "Fuck," she mumbled, "I've made a mess of my life." She grabbed tufts of her short locks and slowly shook her head.

Jo looked first at the scene unfolding on the other side of the room and then back at Lise, who again moved her hand to her drink. Jo pushed the nearly empty glass out of her reach and gently placed her hand over Lise's, keeping her from reaching for it again. "I think you've had enough for one night."

Lise's tear-stained face gazed at the drink and then back at Jo. "This is the story of me, now. It's the only way I can get through a day."

Despite the pain Lise had caused, Jo felt pity for her. She fought back her own tears as she remembered what they'd shared together, and how far Lise had fallen. She forced her thoughts to the present. "I think it's time you went to your room. I don't think you really feel like going to the function now. Maybe you can order some room service. Are you staying here?"

"Yeah, by myself, thankfully." Lise laughed but there was no humour in the sound and she struggled to stand. She sank back down into the seat, puzzled. "There seems to be a problem with my balance."

Jo smothered a nostalgic smile at Lise's often-used phrase for when she'd had too much to drink. *All the same, I don't think I've ever seen you as bad as this.* Jo got up. "Here, let me help you." She pulled Lise upright and placed a steadying hand around her waist.

Lise smiled wistfully. "Just like old times, hey?"

Jo moved her toward the door, Lise's meandering gait making hard work of the process. "No, not like the old times. Never again like the old times."

LAUREN GAZED ACROSS the room just in time to see Jo stand and put her hand around Lise's waist. *I don't know what's going on there but I'm sure as hell going to find out.* As she made to stand Pat moved even closer, insinuating her body between Lauren's legs.

Pat nodded toward Jo and Lise as they made their way out of the bar. "I expect they're off for some fun this evening. Hopefully they won't be the only ones."

Lauren stood, determined to follow Jo.

"Hey, where are you going? I'm sure those two are more than capable of making their own entertainment." Pat placed a proprietary hand on Lauren's hip. "What say you and I remember the old days a little?"

It took a moment for Lauren to realise Pat had no idea who Jo was, nor the frustration Lauren was feeling at Jo's sudden departure with her ex-girlfriend. She looked down at the hand on her waist. "This," Lauren motioned to where Pat's hand rested, "was never about the old days. You were always very careful about keeping your sexual orientation secret," she challenged.

Pat's finger traced the outside seam of Lauren's pants. "Some things change," she said, her meaning clear.

Lauren pulled away from Pat's touch, her back against her barstool. "You're damned right, they do." Anger swelled in her throat and she wasn't sure whether it was focused at Jo or Pat, or both.

Pat took a rice snack from the bowl. "So where did you go that day?" She popped the rice snack into her mouth. "You were nowhere to be found."

Lauren took a long swig of her gin and tonic. "You really don't want to have this conversation here," she replied, in clipped tones.

Pat, completely misreading Lauren's words, again breached Lauren's personal space. "Why don't we go somewhere a little more private, then?"

Lauren shook her head, disgusted. "I was thinking more along the lines of the balcony." *Maybe we're up high enough so I can throw you off!* She headed for the balcony door, Pat following. As they passed the entrance to the bar, Lauren checked the foyer and saw Jo standing near the elevators, her hand around Lise's waist, and Lise's head on her shoulder. Lauren paused. She felt Pat's hand stroke the small of her back.

"What's the matter?" Pat queried.

Lauren took one last glance at Jo, feeling sick to her stomach, and then turned away, continuing to the balcony. She strode across the sandstone paving, halting when she reached the balcony's edge. She gripped the railing so tight her fingers hurt. *What the hell is going on between Jo and Lise?*

Oblivious to Lauren's preoccupation, Pat sidled up beside her. She reached up and teased a lock of Lauren's hair. "Where did you go that day? I looked and couldn't find you anywhere."

Lauren jerked her head away and faced Pat, front on. "Bullshit! You did nothing of the sort."

Pat held out her hands, her face a study of innocence. "Of course, I had to wait until the award ceremony was over, but then I searched for you everywhere."

Lauren folded her arms across her chest and lifted her head to the night sky. She released a deep breath and glared at Pat. "Your excuse might have worked ten years ago, but not now. Do you even remember the last day of play?"

Pat placed her hands in her pockets. "Of course I do. You were leading after the first nine, and with the back nine to play it began to rain."

Lauren stepped toward Pat, barely masking the rage she felt. "Is that *all* you remember?"

Pat instinctively took a step back. "I remember we had that arrangement," she replied, "where I was to finish first and you second, but your game just seemed to go to pieces out there. I was worried about you afterward."

Lauren stared at her in disbelief. "The more you say, the deeper the hole you dig for yourself. Do you remember what you said to your caddy in the changing room?"

Pat dismissively waved her hand. "I don't know what you're talking about."

"Let me remind you. They're words that just about gutted me, and I've never forgotten them. I was there, in the showers, when you said I'd been a wonderful stepping stone and a gratifying fuck. But now it was time for you to move on. And given there'd only ever been one openly gay woman in the Hall of Fame, you couldn't afford for anyone to find out about you. I was *there* Pat. I heard every damned word you said!"

Pat stepped away from Lauren, her easy-going façade forgotten. "What the hell did you *expect* was going to happen? There's no room for 'happily ever after' in this sport, especially not between lesbians on the tour. I needed you and you needed me. It was a mutually beneficial agreement."

"Mutually beneficial, my arse," Lauren shouted, her face mere centimetres from Pat's. She shoved her hands into the front pockets of her pants, rather than around Pat's throat, where she so desperately wanted to put them.

Lauren's eyelids narrowed as she thought about seeing Pat's name that afternoon. *Hall of fame candidates or members are normally noted in a tournament field by a green star for candidates, and a red wreath for members. There was just one member on the board, and it wasn't you.* "I saw the final list this afternoon. Have you made the Hall of Fame yet?" she questioned, a satisfied smile on her lips.

Pat's features hardened. "You bitch," she hissed. "If you saw the board then you know the answer."

Lauren removed her hands from her pockets. "So much for your 'mutually beneficial agreement.' Now it makes sense. The tournament points here figure in the tour standings, so how many points are you short? Or are you lacking in other areas as well?"

"Damn you and your bloody game! I hope you choke tomorrow, just like you did ten years ago, except this time I'll be able to publicly enjoy your pain," Pat's voice was low and dangerous.

"And I yours, you damned has-been." Lauren turned and walked back through the bar and into the foyer, where she impatiently waited for the elevator, feeling for the first time in years as if she'd been released from the emotional millstone that had hung around her neck.

I can't wait to tell Jo. And then she remembered. Jo and Lise, Jo's arm around Lise's waist. Lauren released a deep-throated growl as she stepped into the elevator and punched the button.

LAUREN WALKED PAST Jo's room, the absence of any light beneath the door leaving her both angry and cold. She entered her room, loudly closing the door behind her. She kicked off her shoes and flicked the switch that turned on the small lamps on either side of her bed. She pulled her blouse from her pants and began unbuttoning it. As she did, a soft knock sounded from the door adjoining Jo's room.

Composing herself, she opened the door and glared at Jo then walked through the entrance and looked around.

Jo leant against the doorframe. "What do you think you're doing?"

"I'm just seeing if you're alone." She returned to her own suite.

Jo threw her hands in the air in an exasperated gesture. "You really don't get it do you? I'm not like that. How many times do I have to tell you?"

Lauren whirled, hands on hips. "What do you think I'm supposed to get, when I see the two of you together like you were, your arm around her waist, her head on your shoulder? Damn, I thought you were smarter than to fall for that old trick."

"Christ, Lauren," Jo said, clearly irritated. "She was drunk and needed someone to speak to. Especially after slamming three scotches down and God knows how many more before I got there. She's in a bad way and needed to talk about the mess she's made of her life."

Lauren started pacing in an attempt to calm herself. "It must have been convenient when *you* came along, then."

"I could say the same for you." Jo jabbed her finger at her. "Why didn't that British bitch just jump into your lap and be done with it? Thank Christ it was a public place, or who knows where she would've taken things."

"At least I wasn't escorting someone upstairs, to God knows where," Lauren challenged.

"She was in no fit state to walk. I was merely helping her to her room." Jo sighed and rubbed the centre of her forehead. She took a deep breath and released it through her nose. "Are you ever going to accept I'm not like that? I tried to tell you this morning, but you seem to be bloody clueless. I'm in love with you. Why the *hell* would I be interested in anyone else?"

Lauren stopped pacing, not sure she had heard correctly. A mixture of hope and relief surged through her veins.

Jo slowly closed the distance between the two of them, halting just out of arm's length, in front of Lauren.

"The moment I first saw you in the foyer at The Retreat I felt something for you. I tried to fool myself into believing it was just a passing attraction, tied up with securing your story." Jo smiled, rueful. "It was Ben who actually saw what was going on, the night he arrived. He knew I was falling in love with you and, truth be told, so did I. And I really didn't want to stop my feelings."

Jo paused and she lowered her gaze for a moment then studied Lauren's face again. "But you've confused the heck out of me. That evening, after the day of the golfing clinic with Ben, we really seemed to be starting something. Then, after the confrontation with Annie, everything seemed to go south, and we were back where we started, as if nothing had happened between us." She shoved her hands in her pockets. "And then there's how you acted with Lise at the golf tournament today, and your words just now. No one can be as jealous as you are and not at least *like* the other person."

Lauren gazed down at her hands and raised her eyes to Jo's. "I'm sorry about how I acted. And I don't just like you," she said softly, moving closer. "I love you. I've been trying to convey this through my actions, but obviously I was a little off-kilter." Lauren cupped Jo's face. "Maybe this will help." She brushed her lips over Jo's, seeking permission for something deeper.

Jo's eyes closed and she captured Lauren's lower lip in her own, sucking it as she deepened the kiss between them. She encircled Lauren with her arms, pulling her closer.

Lauren cupped Jo's backside, increasing the contact, needing to feel more of her, as her lips traced a path to Jo's ear. "I love you so much," she whispered as she nibbled Jo's earlobe. She smiled when she heard Jo's breathing quicken. Jo tilted her head, offering her neck to Lauren. Her hands snaked under Lauren's loosened blouse, and she lightly stroked Lauren's back.

Lauren's hips involuntarily responded to Jo's soft touch. She reached down and nipped Jo's neck, then delicately blew on the small bite.

"Oh, that feels good." Jo released Lauren's bra clasp. "Just a little harder."

Lauren tenderly licked Jo's neck. "I don't want to mark you."

"I don't care. I want everyone to know I'm yours." Jo reached under the bra's silky material and cupped Lauren's breasts. "Just as they're going to know you're mine." She ran her thumbs across Lauren's nipples.

Lauren trembled at Jo's touch. "Trust me. They'll know I'm yours." She pulled Jo's blouse free from the confines of her pants and teased Jo's lips, again seeking entry.

Jo moaned as Lauren's tongue began an erotic dance with her own. She removed her hands from Lauren's breasts and undid the rest of the buttons on Lauren's blouse. Jo impatiently pulled open the blouse, stripped it from Lauren's shoulders, and tossed it aside, with

Lauren's bra closely following the path across the room which the blouse had taken.

Jo stepped back, her gaze feasting on Lauren's form. "God, you are so beautiful." She trailed her lips down Lauren's chest. Lauren swallowed heavily, feeling like she might pass out from the sensation.

Lauren's heart was beating so hard she wondered how Jo couldn't hear it, and she eased herself back from Jo. "I want to see you, too. Raise your arms." She pulled Jo's blouse over her head and dropped it onto the floor. "I can hardly breathe at such a sight," she said, staring longingly at Jo. Smiling, she leant down and kissed Jo's nipples through the confines of her bra.

Jo arched into Lauren's kiss and unfastened her bra, offering her breasts to Lauren. "Oh, yes," she breathlessly sighed when Lauren's lips settled over one of her nipples. She cupped Lauren's head with her hands, as if to increase the contact. Lauren rewarded her with feather-light nips to her tender flesh. "Oh God, I feel as if I'm melting."

Lauren knelt in front of Jo, drawing a path of nips and kisses over her stomach. Her fingers traced sensual lines over Jo's backside, her touches coming closer to Jo's centre. Lauren drew in a breath at the heat radiating from Jo. She rested her head against Jo's stomach and smiled.

Jo reached down and stroked Lauren's face. "Are you all right?"

Lauren stared at Jo's part-naked form and rose. "Standing here with the woman I love, knowing she loves me, I couldn't be better." She pulled Jo to her, relishing the delicious contact of skin upon skin.

Jo nibbled Lauren's earlobe as one of her legs hooked itself around Lauren's. "Thank God you're a little taller than me." She pulled Lauren's hips to her. "Make love to me. Please."

Lauren passionately claimed Jo's lips with her own. Without breaking their contact, she unbuttoned Jo's trousers and lowered Jo's zipper. She hooked her thumbs in Jo's pants.

Jo uncurled her leg from Lauren and slipped out of her shoes, in turn allowing her pants and underwear to pool on the floor at her feet. She stepped out of them and reached for Lauren's belt, all the while backing Lauren toward her bed. "There'll be no towels in my way tonight," Jo said. "I want to see all of you this time."

She made short work of Lauren's zipper then knelt and slowly peeled the pants down Lauren's legs, failing to suppress her giggle.

Lauren stepped out of her trousers. "What?"

Jo looked up. "You've got little golf clubs on your underwear. How cute."

"They're my lucky underwear," Lauren mumbled, a little self-conscious. "I always wear something like them at tournaments.

Jo's eyebrows raised as her mouth formed a perfect O. "Crap, I completely forgot. Isn't there something about athletes and sex before a big game?"

Lauren stroked Jo's face and curled a length of Jo's hair around her finger. "I've heard differently. And right now, the damned golf course could burn up and I wouldn't give it a second thought."

Jo chuckled. "So, it would be okay if I did this?" She reached out a finger and traced the tiny clubs decorating the front of Lauren's panties.

"Oh, God," Lauren moaned as Jo's fingertip stirred longings she hadn't felt in such a long time. She widened her stance. "They're all over my pants, you know."

Jo raised an eyebrow. "Are they?" Her fingers teased along the seam of Lauren's pants, lightly stroking between her legs. An inaudible sound passed her lips. "Oh baby, you're so ready."

Lauren reached down and pulled Jo from the floor. "I've been ready for a long time. I just didn't know it." Lauren removed her panties and then pulled Jo on to the bed.

Jo eased herself off Lauren, her gaze trailing over Lauren's body. She ran her fingers between Lauren's breasts, allowing them to come to rest in a series of lazy strokes below Lauren's belly button. "Ben was right about you."

Lauren raised a finger to her lips and licked it, then reached across and teased Jo's nipple with the damp finger. "Right about what?" She moved closer to Jo's lips, quivering as Jo's fingers gently explored her wet heat.

"You're a keeper," Jo replied, catching Lauren's lips with her own.

Lauren deepened the kiss, her mind torn between Jo's touch and the interplay of their tongues. She raised her leg, allowing Jo a greater freedom of entry. "Faster, baby," she gasped between kisses. Unable to contain herself, she threw her head back, her breathing ragged, her hips moving uncontrollably at Jo's demanding touch. She desperately pulled Jo to her as the erotic tension mounted.

"Just there," Jo asked, her fingers gently entering Lauren as her thumb danced over Lauren's sensitive flesh.

"Oh yeah," Lauren cried. For a moment time seemed to stand still, as if she were on an emotional precipice, before she climaxed, riding the passionate rollercoaster Jo's touch created.

Lauren shuddered and twitched under Jo's ministrations as Jo slowed her movements. She rested her head on Lauren's stomach, filling it with feather-light kisses. "Are you okay?"

"Mmm hmm." Lauren wiped the sweat from her brow and sighed contentedly. "But it'll be your fault if I can't swing a golf club tomorrow, let alone walk the course."

Jo gently removed her fingers and sat up. "But you said it was okay." As Lauren's face broke into a smile, she slapped her stomach.

"Come here." Lauren pulled Jo onto her, sighing with pleasure at the feel of their bodies melding as one. She placed a kiss on Jo's nose. "I love you. Thank you for being patient with me."

Jo snorted. "Yes, well I'm sure lesser women wouldn't have held out this long."

"Didn't someone say something about good things coming to those who wait?" Lauren strummed her fingers along the length of Jo's back.

"In more ways than one," Jo chuckled and placed a tender kiss on Lauren's chest.

"Really?" Lauren said, moving her leg between Jo's and raising it to meet Jo's centre.

"Really." Jo angled her hips, increasing the contact. She gasped as Lauren tightened the muscles in her leg. "Definitely worth the wait," she managed between heavy breaths.

Lauren cupped Jo's breasts, matching Jo's slick movements with gently applied pressure to her nipples. Lauren pulled a nipple into her mouth and sucked, running her tongue over its tip.

"That's so good," Jo groaned as she shifted her body, shamelessly offering her other breast to Lauren's lavishing care.

Jo's breathing hitched as Lauren clutched her backside while further tightening the muscles of her leg. Jo moaned at the contact and the speed of her hips increased with Lauren's pressure.

"Come for me, honey. Just for me." Lauren began to thrust in concert with Jo's movements, feeling herself once again close to climax. Lauren pulled Jo close as they crested together, their movements eventually slowing.

"Stop, please." Jo shuddered. "Or *I* won't be able to walk tomorrow."

As Jo came to rest on top of her Lauren kissed the sweaty tendrils of hair from Jo's forehead. "I love you," she whispered, kissing her gently on her nose and wrapping her arms around her.

Jo snuggled her head under Lauren's chin. "I love you, too."

Lauren sighed in mock disappointment. "Of course, now I definitely won't be able to play golf tomorrow, not after such a workout."

"What? You said—" Jo raised her eyes to Lauren's, concern written all over her face. At Lauren's grin, she swatted her and broke into a cheeky laugh. "You are so bad. But you know that, don't you?"

"Only for you my love, only for you."

Chapter
Sixteen

JO AWOKE TO the sounds of soft music, courtesy of the alarm clock beside Lauren's bed. She snuggled closer against the body she was sprawled over, lightly kissing Lauren's chest. "What time is it?" She hooked one of her legs over Lauren's.

"Six-thirty." Lauren laughed softly at Jo's groan, and she trailed her fingers down Jo's back. "I'm sorry, but *you* were the one who thought a golf tournament would be a good idea."

Jo raised herself up on one elbow and yawned. "You're not going to let me forget that, are you?" She leant forward and kissed Lauren. "How did you sleep?"

Lauren stretched. "Very well, thank you." She reached up and stroked Jo's face. "It makes a difference waking up next to the woman I love, and knowing I get to spend the day with her."

"I like the way that sounds." Jo snuggled against Lauren's warm body. "So how do you think today will go?"

"With seven leaders it's anyone's tournament. But if I don't get a move on there'll only be six leaders teeing off. As much as I'd love to spend the rest of the day like this with you," Lauren softly groaned when Jo's leg insinuated itself between her own "I think we'd better get downstairs."

Jo nuzzled Lauren's chest. "Trust me when I tell you there'll be more of these mornings."

"There'd better be," Lauren said, smiling, as she disengaged herself from Jo's warm embrace. "I'll take first shower if you like."

Jo sat up in bed, lasciviously watching Lauren as she headed, naked, to the bathroom. "Do you want me to call room service for some herbal tea?"

"Not unless you want some. I shouldn't be too long."

"Do you want me to shower with you? It'll save time." Jo swung her legs out of the bed.

Lauren turned and arched her brow. "If you shower with me this morning then we're likely to drain the hotel dry of warm water, not to mention miss a tournament. Can I take a rain check?"

Jo clicked her fingers together in mock disgust and flopped back down on the bed. "Darn, foiled again."

Lauren laughed. "There's no stopping you, is there?" She continued into the bathroom.

As the sound of the shower filled the room, Jo lay on the bed, hands entwined behind her head. She stared at the ceiling, a permanent smile on her face. The familiar ring of a cell phone interrupted her reverie, and she rose and opened the door between the two rooms. She checked the caller ID, took a seat on the bed in her room and flicked open her phone. "Hi Ros, how are you? I completely forgot to call you yesterday."

"Where have you been? I tried to call you last night and it went straight to voice mail. Is everything okay?" Ros sounded worried.

Jo drew her fingers through her hair, trying to give it some semblance of order. "Everything's fine. Lauren did really well in the first round yesterday."

"I know. The tournament got a bit of media coverage up here. She's a co-leader, isn't she?"

Jo leant against the doorframe. "Sure is. There're seven in all. We haven't checked who she's teeing off with yet. We'll find out when we head down to breakfast."

"Keep us posted. It'd be opportune if we could utilise the current television coverage to advertise the episode. Speaking of which, when do you think you'll be in a position to deliver the final part in the series?"

Jo canted her head. "It shouldn't be too much longer. Ben's been capturing some great footage. Now it's just a matter—" Jo's words caught in her throat when Lauren exited the bathroom toweling her hair, her body slightly pink from the heat of the shower.

"Just a matter of what? Jo are you there? Is everything okay?" Ros's concerned tones echoed down the line.

Try as she might, Jo failed to tear her eyes from Lauren's naked form as she padded shamelessly around the room, pulling out her outfit for the day.

"Jo!"

"I'm sorry," Jo absently replied. "Lauren's just walked out of the shower."

Lauren turned and looked at Jo, her eyebrows raised in a question.

Jo's eyes widened when she realised what she'd just said and she covered the mouthpiece of the cell. "Did I just say that out loud?"

Lauren nodded.

"What did you just say?" Ros asked.

Jo glanced at Lauren and mouthed an apology.

Lauren walked over and lightly kissed Jo's forehead. "It's okay. You'd better finish your discussion or she'll be on the next plane down here."

"Did you say that Lauren just walked out of the shower? What are you doing in her room at this time in the morning, or is that a silly question?"

A blush rapidly suffused Jo's features. "Ah, we had some early morning things we needed to go over before we started the tournament."

"Really? Are you sure that's all there is? It seems pretty early to be discussing golf stuff, especially with her walking around naked."

Jo continued to track Lauren's form moving around the room, laying her clothes out on the bed. "We're pressed for time. Uh – you know how it is."

Ros's chuckle filtered down the line. "I know *exactly* how it is."

"Ros, that's not entirely the case." Jo backpedaled, trying to avoid the inevitable.

Lauren held out her hand. "Can I have the phone for a moment?" Jo silently handed it over.

"Hello, Ros? This is Lauren. Jo's standing in my room because it's where she slept last night. I'm assuming I don't need to paint a picture for you." Lauren's eyes seemed to sparkle and a little smile pulled at her lips. She nodded in response to whatever Ros said.

"I'm sure there'll be plenty of time for her to fill you in later, but right now we do need to get moving." Lauren paused, listening. She raised her gaze to Jo and smiled again. "Yes, she is very special. I'll put her back on. I've got to get dressed."

Lauren handed the phone back to Jo but leant in for a quick kiss before she continued to get ready. A little tingle shot down Jo's spine.

"So mate, it's happened." Ros sounded positively gleeful.

"Uh, yeah." Jo replied. "And I couldn't be happier." She watched the muscles move under Lauren's skin as she dressed.

"What does she look like?"

"Ros! You're straight, for God's sake. Why are you interested in what my partner looks like?" *Hmm. I like the way that sounds.*

Ros snorted. "It doesn't mean I can't appreciate the female form."

Jo laughed. "Well, you can appreciate it in your imagination."

"Is Lauren always so bossy?"

Jo shrugged and moved across the room, picking up Lauren's polo from where it had slid off the bed. "Sometimes. Not always, though."

"It must be hard for you to take," Ros parried.

"Always quick with the smart remark, aren't you? I'll call you after the tournament and give you a report."

"There's no need. I'm sure I'll see it on the television. Just call me when you think we can start advertising the final episode."

"No worries. I'll let you know as soon as Ben's put the final footage together." Jo headed to the bathroom for her own shower.

"Oh, and Jo?"

"Yes?"

"I'm really happy for you, kiddo. If this *is* the one, then I hope it's everything you want it to be," Ros said, a smile in her voice.

Jo looked at Lauren as she pulled on a clean pair of underpants, which were decorated with tiny golf balls. "She's the one, all right. I have absolutely no doubt."

JO LAUGHED AS Ben impatiently tapped his watch. She waved dismissively at him as she and Lauren approached. "We're five minutes late, mate. The way you're acting you'd think we'd been an hour late."

Ben slapped his stomach. "Not being on time might be okay for you two, but a man's gotta eat." He headed toward the restaurant and then turned back, almost in afterthought. "Have you seen the pairings for today yet?"

"I haven't," Lauren replied. "Jo?"

Jo shook her head. "They came out last night during the function. I, er, didn't hang around to see."

Ben looked at them as they shared a shy smile. He scratched the side of his head and frowned. "Okay, do you want to do it before we head into breakfast?"

Jo nudged Ben. "I don't know. Are you likely to drop dead of food deprivation if we make a slight detour?"

"Stop teasing him, Jo. Let's go and have a look." Lauren headed in the direction of the room where the players' board was located, Jo and Ben close behind.

Ben looked at Lauren's back and over to Jo, his brows raised in question. Jo smiled and put a silencing finger to her lips.

"Ros called me this morning," Jo said as she entered the room. "She was wondering when you'd be finished with the filming. She's keen to air the final program as soon as possible."

"Once we wrap this up today it shouldn't be much longer. We need to sit down and go over what you want to keep in the episode and then we need to ensure Lauren's happy with the final product."

"Oh, shit," Lauren said, exasperated, as she leant toward the board.

Jo was quickly at her side. "What is it? Are you the last to tee off?"

Lauren stepped back, allowing Ben and Jo access to the pairings. "Yes, but that's not the problem. See for yourself."

Jo exhaled in consternation at Lauren's partner for the day. "Pat bloody Morgan. Isn't this going to be cosy."

Ben looked at the board and at Jo, a frown on his face. "Who's Pat Morgan?"

Jo looked at Lauren, posing the question with her expression. At

Lauren's nod, Jo checked to ensure the three of them were the only ones in the room. "Pat's Lauren's ex, and a key reason why she left the tour. She's an unmitigated bitch." Jo watched Lauren walk away, to one of the large windows dominating the room.

"Is she going to be okay?" Ben said under his breath..

"I don't know. Can you grab us a table? I'll have a talk with her."

"Sure, I'll meet you in there." Ben rubbed Jo's arm as if in reassurance. "Don't worry, mate," he softly replied. "She's made of tougher stuff than what an ex can drag up."

Jo watched his back as he left. "I hope so," she said to herself. She turned and joined Lauren at the window. "You okay?" She traced soothing circles in the small of Lauren's back.

Lauren stared out the window. A small mob of kangaroos grazed on the fairway's edge, oblivious to what was to be played out there that day. She turned to Jo and smiled. "I'll be fine. She has no hold over me anymore. I purged those demons last night." Lauren softly stroked Jo's cheek. "Now it's about you and me. Not her."

The soft clearing of a throat broke the tableau. Jo looked up. "Oh—hi, Lise." The look on Lise's face was testimony to the fact that she'd overheard Jo's conversation with Lauren.

Lise, a new awareness in her eyes, looked at Lauren. "Could I have a moment with Jo, please? Would you mind?"

Lauren gazed at Jo and back at Lise. She squeezed Jo's hand. "Sure. I'll see you at breakfast." She moved away, sparing one more glance for Lise before she left.

"It's more than just a professional relationship, isn't it?"

Jo blinked, returning her full focus to Lise. "Much more."

Lise lowered her head and released a sigh then looked up again. "I was hoping when I saw you yesterday there might still be something between us." A fleeting, wistful expression crossed Lise's face

Jo bit back the immediate response that came to mind regarding Lise's current marital status.

"I'm sorry," Jo said, trying to be gentle, "but I think we both know we can't go back to where we were all those years ago. You need to move on, Lise, both personally and professionally. You can't spend the rest of your life unhappy, and something tells me that as long as you stay with him, you will be."

Tears welled in Lise's eyes. "I just don't know. It's such a risk."

"I've no doubt your reporting credentials are impeccable and your name has buying power for any major station. You really do need to look elsewhere." Jo lightly patted her shoulder. "You need to be willing to take risks with your life. After you, I didn't realise how safe I was playing everything until I found Lauren. Trust me, it's a gamble worth taking."

Lise sadly smiled. "I should never have let you go and it's

something I've got to learn to live with."

"There's someone out there for you. You've just got to be willing to walk out of the self-destructive cycle you're in now. Honestly, I've never seen you drink as much as you did last night. If what you said was true about doing it on a regular basis, then it's going to kill you. Stop drinking and get on with your life. That bastard and the damn station have had a hold on you for way too long. You've *got* to move on."

Lise ran her hand through her stylishly cropped locks and released a sigh. "I'll try."

"Don't try, *do*." Jo glanced over her shoulder at another group entering the room. "I'd better get back to Lauren or we'll never get this day underway." She patted Lise's arm again. "You'll be okay. Just be willing to give your life another chance."

JO SAT DOWN at the table next to Ben. "Where's Lauren?"

"She's at the omelette bay getting breakfast." He motioned at the juice in front of her. "She mentioned something about needing the energy."

Jo reached for the glass, unsuccessfully trying to hide the blush creeping across her features. She took a sip, aware of Ben's curious gaze.

"Can I gather by the look on your face something significant has finally happened between you two?"

Jo raised her napkin and dabbed the moustache of juice on her upper lip. "Yes, you can, but I don't want any ribbing from you or I swear you'll wear my breakfast."

Ben laughed. "I can hear the hearts breaking now at the prospect of Jo Ashby being off the market."

"Ben," Jo hissed as she leant forward. "You know it's not like that."

"I know, but I do love to tease you and this may be my last opportunity."

Lauren put an omelette down in front of Jo, then put her own plate at the place setting beside her. "Last time for what?" She took a seat.

Ben reached for his coffee. "Nothing. I was just congratulating Jo on finally coming to her senses over you."

Lauren blushed at Ben's gaze. "I take it you approve?" She removed the Haskell ball from her pocket and placed it beside her on the table.

"I do, but it wouldn't have mattered whether I did or not. Jo's always been her own woman, and one with impeccable taste I might add." Ben dodged Jo's mock swipe and they laughed. "What's that?" He pointed at the Haskell.

Lauren smiled at Jo and then looked at Ben. "It's my good luck charm. It belonged to a friend of a very good friend."

"I didn't know you were superstitious." Ben piled a helping of bacon and fried eggs on to his fork.

"Oh she's really superstitious. You should see her *other* lucky— ow!" Jo reached down and rubbed her shin, where Lauren had just kicked her.

"Why don't you have something to eat before you put your foot too much farther in your mouth," Lauren teased.

"I'd better, because if you kick me again I just might not be able to carry your bloody bricks today." As she finished a shadow crossed Lauren's features.

"Well, well, well. Imagine meeting you here." Pat smirked at Lauren, even as her gaze shamelessly tracked down Jo's torso. Jo placed a restraining hand on Lauren's thigh, out of sight of Pat's gaze.

"If how things were progressing in the bar yesterday evening are any measure of your success then I'd have to say you must have enjoyed yourself last night."

For a moment Jo's mind raced, trying to figure out how Pat had found out about her and Lauren. *Wait. She saw me last night with Lise. She thinks I slept with her.* "I had more fun than you can imagine," Jo replied.

"Oh I don't know. I have a pretty good imagination. Don't I, Lauren?" Pat scanned the room. "Where is your blond friend?"

"She's taken," Jo tersely replied.

Pat dismissively shrugged. "There's plenty more where she came from." She looked over at Lauren. "I see we're playing together. Just like old times."

This time Lauren put a restraining hand on Jo's thigh. Jo knew that was a good thing as her desire to stand and thump this woman senseless was almost too much to bear.

"Playing together again, yes, but not at all like old times Pat," Lauren replied in clipped tones.

"It mightn't be, but I can assure you, the result will be the same." Pat paused, practically oozing condescension. "Gone a little quiet have we?"

Lauren glared at her nemesis. "Actually I'd prefer to do my talking where it counts—on the golf course."

Pat harshly laughed. "We saw how it worked out last time, didn't we?"

Ben stood before the stand-off progressed into something a lot more physical. "Good morning, Miss Morgan, I don't think we've met." He held out his hand. "I'm Ben Redbourne and I'll be filming your group today. You don't mind, do you?"

Pat's visage changed and she graciously took Ben's hand, as if the previous conversation had never happened. "It's a pleasure to meet you. Thank you, I'd be happy to have you follow us and film me."

Ben released her hand. "That's great. I've just got one question for you, if I could."

"Certainly," Pat courteously waited.

Ben frowned and made a show of tilting his head, looking at one side of Pat's face and then the other. "Do you have a good side? It's hard to tell."

Pat's eyes seemed to morph into chips of ice. "I suggest you focus your filming on the eighteenth hole, Mr. Redbourne. It's all that's going to matter today." She stormed off.

Ben sat down and piled another mound of baked beans and bacon on to his fork. "That certainly broke the monotony." He shoved the food in his mouth and chewed enthusiastically.

Lauren exhaled and squeezed his free hand. "Thanks. I think you caught her by surprise there."

Jo huffed. "She deserved it. I hope she chokes on her breakfast. At least then we wouldn't have to put up with her for the day."

Lauren reached for her glass. "It'll be fine. She won't show her claws when the cameras are rolling. She's way too cunning to be caught so easily." She placed a forkful of omelet in her mouth.

Jo forced herself to calm down. "I swear if she'd have said another thing she would've worn my orange juice down the front of her prissy pink top." She checked her watch. "You've still got three-and-a-half hours before you tee off. What do you want to do?"

"I'm going to get some chipping and putting practice in. I didn't seem to have much problem getting distance on the fairway yesterday, but there's still room for improvement in my short game."

"Of course there is," Ben joked. "God forbid someone who barely plays anymore can't better a four under par score. I'll leave you to it. I've got stuff I need to prepare before the game starts." He drained the remainder of his coffee and rose. "I'll meet you on the first tee."

"No worries, we'll see you there."

He waved and made his way through the room. Jo returned her gaze to Lauren. "Are you going to be okay today?"

Lauren surreptitiously ran her foot up the side of Jo's shin. "With bodyguards like you and Ben, why wouldn't I be?"

"Good question," Jo winked. "No reason," she replied, and dug into her food.

JO JOINED BEN on the side of the fairway. "How's the filming going?"

"Fine, although now Lauren's pulled ahead of the rest of the pack by two, it's getting hard to dodge the spectators." He tapped the plastic card around his neck. "Thank God for this bloody press pass. How's Lauren handling things?"

"She's fine. Pat's tried to goad her a couple of times but Lauren's just flat-out ignored her." Jo removed her cap and wiped her brow. "I can't believe how focused she is."

"I can. This is obviously how she managed to get through tournaments when she was on the circuit. Isn't this the hole where she hit it right yesterday?"

Jo looked down the fairway toward a green flanked by steep slopes either side. "Yep, but that shot had more to do with a bloody cell phone going off." She watched Lauren turn, as if looking for her. She patted Ben's arm. "I'd better be getting back. It looks like the green's cleared ahead of us."

Jo jogged back to Lauren, re-positioning the golf bag. "What club would you like?"

Lauren squinted as if measuring the distance between her and the green. "I think a nine iron will be fine. But we'll have to wait for Pat. Is everything okay with Ben?"

Jo nodded. "We were just discussing the growing crowd."

Lauren took a practice swing, clicking her tongue in disgust at the inordinate time Pat was taking with her shot on the opposite side of the fairway. "At this rate it'll be dark before we finish." She wiped the club face. "I expect the increase in crowd numbers means the two of us aren't doing too bad."

Jo tilted her head. "Do you want to know?"

"If it's close, someone will shout it out sooner or later. I'd prefer to hear it from you," she said softly when Pat lined up for her shot for the third time.

"Both of you have moved away from the rest of the group by two shots," Jo whispered when Pat began her downward swing, cleanly connecting with the ball.

The ball hit the front of the green, stopping no more than what seemed to be six feet from the hole. Lauren took one more practice shot. "I'd better make this a heck of a lot better than yesterday's hit."

Lauren addressed the ball, relaxed, and connected cleanly with its surface. She followed the ball's high arc to where it finished, left of the hole, almost equidistant to Pat's shot from the pin. "At least it's better than yesterday's effort, especially given the pin placement so close to the right side of the green." Lauren handed the club to Jo and Jo stowed it in the bag. They walked down the centre of the fairway, not far from where Pat and her caddie were walking.

"What're the chances of a birdie here?" Jo queried.

Lauren shrugged. "It's a wicked sloping green from where I'm positioned. I'll be happy if I can hole it, but I'd be just as happy with a par."

"Settling for mediocrity again, I see," Pat sneered, passing them with her caddie. "I shouldn't have expected any different." She motioned to where her ball lay. "This is when I start to pull away from you, Wheatley. Don't you forget it." Pat shared a laugh with her caddie and walked to where her ball lay on the green.

"Which one of these things is your least favourite club," Jo growled.

"The four iron. Why?" Lauren moved to a space behind her ball.

"I just want to know which one I can use to beat the crap out of her if she says something like that again." Jo pulled the putter from the bag and removed its cover.

Lauren chuckled. "She's only trying to get a rise out of me. Don't let her get to you." She crouched a distance behind the ball, studying the green.

Jo tried to dismiss her violent thoughts and crouched beside Lauren. "What do you reckon?"

"I've got to be right on. If I hit this too much then the ball's just as likely to keep on going." Lauren cupped both hands to her face, in turn allowing her a more pure read of the green. She nodded, rose and took the putter from Jo.

Jo moved away, careful to not step on Lauren's or Pat's line of putt. She removed the flag from the hole and stood off to one side, on the apron. She held her breath when Lauren connected with her ball, only releasing it when the ball slowed, tantalisingly close to the hole.

Lauren walked across and silently asked a question of Pat, who in turn nodded. She again lined up the ball and sank it. Lauren recovered it and walked to where Jo stood. "Close, but not close enough."

Jo took the ball from Lauren and wiped it free of the minute pieces of dirt and grass stuck to it. "She's still got to make hers yet."

"It's a flat putt with no slope. This is a gimme for her." Lauren handed the putter to Jo and they waited for Pat to complete her shot.

Pat again took an inordinate amount of time to commit to the stroke. She finally hit the ball, on a path and speed directly aimed at the hole. It was no more than two feet from its inevitable destination when it seemed to veer away, off to the right. At first the movement was slight. But then the ball seemed to gain momentum, reaching the apron of the green and quickly picking up pace before it rolled down the steeply sloping right side off the green, finally slowing halfway down the slope.

Jo stared, shocked. "What the hell happened there?"

Lauren shook her head, puzzled. "I have no idea. I've never seen a ball do that on this green. She must have hit a bump or something."

Pat muttered something to her caddie as she snatched the sand wedge from her caddie's hands.

Jo cursed under her breath when Pat's pitch shot proved to be right on the mark. She looked around at the crowd, who registered appreciation for the shot as it rolled into the hole. "Damn, I thought it was going to be a bogey for sure."

Lauren began the walk to the next tee. "She always did have good chipping ability. At least we're still on the same score. It could've been worse."

The next few holes continued to proved challenging, as Pat continued her incessant niggling. Strangely though, it was an interruption from an unexpected quarter that finally had an effect on Lauren's game at the tenth hole.

"Don't worry about it." Jo patted Lauren's back as they walked to the tenth green. "How were you to know your female cheer squad from yesterday would call out when they did?"

Lauren sighed with frustration. "It was just such a clean shot for a par three birdie. Now I'll have to settle for par. And the British bitch over there has the absolute easiest of birdie shots."

Despite Lauren's best attempts, Jo sensed Pat's ongoing barrage of snide remarks was beginning to get under Lauren's skin. While it wasn't affecting Lauren's game, it was making her increasingly short-tempered.

"Just remember, she might get this one but there are still eight holes to play. And besides, no one else is within cooee of the two of you." She handed Lauren her putter. "Don't let her see your frustration. The minute she does, she's won." Jo set the bag down and walked with Lauren to the far edge of the green where her ball lay, thankfully devoid of the milling crowd.

"Hey," Jo whispered, cognizant of their surroundings.

Lauren turned, frowning.

"I love you," Jo said.

Lauren's face lost the remnants of frustration that had only so recently resided there and a little rush of pleasure filled Jo's chest.

Lauren smiled. "You sure know how to defuse a situation, don't you?"

"How about you show me your putting prowess now?" Jo walked the twenty feet to where the flag rested in the green's cup. She held it until she received the nod from Lauren, only then removing it and walking to the side of the green.

Lauren's putt was on line, but the distance robbed her of the birdie she so desperately wanted. She marked the ball's position less than two feet from the hole, read the green, and putted in for par. She moved to Jo's side.

"Not too bad for a weekend golfer," Jo joked.

Lauren quirked an eyebrow and smiled. "I'll give you weekend golfer, woman," she said, softly chuckling when Pat lined up for her shot. "She won't miss this. It's way too close."

Both watched Pat use her putter to tamp down any bumps between her ball and the twelve-inch path to the hole. Jo quietly placed the putter cover back on Lauren's club, her eyes never leaving Pat's shot.

The ball began its slow but unerring movement toward the hole.

Pat had already tossed her putter back to her caddie, expecting the result to be a foregone conclusion when a collective gasp came from the crowd. The ball stopped dead, less than an inch from the hole.

Jo looked around at the surrounding crowd. "What the hell," Jo muttered. "It's like the ball hit a brick wall."

As Pat sank her putt, Lauren glanced around her surroundings, as if looking for something. Her gaze settled on a copse of roped-off trees near the eleventh tee and she muttered a barely audible curse.

"What's wrong?" Jo queried as they walked off the green, gazing in the direction that Lauren had been looking.

"Annie's here."

"What?" She collected herself when the marshal leading them to the next green turned back to her, a questioning look on his face. She smiled at him and returned her focus to Lauren. "What do you mean, Annie's here?" she nervously whispered. "You said she couldn't leave the park."

"I didn't think she could. I mean, I've never sensed her presence before when I've been away from the park for a couple of days. But the last shot and the shot on the other green, when the ball turned right angles—they weren't natural shots."

The marshal escorting them to the eleventh tee walked back to the group, just as Pat caught up with Lauren and Jo. "I'm sorry, ladies, but there's a slight delay. We should be underway in another five minutes or so."

Pat and her caddy moved off to a private area, Pat's gesticulating hinting at the frustration she was feeling. Despite the situation, Jo took a perverse pleasure at Pat's misfortune. "How is it she can leave the park?"

Lauren hesitated, thinking. She raised her face to the sky and clicked her tongue. "Shit."

"What?"

"It's the Haskell. It has to be. Remember I told you about the other day, before I left the park to come here, when I went to the cabin to get the ball? When Annie and I spoke?"

Jo nodded.

"She said she'd always be there for me. I've never taken anything of hers from the park, so I can only assume she's here somehow through the ball."

Jo closed her eyes and rubbed her eyebrows. "How the hell can that happen?"

"You're asking me? I haven't got a clue, but she's here. I can sense her and she's not happy with Pat."

"At least it's not *me* this time." She reached out and gripped Lauren's forearm. "You say she's here, somehow channeling through the ball?"

Lauren nodded an affirmative.

"And the ball's normally in your bag, which was in your room last night."

Lauren nodded again.

"It means she was there when, you know." Jo waggled her brows and tilted her head.

Lauren pursed her lips as if in thought. "She probably was."

"Ew!" Jo pulled Lauren away from the marshal's questioning gaze. "She could've been watching the whole thing," she whispered. "I'm not used to threesomes or voyeurs, for that matter."

Despite Jo's reaction Lauren laughed, holding up her hands when Jo scowled at her. "I'm sorry, but you should see the look on your face."

"This is serious, Lauren. What if she turns on me?"

Lauren looked around and moved closer. "Reverse the paradigm, honey," she said, the words meant for Jo's ears alone. "If she was there and she did see us making love, then what she said to me in the hut the other day was true. She realises you're my future and she's at least accepting of that."

Jo mulled on the idea, realising the validity of Lauren's words. She released a shuddering breath. "Okay, I believe you. But what about her and Pat?"

Lauren shrugged. "I need to try and talk to Annie. I don't want her to sabotage Pat's round, no matter how much she deserves it. If I'm going to win this, then I'll do it on *my* terms."

Before they pursued the matter any further, the marshal motioned both players back to the eleventh tee.

Lauren reassuringly rubbed Jo's arm and headed in his direction. Jo followed and pulled the driver from the bag. She removed the head cover and handed the club to Lauren, who swung a few times then took her shot. The ball sailed straight down the fairway. She politely acknowledged the crowd and moved to where Jo stood, out of Pat's line of sight. Pat addressed the ball and prepared to take her shot.

Jo wasn't sure what happened next. The split second before Pat's driver was due to connect, the ball rolled off the tee, which resulted in Pat connecting with nothing but air. She almost spun in the opposite direction to where she was supposed to be facing.

Titters and whispers spread through the crowd. Pat glared, disbelieving, at the ball and Jo leant toward Lauren. "I suggest you find Annie soon, or this is going to turn into a circus if she has anything to do with it."

THE MARSHAL ONCE again walked over to the foursome, his hands outstretched in placation. "I'm sorry, ladies, but there's been a hold up on the eighteenth, and it's halting play on all preceding holes.

Lauren shrugged. "It can't be helped. We'll just wait over here."

She motioned to a small copse of trees.

"I'll call you forward when they're ready. Hopefully, the delay shouldn't be more than ten minutes."

"What sort of bloody tournament are you running here? Call players through, for God's sake," Pat demanded, hands on hips.

"I'm sorry," he said, trying to placate her. "But there's nothing I can do about it back here. I'll keep you advised of any changes in play."

Pat stomped off in the opposite direction and Lauren shared a sympathetic look with the marshal as he turned and trudged to the tee. "Jo, let's go and sit down over there."

Jo picked up the bag. "It looks like this afternoon's drama is starting to take its toll on Pat."

Lauren nodded and took a seat on a log, in the shade of the trees. "I've no doubt some of those shots she's muffed have been courtesy of Annie. Plus, the chuckles from the crowd aren't helping."

Jo consulted the card, checking both Lauren's and Pat's scores. "All the same, she's still managed to play decent golf. She's only one shot behind you."

Lauren removed her cap and ran her fingers through her hair. "Yes, but this isn't the way I'd like to win this, if I do."

"Has Annie answered you when you've tried to call her?"

"No, she's deliberately avoiding me. But I know she's *here*," Lauren replied, emphasising her last word.

Jo scanned their immediate surroundings. "Thank God, a portable toilet. I was beginning to go cross-eyed trying to hang on until we reached the clubhouse. Do you need to go?"

Lauren smiled, relieved for a break in the tension. "No. You go and I'll look after the bag." She'd barely finished her sentence when Jo was up and walking with a decidedly cross-legged gait toward the conveniences.

Lauren focused again on the small copse of trees. It was a roped-off area far enough away from the spectators, enabling competitors some breathing space for any unexpected interruption in play. She slowed her breathing and closed her eyes, trying to pick up on the subtle nuances of sound and wind around her.

"I know you're here. You've been following us since the air swing on the eleventh tee." Lauren opened her eyes and glanced at an area within the dappled light of the trees. In the shadows she made out Annie's form. Lauren looked to ensure no one was watching, and then walked to where Annie stood.

"You've got to stop doing this. It's not fair to her."

Annie folded her arms. "It's not fair to *her*? Maybe she should have thought about how she treated you ten years ago. Now she can feel some of the pain and frustration you went through."

"I think you've achieved that. But I want to win because I

outplayed her, not because you keep on interfering with her shots," Lauren countered.

"I've only interfered with three. The rest we're her own doing." Annie snorted disdainfully. "Why, even my Marta would have been able to beat such a sub-standard player."

"Will you at least promise me you'll let me win on my terms?"

Annie seemed to fight a battle between what was right and what she really wanted to do.

Finally, she shoved her hands in her pockets and sighed as if in resignation. "I will, but if she starts again with her snide comments, then I won't be held responsible for my actions."

Lauren graciously nodded her head. "Thank you, I really —" her next words were cut short at the sound of the marshal's voice, calling them to play. "I'd better get going. Thanks, Annie."

Annie smiled. "Good luck. Marta would be proud of you. Oh, and Lauren?"

Lauren looked back over her shoulder. "Yes?"

"Tell Jo to use a wood if she does hit that woman. It has a much greater range."

Lauren stifled a laugh and returned to her bag where it rested against the log.

Jo returned and picked up the golf bag. "Are you ready to go?"

"Yes, in more ways than one," Lauren replied.

"Hmm?"

"Annie and I have spoken. There'll be no air swings or putted balls turning at right angles. These last three holes will be just me and Pat."

JO WATCHED AS Lauren waved to the cheering crowd along the eighteenth fairway to the easy birdie putt awaiting her. Too excited to contain herself but trying not to get too physically close to Lauren, Jo punched her on the arm instead.

"Ow!" Lauren turned. "What was that for?"

Jo started laughing. "It's because I can't kiss you senseless just yet and, well, I had to do something or I was going to explode! Your play on these last three holes was nothing short of fantastic."

Lauren blushed. "Thanks. I think I just kicked it into another gear and left Pat behind me."

"Behind you," Jo scoffed. "She's been eating your dust for most of the day, Annie or no Annie. It's about time Pat got a taste of her own medicine."

"Annie said much of the same thing when we spoke. Maybe she was right. What goes around comes around."

Jo pulled the putter from the bag for the final time and removed the head cover with a flourish. She handed it to Lauren. "After this is over, those clubs, the bag *and* the Haskell ball go in the four-wheel drive. Tonight it's just you and me."

Lauren threw back her head and laughed, seemingly oblivious to Pat's glare. Jo lowered the bag to the ground and the crowd fell into silence as Pat went into her putting routine. Her par was met with polite clapping from the crowd, most of who were obviously waiting to break loose after Lauren's final shot for birdie.

Lauren's ball had barely hit the hole when the crowd erupted, applause, whistles and screams making it almost impossible to hear anything on the green.

Jo walked to Lauren's side, fighting to keep her emotions in check. Wary of the media coverage, she held out her hand to congratulate her.

Lauren took her hand but also pulled Jo into her embrace. "I wouldn't be here if it wasn't for you. Thank you for believing in me."

"You did all the hard work. Congratulations. I love you so much."

Lauren removed Jo's cap, tossed it aside, and ran her fingers through Jo's hair. "And I love you," she said, lowering her lips to Jo's.

Jo's ears barely registered the even louder roar from the crowd at Lauren's searing kiss. Pat's voice brought Jo back to the present.

"You're a bit free with your body aren't you?" Pat said sarcastically.

Jo turned in Lauren's embrace. "Only with the woman I love. But I suppose love's something you're not too familiar with, is it?"

Lauren disengaged herself and shook Pat's hand. She looked to where the nearest cameraman stood, far enough away to not pick up any discreet conversation. "Now you know what it feels like."

"Do I now," Pat sneered. "You had a lucky day, nothing more."

Lauren moved toward Pat and for a moment Jo thought Lauren might actually hit her. "Lucky day, my arse," Lauren growled. "But, just in case, you let me know the course and date. I'll play you anywhere, any time, and the result will always be the same. You're a spiteful has-been and I hope you reap every bloody pain you've sown."

Lauren briefly shook Pat's caddy's hand and then turned back to Jo. "Now, let the real celebration begin." She took the ball she'd played the round with and tossed it into the crowd, which brought yet another cheer.

Ben met them as they left the green. "That was bloody fantastic! I can't wait to check some of the footage. Lauren, do you have time for a quick interview with Jo?"

Jo held up her hands. "Hang on a minute, mate, I can barely walk, let alone conduct an interview.

"It's not *my* fault that you didn't pace yourself last night," Ben replied with a cheeky grin.

Lauren looked at them. "You're incorrigible, the two of you. Ben,

I've got to check my final scores in with the marshal, and then I've got a raft of interviewers waiting in line out there." She motioned over her shoulder. "Do you think it can wait?"

Ben looked as if he was weighing his answer. "Lauren, love, winner of the Gracemere Wells Charity Golf Tournament, I'd do anything for you."

Jo punched him on the shoulder. "We'll meet you back at the hotel. The official award ceremony's in about two hours. We'll catch you then."

Ben checked his watch. "It'll give me time to check the final footage. See you then."

He hefted his camera and headed into the crowd.

Lauren softly stroked Jo's arm. "Will you wait here while I turn in my card? I won't be long and then we'll hit the interview line."

As she went to move away Jo snagged her shirt. "How do you want to deal with what happened out there between us?"

Lauren shrugged. "With absolute honesty, that's how. I don't know of anyone else who won a tournament not sharing the moment in a similar way with their partner. Are you okay with that?"

Jo smiled and stroked Lauren's face. "I'm more than okay. I just wanted to make sure we're singing off the same sheet of music."

After Lauren returned from handing in her card they started down the line of interviewers, who seemed to have proportionately grown from the day before. By the time they'd reached the last one Jo felt like she was ready to drop.

"I'm sorry, Miss Wheatley, can you wait a second? My cameraman's got a slight glitch in his recording equipment."

"Sure," Lauren good-naturedly replied.

The gratitude at even a minor break in talking didn't escape Jo's gaze. "Are you okay?"

Lauren smiled. "I'm fine, just happy this is the last one. I have to say I'm a bit surprised there haven't been too many questions about our kiss out there."

Jo shrugged. "Tasmania's a pretty open state, even if it wasn't always the case."

"Excuse me, Miss Wheatley, we're ready now."

Lauren gave her full attention to the interviewer. Listening on the periphery to the questions he was posing, Jo scanned the crowd, her eyes coming to rest on Lise, who was in animated conversation with a female camerawoman. Jo smiled as Lise laughed and touched the woman's arm. *For anyone who doesn't know her, that was a passing touch, but I know better. Maybe she is taking a little of what I said to heart.* A pause in the questioning brought her attention back to Lauren.

"I'm sorry, could you repeat what you just said? The noise here's incredible." Lauren leant in closer to the interviewer.

"I said, is this the beginning of a comeback for you?"

Lauren resolutely shook her head. "Not in the least. I set out to do something over the past couple of days and I've achieved it. I'm more than happy with what I do now, where I am in my life, and where I live, here in Tasmania."

The interviewer nodded. "I hope you don't mind me asking, but I and thousands of others couldn't help but notice the kiss you shared with your caddy after you sank your last putt. Is she living with you in Tasmania? Is there a future between the two of you? I mean, Miss Ashby, you're a mainland girl, aren't you?"

Jo looked at Lauren who seemed to struggle with a way to answer the question without sounding too presumptuous.

"I suppose time will tell," Lauren replied, her eyes searching Jo's for an answer.

Chapter
Seventeen

JO BALANCED A tray of coffee and biscuits as she nudged open the door to her mother's lounge room. She settled the platter on the table between them and took a seat.

Margaret spooned sugar into both of the mugs on the tray. "I could've helped you with that."

"Of course you could, while precariously holding on to your crutches," Jo quipped.

Margaret raised a crutch and shook it at Jo, as if she was wielding a weapon. "You be careful, young lady, or I'll show you just how good I am with these things."

Jo chuckled and poured coffee into the two cups, topping each with a dash of milk. "I'm sure you're more than capable with them. Speaking of which, when are you due to see the doctor again? Shouldn't you be going to a half-cast soon?"

Margaret's eyes sparkled. "I called him the other day and I have an appointment next week. You remember I told you how when I last saw him he said the bone was knitting well, especially given my age? He's going to take another set of x-rays and unless there's a setback, he said he'd put me into a half-cast."

"That's great news. Will you still need crutches?" Jo snagged a chocolate biscuit from the tray on the table.

"I'll need them for a little bit yet. But Andrew's already coming up with ways to celebrate my transition to a different cast."

Jo wiped the crumbs from the front of her shirt. "Like what?"

Margaret sipped her coffee, deliberately avoiding Jo's gaze. "He's talking about a trip to Leura in the Blue Mountains." She paused. "An overnight trip," she whispered.

Jo made a pretense of looking around the room and at the door. "Mum, unless there's something you're not telling me, then there's no need to whisper. We're the only ones in the house."

Margaret quirked her mouth. "I know, but this is all new to me again, if that makes sense. I haven't done something like this since your father died." Margaret looked around the room and then back at Jo, her indecision clear on her face.

"Andrew made a point of letting me know he was booking the one room. And, from the way he said it, I don't think the room's a double."

Jo raised her brows, masking her own surprise at Andrew's presumption by taking a sip of her coffee. She warred with her desire to protect her mother from any possible hurt, but at the same time she sensed pain wasn't something her mother would get from Andrew. *And, face it Jo, if you wait for your mum to act on her feelings then Andrew might be long gone by then.* "How do you feel about his idea?"

Margaret slowly sipped her coffee. "Truthfully, I don't know." She patted Jo's knee. "But enough about me. What about you? I know I don't watch a lot of golf, but I'm assuming golfers and caddies aren't always *that* demonstrative when they win a tournament."

Jo fought a blush, to no avail. "No, not usually, but don't change the subject. How do you feel about Andrew's plans?"

Margaret idly traced the rim of her cup with her fingers. "I think — no, I *know* I'm falling in love with him. But I still can't help but think it's too soon. What would your father say?"

Jo shook her head in exasperation. "Mum, I know you loved Dad, we all did. But he's gone. You have to move on. I've said this to you before, but if I know anything, it's that Dad would be unhappy to know you're holding the rest of your life to his memory. It's not fair to you, and it's certainly not fair to Andrew."

Margaret sighed. "I know. Andrew's given me a couple of days to think the idea over." She gazed around the room, her eyes coming to rest on her wedding photo on the mantelpiece. "I really want to. It's just so hard."

"You're right, love is never easy and my most recent experience has taught me that."

"So how are things between you and Lauren? If the golf celebrations are any indication, then I guess they're going well."

Jo held up her hands and laughed. "Okay, I can see I'm not going to get any rest until I answer your questions. Things are going reasonably well between us."

Margaret shifted in her seat, attempting to adjust her broken leg. "Only reasonably well? Is her friend Annie still causing you trouble?"

"She was a bit of trouble at the golf tournament but, thankfully, not for me. Lauren says Annie's accepted what's happening between the two of us."

Margaret topped up her cup with more coffee. "So, has she moved on?"

"I don't think so. The other night when Lauren and I spoke she said she'd sensed Annie while she was guiding a tour through the park."

Margaret furrowed her brows. "I don't know too much about this stuff, but I suppose I figured Annie would've moved on, once things had settled between you and Lauren."

Jo shook her head. "From what you experienced with your own mum's psychic ability, you know more than me. I don't know if I told you, but Annie had a partner. Her name was Marta and she died in the park early in the twentieth century. Lauren says Annie's still searching for her. Maybe it's why she hasn't—" Jo frowned, searching for the right term—"crossed over."

"How terrible, especially when you think Annie's been without Marta for such a long time."

Jo's forehead furrowed as the kernel of an idea began to form in her mind. She was so pre-occupied she missed her mother's next question. "I'm sorry. What did you say?"

"I asked you when you last spoke with Lauren."

"Last night and she was a little distant." Jo raked her fingers through her hair, relaying to her mother the mainly monosyllabic conversation they'd shared.

"It's been two weeks since you returned from Tasmania hasn't it? Is this the first time you've called her?" Margaret arched a brow. "I mean, I know what you can be like, keeping in contact with people."

Jo shot a mock glare at her. "I'll have you know, I've called her every second night. All the same, I can't help but worry that our conversations seem to be getting shorter with every passing day. It's like she's preparing for the possibility I won't return."

Margaret leant forward. "Are you going back?"

"Of course I am. There's no doubt about it and I've told her so. I think it's just her past insecurities resurfacing again. But there was some business I needed to finish up on the mainland, not the least of which was the finalising of the editing of Lauren's story." Jo drained her cup and took another biscuit from the tray.

"Have you finished the editing?"

"Yes, and in fact I'm due to meet Ben at Ros's offices so she can view the final product." Jo consulted her watch. "Speaking of which, I'd better get myself ready or I'll be late yet again."

Margaret chuckled. "You never could make it to meetings on time."

"Thanks for your faith in me." Jo smiled and picked up the tray. "I'll move this into the kitchen and then help you back up the stairs."

"There's no need, love. I can manage."

Jo placed her mother's cup on the tray. "I've no doubt you can. But there are people here who both care about and love you." She watched her mother's face for evidence that the underlying meaning of her words had sunk in. She placed the tray back down and knelt by her side. "I'm very happy you're falling in love again and Dad would be, too. Just remember that before you make a decision with regard to Andrew's idea."

Margaret softly patted the hand covering her own. "I will. I promise."

JO SETTLED NEXT to Ros as Ben placed a tape in the recorder. "I know it's been a long time coming, but I think you'll agree it was worth the wait."

Ros rolled her eyes and laughed. "It had better be worth the wait, let alone the cost of this. This episode just about mirrors the cost of your last one with the sharks."

Ben picked up the remote and took a seat on the other side of Ros. "It is. Trust me."

For the next sixty minutes they watched the results of the weeks of filming, culminating with the golf tournament.

Ben pressed the stop button when the credits began to roll.

Ros nodded as she reached for her coffee. "The tournament's a nice ending to the story, as if her life's gone the full circle. Your narrative on where her future lies is also nicely done."

Jo smiled, appreciating Ros's comments. "Thank you. I think it was important to emphasise, even though she's still got her golfing skills, that she's moved on with her life and is happy with the direction it's heading."

Ros looked at her. "You mentioned there were some issues with Annie at the golf tournament. Ben, did you capture any footage of her?"

Jo cut off his reply. "Regardless of whether there was footage or not, I've an agreement with Lauren that no such film would be shown in the episode. There's no way she'd agree to such a thing."

Ros held up her hand. "Hang on, there. I wasn't suggesting we do anything of the sort. I was just asking whether the uncut footage showed evidence of Annie." She folded her arms, a small pout on her lips. "I mean, you two have seen her and I *still* haven't."

Jo shook her head. "I'm sorry. I should've known you better than to think you'd want to use such footage. I'm a bit sensitive about Lauren and Annie's situation at the moment."

"Sensitive's not the word for it." Ben sat back, a smug smile on his face. "Love-struck is more like it." As Jo moved to whack him, he dodged and went to the tape recorder. He ejected the tape and put it in its jacket then handed it to Ros. "Here," he said, retrieving a disc from his bag and popping it into the DVD player. "I'll forward to the unedited elements of the golf tournament. Annie's not as clear here as in the footage I took in the park, but you'll see something."

They watched the footage, evidence of Annie clear in the slight distortions at certain points in the episode. Ben paused the film at Pat's wild swing and pointed at the screen. "Jo, you asked me to check when Annie might have directly interfered with Pat's play. Using the distortions as the basis for interference, she only did it three times. The first two were the putts she missed and the third was this air swing. I mean, Annie was off to the side in a lot of the wide shots I filmed, but I managed to dub the footage so the distortion isn't obvious."

Jo nodded, relieved. "Thanks. I think Lauren's still doubtful she won the tournament through her own efforts."

Ros snorted. "There's no way Pat could've beaten her, even without Annie's intervention. I watched the final round and Lauren was on a roll that day. I doubt anyone was capable of catching her."

"I know, but it's still a hard slog to convince her. Ben, is it possible I could have a copy of the uncut version?"

Ben ejected the disc and put it in its protective sleeve and retrieved a second disc from his bag, holding the two out to Jo. "This is your edited copy and the second disc is the complete unedited copy of the actual episode. I figured you'd need to show it to Lauren before it could be shown on television."

Jo gratefully accepted the two discs and placed them in a secure compartment of her daypack. "Thanks. It was part of the deal we made. I don't think she's going to have any problems with the final version, though."

Ben checked his watch and looked at Jo and Ros. "If you don't have any other questions, I'm due at an interview for my next job. Thankfully this one doesn't include wandering around the countryside or filming ghosts."

Jo rose and hugged him. "Admit it, you enjoyed every minute of it."

"It was a heck of a lot more fun than being shark bait." He grinned at her. Jo lightly kissed him on the cheek. "Thanks again for your support and your discretion with this story."

Ben smiled and disengaged himself from Jo's arms. "No worries, cheeky chops. You know me, discretion's my middle name." He jumped back, dodging another blow from her.

Ros addressed Ben. "Thanks for your work. As usual, it was first-rate."

Ben blushed. "God, I'd better get out of here before the two of you start crying over my imminent departure." He picked up his bag and turned to Jo, his face serious. "Best of luck, kiddo, whichever way things go with you and Lauren. And remember, any time you need a cameraman, just call."

Jo nodded. "Thanks, mate. I really do appreciate it."

She and Ros waited as Ben gave them another wave as he left the room.

Ros sat back down and glanced across at Jo. "When are you looking at getting the final clearance from Lauren? We're a little behind the release time with this one, and I'm keen to air it."

Jo sat down. "I'm due to head back down to Tasmania by the end of this week. I've just got a couple of loose ends I have to tie up here first. Lauren's working the full week so she could free up her weekend. She's expecting me on Friday."

Ros raised a brow. "I'm assuming you won't need a room at The Retreat?"

"No, I expect I'll be staying with Lauren."

"Is everything okay between the two of you?"

Jo shrugged. "They seem to be okay. I'm calling her every second day, but I sense she's starting to distance herself a bit. I mean, I keep telling her I'm coming back, but I've just got to get some things finalised here first before I do so."

Ros frowned. "What things?"

Jo avoided Ros's gaze, and focused instead on the cuff of her shirtsleeve. "I'd prefer to talk to Lauren about those things first."

Ros searched Jo's face. She narrowed her eyes and then slowly nodded as much to herself as to anyone else. "You know, someone in your profession can work from anywhere."

Jo coyly smiled and stood. "I suppose I can, as long as there's connectivity with the outside world. I'll give you a call once I've shown Lauren the episode."

Ros got up as well and gave Jo a hug. "Thanks. Don't forget about your friends on the mainland."

"You make it sound like I'm leaving the mainland for good."

Ros folded her arms, a knowing smile on her face. "Aren't you?"

JO HAD BARELY finished the first knock on the door when it flew open and Lauren enveloped her in an all-encompassing hug. She passionately kissed Lauren, revelling in their reconnection.

Jo lightly stroked Lauren's face. "Hey, babe," She said, butterflies dancing in her stomach.

Lauren disengaged herself and picked up Jo's bag. "Where have you been? I thought you were going to be here an hour ago."

"I was, but there were some issues with the car hire company at the airport."

Lauren placed Jo's bag on the lounge. "I could've taken the day off and come and picked you up, you know."

Jo smiled and closed the door. "I know, but I brought someone with me and I expect she'll need the car in a couple of days." She snuggled against Lauren's back. "Besides, you said you'd been working back-to-back shifts so we could have some time together when I got here."

Lauren turned and placed a light kiss on Jo's head. "Who did you bring?"

"Her name's Shannon McClean." Jo nuzzled Lauren's shirt.

"Is she on holiday at The Retreat?"

"Not exactly. I've arranged for us to meet tomorrow. But in the meantime, what does a girl need to do to get a coffee around here?"

"Just ask." Lauren kissed her again and went into the kitchen. "Why do you want me to meet her?"

Jo hopped up onto a stool at the breakfast bay, content to watch Lauren as she put the electric jug on its base and flicked the switch.

"You'll find out tomorrow, but I promise it doesn't involve filming or interviews."

Lauren pulled two mugs down from one of the cupboards, along with a coffee plunger. "Speaking of which, did you bring the film?" She reached into the fridge and retrieved a container of fresh coffee.

"Of course. In fact, I bought two copies." Jo reached down into the pack by her side, retrieving the DVDs. "The edited and the unedited version."

Lauren took the two discs from Jo, studying them with a pensive expression. "Is there anything of Annie on these?"

"Yes, but only on the unedited version. Ben did a great job of dubbing and filming around Annie. I think you'll be happy with the final product. God only knows Ros is."

"She must be jumping out of her skin, waiting for my go-ahead."

Jo shrugged. "Ros knew the deal from the get-go. The episode wouldn't be shown until you've approved the final product."

Lauren looked at the discs, both clearly defined by their titles. "Are you happy with the final product?"

"I'm more than happy. It tells your story in a very positive light, yet gives nothing away about you that would give you cause for concern. It's just as we agreed. Trust me."

Lauren turned the episode disc over and pursed her lips, a slight crease on her forehead. She slowly exhaled and handed the DVD back to Jo. "I do trust you. You can tell Ros she can show it whenever she wants to."

Jo raised her brows as she took the disc from Lauren. She glanced at the DVD and blinked back a tear at Lauren's faith in her. "Thank you. That means a lot to me." She took Lauren's hand. "And I figure you know I'm not talking about the episode."

Lauren bowed her head but not before Jo caught the ghost of a smile on her face. The whistle of the kettle broke the tableau and Lauren reluctantly removed her hand from Jo's reassuring grasp. "What have you been up to over the past couple of weeks?" She turned off the kettle and poured three measured spoons of ground coffee into the plunger.

"Oh, just stuff. Nothing terribly interesting," Jo deflected, grateful Lauren wasn't facing her when she told what she knew was a white lie. "I spent a lot of time with my mum."

"How is she?" Lauren poured a generous measure of water from the kettle into the plunger and then placed the lid on the press.

Jo rested her elbows on the bench and cupped her cheeks. "Her leg's healing well. Things are also moving along between her and Andrew, although she's still a little preoccupied about what Dad would think."

Lauren poured a dash of milk into the two mugs. "What do you think?"

"I couldn't be happier for her. I'm just a bit worried Andrew's patience may end up wearing a little thin and he'll walk away."

Lauren picked up the two mugs and headed for her sofa. Jo grabbed the unedited disc from the counter and followed her.

"From what you've said, if he's hung around *this* long, I don't think he'll give up easily." Lauren held a cup out to Jo. "Especially if he's taken any lessons from you." She winked.

Jo took the proffered coffee and took a sip. "Thanks. Patience is a virtue of mine, you know."

"One of your many." Lauren motioned at the disc on the table. "Can we watch it now?"

"Sure." Jo tucked her legs beneath her, making herself comfortable on the couch.

Lauren set the DVD up in the player then grabbed the remote and headed back to where Jo had eased herself into the softness of the sofa. She took Jo's hand and pressed the play button.

For the next eighty minutes the two sat through the uncut footage of the actual episode, replete with Annie's presence and more than a few comical outtakes. Lauren hit the pause button as the footage faded to a blue screen.

"I trust the picture of me sitting in the pond after the water shot with my wig of pond weed didn't make the final cut," Lauren deadpanned, obviously fighting to keep the smile from her face.

Jo kissed the tip of Lauren's nose. "No, that one's for private viewing only."

Lauren gazed at the remote and then at the panoramic window, usually affording a view of Cradle Mountain. At that moment it was no more than an inky black sheet of glass. "Annie was only really close in those two putts and then at the tee."

"Yes she was. Your skill won you the tournament, not Annie's antics, although they do make for entertaining viewing."

Lauren lapsed into silence.

"You didn't doubt your ability, did you?"

Lauren looked down at her hands then at her. "I suppose in a little way I did."

"Annie was good to her word, at least most of the time. She was there for you. She just kept her distance."

"Yes, she was, wasn't she?"

"Have you seen her recently?"

"No, but I know she's still around. I can still sense her." Lauren raised her hand, attempting unsuccessfully to stifle her yawn. "I'm sorry, but it's been a long day and an equally long week. I know we should head up to the tavern for dinner, but can I interest you in soup instead?"

Jo stood and held out her hand to Lauren, who took it and rose. "Why don't you show me where the soup is and I'll make us some."

She made a pretense of leaning forward and sniffing Lauren's shirt. "In the meantime, you get yourself showered and changed and out of your work clothes."

Lauren pulled her shirt away from her chest and sniffed. "I suppose I could do with a wash, couldn't I?" She smiled apologetically and picked up Jo's suitcase. "I'll put this in the bedroom then?"

Jo felt her heart miss a beat, quietly liking the way Lauren's question sounded. "Thanks. I guess I just assumed —"

Lauren put a finger against Jo's lips, effectively halting further comment. "You assumed correctly. If you think for one moment you were going to be staying up at The Retreat and I here, then you're sorely mistaken, missy." She motioned with her head toward the kitchen. "Check the long cupboard just to the left of the fridge. You'll find an impressive supply of tinned soup there."

"By the sounds of that, I think we're going to be doing some shopping before too long." Jo smiled at Lauren's reaction to the implication behind her words.

Lauren lightly touched her lips to Jo's. "I couldn't think of anything better." She headed toward the bedroom and a shower.

JO SPOONED LAUREN and smiled when Lauren grabbed her hand. Jo proprietarily moved her fingers to Lauren's breast. She placed a series of feather soft kisses between Lauren's shoulder blades, while simultaneously stroking Lauren's nipple. Her efforts were rewarded when Lauren rolled over, effectively pinning Jo beneath her.

"Can't anyone get some sleep around here?" Lauren growled as she lowered her head and nuzzled Jo's throat.

Jo angled her head, granting Lauren greater access. She ran her fingers through Lauren's hair. "I thought you got enough sleep last night."

Lauren nipped at Jo's neck then kissed the skin of her neck before raising her eyes to Jo's. "I'm sorry. I couldn't believe how tired I was."

Jo's heart swelled with a love that filled her every being. "You weren't the only one who was tired. I love the idea that you felt comfortable enough to fall asleep like you did. And besides, our relationship's more than just the physical element. Although I do enjoy *that* part of it." She squirmed when Lauren reached down and tickled her ribs. "It's about supporting one another as well."

Lauren teased Jo's lips with her tongue in unspoken question.

Jo moaned and she opened her mouth, granting Lauren entry. Without thinking she arched her hips and her tongue began a slow intense dance with Lauren's.

Lauren raised her head, chuckling when Jo's lips seemed to pursue her own. "So, can I cash in my rain check now?"

Jo gently toyed with Lauren's nipple. "What rain check?"

Lauren looked down at Jo's errant hand and released a shuddering breath. "The one you gave me on the final day of the tournament. I was figuring we'd better be clean when we meet your friend." She waggled her eyebrows as if in invitation. "Care for a shower?"

Jo took Lauren's nipple between her lips, softly biting the tender flesh before letting go. "I thought you'd never ask. Does your water heater have enough capacity?"

Lauren laughed. "I expect we're just about to find out." She eased herself off Jo.

Jo shivered as she climbed out of the bed.

Lauren wrapped Jo in the duvet. "I'd forgotten how cold it can get in the mornings. I suppose I'm used to it."

Jo snuggled into the duvet's warmth. "I can really tell the difference in the weather from when I was last here."

Lauren pulled on a flannel night shirt that settled mid-thigh and motioned Jo to the window. She pointed toward Cradle Mountain. "There's the reason. The peak of the mountain had its first decent snow on Wednesday. Give it another two weeks and we should get our first solid ground cover over the rest of the higher areas."

Jo scooped Lauren into the duvet and hugged her from behind, relishing the feel of the soft flannel on her skin. "How about that shower?"

Lauren took Jo's hand and led her back into the bedroom. "Wait while I get it ready. I don't want you standing in there freezing, while I'm waiting for the water to heat up."

Shortly thereafter, Lauren appeared and held out her hands to Jo. "All set." She smiled and Jo rose, allowing the duvet to pool around her feet, and she stepped over the pile. She gently snatched the edge of Lauren's flannel night shirt, and pulled it clear of her body, dropping it. She silently followed Lauren into the bathroom and stepped into a reasonably generous shower recess.

"Thank God for the size of modern showers." She pulled Lauren against her, the warm water sluicing over their bodies. She tilted her head back, allowing the water to dampen her hair.

Lauren nibbled at Jo's exposed neck and pulled her closer, hands on her back. Jo picked up the bar of soap, lathered her hands, and returned it to its holder. She began a leisurely cleansing of Lauren's back, while at the same time licking and sucking Lauren's nipples.

"God, that feels good." Lauren took the soap and rubbed it between her own hands. She made room between them, and a spray of water splashed between their bodies. With both hands, Lauren splayed her fingers over Jo's collar bone, making a soapy circular trail to Jo's breasts. "You're so beautiful. Sometimes I wonder how I've managed to be so lucky."

Jo curved herself into Lauren's caresses. "No, I'm the lucky one. I never thought I'd find someone I wanted to spend the rest of my life with, and now I have."

Lauren paused and she searched Jo's face, as if measuring the earnestness of her words. "I couldn't think of anyone else I'd like to spend my life with." She slowly turned Jo around, so the water could rinse the soap from Jo's chest and from her own hands. She kissed the back of Jo's neck as her fingers strummed Jo's front, dipping lower with each tender kiss, until they reached their destination.

"Yes," Jo gasped when Lauren slid her fingers into Jo's heat. She raised her leg and placed her foot on the small footrest in one of the corners of the shower, affording Lauren greater access. "Inside," she whispered, "go inside."

Lauren coated her fingers in Jo's wetness and slowly entered her. Jo's knees buckled at the contact and Lauren wrapped her other arm around Jo's waist. She began a slow but steady rhythm, while softly drawing her thumb across Jo's sensitive skin.

"A little faster," Jo cried, her hips moving in synchronization with Lauren's efforts.

Lauren moaned as Jo began to undulate. "Let go, baby," she whispered, her breathing ragged. "Let go."

Jo screamed in release and slowly sank to the floor of the shower, taking Lauren with her. As the two of them lay beneath the warm spray, Jo's body continued to twitch at Lauren's ministrations, and she placed a steadying hand over Lauren's. "Stop or I'm not going to be able to walk," she joked.

"Have you any idea what hearing you let go like that does to me?" Lauren passionately kissed Jo as she gently removed her fingers.

Without breaking the kiss, Jo turned and trailed her fingers down the front of Lauren's body. Lauren moaned as Jo reached the top of her tender flesh. Jo broke their kiss. "Stand for me."

Lauren silently stood and braced her back against the wall as she gazed lovingly at Jo.

"Yeah, like that." Jo knelt and kissed Lauren's stomach. She gripped Lauren's backside, intimately stroking between Lauren's cheeks, all the while bringing her kisses lower, toward Lauren's centre.

Lauren closed her eyes and snapped her head back, in turn connecting with the wall.

Jo's tongue lightly teased Lauren, only interrupting her actions when she raked her teeth across Lauren's centre. Feeling Lauren's hand on the back of her head, as if holding her in place, Jo smiled and nuzzled closer.

In concert with her tongue, Jo covered her fingers with Lauren's moisture. She laved her tongue against Lauren as her fingers entered her, sucking Lauren as she curled her fingers back toward her.

"Oh, Jesus, not much longer," Lauren managed, her hips bucking.

Jo's fingers plunged deeper as she again lightly drew her teeth over Lauren.

Lauren braced her hands against the edge of the shower and shuddered as she came, barely managing to remain standing as Jo continued to caress her, using her tongue. She reached down and steadied Jo's head.

"Enough or I'll be the one who won't be able to walk." Lauren gradually sank to the floor and kissed Jo, shuddering again as she tasted herself on Jo's mouth.

Lauren tipped her head back into the cascade of water. She shook the water from her eyes and gazed at Jo. "Meeting with your friend doesn't involve too much walking, does it?"

Jo smiled enigmatically. "It might."

Chapter
Eighteen

LAUREN WAVED TO the desk clerk of The Retreat as she and Jo walked through the front doors of the lodge. Jo picked up one of the complimentary papers and walked to where the clerk stood. "I know I'm not officially a guest, but I'd be happy to pay for this."

The clerk dismissively waved her hand. "Don't worry about it, Miss Ashby. You were a guest long enough to earn at least *some* privileges."

Jo nodded her thanks and followed Lauren into the Cowle Lounge, where they took a seat in the plush leather chairs by the fire.

Lauren crossed her legs and looked around. As it was still early in the morning, the only other people in the room were the staff, tidying up from the previous night's activities. She returned her gaze to Jo. "You haven't told me yet what we're doing here, and who your friend is."

Jo scanned the local paper, seemingly preoccupied by its contents. "I told you. Her name's Shannon McClean. You'll like her."

Lauren released a slightly exasperated breath. "That's about *all* you've told me."

"Hey, look at this." Jo sat forward in her seat, pointing to an article on the second page of *The Tasmanian Daily*. "Apparently the major television network here has gained themselves a new news anchor, Lise Crowley." Jo's finger traced down the article, focusing on the salient elements of information. "It says she amicably separated from her husband. The evening news network in Tasmania provided a new start for her."

Jo smugly smiled and placed the paper on the seat beside her. "It looks like she listened to my advice after all. I told her to move on."

"You do possess the innate ability to wear people down. Look at me, for instance."

Jo scanned the room and then leant forward. "I intend to wear you down every day for the rest of your life," she whispered, "and this morning was only the beginning."

Lauren's eyes sparkled. "I didn't mean that, but I like the idea. Now, are you going to tell me anything more about this Shannon McClean?"

"I should've told you sooner, but I wasn't sure I'd get you here." She reached for Lauren's hand and nervously cleared her throat.

Lauren frowned and took Jo's hand. "What's wrong?"

"Nothing's wrong. It's just...hell, on the mainland this seemed like such a good idea." Jo lowered her head.

Lauren bent her head to try to meet Jo's gaze. "Babe, you're beginning to scare me. What's a good idea?"

Jo sighed and met Lauren's gaze. "Shannon's a medium." She hung on to Lauren's hand even as she felt her begin to withdraw. "Please, hear me out. Shannon and her partner Andrea have been good friends of mine for years now and, from what her partner says, she's very good at what she does."

Lauren pulled her hand from Jo's and looked at the fire. "What did you tell her?"

"Only enough for her to help. I told her you had a spirit guide in the park, who followed you around. I didn't mention anything else about your relationship with Annie. I'd never do that."

Lauren sighed and shook her head. "If she's as good as you say she is, then it won't take her long to figure it out."

Jo again took Lauren's hand, and softly stroked it. "Trust me when I tell you she's not one to discuss what she does for a living. Andrea says Shannon takes her ability very seriously. Hell, sometimes even Andrea doesn't know who she's been helping."

Lauren closed her eyes and craned her neck. "I don't know. Why did you do this?"

"The other day I was surprised when you mentioned that Annie was still around. I called Shannon, hoping I might be able to help you both. I honestly thought Annie would've moved on by now, but then something you'd said earlier during my trip dawned on me. She's still looking for Marta. I thought that maybe Shannon could find Marta for her." Jo stroked Lauren's cheek with her free hand. "I did this because I love you, not because I wanted to get rid of Annie. The idea of her looking for Marta for the rest of eternity can't be something you want, is it?"

Lauren looked down at their intertwined hands and then at Jo. "No, it isn't. So how does Shannon do this?"

Jo rose. "Here she is now. She can tell you herself. Hey, Shannon." Jo waved at the woman entering the lounge.

"Hi, Jo." Shannon's short, athletic frame wound its way around the maze of chairs and ottomans. She smiled at Jo and then looked at Lauren. "You must be Lauren." She held out her hand.

Lauren shook Shannon's hand. "I am. It's nice to meet you, though I have to say Jo's only *now* told me what you're here for."

Shannon chuckled. "Jo can be a little short on details sometimes. Why don't we sit down and, if it's okay, I'll ask you a few questions."

Lauren seemed to relax and Jo released a breath she didn't realise she was holding. *You always had the ability to put people at ease, didn't you Shannon.*

Shannon scrutinized Lauren. "I'm figuring you've never really spoken with a medium before."

"No." Lauren's hand gripped Jo's.

"Let me put some fears to rest. I don't have a black cat, nor do I own a great big cauldron or a bottle of eye of newt. And I don't dance naked under the full moon." Shannon's eyes twinkled mischievously. "Although I expect my partner wouldn't be too disappointed if I acted out the last one. I used to be a five-star chef, but these days I'm a full-time wife to Andrea and full-time mum to my children. And boy, can they be a handful."

Lauren eased back into her chair. "How did you find out you were, you know, a medium?"

"I knew I was different when I was young. I could see and talk with people who my friends couldn't see." Shannon flicked a lock of her short brown hair out of her slate-blue eyes. "Plus, it was to be expected. It's an ability all the women of my family share. Jo tells me you've both seen Annie and can sense her presence."

"She's helped me on the mountain a number of times with rescuing people. I've known her for the better part of nine years." Lauren bit her bottom lip then released it. "Did Jo tell you about Annie and Marta?"

"Yes."

Lauren leant forward toward Shannon. "Is there the possibility you'll be able to talk with Annie, and at least find out what happened to Marta?"

"Talking to Annie and working out Marta's predicament are two separate issues. While I might be able to pick up on Annie's presence, I'll only be able to talk to her if she wants to talk to me."

"Like she did with me during the last rescue at the lake," Jo interjected. "I saw her but it wasn't until the hut that she actually spoke with me."

Shannon smiled. "Often it's the spirit who makes the decision as to who they connect with. She sounds like she's reasonably approachable and that's a good thing."

"I wouldn't go that far," Jo grumbled, settling back in her chair.

Lauren patted Jo's shoulder and returned her attention to Shannon. "What about finding Marta?"

"I don't necessarily need Annie to do that. And, if what Jo's told me is true, Annie mightn't be of too much use, especially if she hasn't managed to find her after all these years." Shannon scratched her chin as if in thought. "In fact, there's every possibility Marta's already crossed over and Annie just doesn't realise it."

Lauren reached for Jo's hand. "If you find where Marta died, will Annie cross over?"

"She may. It's usually what happens in situations like this."

Jo felt Lauren's hand again grip hers at Shannon's last words. She gently touched Lauren's arm. "Are you okay with that?" Several emotions crossed Lauren's face. "Shannon, can you give us a minute?"

"Sure. I'll just go and grab a coffee and be right back."

Jo watched Shannon to leave. She turned to Lauren and gently stroked her hand. "What's on your mind?"

Lauren exhaled. "I just don't know if this is a good idea."

"Honey, I understand what you're thinking, but you've got to let Annie go. It wouldn't be fair to do anything else."

Lauren lowered her head. "I know, but it's just hard to believe I might lose her after knowing her for so long."

"You might lose her, but you'll never lose her memories, just as she'll never lose the ones she has of you." Jo raised Lauren's hand to her lips and placed a feather-light kiss on Lauren's knuckles. "You understand, don't you?"

Jo watched an internal battle play itself out on Lauren's face. After what seemed like an interminable silence, Lauren finally spoke.

"I understand, and you're right. Annie needs to move on." She raised her face to Jo's and sighed. "Let's find Shannon and be on our way."

JO GOT OUT of Lauren's four-wheel drive and zipped up her parka. She retrieved a beanie and gloves from the jacket's pockets and put them on. "It's a heck of a lot colder than when I was last here."

Lauren locked the vehicle and motioned at Cradle Mountain. "The snow and the wind off Dove Lake aren't making things any easier."

"This is a lot chillier than Sydney." Shannon pulled on a pair of gloves. "Of course, the good side is, I expect it keeps the tourists away and makes my job a little easier." She turned to Lauren. "Is there anywhere we can go to get out of this wind?"

Lauren motioned to the weather-beaten boatshed on the right forward shore of the lake. "We can try there. It won't be completely cosy, but it'll give you some protection."

In less than five minutes they stood in the cold shed, relieved to be out of the wind.

Jo looked at Shannon. "What do we do now?"

Shannon held up her hand. She seemed to reach out to the open space in front of her, much like Jo had seen Lauren do so many times before. Shannon squinted and then smiled. "Hello, Annie."

Jo looked over at Lauren for confirmation.

Lauren nodded. "She's here."

"Here? In the boat shed?" Jo tried to remain calm.

"Not exactly," Lauren squeezed Jo's arm. "But she's close by."

Shannon moved to the edge of the boat shed and turned her face into the wind. "Annie, I'm Shannon. Lauren's told me what happened and I'm terribly sorry for your loss. I'd like to try and find Marta, if you'll allow me to."

A silent exchange seemed to occur between Shannon and Annie. Jo nudged Lauren. "Can you hear what they're saying?"

Lauren nodded. "Annie's asking Shannon what makes her so sure she can find Marta when Annie's been trying to find her for years."

"I can't guarantee I'll find her," Shannon replied. "But will you at least let me try?" She waited a beat. "Thank you, Annie. I'll do my best."

Jo and Lauren followed Shannon to the leeward side of the boat shed. Shannon gazed out across the expanse of Dove Lake and then frowned before she slowly nodded. "Whatever happened to Marta happened near water."

"What do you mean, what happened?" Jo asked.

"Marta's death. She died near water, here on the mountain." Shannon turned and headed to the path that led to the car park.

Jo scrambled after her. "Was it here, at Dove Lake?"

Shannon looked behind her. "No. This lake's too big."

"There are six other bodies of water in this part of the park," Lauren said as they made their way to the car park. "It could be any one of them."

Shannon pursed her lips as if in thought. "It may be, but I get the feeling it's out of the way, somewhere tourists wouldn't normally walk."

Lauren bit her lip in contemplation. "That narrows it down a little bit."

Shannon scanned the surrounding terrain and then suddenly turned. "It's over this way," she pointed to her left, "along the track."

Jo pulled out her map of the mountain and tracked her finger along a path. "Other than Dove Lake, there are three other lakes along or near this track."

Shannon raked her fingers through her hair and narrowed her eyes. "I'm hearing a surname." She turned to Lauren. "Does that help?"

"Lake Wilks is along the path," Lauren offered.

Shannon gazed at the left side of the lake. "No, it doesn't sound right."

"What about Lake Hanson?" Jo queried. "It's the only other one on the left side with a surname."

"It's still a fair size of water but it is smaller than Dove Lake," Lauren agreed.

Shannon shrugged. "I'm sorry this isn't a more exact science, but I suppose there's only one way to find out which lake's the right one."

Jo folded her map and stowed it in her pocket. "Lauren, if we're going to climb to Lake Hanson then shouldn't we sign out at the walkers' hut?"

Lauren looked toward the hut and then doubtfully at Shannon. "It's a bit of a climb."

Shannon put her hands on her hips and smiled. "I might look out of shape, but believe me, as a result of my current job of house spouse to two unruly children and, sometimes, an equally unruly wife, I'm a lot more robust than I seem. But I expect it's something you two will learn when you have children of your own."

Lauren's eyes goggled at Shannon's last comment and Jo gulped. "Are you trying to tell us something?"

Shannon knowingly smiled. "I expect it's for me to know and for you to find out." She turned to Lauren. "Let's get moving before my butt permanently turns into a block of ice."

JO SCRAMBLED ACROSS the track and onto a rocky outcrop affording a view of the choppy waters of Lake Hanson. The perimeter of the lake was dotted with button grass scrub, and only the occasional King Billy pine, with the remaining area liberally sprinkled with craggy rock formations. She turned as Lauren stood beside her. "I can see how something could happen here. Aside from a track you'd almost have to be a psychic to be able to follow, the ground here isn't all that forgiving."

Lauren offered a hand-up to Shannon. "No, it isn't. It's a pretty exposed area. Despite regular maintenance on the track, the markers always seem to wear here more readily than anywhere else on the mountain."

"And," Shannon wiped the mud from the knees of her walking pants, "if I'm guessing correctly, then in Annie and Marta's time this track wasn't marked at all."

"You're probably right," Lauren said, "though it would've been known to the local walkers of the area. Even today it can still be treacherous if you stray from the path. Can you sense anything?"

Shannon glanced around. "There's a lot of energy here." She motioned to a point on the lake that seemed to disappear over the edge of the escarpment. "Can we get to that spot?"

Lauren nodded. "Yes, but it's not a formed track, so there'll be a bit of bush-bashing needed to get there."

Jo lightly touched Lauren's arm. "What about wandering off the allocated tracks? We're not supposed to do that, are we?"

Lauren smiled and bumped her gently with her shoulder. "I know we're not, but if we stay pretty close to the edge of the lake and I lead the way, then that should ensure we don't do too much damage."

After another half-hour of concerted, careful walking they stood at their destination. Shannon glanced at the narrow avenue of moss-covered rocks that separated the lake from their location and the precipice below.

Lauren reached down and picked up two lichen-covered stones, handing one to Jo and the other to Shannon. "When the snow melts the water runs over this part of the mountain." Jo ran her fingers over the rock's slippery surface. "This is why," Lauren continued, "we don't have a path here. It's too easy to lose someone over the edge."

Jo's eyes widened. "Do you think —" she stopped when Shannon handed the rock she was holding to Lauren.

Shannon cautiously moved forward and out onto a rocky outcrop. She crouched down and placed her palm on the grey-green surface.

Lauren instinctively reached out toward her. "Please don't go any farther. The ground underfoot is fairly unstable past where you're currently standing."

Shannon nodded. She bent her head, closed her eyes and then straightened. "This is where it happened."

Jo looked past Shannon's shoulder. "Marta died here," she whispered.

Shannon held up her hand and inclined her head, as if listening.

Jo turned to Lauren, who had taken up a similar stance to that of Shannon. "What's going on?"

"Annie's telling Shannon she never searched for Marta here because Marta very rarely walked this track."

Lauren grimaced as if in pain. She glanced across the narrow avenue of rocks to a spot twenty-five metres from where they stood.

"It's not your fault you never looked here, Annie," Lauren said. "You know as well as I do just how big this mountain is. Marta's death could've happened anywhere."

Shannon nodded. "Lauren's right." she held up her hand. "And that's not me speaking, Annie. It's Marta."

Jo gasped and a chill ran up her spine. She'd barely recovered from Shannon's words when Annie materialised on the spot where she'd been looking. Shannon calmly gazed at Annie, as if ghosts appearing were an everyday event. "Marta's saying you have to believe her. If she hadn't been so stubborn on the day the two of you argued, then her death wouldn't have happened. But when the fog came in she lost sight of the track. She says she wandered off it and fell."

Annie desperately looked around, as if searching for Marta. Frustration gathered on Annie's face and the wind began to pick up, buffeting the group where they stood.

Lauren pulled Shannon back from the outcrop, simultaneously steadying Jo with her other hand. "Annie, listen to Shannon. Marta says it was *her* fault, not yours."

As Annie folded her arms across her chest a passing cloud covered the sun, reducing the surrounding light to a cold dullness. "How do I know you're not making this whole scenario up?" She pointed at Shannon. "Why can you hear Marta and I can't?"

"It's because she's left this earth. She's crossed over. She's using me to speak with you." Shannon took a step toward the moss-covered bridge that separated her from Annie. It was only Lauren's grip on her arm that stopped her.

"Can you hear Marta?" Jo whispered to Lauren.

"No, just Annie. But what Shannon's saying about Marta's accident makes sense. Marta isn't the only one who's died in this spot. We've lost two other walkers here in similar circumstances over the years."

Shannon shook herself free of Lauren's grip. "I won't go any farther than where I am, I promise."

Lauren nodded her assent before returning her gaze to Annie. "Marta's waiting for you Annie." she said.

Annie alternated her focus between Lauren, Shannon, and the edge where Marta had fallen to her death. "Lauren, what do I do?"

Shannon turned to Jo and frowned. "You mentioned Annie showed herself to Lauren and helped her in the park. Is that *all* there is to the friendship between the two of them?"

Jo quickly glanced at Lauren.

"No, Annie loves me," Lauren replied, "and, for a long time, I felt the same way."

Shannon stared at Jo. "Given your profession as a journalist I should've *known* there was more to this than what you told me." She turned to Lauren. "If I'm guessing correctly, then Annie won't go while you hold her here. It must be you who releases her from this world, or she'll never go to Marta."

Jo took Lauren's hand, trying to convey the strength Lauren needed to make such a choice. "I know this is hard, but you've got to do it."

Lauren's eyes welled with tears.

Shannon took a step backward toward the two. "I can't keep the connection with Marta forever. I can already feel her pulling away. If you're going to do something Lauren, then you've got to do it *now*."

Lauren stepped around Shannon, and focused on Annie. "Marta's waited for you long enough. You need to go now, Annie."

Indecision was clear on Annie's features. "I'll always love you."

Lauren softly smiled and nodded. "I understand, but now you need to be with your *true* love."

Annie lowered her hands to her sides and sadly smiled. She raised one arm in farewell to the group and faded into the surrounding landscape. As she did, the clouds began to clear away from the sun and the wind died down, leaving them in silence.

Lauren turned back to Shannon. "They're together?"

Shannon closed her eyes and again seemed to centre herself. After a moment she opened her eyes. "Yes, they are."

"Thank you." Lauren pulled Jo into a hug and kissed her cheek. "Thanks for your help. I don't know why I didn't think of this sooner."

Jo gently wiped the tears from Lauren's face. "Even if you had, I don't think either of you were ready yet for what happened today. Now you're both ready to move on."

"I love you," Lauren replied, softly kissing Jo's lips. Jo pulled away and lovingly cupped Lauren's face with her palm. "I think we'd better be heading down before the weather changes."

"You're right again, of course." She entwined her fingers with Jo's. "Come on Shannon, we'd better get you out of here before your butt really does freeze."

Shannon held up her hand. "Hang on a minute. Marta says there's someone else. Someone who needs to talk to Jo."

Jo looked at Lauren and then Shannon. "I don't understand."

Shannon vigorously waved her hand, as if to clear her thoughts. "I'm losing contact, but—" she looked toward Jo, a soft smile on her lips. "It's Liam."

Jo's bottom lip quivered as tears welled in her eyes. "Daddy?" she whispered, her voice full of hope. She felt Lauren's comforting touch in the small of her back.

"He says, yes, pumpkin, it's him," Shannon said. He wants you to tell your mum it's okay. It's time for her to move on."

With Shannon's last words Jo's tears began to flow. "Daddy, I'm sorry I wasn't there for you."

"He says you were there in his heart. You're always there," Shannon gently replied.

Jo gazed around her surroundings vainly hoping her father would appear. "I love you, Daddy," she sobbed.

"He says he loves you, too, pumpkin and he'll always be there for you." Shannon sighed. "I'm sorry, but he's gone. The connection's broken."

Jo turned into Lauren's arms and cried in earnest. In their silent surrounds Lauren stroked her back until Jo's tears gradually subsided. She reached into her pocket, pulled out a handkerchief, blew her nose, and cleared her throat. "I'm sorry."

"Hey," Lauren placed a finger under Jo's chin and raised it so Lauren's eyes were locked with hers. "There's nothing to be sorry for. I would've done the same if my mother and father had turned up."

Shannon touched Lauren's arm. "I'm sorry, but I didn't pick up anything else. The connection was pretty tenuous at the end, but I do know Annie's finally reached Marta."

This time it was Lauren who sniffled, before she swallowed and rubbed her eyes. "I'm glad." She gathered herself then quietly said, "We'd better start heading down."

JO EASED HERSELF out of Lauren's four-wheel drive, in front of Shannon's guest cabin. She moved around to Shannon and hugged her hard. "Thanks for your help. What you've given all of us — Lauren, my mum, me — can never be repaid."

Shannon smiled. "I've already received my payment and it's the look on the faces of the two of you."

"All the same," Lauren grabbed Shannon and hugged her. "Thank you from me, Jo, and Annie. I can't tell you how much it means to me to know Annie's where she finally needs to be."

Shannon pulled gently away. "I'm just glad things ended as well as they did." Her face sobered. "Sometimes they don't."

Jo wondered at that, but didn't address it. "What are your plans for the rest of the day?"

Shannon picked up her daypack. "First, I'm going to have a little sleep and then have a long hot soak. Some days I think I'm getting too old for climbing up and down bloody great mountains."

They laughed and Jo poked her playfully in the shoulder. "You are joining us at the lodge for dinner aren't you? It's my treat."

Lauren placed her arm around Jo's shoulders. "No, it's mine. It's the least I can do."

"Hey, I said it first."

Shannon laughed, attempting to defuse a potential disagreement between them. "You two work it out." She headed for the steps of her cabin. "In the meantime," she called over her shoulder, "I'm going to have a nap."

JO FOLLOWED LAUREN as she entered the cabin and turned on the radio. She tossed her keys onto the coffee table. Jo held her hands up in defeat. "Okay, you can buy dinner, if we can go out grocery shopping tomorrow. You're in dire need of some decent nutrition."

Lauren pulled Jo to her. "You're all the sustenance I need."

"Thanks for the compliment, but I doubt it."

Lauren slowly ran her fingers through Jo's hair. "When are you going to tell your mum about what happened today?"

"I'll call her on my cell at the lodge tonight. The mobile phone reception inside the park's non-existent. I can't wait to hear what she says."

Before Lauren replied, the park's two-way radio sputtered to life.

"Lauren, this is park base. Are you there?"

Lauren groaned softly. "I'm definitely off-duty today. They can find the on-duty rescue guide," she muttered. "This is Lauren," she tersely replied.

"Lauren, is Jo there with you? We have a message for her."

Lauren frowned, puzzled, at the microphone then silently handed the mouthpiece to Jo.

"Yes, I'm here. Is anything wrong?"

"Hi, Jo. We have a message from a Melissa Rylatt for you. She said to pass on that the contract's been signed."

Jo fought to contain her excitement, and dropped the microphone. She quickly retrieved it and pressed the talk switch. "That's great news! Thanks."

"No worries, we're happy to be of service. Out."

Lauren put her hands on her hips as Jo jigged around the room in a little dance. "What's going on?"

"I told you my phone doesn't work well in the park, so I asked the ranger on duty if I could leave Melissa their number so she could contact me when the contract was signed."

Lauren shook her head. "I still don't get it. What contract? Are you off on another shoot already?"

Jo picked up Lauren's keys from the coffee table. "No, I'm not off on another shoot. But it's probably easier if I show you." She tossed the keys up and caught them again. "Can I drive?"

Lauren rolled her eyes in mock exasperation. "Sure. What's one more surprise today?"

It wasn't long before Jo pulled the vehicle to the side of the road, just outside the park proper. She checked her rear vision mirror for oncoming traffic and then turned to Lauren. "Follow me." She got out and walked toward an old wooden gate, Lauren close behind.

Jo made a show of opening the gate and motioning a confused Lauren through it. Looking toward a sign just inside the gate, Jo headed right for it. She bent over, gripped the sign's post, and began pulling at it with all her might.

Lauren stood hands on hips, barely managing to keep the laughter from her voice. "What on *earth* do you think you're doing?"

"I'm —" Jo bent her knees more and tightened her grip — "trying..." she grunted, "to get rid of this!" Her final words were met with success as the stubborn post left the ground. She and the sign fell backward onto the damp earth.

Lauren quickly walked to Jo's side and helped her up. "Are you all right?"

Jo wiped dirt from the seat of her pants. "I'm fine, but I didn't think that sucker was ever going to come out."

Lauren glanced down at the sign and then back at Jo. "That's a For Sale sign. You could be charged with trespassing."

"Maybe yesterday. Maybe even half an hour ago." Jo slapped the dirt from her hands. "But not now." She gestured around her. "This is why I've been stuck on the mainland for the past two weeks."

Lauren's eyes widened. "You mean you bought this?"

Jo smiled and wiped her cheek, leaving a smear of dirt in its place. "I wasn't only wrapping up the filming. I was wrapping up business matters as well." She took Lauren's hand. "I didn't just buy this for me. I bought it for *us*. This is where I want to be, where the two of us can live together. I know you need to be near the park and this was about the closest I could get and still be able to get reception so I can continue my work. It's ten acres and it's all ours."

Lauren shook her head in disbelief. "I don't know what to say."

Jo reached up, snaked her hand around the back of Lauren's neck and pulled her close. "Just say you love me, you crazy woman," she uttered and brought her lips to Lauren's.

Jo wasn't sure how long they remained locked together, and it was only the enthusiastic honking of a passing car's horn that broke the intimate embrace. She snuggled into Lauren's jacket.

"I love you, but I do think there're going to be some problems," Lauren replied, a hint of teasing in her voice.

"What?"

Lauren stroked Jo's hair. "Fluff the wombat, for one. I think she's used to being just outside my back door."

Jo chuckled and mock growled. "If I can bloody-well move, then so can she." She once again captured Lauren's lips with her own.

The End

ANOTHER HELEN MACPHERSON TITLE

Colder Than Ice

Allison Shaunessy is a woman on the edge. As an archaeologist with the Flinders Museum of Australasian Exploration, she and her team are racing against time to secure funding for an unprecedented excavation in Antarctica. Despite her best attempts, she despairs when she falls short of her financial goal.

In America, Michela DeGrasse, a psychologist with the International Space Research Institute, is involved with studying the interaction of humans in extreme environments. When Michela learns of the possibility of the Antarctic research, she attempts to join Allison's expedition but is met with resistance. Only the fact that she is able to provide the needed funding allows Michela to join the expedition to continue her studies.

Allison and Michela instantly clash regarding the focus of the expedition and who should lead the team. They settle into a grudging working relationship that gradually deepens into a fragile friendship, but what they find at the expedition site defies all expectations. With hardship, extreme cold, and rivalry standing in their way, will the two women see past their own stubbornness long enough to allow their friendship to develop any further?

ISBN 978-1-932300-29-1
1-932300-29-5

Another Yellow Rose title you might enjoy:

Family Ties
by Vicki Stevenson

Fleeing from her abusive husband, Jill Dewey impulsively returns to her small hometown. A chance encounter with a former teacher leads her to the safety of a local dude ranch, where she accepts work as a chef. Through an intermediary, she notifies her parents that she is well and does not wish to be found.

Ranch owner Casey McQuaid is pleased with Jill's performance as a chef and enjoys her company as a friend. Jill is drawn to the warmth and support of Casey's LGBT family. As she becomes involved in the family's struggle against a powerful adversary of the gay community, she is increasingly obsessed by unexpected feelings for Casey.

While Jill grapples with her newly emerging emotions, her parents and husband discover her whereabouts and work relentlessly and viciously to compel her to return. And as the battle against the homophobic enemy proceeds, Casey and Jill must confront the nature of the relationship that has developed between them.

ISBN 978-1-935053-03-3
1-935053-03-5

OTHER YELLOW ROSE PUBLICATIONS

Sandra Barret	Lavender Secrets	978-1-932300-73-4
Georgia Beers	Thy Neighbor's Wife	1-932300-15-5
Georgia Beers	Turning the Page	978-1-932300-71-0
Carrie Brennan	Curve	1-932300-41-4
Carrie Carr	Destiny's Bridge	1-932300-11-2
Carrie Carr	Faith's Crossing	1-932300-12-0
Carrie Carr	Hope's Path	1-932300-40-6
Carrie Carr	Love's Journey	978-1-932300-65-9
Carrie Carr	Strength of the Heart	978-1-932300-81-9
Carrie Carr	The Way Things Should Be	978-1-932300-39-0
Carrie Carr	To Hold Forever	978-1-932300-21-5
Carrie Carr	Something to Be Thankful For	1-932300-04-X
Carrie Carr	Diving Into the Turn	978-1-932300-54-3
Jennifer Fulton	Passion Bay	1-932300-25-2
Jennifer Fulton	Saving Grace	1-932300-26-0
Jennifer Fulton	The Sacred Shore	1-932300-35-X
Jennifer Fulton	A Guarded Heart	1-932300-37-6
Anna Furtado	The Heart's Desire	1-932300-32-5
Anna Furtado	The Heart's Strength	978-1-932300-93-2
Lois Glenn	Scarlet E	978-1-932300-75-8
Melissa Good	Eye of the Storm	1-932300-13-9
Melissa Good	Hurricane Watch	978-1-935053-00-2
Melissa Good	Red Sky At Morning	978-1-932300-80-2
Melissa Good	Thicker Than Water	1-932300-24-4
Melissa Good	Terrors of the High Seas	1-932300-45-7
Melissa Good	Tropical Storm	978-1-932300-60-4
Maya Indigal	Until Soon	1-932300-31-7
Lori L. Lake	Different Dress	1-932300-08-2
Lori L. Lake	Ricochet In Time	1-932300-17-1
K. E. Lane	And, Playing the Role of Herself	978-1-932300-72-7
J. Y Morgan	Learning To Trust	978-1-932300-59-8
J. Y. Morgan	Download	978-1-932300-88-8
A. K. Naten	Turning Tides	978-1-932300-47-5
Lynne Norris	One Promise	978-1-932300-92-5
Paula Offutt	Butch Girls Can Fix Anything	978-1-932300-74-1
Surtees and Dunne	True Colours	978-1-932300-52-9
Surtees and Dunne	Many Roads to Travel	978-1-932300-55-0
Vicki Stevenson	Family Affairs	978-1-932300-97-0
Vicki Stevenson	Family Values	978-1-932300-89-5
Cate Swannell	Heart's Passage	1-932300-09-0
Cate Swannell	No Ocean Deep	1-932300-36-8

About the Author

Born in Australia, Helen lives and works in Canberra, Australia's capital. When she isn't tied to her work she enjoys traveling, reading, writing and bushwalking. She's an avid sportswoman, in her younger years having competed in soccer and softball at a representational level. Most recently age and injury have made her more of a spectator than participant. She currently lives with her partner of fifteen years and their two cats.

VISIT US ONLINE AT

www.regalcrest.biz

At the Regal Crest Website You'll Find

- The latest news about forthcoming titles and new releases

- Our complete backlist of romance, mystery, thriller and adventure titles

- Information about your favorite authors

- Current bestsellers

Regal Crest titles are available from all progressive booksellers and online at StarCrossed Productions, (www.scp-inc.biz), Bella Distribution and many others.

Printed in the United States
205401BV00001B/454/P

9 781935 053040